'Hoyle demonstrates ... but the personal allure of transcendental intoxication. His appeal is straightforward. In his hands, sf does not explain. It releases'

Encyclopedia of Science Fiction

'The John Buchan of science fiction. His fantasies are not only firmly rooted in scientific possibilities but are told at galloping pace and with an appealing no-nonsense authority'

Sunday Times

'A first-class novel, original and disturbing. It is a brightly written, really exciting tale with the added inducement of scientific accuracy'

Weekly Science Diary

SF MASTERWORKS

The Andromeda Anthology

A for Andromeda
Andromeda Breakthrough

FRED HOYLE AND JOHN ELLIOT

This edition first published in Great Britain in 2020 by Gollancz
an imprint of the Orion Publishing Group Ltd
Carmelite House, 50 Victoria Embankment
London EC4Y 0DZ

An Hachette UK Company

1 3 5 7 9 10 8 6 4 2

A for Andromeda copyright © Fred Hoyle and John Elliot 1962
Andromeda Breakthrough copyright © Fred Hoyle and John Elliot 1964
Introduction copyright © Kim Newman 2020

A CIP catalogue record for this book is
available from the British Library.

ISBN 978 1 473 23011 8

Printed and bound in Great Britain by Clays Ltd,
Elcograf S.p.A.

www.sfgateway.com
www.gollancz.co.uk

CONTENTS

INTRODUCTION
Kim Newman

The popular and critical success of Nigel Kneale's BBC-TV Quatermass serials – *The Quatermass Experiment* (1953), *Quatermass II* (1956), *Quatermass and the Pit* (1959) – encouraged British television channels (both of them) to commission more science fiction, often following Kneale's lead by combining s-f concepts with gothic horror and British boffinry. ITV's *The Trollenberg Terror* (1956) and *The Strange World of Planet X* (1956) followed Quatermass from the small screen to the movies, but – oddly – there was no cinema adaptation of the BBC's most significant post-*Quatermass*, pre-*Doctor Who* science fiction franchise – the Andromeda saga.

Scripted by astronomer-novelist Fred Hoyle (*The Black Cloud*) and TV writer-producer-director John Elliot (*The Trouble-shooters*), *A for Andromeda* was a ratings hit on its broadcast in seven episodes in the Autumn of 1961. Twenty-year-old Julie Christie, cast in a dual role, was propelled to stardom by the serial, dominating its later stages as the unearthly Andromeda. The show offered three contrasting boffins – stereotypical foreign-sounding Einsteinian genius Ernest Reinhart (Esmond Knight), unstereotypical female big thinker Madeleine Dawnay (Mary Martin), and virile (if vacillating) young John Fleming (Peter Halliday). It seems likely that Fleming is Hoyle's fantasy self-image. A year later, the BBC broadcast *The Andromeda Breakthrough*, a sequel with similarly blonde Susan Hampshire replacing Christie and a storyline with a more global reach. Hoyle and Elliot concentrate on the political, technical and social implications of contact with a perhaps-malignant alien intelligence rather than go for the viral mutation or dyed-in-the-DNA Martian evil of the Quatermass serials... but Andromeda is as disruptive and dangerous in her own way as the metastising cactus creature that threatens to turn the world into a vast carpet of undulating, tentacular biomass in *The Quatermass Experiment*.

Whereas Kneale allowed publication of his Quatermass scripts, Hoyle and Elliott did the work of novelising their Andromeda stories for tie-in books – an approach Kneale wouldn't take until his fourth, late in the day serial *Quatermass* (1979). *A for Andromeda* (1962) is subtitled 'a novel of tomorrow', while *Andromeda Breakthrough* (1962) – note the slight title change – becomes 'a novel of Tomorrow's Universe'. Review extracts or publicity blurbs on the back covers, sleeves and prelims work hard to take any sting out of the lowly status generally accorded TV novelisations, stressing the authors' CVs as 'an astro-physicist of world-wide reputation and a talented dramatist whose work for British television has received the highest critical recognition'. Over and over, the selling copy hits the expected beats ('originality, excitement, pace') but more than anything stakes a claim for 'scientific accuracy' that seems like a veiled rebuke of those fanciful ninnies who turned out stuff like *The Trollenberg Terror* (featuring monsters who inspired the US release title *The Crawling Eye*) or the wholly wonderful *Devil Girl From Mars* (1954) in which a PVC-clad dominatrix and her giant robot invade a pub in Scotland in search of human males. Ungrateful science fiction fans of the day carped that the BBC's high-tech genesis chamber looked like a washing machine onscreen, but obviously the novel version of the story is free to come up with something beyond criticism.

Unusually for such ephemera, the Andromeda novels stayed in print for decades – a Google image search will show up a wealth of cover designs, surprisingly few of which feature Julie Christie's face (or even Susan Hampshire's). By the 1970s, tie-in images from the serials or stylised starscapes are replaced by decade-appropriate psychedelic imagery, invariably featuring the beautiful nude female half-alien Andromeda. Paperback blurbs even stopped mentioning that these were 'as seen on TV' properties. My 1972 Corgi paperback has a wonderfully blaring back cover blurb – 'From two hundred light years across the universe comes a message of terror', in big blue on black script with the word 'terror' highlighted in white.

Hoyle and Elliot's premise proved influential. The movie *Species* (1995), also has a signal from deep space instruct scientists to create a human-alien hybrid which looks like a stunning blonde woman and might pose a threat to all life on Earth. And, in the 'scientists receive instructions from space' sub-genre, Hoyle and Elliot fit in between Raymond F. Jones' *This Island Earth* (1952) and Carl Sagan's *Contact* (1985). The Andromeda stories also feature one of the first evil corporations (as opposed to evil tycoons) in drama; Hoyle and Eliot's ruthless multinational Intel is a model for many subsequent concerns (eg: the Parallax Corporation of *The Parallax View*, ConSec of *Scanners*, Roxxon Oil in Marvel Comics, Omni Consumer Products of *Robocop*).

Sadly, the original *A for Andromeda* is lost but for one full episode ('The Face of the Tiger'), snippets from earlier shows, still photographs taken off air ('telesnaps') and the fifteen-minute climax of the finale 'The Last Mystery'. *The Andromeda Breakthrough* survives complete, and can be found along with what's left of the first serial on a now-OOP-and-pricey *Andromeda Anthology* DVD set. The curious are also referred to two official remakes of the original – Vittorio Cottafavi's *A come Andromeda* (1972), an Italian serial with Nicoletta Rizzi as Andromeda, and Richard Fell's TV movie remake *A for Andromeda* (2005), with Kelly Reilly as Andromeda, Jane Asher as Professor Dawnay and Tom Hardy as a very eccentric Fleming.

The serials are astute politically, even if they fail to foresee the social changes of the 1960s – the British Prime Minister of the near future (unspecified in print, 1971 on TV) sounds a lot like Harold Macmillan, for instance. Andromeda (aka Andre), the saga's most interesting character and creation, sometimes tends to get lost in all the earthly intrigue. Hoyle seems to have deliberately excluded the gothic or horrific elements Kneale deploys so effectively – and the Andromeda stories sometimes seem to be engaging in a debate with the Quatermass sagas. A professional scientist, albeit one with an attraction to extreme theories, the astronomer was plainly concerned with realistic depiction of laboratory work (though the deadly exposed terminals which are vital to the plot seem unlikely, despite the warning signs). Michael Hayes, who directed the first serial, noted that the Hoyle-Elliot scripts were literate, but seldom concerned with sounding like real people talking (as Nigel Kneale's usually were). The director may have moderated this stiffness a little, since the follow-up, co-directed by John Elliot and John Knight, seems to witter on more.

The novels are smart, sharp, fast reads – idea-driven s-f, but with a sense of the real world outside the concerns of pulp. Hoyle was an unusual figure as a science fiction writer and even as a scientist – a mainstream TV personality and commentator (like a grown-ups' Patrick Moore) with ambitions for an audience outside the fans who stereotypically consumed s-f paperbacks. In the 1970s, *The Black Cloud* – of all possible s-f texts – was on my school English curriculum (along with *The Lord of the Flies*, *Fahrenheit 451* and *The Trouble with Lichen*). Other science fiction was as liable to be confiscated as a *Pan Book of Horror Stories* or *Skinhead* paperback, but Hoyle was a proper scientist and got a pass – just as William Golding and Ray Bradbury were proper writers (John Wyndham, at least, was published by Penguin).

In the early 1960s, most television programs were as ephemeral and random as signals sent to (or from) Andromeda (even if they weren't wiped by the BBC). The serials were seen once (oddly, they weren't even given the Equity-approved one-off repeat), then remembered (or misremembered) for years after . . . mostly for that first luminous look at Julie Christie.

Meanwhile, these novels survived, and became the definitive Andromeda transmissions.

A for Andromeda

One

ARRIVAL

LIGHT was soaking out of the sky when they drove up to Bouldershaw Fell. Judy sat beside Professor Reinhart in the back of the staff car as it slid up the road from Bouldershaw town to the open moor; she peered hopefully out of the windows, but they were nearly at the crest of the hill before they could see the radio-telescope.

Suddenly it stood in front of them: three huge pillars curving together at the top to form a triangular arch, dark and stark against the ebbing sky. Hollowed out of the ground between the uprights lay a concrete bowl the size of a sports arena, and above, suspended from the top of the arch, a smaller metal bowl looked downwards and pointed a long antenna at the ground. The size of the whole thing did not strike the eye at first; it simply looked out of proportion to the landscape. Only when the car had drawn up and parked beneath it did Judy begin to realise how big it was. It was quite unlike anything else she had seen—as completely and intensely itself as a piece of sculpture.

Yet, for all its strangeness, there was nothing particularly sinister about the tall, looming structure to warn them of the extraordinary and disastrous future that was to emerge from it.

Out of the car, they stood for a moment with the soft, sweet air filling their heads and lungs, and gazed up at the three huge pylons, at the metal reflector that glistened high above them, and at the pale sky beyond. Around them a few low buildings and smaller arrays of aerials were scattered about on the empty moor-top, enclosed by a wire-link fence. There was no sound but the wind in the pylons and the curlews calling, and they could almost feel the great concrete-and-metal ear beside them straining to listen to the stars.

Then the Professor led the way to the main building—a low stone-faced affair with a half-finished entrance and a newly-laid approach. Men were putting in gateposts and direction notices and painting them: it all looked very new and sharp against the soft, dark hilltop.

" There's all sorts of subsidiary gubbins," said the Professor, with a small delicate wave of his hand. " This houses the main control room."

He was a man in his sixties, small, neat and cosy, like a family doctor.

" It's quite a baby," said Judy.

" Baby? It's the biggest baby I've ever given birth to. A ten years' labour."

He twinkled at her and his small black shoes pattered up the steps into the control building.

The entrance hall had an unfinished but at the same time familiar look: inevitable pegboard ceiling, inevitable composition floor, plain colour-washed brick walls and fluorescent lighting. There was a wall telephone and a drinking fountain; there were two small doors in the side walls, and there were double-doors facing the entrance; and that was about all. A faint hissing noise came from behind the double doors. When the Professor opened them the hissing became louder. It sounded like atmospherics from a radio.

As they went through the double doors a man in a cleaner's brown coat came out. His eye met Judy's for a moment, but when she parted her lips he looked away.

" Good-evening, Harries," said the Professor.

The room they entered was the control room, the centre of the observatory. At the far end an observation window gave a view of the gigantic sculpture outside, and facing the window was a massive metal desk, like an organ console, fitted with panels of buttons, lights and switches. Several young men were working at the desk, referring from time to time to the two computers which stood in tall metal cases on each side of it. One side wall was covered with enlargements of optical-telescope photographs of stars, and the other was two-thirds glass partition behind which more young men could be seen working at equipment in an inner room.

" The opening ceremony will be in here," said Reinhart.

10

"Where does the Minister break the champagne bottle, or cut the ribbon, or whatever he does?"

"At the desk. He presses a button on the control desk to start it."

"It isn't working yet?"

"Not yet. We're running acceptance tests."

Judy stood by the doorway taking it in. She was the sort of good-looking young woman who is more often called handsome than pretty, with a fresh complexion and alert, intelligent face and a very positive, slightly ungainly, way of standing. She might have been a nurse, or an officer in the Services, or simply the product of a good hockey-playing school. She had rather large hands and deep blue eyes. Under one arm she held a bundle of papers and pamphlets which she pulled out and looked at, as if they might explain what she saw.

"It's the biggest radio-telescope, well—anywhere." The Professor smiled happily round the room. "It's not as big as an interferometer, of course, but you can *steer* it. You can shift your focus by the small reflector up top, and by that means you can track a source across the sky."

"I gathered from these," Judy tapped her papers, "that there are other radio-telescopes operating in the same way."

"There are. There were in nineteen-sixty, when we started this—and that's several years ago. But they haven't our sensitivity."

"Because this is bigger?"

"Not entirely. Also because we've better receiving equipment. That should give us a higher signal-to-noise ratio. It's all housed in there."

He pointed a small, delicate finger to the room behind the glass panel.

"You see, all you pick up from most astronomical sources—radio stars for instance—is a very faint electrical signal, and it's mixed up with all kinds of noise, from the atmosphere, from interstellar gas, from heaven knows what—well, heaven indeed."

He spoke in a precise, matter-of-fact tenor voice; he might have been a doctor discussing a cold. The sense of achievement, of imagination, was all hidden.

"You can hear sources other people can't?" asked Judy.

"Hope to. That's the idea. But don't ask me how. There's

a team evolved it." He looked modestly down at his little feet. " Doctors Fleming and Bridger."

" Bridger?" Judy looked up sharply.

" Fleming's the real brains. John Fleming." He called politely across the room. " John!"

One of the young men detached himself from the group at the control desk and wandered towards them.

He said, " Hi!" to the Professor and ignored Judy.

" If you have a moment, John. Dr. Fleming. Miss Adamson."

The young man glanced at Judy, then called across to the control desk.

" Turn that flaming noise down!"

" What is it?" Judy asked. The atmospherics reduced themselves to a faint hissing. The young man shrugged.

" Interstellar hiss, mainly. The universe is full of electrically charged matter. What we pick up is an electrical emission from these charges, which we get as noise."

" The background music of the universe," Reinhart added.

" You can keep that, Prof.," said the young man, with a sort of friendly contempt. " Keep it for Jacko's press handouts."

" Jacko's not coming back."

Fleming looked faintly surprised, and Judy frowned as if she had mislaid some piece of information.

" Who?" she asked the Professor.

" Jackson, your predecessor." He turned to Fleming. " Miss Adamson's our new press officer."

Fleming regarded her without relish. " Well, they come and go, don't they? Inheriting Jacko's spheres?"

" What are they?"

" Dear young lady, you'll soon find out."

"I'm showing her the layout for Thursday," the Professor said. " The official opening. She'll be looking after the press."

Fleming had a dark, thoughtful face which was less surly than preoccupied; but he seemed tired and bitter. He grumbled away in a thick Midland accent.

" Oh yes—the Official Opening! All the coloured lights will be working. The stars will sing ' Rule Britannia ' in heavenly chorus, and I'll be round at the pub."

" You'll be here, John, I hope." The Professor sounded slightly irritated. " Meanwhile, perhaps you'd show Miss Adamson round."

"Not if you're busy," said Judy in a small, hostile voice. Fleming looked at her with interest for the first time.

"How much do you know about it?"

"Very little yet." She tapped her papers. "I'm relying on these."

Fleming turned wearily to the room and spread an arm wide.

"This, ladies and gentlemen, is the largest and newest radio-telescope in the world—not to say the most expensive. It has a resolution of fifteen to twenty times greater than any existing equipment and is, of course, a miracle of British science. Not to say engineering. The pick-up elements"—he pointed out of the window—"are steerable so as to be capable of tracking the course of a celestial body across the heavens. Now you can tell them everything, can't you?"

"Thank you," said Judy icily. She looked at the Professor, but he seemed only a little embarrassed.

"I'm sorry we worried you, John," he said.

"Don't mention it. It's a pleasure. Any time."

The Professor turned his kindly general-practitioner's attention to Judy.

"I'll show you myself."

"You do want it operating by Thursday, don't you?" said Fleming. "For His Ministership."

"Yes, John. It'll be all right?"

"It'll look all right. The brass won't know if it's working. Nor the news touts."

"I should like it to be working."

"Yeh."

Fleming turned away and walked back to the control desk. Judy waited for an explosion, or at least some sign of affront, from the Professor, but he only nodded his head as if over a diagnosis.

"You can't push a boy like John. You may wait months for an idea. Years. It's worth it if it's a good one, and it generally is with him." He looked wistfully at Fleming's receding back: sloppy, casual, with untidy hair and clothes. "We depend on the young, you know. He's done all the low-temperature design, he and Bridger. The receivers are based on low-temperature equipment and that's not my subject. There's a hand-out on it somewhere." He nodded vaguely at her bundle of papers. "We've run him a bit ragged, I'm afraid."

He sighed, and took her off on a conducted tour of the building. He showed her the wall photographs of the night sky, telling her the names and identity of the great radio stars, the main sources of the sounds we hear from the universe. " This," he explained, pointing to the photographs, " is not a star at all, but two whole galaxies colliding; and this, a star exploding."

"And this?"

" The Great Nebula in Andromeda. M.31 we call it, just to confuse it with the motorway."

" It's in the Andromeda constellation?"

" No. It's way, way out beyond that. It's a whole galaxy in itself. Nothing's simple, is it?"

She looked at the white spiral of stars and agreed.

" You get a signal from it?"

"A hiss. Like you heard."

Near the wall was a large perspex sphere with a small dark ball at its centre and other white ones set around it like the electrons in a physicist's model of the atom.

" Jacko's spheres!" The Professor twinkled. " Or Jacko's folly, they call it. It's a display of things in orbit near the earth. All these white units represent satellites, ballistic missiles and so on. Ironmongery. That's the earth, in the middle."

The Professor waved it daintily aside.

"A gimmick, I think you'd call it. Jacko thought it would interest our government visitors. We have to keep tabs, of course, on what's happening near the earth, but it's a waste of a machine like this. Still, the military ask us to, and we don't get the sort of money we need unless we can tap the defence budget." He sounded as though he was being naughty and enjoyed it. He made one of his small, manicured gestures to take in the room and the huge thing outside. " Twenty-five millions or more, this has cost."

" So there's a military interest?"

" Yes. But it's my establishment—or rather, the Ministry of Science's. Not your Ministry's."

" I'm on your staff now."

" Not at my request." His manner stiffened, as it had not done when Fleming was rude to him; Fleming, after all, was one of his own.

" Does anyone else know why I'm here?" Judy asked him.

" I've told no-one."

He steered her away from the subject and into the other room, where he went carefully over the receiving apparatus and the communications equipment.

" We're simply a link in a chain of observatories all round the world, though not the weakest link." He looked around with a kind of pure pleasure at the switchboards and wires and racks of equipment. " I didn't feel an old man when we started to put all this together, but I do now. You have an idea and you think: ' That's what we must do ', and it just seems the next step. Quite a small step, possibly. Then you start: design, research, committees, building, politics. An hour of your life here, a month there. Let's hope it'll work. Ah, here's Whelan! He understands all about this part of it."

Judy was introduced to a pasty-faced young man with an Australian voice who held on to her hand as though it was something he had lost.

" Haven't we met before somewhere?"

" I don't think so." She stared at him candidly with large blue eyes, but he would not be put off.

" I'm sure of it."

She wavered and looked around for help. Harries, the cleaner, was standing across the room, and when she looked at him he shook his head very slightly. She turned back to Whelan.

" I'm afraid I don't remember."

" Maybe at Woomera. . . ."

The Professor piloted her back into the main control-room.

" What was his name?"

" Whelan."

She made a note on her pad. The party at the control desk had split up, leaving only one young man who was sitting in the duty engineer's seat checking the panels. The Professor led her across to him.

" Hallo, Harvey."

The young man looked up and half rose from his seat.

" Good-evening, Professor Reinhart." At least he was polite. Judy looked out of the window to the great piece of gadgetry beyond and the empty moorland and the sky, now growing dark purple.

" You know the principle of the thing?" Harvey asked her. "Any radio emission from the sky strikes the bowl and is reflected to the aerial, and received and recorded on the equip-

15

ment in there." He pointed through the glass partition. Judy did not look for fear of seeing Whelan, but Harvey—keen, dogged and toneless—was soon directing her attention to something else. "This bank of computers works out the azimuth and elevation of whatever source you want to focus on to it and keeps it following. There's a servo link arrangement. . . . ."

Eventually Judy managed to escape to the hall and have a moment alone with Harries.

"Get Whelan moved," she said.

She had left her suitcase at the hotel in the town and driven on up the hill with very little idea of what to expect. She had visited a good many service establishments and served as security officer in a number of them, from Fylingdales to Christmas Island. Whelan, she knew, had met her on a rocket range in Australia. She had worked with Harries on a tour of duty at Malvern. She did not think of herself as a spy, and the idea of informing on her own colleagues struck her as an unpleasant business; but the Home Office had asked for her, or at least for someone, to be transferred from the Ministry of Defence security section to the Ministry of Science, and an assignment was an assignment. Before, the people she worked with had always known what she was, and she had thought of her duty as protecting them. This time they themselves were suspect and she was to be palmed off on them as a public relations stooge who could nose around and ask questions without putting them on their guard. Reinhart knew, and disliked it. She disliked it herself. But a job was a job and this—she was told—was important.

She could act the part without difficulty: she looked so honest, so forthright, so much a team member. She had only to sit back and listen and learn. It was the people she met who discomforted her; they had their own world and their own values. Who was she to judge them or be party to their judging? When Harries nodded and sauntered away to do what was needed, she despised both him and herself.

The Professor left soon afterwards and handed her over to John Fleming.

"Perhaps you'd drop her at the Lion when you go back to Bouldershaw. She's staying there."

They went out on to the steps to see the old man off.

" He is rather sweet," said Judy.

Fleming grunted. " Tough as old nails."

He took a hip-flask from his pocket and drank out of it. Then he handed it to her. When she refused he took another swig himself, and she watched him standing in the light of the porch, his head thrown back, his Adam's apple working up and down as he gulped. There was something desperately keyed-up about him; perhaps, as Reinhart had said, they had run him ragged. But there was something else beside—a feeling of a dynamo permanently charging inside him.

" Play bowls?" He seemed to have forgotten his earlier indifference to her. Perhaps the drink. " There's an alley down at Bouldershaw. Come and join our rustic sports."

She hesitated.

" Oh come along now! I'm not going to leave you at the mercy of these mad astronomers."

" Aren't you an astronomer?"

" Do you mind! Cryogenics, computers, that's really my stuff. Not this airy-fairy nonsense."

They walked across to the small concrete apron where his car was parked. A red beacon light shone on top of the telescope, and in the dark sky behind it stars began to show. Some could be seen through the tall arches of the pylons, as though they had already been netted by man. When they reached the car, Fleming looked back and up.

" I've an idea," he said, and his voice was quieter, quite gentle and no longer aggressive. " I've an idea we've got to the breakaway stage in the physical sciences."

He started to unclip the tonneau cover from his car, a small open sports, while she moved round to the other side.

" Let me help you."

He hardly seemed to notice.

" Some moment, somewhere along the perimeter of our knowledge, we're going to go—*wham!*—clean through. Right out into new territory. And it might be here, on this stuff." He bundled the tonneau cover in behind the seat. " ' Philosophy is written in that vast book which stands forever open before our eyes, I mean the universe.' Who wrote that?"

" Churchill?"

"Churchill!" He laughed. "Galileo! 'It is written in mathematical language.' That's what Galileo said. Any good for a press hand-out?"

She looked at him, uncertain how to take it. He opened the door for her.

"Let's go."

The road dropped down to Lancashire on one side and into Yorkshire on the other. On the Yorkshire side it ran down a long valley, where every few miles a tall old brick mill stood over the river, until they came to the town of Bouldershaw. Fleming drove too fast, and grumbled.

"They get on my wick . . . Flogging Ministers' Opening! . . . The old Prof. sweating on the Honours List; the Ministry bunch all needling and nagging. All it is, really, is a piece of lab. equipment. Because it's big and costs the earth, it becomes public property. I don't blame the old man. He's caught up in it. He's stuck his neck out and he's got to show results."

"Well, won't it?"

"I dunno."

"I thought it was your equipment."

"Mine and Dennis Bridger's."

"Where is Dr. Bridger?"

"Down at the alley. Waiting for us with a lane booked, I hope. And a flask."

"You've got one flask."

"What good's one? They're dry, these places."

As they swung down the dark winding road, he started telling her about Bridger and himself. Both had been students at Birmingham University, and research fellows at the Cavendish. Fleming was a theorist, Bridger a practical man, a development mathematician and engineer. Bridger was a career scientist; he was set to make the most he could out of his particular line. Fleming was a pure research man who did not give a damn about anything except the facts. But they both despised the academic system into which they grew up, and they stuck together. Reinhart had winkled them out, several years ago, to work on his new telescope. As he was, perhaps, the most distinguished and respected astro-physicist in the western world, and a born leader of teams and picker of talents, they had gone along with him without hesitation, and he had backed and encouraged and generally fathered them throughout the long and tortuous business of development.

It was easy to see, when Fleming talked, the mutual trust that tied him to the older man, behind his surliness. Bridger, on the other hand, was bored and restless. He had done his part. And they had, as Fleming said without modesty or conceit, given the old boy the most fabulous piece of equipment on earth.

He did not ask about Judy, and she kept quiet. He waited in the bar of the Lion while she went to her room. By the time they reached the bowling alley he was pretty much the worse for wear.

The bowling alley was a converted cinema which stood out in a wash of neon and floodlighting against the dark old mill-town. Its clientele seemed to have come from somewhere other than the cobbled streets. They were mostly young. They wore jeans and soda-jerks' jackets, crew-cuts, and blouses with slogans on them. It was difficult to imagine them at home in the old terraced houses, the grimy Yorkshire valleys. Their native voices were drowned under a flood of music and the rumble and clatter of bowls and skittles on the wooden planking of the lanes. There were half-a-dozen lanes with ten pins at one end of each and, at the other, a rack of bowls, a scoring table, a bench and a quartet of players. When a bowl pitched down and scored a strike, an automatic gate picked up the skittles again and returned the bowl to the rack at the players' end. Except in the concentrated, athletic moment of bowling, the players seemed uninterested in the game, lounging around and talking and drinking Coca Cola out of bottles. It was more transatlantic than the cinema had been: as though the American way of life had burst out through the screen and possessed the auditorium. But that, Fleming remarked, was just bloody typical of the way things are generally.

They found Bridger, a narrow, pointed man about Fleming's age, bowling on a lane with a curvy girl in a vermilion blouse and tight, bright yellow drainpipes. Her bosom and hair were swept up as high as they would go, her face was made up like a ballet dancer's, and she moved like something in a Hollywood chorus; but when she opened her mouth all Yorkshire came out of it. She bowled with a good deal of muscular skill, and came back and leant on Bridger, sucking a finger.

" Ee, I got a bit o' skin off."

" This is Grace." Bridger seemed slightly ashamed of her. He was prematurely lined and nervous, mousily dressed in dull sports clothes like a post office assistant on Saturday morning. He shook hands tentatively with Judy, and when she said " I've heard of you," he gave her a quick, anxious look.

" Miss Adamson," said Fleming, pouring some whisky into Bridger's Coke, " Miss Adamson is our new eager-beaver—lady-beaver—P.R.O."

" What's your other name, love?" inquired the girl.

" Judy."

" You haven't got a bit of sticking-plaster?"

" Oh, ask at the desk!" said Bridger impatiently.

" One of your team?" Judy asked Fleming.

" Local talent. Dennis's. I've no time."

" Pity," she said. But he appeared not to hear. Taking another swig from the flask, he addressed himself unsteadily to the bowling. Bridger turned confidentially to her.

" What have you heard about me?"

" Only that you'd been working with Dr. Fleming."

" It isn't my cup." He looked aggrieved; the point of his nose twitched like a rabbit's. " I could get five times my salary in industry."

" Is that what you want?"

" As soon as that lot on the hill's working, I'm away." He glanced across at Fleming, conspiratorially, then back at her. " Old John will stay, looking for the millennium. And before he's found anything, he'll be old. Old and respected. And poor."

" And possibly happy."

" John'll never be happy. He thinks too much."

" Who drinks too much?" Fleming lurched back to them and marked up his score.

" You do."

" All right—I drink too much. Brother, you've got to have something to hold on to."

" What's wrong with the railings?" asked Bridger, twitching his nose.

" Look—" Fleming slumped down on to the bench beside them. " You're going to walk along those railings, and then you'll take another pace and they won't be there. We were talking about Galileo—why? Because he was the Renaissance. He and Copernicus and Leonardo da Vinci. That was when they said 'Wham!' and knocked down all the railings and had to stand on their own feet in the middle of a great big open universe."

He heaved himself up and took another of the heavy bowls from the rack. His voice rose above the din of the music and bowling.

"People have put up new fences, further out. But this is another Renaissance! One day, when nobody's noticing, when everybody's talking about politics and football, and money—" he loomed over Bridger, "then suddenly every fence we know is going to get knocked down—*wham!*—like that!"

He made a great sweep with the bowl and knocked the bottles of Coke off the scoring table.

"Oi! Careful, you great clot!" Bridger leapt to his feet and started picking up the bottles and mopping at the spilt drink with his handkerchief. "I'm sorry, Miss Adamson."

Fleming threw back his head and laughed.

"Judy—her name is Judy."

Bridger, down on his knees, rubbed away at the stain on Judy's skirt.

"I'm afraid it's gone on you."

"It doesn't matter." Judy was not looking at him. She was gazing up at Fleming, puzzled and entranced. Then the Tannoy went.

"Doctor Fleming—telephone call, please."

Fleming came back after a minute, shaking his head to clear it. He pulled Bridger up from the bench.

"Come on, Dennis boy. We're wanted."

Harvey was alone in the control-room, sitting at the desk adjusting the receiver tune. The window in front of him was dark as a blackboard, and the room was quiet except for a constant low crackle of sound from the loudspeaker. From outside—nothing, until the noise of Fleming's car.

Fleming and Bridger came pushing in through the swing doors and stood, blinking, in the light. Fleming focused blearily on Harvey.

"What is it?"

"Listen." Harvey held up a hand, and they stood listening.

In among the crackle and whistles and hiss from the speaker came a faint single note, broken but always continuing.

"Morse code," said Bridger.

"It's not in groups."

They listened again.

"Short and long," said Bridger. "That's what it is."

"Where's it coming from?" Fleming asked.

"Somewhere in Andromeda. We were sweeping through—"

"How long's it been going on?"

"About an hour. We're over the peak now."

"Can you move the reflector?"

"I expect so."

"We're not supposed to," said Bridger. "We're not supposed to start tracking tests yet."

Fleming ignored him.

"Is the servo equipment manned?" he asked.

"Yes, Dr. Fleming."

"Well, try to track it."

"No, listen John." Bridger put an ineffectual hand on Fleming's sleeve.

"It may be a sputnik or something," said Harvey.

"Is there anything new up?" Fleming disengaged himself from Bridger.

"Not that we know of."

"Someone could have put something fresh into orbit—" Bridger started, but Fleming cut him off.

"Dennis—" He tried to think clearly. "Go and get this on to a recorder, will you? There's a good chap. Get it on a printer too."

"Hadn't we better check?"

"Check after."

Fleming walked carefully out into the hall, bent his face over the drinking fountain and sluiced it with water. When he returned, fresh and shining and remarkably sober, he found Bridger already setting up in the equipment room and Harvey phoning the duty engineer. There was a dip in the lights as the electric motors started. The metal reflector high up outside swung silently and invisibly, its movement compensating for the motion of the earth. The sound from the speaker grew a little louder.

"That the best you can get?"

"It's not a very strong signal."

"Hm." Fleming opened a drawer in the control desk and fished out a catalogue. "Have its galactic cordinates shifted at all?"

"Hard to say. I wasn't tracking. But they couldn't have shifted very much."

"So it's not in orbit?"

"I'd say not." Harvey bent anxiously over the faders on his desk. "Could it be some ham bouncing morse code off the moon?"

"Doesn't really sound like morse code, and the moon isn't up."

"Or off Mars, or Venus. I hope I haven't brought you out on a wild goose chase."

"Andromeda, you said?"

Harvey nodded. Fleming turned the pages of the catalogue, reading and listening. He became quiet and gentle again as he had been earlier with Judy at the car. He looked like a studious small boy.

"You're holding it?"

"Yes, Dr. Fleming."

Fleming walked across to the desk and flicked on the intercom.

"Getting it, Dennis?"

"Yes." Bridger's voice came tinnily back. "But it doesn't make sense."

"It may by morning. I'm going to try to get some idea of the distance."

Fleming flicked back the key and crossed, book in hand, to the astronomical charts on the back wall.

They worked for a while with the sounds from space the only noise in the room, Fleming checking the source and Harvey holding it with the great silent telescope outside.

"What do you think?" Harvey asked at last.

"I think it's coming from a long way out."

After that they simply worked and listened, and the signal went on and on and on, endlessly.

Two

ANNOUNCEMENT

In the late nineteen-sixties, when these things happened, the Ministry of Science was moved into a new glass-walled building near Whitehall. It was elegantly furnished and staffed, as if to prove that technology was on a par with the arts, and the Permanent Under-Secretary of State, Michael Osborne, was one of the most cultivated of its many cultivated servants. Although he wore tweeds in the office, they were the smoothest and most formal of tweeds. He seldom sat at his huge desk—more often in one of the low easy chairs by the low marble-topped coffee-table.

He sprawled there, decoratively, the morning after the message had started to come through at Bouldershaw Fell, talking with General Charles G. Vandenberg of the U.S. Air Force. The light from the venetian blinds fell across him in neat lines.

England by that time was something like the advance headquarters of a besieged land: an area consisting of Western Europe and North America. Pressure from the East, and from Africa and Asia, had pushed western civilisation up into one corner of the globe, with America north of Panama a fairly secure centre and Western Europe an embattled salient. Not that anyone was officially at war with anyone else; but economic sanctions and the threat of bombs and missiles gripped the remains of the old world in a fairly acute state of siege. The lifeline across the Atlantic was maintained almost entirely by the Americans, and American garrisons in Britain, France and Western Germany held on with the same desperate tenuousness as the Roman legions in the third and fourth centuries.

Protocol insisted that Britain and her neighbours were still sovereign states, but in fact initiative was fast slipping out of their hands. Although General Vandenberg was modestly styled representative of the Defence Co-ordination Committee, he was, in effect, air commander of a friendly but dominant occupying power to whom this country was one square on a large chess-board.

An ex-bomber-boy, bull-necked and square-headed, he still looked brash and youthful in middle age; but there was nothing brash about his manner. He was a New Englander, quietly spoken and civilised, and he talked with authority, as if he knew more about the world than most of the people in it.

They were speaking about Whelan. A note about him hung limply from Osborne's hand.

" I can't do anything now."

" There is a kind of priority—"

Osborne heaved himself up out of his chair and called his secretary through the intercom on his desk.

" The Defence Co-ordination Committee have a low boiling-point," Vandenberg observed.

" You can tell them we'll cope."

Osborne gave the note to the secretary as she came in.

" Get someone to look after that, will you?"

She took it and put a folder of papers on his desk. She was young and pretty and wore what looked like a cocktail dress: the civil service had moved on.

" Your papers for Bouldershaw."

" Thanks. Is my car here?"

" Yes, Mr. Osborne."

He opened the folder and read:

" The Minister's party will arrive at Bouldershaw Fell at 3.15 p.m. and will be received by Professor Reinhart."

" That's to-morrow," remarked Vandenberg. " Are you walking up?"

" I'm going a day early to meet Reinhart." He stuffed the folder into his brief case. " Can I give you a lift to the top of Whitehall?"

" That would be a Christian deed."

They were wary of each other, but polite—almost old-fashioned. As he rose, Vandenberg asked casually:

" Do you have an operational date for it?"

" Not yet."

" This grows a little serious."

" The stars can wait. They've waited for a long time."

" So have the Defence Co-ordination Committee."

Osborne gave a shrug of sophisticated impatience. He might have been a Greek arguing with a Roman.

" Reinhart will undertake military programmes as and when he can. That's the arrangement."

" If there's an emergency . . ."

" *If* there's an emergency."

" You read the newspapers?"

" I can never get beyond the magazine section these days."

" You should try the news pages. If there's an emergency we'll need all the ears we can grow this side of the Atlantic." Vandenberg nodded to an artist's impression of the radio-telescope on the wall of the office. " It's not a kid's toy to us."

" It's not a kid's toy to them, either," said Osborne.

After they had gone, Fleming phoned through from Boulder-shaw Fell; but it was too late.

Judy arrived at the radio-telescope just before Osborne and Reinhart, and had a quiet chat to Harries in the hall.

" What about Bridger?"

Harries tried to look as though he were polishing a door-handle.

" Two or three visits to a back-street bookie in Bradford. Apart from that, nothing."

" We'd better watch him."

" I'm watching him."

When Osborne and Reinhart arrived, they took her into the control room with them. The place was quiet and almost empty; only Harvey sat tinkering at the desk, surrounded by a litter of papers and cigarette-ends and empty drinking-cups. Reinhart clucked at it like a disturbed hen.

" You'll have to keep this place clean."

" Will they be able to swing the focus for the Minister?" Osborne asked.

" I hope so. We haven't tested the tracking apparatus."

Reinhart pottered round busily while Harvey tried to attract his attention.

" You look as if you've been up all night, Harvey."

" I have, sir. So have Dr. Fleming and Dr. Bridger."

" Struck a snag?"

" Not exactly, sir. We've been tracking."

" On whose instruction?"

" Dr. Fleming's." Harvey was quite casual about it. " We're lining up again now."

" Why wasn't I told?" Reinhart turned to Osborne and Judy. " Did you know about this?"

Judy shook her head.

" Fleming appears to make his own rules," observed Osborne.

" Where is he?" Reinhart demanded.

" In through there." Harvey pointed to the equipment room. " With Dr. Bridger."

" Then ask him to spare me a minute."

While Harvey spoke into a microphone on the desk, Reinhart paced to and fro on his small feet.

" What were you tracking?" he asked.

" A source in Andromeda."

" M.31?"

" Not M.31, sir."

" What then?"

"Another signal near there. An interrupted signal."

" Have you heard it before?"

" No, sir."

When Fleming came in he was tired and unshaven, sober but very excited in a subdued way. He held in his hand a bunch of papers from a line-printer. This time Reinhart made no allowances.

" I gather you've taken over the telescope."

Fleming stopped and blinked at them.

" I beg your pardon, gentlemen. I didn't have time to fill in the proper forms in triplicate." He turned to Osborne. " I did telephone your office, but you'd gone."

" What have you been doing?" asked Reinhart.

Fleming told them, throwing the papers down on the desk in front of them.

"—And that's the message."

Reinhart looked at him curiously.

" You mean signal."

" I said message. Dots and dashes—wasn't it, Harvey?"

" It did sound like that."

" It went on all night," said Fleming. " It's below the horizon now, but we can try again this evening.

Judy looked at Osborne. but got no help from him.

" What about the opening?" she asked diffidently.

" Oh, to hell with the opening!" Fleming turned on her.
" This is something! This is a voice from a thousand million,
million miles away."

"A voice?" Her own voice sounded weak and unreal.

" It's taken two hundred light-years to reach us. The Minister can wait a day, can't he?"

Reinhart seemed to have recovered himself. He looked up at
Fleming with amusement.

" Unless it's a satellite."

" It's not a satellite!"

Reinhart wandered over to Jacko's folly.

" Before you get too excited, John, let's check on the ironmongery in orbit."

" We have."

Reinhart turned to Osborne.

" You haven't heard of anything new going up?"

" No."

" Look," said Fleming, " if it were a satellite it wouldn't
have stayed put all night, in the middle of the Andromeda
constellation."

" You're sure it wasn't the Great Nebula?"

" We located that separately, didn't we, Harvey?"

Harvey nodded, but Reinhart still looked unconvinced.

" It could have been pattern interference—anything."

" I know a message when I meet one!" Fleming said.
" Besides, there's something about this message I've never seen
before. Between the groups of dots and dashes there's a
fantastic amount of fast, detailed stuff. We'll have to lash up
special receiving gear to record that."

He keyed down the intercom and called Bridger to come
from the other room, then he picked up the papers and pushed
them into Reinhart's hand. " Have a look! Ten years or more
people have been waiting for this. Ten centuries for that matter."

" Is it intelligible?" asked Osborne in his detached civil-
servant's voice, high and whinnying.

" Yes!"

" You can decypher it?"

" For heaven's sake! Do you think the cosmos is populated
by Boy Scouts sending morse code?"

Bridger came in looking pale and twitchy, but his presence seemed to calm Fleming and he confirmed Fleming's reports.

"It could be from a very distant probe," Osborne suggested. Fleming ignored him. Judy plucked up her courage.

"Or another planet?"

"Yes!"

"Mars or somewhere?"

Fleming shrugged: "Probably a planet going round some star in Andromeda."

"Signalling to us?"

Reinhart handed the papers to Osborne.

"It's certainly a coherent form of dots and dashes."

"Then why has no-one else picked it up?"

"Because no-one else has got equipment like this. If we hadn't given you a thundering good piece of circuitry, you wouldn't be getting it now."

Osborne sat down on a corner of the control desk, looking at the papers in a dazed sort of way.

"If some sentient being is trying to communicate . . . No, it doesn't make sense."

"It's possible." Reinhart glanced down at his small delicate fingers, as if this were something he would prefer not to talk about. "If there are other creatures—"

Fleming interrupted him: "Not creatures—another intelligence. It doesn't have to be little green men. It doesn't have to be organic at all; just an intelligence."

Judy shuddered, then pulled herself together.

"Why do I shiver?"

"For the same reason I do," said Fleming.

Osborne came out of his daze.

"For the same reason everyone will, if it *is* an astronomical source."

They decided in the end to listen for it again that night. The message had not stopped, merely faded as the rotation of the earth had swung the telescope away from it. The chances were that it would still be going on. Once he had accepted the possibility, Reinhart became calm and businesslike. He and Fleming and Bridger spread out the papers and examined them.

"You know what it might be?" Fleming said. "Binary arithmetic."

"What's that?" asked Judy.

"It's arithmetic expressed entirely by the figures 0 and 1, instead of the figures 1 to 10, which we normally use and which we call denary. 0 and 1, you see, could be dot and dash. Or dash could equal 0 and dot 1. The system we use is arbitrary, but the binary system is basic; it's based on positive and negative, yes and no, dot and dash—it's universal. Strewth." He turned on her with his eyes bloodshot and feverish with strain and excitement. "'Philosophy is written in mathematical language!' Remember? We're going—Wham!—clean through on this!"

"We'd better put off the opening," said Osborne. "We don't want this in the *Social Gazette*."

"Why not?"

Osborne looked pained. Nothing in his world was as simple as that; nothing could be said or done without permission. On his files, what happened at Bouldershaw Fell was one small part of an intricately complex pattern of arrangements, and behind them loomed everything that Vandenberg stood for. Everything had to be weighed and considered with caution.

"What do I tell the press?" Judy asked him.

"Nothing."

"Nothing?"

"Are we a secret society or something?" Fleming regarded him with contempt, but Osborne managed to sound at the same time official and reasonable.

"You can't throw this kind of undigested information about. There are other people to consult, and besides there might be a panic: space-ships, saucers, bug-eyed monsters. Every idiot in the country will be seeing them. Or it may be someone up to something. Nothing must appear in the press, Miss Adamson."

They left Fleming seething, went to the Professor's office to telephone the Ministry, and drove away.

At the Lion at Bouldershaw the press had already begun to arrive to cover the opening ceremony. Judy piloted Reinhart and Osborne round by the back door to a small room where they were given dinner rather late and were able to dodge the growing phalanx of scientific correspondents living it up in the lounge. Osborne made covert dashes to the phone box between each course and came back each time looking more harassed and depressed.

"What did the Minister say?"

"He said—ask Vandenberg."

They ate through some tepid meat and he went off again.

" What did Vandenberg say?"

" What did you imagine he'd say? ' Keep quiet about it.' "

Judy was to tell the press, the next morning, that the opening had been cancelled because of a technical hitch, nothing more. Any other statement would be made from London to the Fleet Street desks. They contrived to slip out again, unnoticed, by the back door.

Half an hour later, Fleming's car pulled up outside and Fleming, tired and thirsty, disappeared into the lounge.

The message was picked up again that evening. It went on all through the night and was recorded by Fleming and Bridger in turns, not only the audible dots and dashes, but the high speed part of the message as well. The next morning Dennis Bridger went down by himself to Bouldershaw and Harries followed him. After leaving his car in the Town Hall car park Bridger walked down a cobbled side-street to the lower part of the town. Harries followed him on foot at a distance of one street corner. With a raincoat in place of his overall, Harries looked more like an Irish gunman than a lab. cleaner and he was careful not to let Bridger see him. Harries himself did not notice a couple of men standing on the pavement on the opposite side of the road to a small doorway marked JAS. OLDROYD, TURF ACCOUNTANT. There were a number of people around; two men talking were not conspicuous.

Bridger turned in at the doorway and entered a narrow dark passage with stairs with linoleum treads running up to the floor above and a door with a frosted glass panel near the foot of the staircase. When he closed the outer door, the noise of the street was sealed off, leaving the passage as solitary as a crypt. The door with the frosted glass bore the same lettering for Jas. Oldroyd. It also said *Knock and Enter*; Bridger did so.

Inside, Jas. Oldroyd was having a late breakfast at his desk. An elderly man in rolled-up sleeves and a dim colourless cardigan, he was sopping up fried egg with a piece of bread on the end of a fork when Bridger walked in. There was no-one else in the office, yet the small room seemed full, with a litter of papers, telephones, an adding machine, a ticker-tape and a teleprinter. Several tradesmen's calendars hung on the walls, torn off at different months, but there was a prominent, very accurate clock. Mr. Oldroyd looked up from his web of old litter and new equipment and eyed Bridger for a moment.

" Oh, it's you."

Bridger nodded towards the teleprinter machine.

" O.K.?"

Mr. Oldroyd put the piece of egg-soaked bread in his mouth by way of answer and Bridger set to work on the telex.

" How's business?" he asked as he switched it on and dialled a number. It sounded like a stock greeting between old acquaintances.

" Chancy," said Mr. Oldroyd. "Horses 'ave no sense of responsibility. If they're not bunchin' they're crawlin', like t'ruddy buses."

Bridger typed: KAUFMAN TELEX 21303 GENEVA. Then he became aware of a scuffling in the passage outside. A single head was silhouetted for a moment against the glazed panel of the door. Then there was a grunt and a groan, and the head was pulled away by other less distinct figures. Bridger glanced at Oldroyd, who appeared to have noticed nothing and was cutting the rind off a piece of curled up bacon. He went back to the printer. When he had finished typing, he stepped cautiously out into the passage. It was empty. The street door was swinging open, but in the street outside there was no sign of anything unusual. There was no-one standing opposite, no-one watching from the corner. A car driving away might or might not have had something to do with it.

Dennis Bridger set off towards the car park, his legs shaking.

News of the message came out through one of the wire agencies in time for the evening papers. By the time General Vandenberg called on the Minister of Science to protest, a government statement was being broadcast on television. The Minister was out. Osborne stood with Vandenberg in his senior's office watching the newsreader mouthing earnestly out of the screen in the corner of the room.

The government of the time was a well-sounding but purposeless coalition of talents, nicknamed the Meritocrats, a closing of ranks in time of crisis. They were able men and women with no common principle except survival. The Prime Minister was a liberal Tory, the Minister of Labour a renegade trade-unionist; key posts were held by active and ambitious younger men like the Minister of Defence, others by less capable but publicly impressive figures with a good turn of phrase, such as the Minister of Science. Party differences had been not so much sunk as mislaid: possibly it was the end of party government in this country. Nobody cared much, the whole nation was apparently sunk in hopeless apathy in the face of a world that had got beyond its control. Some remaining left-wing anti-Establishment movements caused *Vichy* to be chalked up occasionally on Whitehall walls, but that was the only visible sign of spirit. People went quietly about their lives and an odd silence fell over public affairs. Someone said it was so quiet you could hear a bomb drop.

Into this vacuum fell the news of a message from space. The newspapers inevitably got it hopelessly wrong. SPACE-MEN SCARE: IS THIS AN ATTACK? they asked. The young man on the screen earnestly read out the official statement:

"The government this evening forcibly denied rumours of a possible invasion from space. A Ministry of Science spokesman told reporters that, while it was true that what appeared to be a message had been picked up by the new giant radio-telescope at Bouldershaw Fell, there was no reason to believe that it originated from either a space-ship or a nearby planet. If indeed the signal received was a message, it came from a very distant source."

There was no satisfactory explanation for the leak. Reinhart knew nothing about it and the Ministry of Defence's security man on the spot—Harries—was unaccountably missing. The military, however, were after heads. Vandenberg produced two dossiers which he opened on the Minister's table.

"'Fleming, Dr. John—1960 onwards: anti-N.A.T.O., pro-African, Aldermaston marcher, civil disobedience, nuclear disarmament.' Do you call that reliable?"

"He's a scientist, not a candidate for a police commission."

"He's supposed to be responsible. Look at the other." The General riffled through the other folder, not without relish. "Bridger—Communist Party 1958 to '63. Then he swung right round and started doing jobs for one of the international cartels. But one of the dirtiest: Intel. You could lose him anyway."

"Fleming won't work without him."

"That figures." The General gathered up the files. "I'd say we're vulnerable in that area."

"All right," said Osborne wearily, and picked up the Minister's phone. He spoke into it gently, as if ordering flowers. " Bouldershaw Fell."

In the control room the message was coming through again. Harvey was out in the recording bay, looking after the tapes, and Fleming was alone at the control desk. They were short-handed: Whelan had suddenly been posted away and even Harries was absent. Bridger hovered about in corners looking petulant and uneasy and twitching a good deal. Finally he faced up to the other man.

" Look, John, this could go on for ever."

" Maybe."

The sound from the stars went on over the loudspeaker.

" I'm going to bale out." Fleming looked up at him. " The design's finished. There's nothing more for me to do here."

" There's everything for you to do!"

" I'd rather move on."

" How about that?"

They listened for a moment to the speaker. Bridger's nose twitched.

" Could be anything," he said off-handedly.

" But I've an idea what."

" What?"

" It could be a set of instructions."

"All right, you work on it."

" We'll work on it together."

At that moment Judy broke in on them. She marched across from the door, her high heels clicking on the flooring like a guardsman's, her face set and furious. She could hardly wait to get to them before she spoke.

" Which of you told the press?"

Fleming stared at her in amazement. She turned to Bridger.

" Someone has leaked the information—*all* the information —to the press."

Fleming clicked his tongue deprecatingly. Judy gave him a blazing look and turned back to Bridger.

" It wasn't Professor Reinhart and it wasn't me. It wasn't Harvey or the other boys—they don't know enough. So it must be one of you."

" Q.E.D." said Fleming. She ignored him.

" How much did they pay you, Dr. Bridger?"

"I—"

Bridger stopped. Fleming got up and barged his way between them.

"Is it your business?" he asked her.

"Yes. I—"

"Well, what are you?" He pushed his face close up to her and she realised that his breath smelt of drink again.

"I—" she faltered, "I'm the press officer. I'm carrying the can. I've just had the biggest rocket of all time."

"I'm very sorry," said Bridger.

"Is that all you can say?" Her voice rose unsteadily.

"Do yourself a favour, will you?" Fleming stood with his legs apart, swaying, and grinning contemptuously down on her. "Take your talons out of my friend Dennis."

"Why?"

"Because *I* told them."

"You!" She stepped back as if she had been slapped in the face. "Were you drunk?"

"Yes," said Fleming and turned his back on her. He walked to the door of the recording room and then looked round. "It wouldn't have made any difference if I'd been sober."

As he went out of the door he called back at her: "And they didn't pay me!"

Judy stood for a moment without hearing or seeing. The loudspeaker hissed and crackled, fluorescent lighting shone down on the sparse angular furniture. Outside the window, the arch of the telescope reared up into a darkening sky: only three evenings ago she had come to it, uninitiated and uninvolved . . . She became aware of Bridger standing beside her, offering her a cigarette.

"Lost an idol, Miss Adamson?"

Judy, as press officer, had to report to Osborne, and Osborne reported to his Minister. Nothing was heard of Harries, and his disappearance was not announced. The press were persuaded that the whole thing was either a mistake or a hoax. After a series of painful meetings between ministers, the Ministry of Defence were able to assure General Vandenberg and his masters that nothing of the kind would occur again: they would take full responsibility. The search for Harries was intensified, and Fleming was summoned to London.

At first it seemed possible that Fleming was shielding Bridger, but it was soon established that he had in fact told the whole story over drinks in the Lion to an agency reporter called Jenkins. Although Bridger tendered his resignation, he had three months' notice to work out and he was left in charge of Bouldershaw Fell while Fleming was absent. The message continued to come in, and was printed out in a code of 0 and 1.

Fleming himself seemed quite unmoved by the commotion around him. He took all the printed sheets with him in the train to London and studied them hour after hour, making notes and calculations in the margin and on odd letters and envelopes that he found in his pockets. He appeared to be hardly aware of anything else. He dressed and ate absent-mindedly, he drank little; he burned with intense preoccupation and excitement. He ignored Judy, and hardly looked at the newspapers.

When he arrived at the Ministry of Science, he was shown up to Osborne's room, where Osborne was waiting for him with Reinhart and a stiff, middle-aged man with grey hair and impatient blue eyes. Osborne rose and shook hands.

" Dr. Fleming." He was very formal.

" Hi," said Fleming.

" You don't know Air Commodore Watling, Security Section, Ministry of Defence."

The stiff man bowed and looked at him without warmth. Fleming shifted and turned enquiringly to Reinhart.

" Hallo John," said Reinhart, in a small, restrained voice, and looked down self-consciously at his fingers.

" Have a seat, Dr. Fleming."

Osborne indicated a chair facing the others, but Fleming stared from one to another of them before he sat, as though he were waking up in a strange place.

" Is this a court of enquiry?"

There was a small silence. Watling lit a cigarette.

" You were advised there was a security barrier on your work?"

" What does that mean?"

" That it was confidential."

" Yes."

" Then why—?"

" I don't go for gagging scientists."

"Take it easy, John," Reinhart said soothingly. Watling went on to another tack.

"You've seen the papers?"

"Some of them."

"Half the world believes little green men with feelers are about to land in our back gardens."

Fleming smiled, feeling the ground firmer beneath him.

"Do you?"

"I'm in possession of the facts."

"The facts are what I gave the press. The straight scientific facts. How was I to know they'd distort them?

"It's not your job to assess these things, Dr Fleming." Osborne had installed himself elegantly and judicially behind his desk. "Which is why you were told not to interfere. I warned you myself."

"So?" Fleming was bored already.

"We've had to send a full report to the Defence Co-Ordination Committee," said Watling severely. "And the Prime Minister is making a statement to the United Nations."

"That's all right then."

"It's not the sort of position we like to be in, but our hand has been forced and we have to allay fear."

"Naturally."

"Our hand has been forced by you."

"Am I supposed to grovel?" Fleming began to be angry as well as bored. "What I do with my own discoveries is my own affair. It's still a free country, isn't it?"

"You *are* part of a team, John," Reinhart said, not looking at him.

Osborne leaned coaxingly forward across his desk.

"All we need, Dr. Fleming, is a personal statement."

"How will that help?"

"Anything which will reassure people will help."

"Particularly if you can discredit your informant."

"This isn't personal, John," said Reinhart.

"Isn't it? Then why am I here?" Fleming looked contemptuously round at them. "When I've made a statement to say I was talking out of the back of my head—what happens then?"

"I'm afraid . . ." Reinhart studied his fingers again.

"I'm afraid we've given Professor Reinhart no choice," said Watling.

"They want you to leave the team," Reinhart told him.

Fleming got up and thought for a moment, while they waited for an outburst.

"Well, it's easy, isn't it?" he said at last, smoothly.

"I don't want to lose you, John." Reinhart made a small, deprecating movement with his tiny hands.

"No, of course not. There's one snag."

"Oh?"

"You can't go any further without me."

They were prepared for that. There were other people, Osborne pointed out.

"But they don't know what it is, do they?"

"Do you?"

Fleming nodded and smiled. Watling sat up even straighter.

"You mean, you've decyphered it?"

"I mean, I know what it is."

"You expect us to believe that?"

Osborne obviously did not, nor Watling; but Reinhart was unsure. "What is it, John?"

"Do I stay with it?"

"What is it?"

Fleming grinned. "It's a do-it-yourself kit; and it isn't of human origin. I'll prove it to you."

He dug into his briefcase for his papers.

Three

ACCEPTANCE

THE new Institute of Electronics was housed in what had once been a Regency square and was now a pedestrian precinct surrounded by tall concrete-and-glass buildings with mosaic faces. The Institute possessed several floors of computing equipment, and after intensive lobbying Reinhart was able to gain Fleming a reprieve and install him and the rest of the team there with access to the equipment. Bridger, nearing the end of his contract, was given a young assistant named Christine Flemstad, and Judy — to her and everyone else's disgust—was sent along with them.

"What," Fleming demanded, "is the point of a P.R.O. if we're so damn top-secret we have to stand on a ladder to brush our own teeth?"

"I'm supposed to learn, if you'll let me. So that when it *is* released . . ."

"You'll be *au fait?*"

"Do you mind?" Judy spoke tentatively, as though she, not Fleming, had been to blame before. She felt bound to him in an inexplicable way.

"I should worry!" said Fleming. "The more sex the better."

But, as he had said at Bouldershaw, he had no time. He spent all his days, and most of the night, breaking down the enormous mass of data from the telescope into comprehensible figures. Whatever deal he had made—or Reinhart had made for him—had sobered him and intensified his work. He drove Bridger and the girl with solid and unrelenting determination and suffered patiently all manner of supervision and routine. Nominally, Reinhart was in charge, and he took all his results obediently to him; but the defence people were never far away, and he even managed to be polite to Watling, whom they called "Silver-wings."

The rest of the team were less happy. There was a distinct coolness between Bridger and Judy. Bridger, in any case, was anxious to be gone, and the girl Christine was openly in the running to succeed him. She was young and pretty with something of Fleming's single-mindedness, and she patently regarded Judy as a hanger-on. As soon as she had an opportunity, she fought.

Shortly after they moved down from Bouldershaw, Harries had turned up: Watling revealed this on one of his visits to the unit. Harries had been set on at the bookie's, bundled into a car, beaten up and dumped in a disused mill, where he had nearly died. He had crawled around with a broken leg, unable to get out, living on water from a dripping tap and some chocolate he had in his pocket, until after three days he had been discovered by a rat-catcher. He did not return to them, and Watling told only Judy the details. She kept them to herself, but tried to sound Christine on Bridger's background.

"How long have you known him?"

They were in a small office off the main computer hall, Christine working at a trestle table littered with punched input cards, Judy pacing about and wishing she had a chair of her own.

"I was one of his research students at Cambridge." In spite of her Baltic parentage, about which Judy knew, Christine spoke like any English university girl.

"Did you know him well?"

"No. If you want his academic references . . ."

"I only wondered . . ."

"What?"

"If he ever behaved—oddly."

"I didn't have to wear a barbed wire girdle."

"I didn't mean that."

"What do you mean?"

"He never asked you to help him do anything, on the side?"

"Why should he?" She looked round at Judy with serious hostile eyes. "Some of us have real work to get on with."

Judy wandered into the computer hall and watched the machines clicking and flickering away. Each machine had its own attendant: neuter-looking young men and women in identical overalls. In the centre was a long table where calculations from the computers were assembled in piles of punched cards or coils of tape or long screeds of paper from the output printers. The volume of figures they handled was prodigious, and it all seemed utterly unrelated to flesh and blood—a convocation of machinery, talking its own language.

Judy had learnt a little of what the team were doing. The message from Andromeda had continued for many weeks without repeating itself, and then had gone back to the beginning and started all over again. This had enabled them to fill in most of the gaps in the first transmission; as the earth was turning, they were only able to receive it during the hours that the western hemisphere was facing the Andromeda constellation, and for twelve hours out of every twenty-four the source went below their horizon. When the message began again, the rotation of the earth was in a different phase to it, so that part of the lost passages could now be received; and by the end of the third repeat they had it all. The staff at Bouldershaw Fell went on monitoring, but there was no deviation. Whatever the source was, it had one thing to say and went on saying it.

No one concerned now doubted that it was a message. Even Air Commodore Watling's department referred to it as " the Andromeda broadcast " as if its source and identity were beyond doubt. The work on it they catalogued as Project A. It was a very long message, and the dots and dashes, when resolved into understandable arithmetic, added up to many million long groups of figures. Conversion into normal forms would have taken a lifetime without the computers, and took a good many months with them. Each machine had to be instructed what to do with the information given it; and this, Judy learnt, was called programming. A program consisted of a set of calculations fed in on punched cards, which set the machine to do the job required. The group of figures to be analysed—the data—was then put in, and the machine gave the answer in a matter of seconds. This process had to be repeated for every fresh consideration of every group of figures. Fortunately, the smaller computers could be used for preparing material for the larger ones, and all the machines possessed, as well as input, control, calculating and output units, a reasonable memory storage, so that new answers could be based on the experience of earlier ones.

It was Reinhart — kind, tolerant, wise, tactful Reinhart — who explained most of it to Judy. After the affair at Bouldershaw Fell he came to accept her with more grace, and to show that he liked her and felt sorry for her. Although he was deeply and precariously involved in the inter-departmental diplomacy which kept them going, his particular qualities of leadership were very apparent at this time. Somehow he kept Fleming on the rails and the authorities at bay and still had time to listen to everyone's ideas and problems; and all the while he remained discreetly in the background, hopping from issue to issue like some quiet, dainty, highly intelligent bird.

He would take Judy by the arm and talk to her quite simply about what they were doing, as though he had all the time and all the knowledge in the world. But there came a point in the understanding of computation where he had to hand over to Fleming, and Fleming went on alone. Computers, Judy realised, were Fleming's first and great love, and he communicated with them by a sort of intuitive magic.

It was not that there was anything cranky about him; he simply had a superhuman fluency in their language. He swam in binary mathematics like a fish in the sea, and made short cuts which it took Bridger and Christine many hours of solid plodding to check. But they never found him wrong.

One day, just before Bridger was due to leave, Reinhart took him and Fleming aside for a longer session than usual and at the end of it went straight to the Ministry. The following morning the Professor and Fleming went back to Whitehall together.

" Are we all met?"

Osborne's rather equine voice neighed down the length of the conference room. About twenty people stood round the long table, talking in groups. Blotters, notepads and pencils had been laid out for them on the polished mahogany and at intervals down the centre of the table were silver trays bearing water-jugs and glasses. At the end was one larger blotter, with tooled leather corners, for the Top Man.

Vandenberg and Watling were in one group, Fleming and

Reinhart in another, and a respectful circle of civil servants in charcoal-grey suits surrounded one dazzling matron in a flowered costume. Osborne surveyed them expertly and then nodded to the youngest charcoal-suited man who stood by the door. The young man disappeared into the corridor and Osborne took his place by the head of the table.

"Aheeem!" he whinnied. The others shuffled into their places, Vandenberg—at Osborne's invitation—at the right of the top chair. Fleming, accompanied by Reinhart, sat obstinately at the far end. There was a little silence and then the door opened and James Robert Ratcliff, Minister of Science, walked in. He waved an affable hand at one or two juniors who started to rise—"Sit down, dear boy, sit down!"—and took his seat behind the tooled leather. He had a distinguished, excessively well-groomed grey head and healthy pink-and-white face and fingers. The fingers were very strong, square and capable: one could imagine him taking large handfuls of things. He smiled genially upon the company.

"Good-morning, lady and gentlemen. I hope I'm not late."

The more nervous shook their heads and muttered "No."

"How are you, General?" Ratcliff turned, slightly Caesar-like, to Vandenberg.

"Old and ailing," said Vandenberg, who was neither.

Osborne coughed. "Shall I go round the table for you?"

"Thank you. There are several fresh faces."

Osborne knew all the names, and the Minister gave a gracious inclination of his head or lift of his hand to each one. The flowered prima-donna turned out to be a Mrs. Tate-Allen from the Treasury, who represented the grants committee. When they got to Fleming the ministerial reaction changed.

"Ah—Fleming. No more indiscretions, I hope."

Fleming scowled the length of the table at him.

"I've had my mouth shut, if that's what you mean."

"It is." Ratcliff smiled charmingly and passed on to Watling.

"We'll try not to take too much of each other's time, shall we?" He raised his fine Roman head and looked down the table to Reinhart. "You have some more news for us, Professor?"

Reinhart coughed diffidently on to his little white hand.

"Dr. Fleming here has made an analysis."

"Excuse me," Mrs. Tate-Allen beamed, "but I don't think Mr. Newby here is entirely in the picture."

Mr. Newby was a small, thin man who looked used to humiliation.

"Oh, well," said Ratcliff, "perhaps you'd fill in the background, Osborne."

Osborne filled it in.

"And now?"

Twenty pairs of eyes, including the Minister's, turned to Fleming.

"We know what it is," said Fleming.

"Well done!" said Mrs. Tate-Allen.

"What is it?"

Fleming looked levelly at the Minister.

"It's a computer program," he said quietly.

"A computer program? Can you be sure about that?"

Fleming merely nodded. Everyone else talked.

"Please!" said Osborne, banging his fist on the table. The hubbub subsided. Mrs. Tate-Allen held up a blue-gloved hand.

"I'm afraid, Minister, some of us don't know what a computer program is."

Fleming explained, while Reinhart and Osborne sat back and breathed relief. The boy was behaving well.

"Have you tried it in a computer?" asked Mrs. Tate-Allen.

"We've used computers to break it down. We've nothing that'll take all of it." He tapped the papers in front of him. "This is simply vast."

"If you had access to a bigger computer—" Osborne suggested.

"It isn't only size. It is, in fact, more than just a program."

"What is it then?" Vandenberg asked, settling more comfortably into his chair. It was going to be a long business.

"It's in three sections." Fleming arranged his papers as if that would make it clearer. "The first part is a design—or rather, it's a mathematical requirement which can be interpreted as a design. The second part is the program proper, the order code as we call it. The third and last part is data—information sent for the machine to work on."

"I'd be glad of an opportunity . . ." Vandenberg extended a hand and the papers were passed to him. "I don't say you're wrong. I'd like our signals people to check your methodology."

44

"You do that," said Fleming. There was a respectful hush as the papers were handed up the table, but Mrs. Tate-Allen evidently felt that some comment was required.

"I must say, this is very interesting."

"Interesting!" Fleming looked explosive. Reinhart laid a restraining hand on his sleeve. "It's the most important thing that's happened since the evolution of the brain."

"All right, John," said Reinhart. The Minister passed it over.

"What do you want to do next?"

"Build a computer that'll handle it."

"Are you seriously proposing," the Minister spoke slowly, choosing his words carefully, as though they were chocolates out of an assorted box, "that some other beings, in some distant part of the galaxy, who have never had any contact with us before, have now conveniently sent us the design and program for the kind of electronic machine—"

"Yes," said Fleming. The Minister sailed on: "Which we happen to possess on this earth?"

"We don't possess one."

"We possess the type, if not the model. Is it likely?"

"It's what happened."

Fleming made a dubious impression on the meeting. They had often seen it before: dedicated young scientists, obstinate and peevish, impatient of committee processes, and yet to be treated with great patience because they might have something valuable on them. These easily caricaturable officials were not fools; they were used to assessing people and situations. Much would depend on what Vandenberg and Osborne and Reinhart thought. Ratcliff enquired of the Professor.

"Arithmetic's universal," said Reinhart. "Electronic computing may well be."

"It may be the only form of computing, in the last analysis," put in Fleming.

Vandenberg looked up from the papers.

"I wonder—"

"Look," Fleming interrupted. "The message is being repeated all the time. If you've a better idea, you go and work on it."

Reinhart glanced uneasily across at Osborne, who was watching the state of play like a scorer at a cricket match.

"You can't use an existing machine?" Osborne asked.

"I said!"

"It seems a reasonable enough question," the Minister observed mildly. Fleming turned on him passionately.

"This program is simply enormous. I don't think you realise."

"Just explain, John," Reinhart said.

Fleming took a breath and continued more calmly. "If you want a computer to play you a decent game of draughts, it has to be able to accept a program of around five thousand order groups. If you want it to play chess—and you can; I've played chess with computers—you have to feed in about fifteen thousand orders. To handle this material," he waved towards the papers in front of Vandenberg, "you need a computer that can take in a thousand million, or, more accurately, tens of thousands of millions of numbers, before it can even *start* work on the data."

At last he had the meeting with him: this was a glimpse of a brain they could respect.

"It's surely a matter of assembling enough units," Osborne said.

Fleming shook his head.

"It isn't just size; it needs a new conception. There's no equipment on earth . . ." He searched his mind for an example, and they waited attentively until he found one. "Our newest computers still work in microseconds. This is a machine that must operate in milli-microseconds, otherwise we'd all be old men by the time it got round to processing the whole of the vast quantity of data. And it would need a memory—probably a low temperature memory—at least with the capacity of the human brain, and far more efficiently controlled."

"Is this proven?" asked Ratcliff.

"What do you expect? We have to get the means to prove it first. Whatever intelligence sent this message is way ahead of us. We don't know why they sent it, or to whom. But it's something we couldn't do. We're just *homo sapiens,* plodding along. If we want to interpret it—" He paused. "If . . ."

"This is theory, isn't it?"

"It's analysis."

The Minister appealed once more to Reinhart.

"Do you think it could be proved?"

"I can prove it," said Fleming.

"I was asking the Professor."

"I can prove it by making a computer that *will* handle it," said Fleming, undeterred. "That's what's intended."

"Is that realistic?"

"It's what the message is asking for."

The Minister began to lose patience. He drummed his square fingers on the table.

"Professor?"

Reinhart considered, not so much what he believed, but what to say.

"It would take a long time."

"But it's what is wanted?"

"Possibly."

"I shall need the best available computer to work with," said Fleming, as though it were all agreed. "And the whole of our present team."

Osborne looked anguished; the issue was very doubtful still, to anyone who knew, and the Minister showed signs of taking offence.

"We can make available university computers," he said, in tones that suggested matters of mere routine. Fleming's patience suddenly snapped.

"University nothing! Do you think universities have the best equipment in this day and age?" He pointed across the table at Vandenberg. "Ask your military friend where the only really decent computer in the country is."

A small frozen pause: the meeting looked at the American general.

"I'll need notice of that question."

"You won't, 'cause I'll tell you. It's at the rocket research establishment at Thorness."

"That's engaged on defence work."

"Of course it is," said Fleming contemptuously.

Vandenberg did not reply. This young man was the Minister's problem. The meeting waited while Ratcliff drummed his fingers on the tooled leather and Osborne totted up the score, not very hopefully. His master was undoubtedly impressed but not convinced: Fleming, like most men of sincerity, was a bad advocate; he had had his chance and more or less thrown it away. If the Minister did nothing, the whole thing would remain a piece of university theory. If he took action, he would have to negotiate with the military: he would have to convince not only the Minister of Defence but also Vandenberg's Allied committee that the effort was worth the candle. Ratcliff took his time. He liked to have people waiting for him.

"We could make a claim," he said at last. "It would be a Cabinet matter."

For some time after the meeting there was nothing for the team to do. Reinhart and Osborne took negotiations forward step by prudent step, but Fleming could go no further. Bridger cleared up his remaining work, Christine sat quietly in the office checking and re-checking the ground they had already been over; but Fleming turned his back on the whole thing, and took Judy with him.

"It's no good fiddling around until they've made up their minds," he told her and dragged her off to help him enjoy himself. Not that he made passes at her. He simply enjoyed having her around and was affectionate and surprisingly pleasant company. The mainspring of his discontent, she discovered, was irreverence of pomposity and humbug. When they got in the way of his job he was sour and sometimes violent, but when he put work behind him they became merely targets for his particular brand of bitten-off salted humour.

"Britain is sinking slowly in the west," he remarked once, when she asked him about the general state of things, and dismissed it with a grin. When she tried to apologise for her outburst at Bouldershaw Fell, he simply smacked her across the bottom.

"Forgive and forget, that's me," he said, and bought her a drink. She endured a good deal for his pleasure: he loved modern music, which she did not understand; he loved driving fast, which frightened her; and he loved looking at Westerns, which frightened her even more. He was deeply tired and restless. They rushed from cinema to concert, from concert to a long drive, from a long drive to a long drink, and by the end of it he was worn out. At least he seemed happy, although she was not. She felt she was sailing under false colours.

They only went occasionally to the little office in the Institute, and when they were there Fleming flirted with

Christine. Not that Judy could blame him. He took no notice of her in any other way, and she was astonishingly pretty. She was, as she confided to Bridger, " In love with his brain," but she seemed not particularly to relish being hugged and pinched. She went on stolidly with her work. She did enquire, however, about Thorness.

" Have you ever been there Dr. Fleming?"

" Once."

" What's it like?"

" Remote and beautiful, like you. Also high-powered, soulless, clueless—not like you."

It was assumed that, if Fleming were allowed to go there, she would go too. Watling had looked over her antecedents and found them impeccable. Father and mother Flemstad had fled from Lithuania when the Russian armies rolled over it towards the end of the Hitler war, and Christine had been born and brought up in England. Her parents had become naturalised British citizens before they died and she had been subjected to every possible check.

Dennis Bridger's activities seemed a good deal more interesting. As the date of his departure drew near, he received an increasing number of unexplained long-distance telephone calls which appeared to worry him a good deal, although he never talked about them. One morning, alone in the office with Judy, he seemed more harassed than usual. When the telephone rang he seized it practically out of her hand. It was obviously a summons; he made some sort of excuse and left the office. Judy watched him from the window as he walked across the precinct to the roadway where a very large, very expensive car was waiting for him.

As he approached, the driver's door opened and an immensely tall chauffeur stepped out wearing the sort of livery that one associated with a *coupé de ville* of the nineteen twenties, a pale mustard high-buttoned cross-over tunic, breeches and polished leather leggings.

" Dr. Bridger?"

He had on dark glasses and he spoke with a soft, indeterminate foreign accent. The car was shining and monstrously beautiful, like a new aircraft without wings. Twin radio masts sprung from its tail fins to above the height of a man—even that man. The whole outfit was quite absurdly larger than life.

The chauffeur held open the door to the back of the car while Bridger got in. There was an immensely wide seat, a deeply carpeted floor, blue-glazed windows and, on the far side of the seat, a short stocky man with a completely bald head.

The short man extended a hand with a ring on it.

" I am Kaufmann."

The chauffeur returned to his place in front of the glass partition and they moved off.

" You do not mind if we drive around?" There was no mistaking Kaufmann's accent: he was German, prosperous and tough. " There is so much tittle-tattle if one is seen in places."

There was a small buzz by his ear. He picked up an ivory telephone receiver that lay across a rack in front of him. Bridger could see the chauffeur speaking into a microphone by the steering-wheel.

" Ja." Kaufmann listened for a moment and then turned and looked out of the rear window. " Ja, Egon, I see. Go in a circle, then, yes? Und Stuttgart . . . the call for Stuttgart."

He replaced the phone and turned to Bridger.

" My chauffeur says we are being followed by a taxi." Bridger looked round nervously. Kaufmann laughed, or at least he showed his teeth. " Not to worry. There are always taxis in London. He will see we go nowhere. What is important is I have my call to Stuttgart." He produced a silver case containing miniature cigars. " Smoking?"

" No thank you."

" You send me a telex message to Geneva." Kaufmann helped himself to a cigarillo. " Some months ago."

" Yes."

" Since then, we do not hear from you."

" I changed my mind." Bridger twitched anxiously.

"And now, perhaps, comes the time to change it back. We have been very puzzled, you know, these past few months." He was serious but agreeable and relaxed. Bridger looked guiltily out of the back window again.

" Do not worry, I tell you. It is looked after." He held a jewelled silver lighter to the end of his cigarillo and inhaled. " There really was a message?"

" Yes."

" From a planet?"

"A very distant planet."

" Somewhere in Andromeda?"

" That's right."

" Well, that is a comfortable way away."

" What is this—?" Bridger twitched his nose as the cigar smoke drifted up it.

" What is this about? I come to that. In America—I was in America at the time—there was great excitement. Everyone was very alarmed. And in Europe—everywhere. Then your government say: ' Nothing. It is nothing. We will tell you later.' And so on. And people forget; months go by and gradually people forget. There are other things to worry about. But there is something?"

" Not officially."

" No, no—officially there is nothing. We have tried, but everywhere is a blank wall. Everybody's lips are sealed."

" Including mine."

They were by now half-way round Regent's Park. Bridger looked at his watch.

" I have to get back this afternoon."

" You are working for the British Government?" Kaufmann made it sound like a piece of polite conversation.

" I'm part of their team," said Bridger.

" Working on the message?"

" Why should that interest you?"

"Anything of importance interests us. And this may be of great importance."

" It might. It might not."

" But you are going on with the work? Please, do not look so secretive. I am not trying to pump you."

" I'm not going on with it."

" Why not?"

" I don't want to stay for ever in government service."

They drove past the zoo and down towards Portland Place. Kaufmann puffed contentedly at his cigar while Bridger waited. As they turned west into Marylebone Kaufmann said:

" You would like something more lucrative? With us?"

" I did think so," Bridger said, blinking at his feet.

" Until your little fracas in Bouldershaw?"

" You knew about that?" Bridger looked at him sharply. "At Oldroyd's?"

"Naturally I knew."

He was very affable, almost sweet. Bridger studied his shoes again.

"I didn't want any trouble."

"You should not be so easy put off," said Kaufmann. "At the same time, you must not lead people towards us. We may be busy with something else."

They turned north again, up Baker Street.

"I think you should stay where you are," he said. "But you should keep in touch with me."

"How much?"

Kaufmann opened his eyes wide.

"Excuse?"

"If you want me to give you information."

"Really, Dr. Bridger!" Kaufmann laughed. "You have no finesse."

The intercom buzzed. Kaufmann picked up the phone.

"Kaufmann. . . . Ja, ja. . . . Das ist Felix? . . ."

They did two more turns round the park and then dropped Bridger off a few hundred yards from the Institute. Judy watched his return but he said nothing to her. He thoroughly distrusted her anyhow.

Half an hour later the taxi which had followed Kaufmann's car drew up at a telephone box and Harries stepped out. His leg was still strapped and he moved stiffly, but he considered himself fit for work. He paid the driver and limped across to the phone box. As the taxi drove away another car drew up and waited for him.

The phone was answered by Watling's P.A., a bored Lieutenant from the Household Cavalry, the Ministry of Defence being, by that time, what was called "integrated."

"I see. Well, you'd better come round and report."

As he hung up, Watling swept in, brisk and bothered from another meeting with Osborne.

"Jabber, jabber, jabber. That's all they do." He slung his brief case on to a chair. "Anything new?"

"Harries has been on."

"And?"

Watling took possession of his desk, a severe metal table in a severe concrete room with fire instructions on the door. The P.A. raised a cavalry-trained eyebrow.

"He says Bridger has been seen with a Known Person."

"Who? You can ditch the jargon."

"Kaufmann, sir."

"Kaufmann?"

"Intel. The international cartel people."

Watling stared at the blank wall facing him. There were still a number of large cosmopolitan cartels in spite of the anti-trust laws and the administration of the Common Market. They were not palpably illegal but they were extremely powerful and in some cases they had very nearly a stranglehold over European trade. At a time when the West was liable to boycott by any or all of the countries it depended on for raw materials, there was a frightening amount of scope for unscrupulous trading agencies, and Intel was generally known and disliked for its lack of scruple. Anything which found its way into its hands was likely to be sold profitably in another capital the next time the market was good.

"Any more?"

"No. They did two or three circuits in Kaufmann's mobile gin-palace and then landed back at base."

Watling stroked his chin as he fitted pieces of thought neatly and methodically together.

"You think that's what he was up to at Bouldershaw?"

"Harries thinks so."

"Which is why Harries was hauled off and pranged and dumped?"

"Partly."

"Well, they're the last people we want genned up on this."

Once anything got into the hands of Intel it was extremely difficult to trace. They had a perfectly legal organisation in London, registered offices in Switzerland and branches over at least three continents. Information slipped along their private wires like quicksilver and there was very little that could be done about it. There were no search warrants for that kind of operation. By the time you were ransacking a Piccadilly office, the thing you had lost was being swapped for manganese or bauxite behind some very unsympathetic frontier. Nothing was sacred, or safe.

" I suppose Bridger'll go on feeding 'em stuff," he said.

" He's supposed to be pulling out," his P.A. reminded him.

" I doubt if he will now. They'll have crossed his palm." He sighed. "Anyway. he'd get it all from Fleming. They're thick as condensed soup."

" You think Fleming's in it?"

"Ach!" Watling pushed his chair back and gave the thing up. " He's just a hopeless innocent. He'll blow the gaff to anyone to show how independent he is. Look at what happened last time. And now we're going to have them in our midst."

" How so?"

" How so? You ought to write a phrasebook. They're moving into W.D. quarters, that's how so. The whole boiling. Fleming wants to build his super-computer at the Rocket Research Establishment at Thorness."

" Oh?"

" That's Top Secret."

" Yes, sir." The P.A. looked languidly discreet. " Has it been agreed?"

" It will be. I can smell a nonsense when I'm down-wind of it. Vandenberg's furious. So are all the Allies, I wouldn't wonder. But Reinhart's all for it and so's Osborne, and so's their Minister. And so will the Cabinet be, I expect."

" Then we can't keep 'em out?"

" We can watch 'em. We'd better keep Harries on it for one."

" They've their own security staff at Thorness. Army," the P.A. added with pride.

The Air Commodore sniffed. " Harries can work in with them."

" Harries wants to come off it."

" Why?"

" He says he's sure they've rumbled him."

" How? Pardon." Watling flashed a smile at him. " How so?"

" Well, they beat him up at Bouldershaw. They probably think he's on to something bigger than this."

" He probably is. Where is he now?"

" Tailing them. He's coming in later to report."

But Harries did not report later, or at all. Judy and Fleming found his corpse the following morning, under the tonneau cover of Fleming's car.

When Judy had been sick and they had both been to the police station and the body had been taken away and dealt with, they went back to the office to find a message for Fleming to go straight round to the Ministry of Science. Judy, waiting with Christine, was interviewed by Watling and felt frightened and miserable. Christine went on with her work, only stopping to give Judy two aspirin with the air of one who dispenses charity regardless of merit.

Before he left for the Ministry. Fleming had kissed Judy on the cheek. She smiled queasily at him.

" Why should they dump it on me?" he said.

" They didn't dump it on you. They dumped it on me, as a warning."

She went to the Ladies and was sick again.

Fleming came back before lunch cock-o'-hoop and bubbling. He pulled Christine out of her chair and held her to him.

" It's through!"

" Through?" Judy remained dazed at the other side of the room.

"Authority in triplicate from Air Commodore Jet-Propelled's superior officers. They've opened wide their pearly barbed wire stockade."

" Thorness?" Christine asked, pushing him away. Fleming bounced his behind on to the trestle table.

" We're graciously allowed in to use their beautiful, beautiful tax-payers' equipment hitherto reserved for playing soldiers."

" When?" asked Judy.

Fleming slid off the table and went across and hugged her.

"As soon as we're ready. Priority A on the big computer—barring what is laughingly called a national emergency. We're excused morning parades, we shall be issued with passes, we shall have our fingers printed, our brains washed and our hair searched for small animals. And we shall build the marvel of the age." He left Judy and held out his arms to Christine. " You and I, darling! We'll teach 'em, won't we? ' Is it proven?' asks His Ministership. We'll prove 'em! ' Come the

four corners of the world in arms, and we will shock them '—
as the lady said in the strip club. Oh—and Silver-Wings is
coming to give us our marching-orders."

He started singing " Silver wings among the gold," and took
them both out to a lunch which Judy could not eat. There was
no sign of Bridger.

Watling called back in the afternoon, composed but severe,
like a visiting headmaster. He made the three of them sit down
while he lectured them.

" What happened to Harries followed directly from his work
with you."

" But he was a lab. cleaner!"

" He was Military Intelligence."

" Oh!"

This was news to Christine, and to Fleming. He reacted with
a kind of savage flippancy.

" Ours, as they say?"

" Ours."

" Charming."

" Don't flatter yourselves that this was all on account of
what you're doing. You're not that important yet." The girls
sat and listened while Watling turned his attention exclusively
on Fleming. " Harries probably ran into something else when
he was covering for you."

" Why was he covering for us if we're not important?"

" People—other people—don't know whether it's important
or not. They know something's on, thanks to you opening your
mouth. It may or may not be of great strategic value."

" Do you know who killed Harries?" Fleming asked quietly.
His own share in the death had perhaps come home to him.

" Yes."

" That's something."

"And we know who paid them to."

" Then you're home and dry."

" Except that we won't be allowed to touch them," said
Watling stiffly. " For diplomatic reasons."

" Charming again."

" It isn't a particularly charming world." He looked round
at them as if performing an unpleasant duty. He was a modest
and unpompous man who disliked preaching. " You people

who've been living a quiet, sheltered life in your laboratories have got to understand something: you're on ops. now."

" On what?" asked Fleming.

"Operations. If this idea of yours comes off, it'll give us a very valuable piece of property."

" Who's ' us '?"

" The country."

"Ah yes, of course."

Watling ignored him. He had heard plenty about Fleming's attitude to the Establishment.

" Even if it doesn't work, it'll attract attention. Thorness is an important place and people will go to great lengths to find out what's going on there. This is why I'm warning you—all of you." He fixed them in turn with his brisk blue eyes. " You're not in the university any more—you're in the jungle. It may just look like stuffy old officialdom, with a lot of smooth talk and platitudinous statements by politicians and government servants like me, but it's a jungle all the same. I can assure you of that. Secrets are bought and sold, ideas are stolen, and sometimes people get hurt. That's how the world's business is done. Please remember it."

When he had gone, Fleming returned to the computers and Judy went down to Whitehall to get her next instructions. Bridger drifted in later in the day, anxious and looking for Fleming.

" Dennis "—Fleming bounced back in from the computer hall—" We're off!"

" Off?"

" Thorness. We're cooking with gas."

" Oh, good," said Bridger flatly.

" The Minister of Science hath prevailed. Mankind is about to take a small step forward into the jungle, according to our uniformed friends. Why don't you change your mind? Join the happy throng."

"Yes. Thank you, John." Bridger looked down at his feet and twitched his nose in an agony of shyness. "That's what I came to see you about. I *have* changed my mind."

By the time Judy reached Osborne, Osborne knew.

Four

ANTICIPATION

No one ever went to Thorness for fun. The quickest way from
London took twelve hours, by air to Aberdeen and then by fast
diesel across the Highlands to Gairloch on the west coast.
Thorness was the first station north of Gairloch, but there was
nothing there but a small decaying village, the wild rocky coast
and the moors. The Research Establishment covered a headland
facing out to the wide gap of water between the Isle of Skye and
the Isle of Lewis, and was fenced in to the landward side by
tall link wiring topped with barbed wire. The entrance was
flanked by guard-huts and guards, and the fence and cliff-top
were patrolled by soldiers with dogs. To seaward lay the grey
Atlantic water, an island inhabited by birds, and an occasional
Royal Naval patrol launch. It was all green and grey and brown
and prone to clouds, and, apart from periodical noises from inside
the camp, it was a silent place.

It was raining when Reinhart and Fleming arrived. A black
staff car driven by a young woman in green uniform met them
at the station and splashed along the open moorland road to
the gates of the camp. There they were checked in by a sergeant
of the Argyll and Sutherland Highlanders who phoned the
Director to let him know they were on the way.

The main offices were in a long, narrow one-storey building standing in the middle of the open compound. Although it
was new and modern in design, it still had something of the
traditional, bleak look of a barracks; but the inside of the
Director's office was a very different matter. The ebony floor
shone, the lights were hooded by white streamlined shapes,
windows were curtained to the floor and maps and charts on the
walls were framed in polished wood. The Director's desk was

wide and beautiful: behind it sat a man with a narrow, lined face, and on it stood a small plaque stating, in neat black letters, DR. F. T. N. GEERS.

He greeted them with politeness but without enthusiasm, and with a patently false deprecation of what he was doing.

" You'll find it a very dull place here," he said, offering them cigarettes out of the polished nose-cap of a rocket. " We know each other by repute, of course."

Reinhart sat warily on one of the visitors' chairs, which were so low that he could hardly see the Director behind his desk.

" We've corresponded, I think, over missile tracking." He had to crane up to speak; it was obviously done on purpose. Fleming regarded the arrangement and smiled.

A physicist by training, Geers had for years been a senior scientific executive on defence projects and was now more like a commanding officer than a scientist. Somewhere beneath the martinet's uniform a disappointed research man lay hidden, but this only made him more envious of other people's work and more irritated by the mass of day-to-day detail that fell upon him.

" It's about time you got your job behind barbed wire, from all I hear." He was peevish. but able; he had plans worked out for them. " It's going to be difficult, of course. We can't give you unlimited facilities."

" We don't ask—" began Reinhart.

Fleming interrupted. " The priorities have been fixed, I understood." Geers gave him a sharp, cold look and flicked ash into a tray made from a piston casting.

" You'll have certain hours set aside on the main computer. You'll have your own work-block and living-quarters for your team. They'll be within our perimeter and you'll be under our surveillance, but you'll have passes and you'll be free to come and go as you wish. Major Quadring is in charge of our security, and I'm in charge of all research projects."

" Not ours," said Fleming, without looking at Reinhart.

" Mine are more mundane but more immediate tasks." Geers, so far as possible, tried to avoid Fleming and addressed himself to the Professor. " Yours is a Ministry of Science affair—more idealistic, though perhaps a little hit and miss."

There was a framed photograph, on one corner of his desk, of his wife and two small children.

" I wonder how they get on?" Fleming said to Reinhart when they left.

It was still pouring outside. One of Geers's assistants led them round the compound, across the wet grass, along concrete paths between rows of low bunker-like buildings half buried in the ground. and up to the launching area at the top of the headland.

" It's quite calm here to-day," he said, as they bent their heads against the sweeping rain. " It can blow a gale as soon as look at you."

Several small rockets rested on their tilted racks, swathed in nylon covers, pointing out to sea, and one larger one stood vertical on the main launching pad, looking heavy and earthbound lashed to its scaffold.

" We don't go in for the really big stuff here. These are all interceptors; a lot of ability packed into a little space. It's all highly classified, of course. We don't encourage visitors in the normal way."

The main computer was an impressive affair, housed in a big laboratory building. It was an American importation, three times the size of anything they had used before. The duty staff gave Fleming a timetable with his sessions marked on it; they seemed friendly enough though not particularly interested. There was also an empty office building for their own use, and a number of pre-fabricated chalets for living-quarters—small and bare but clean and fitted out with service furniture.

They squelched in their sodden shoes across to the personnel area and were shown the senior staff mess and lounge, the shop, laundry and garage, the cinema and post office. The camp was completely self-supporting: there was nothing to go out for but views of heather and sky.

For the first two or three months only the basic unit moved up: Fleming, Bridger, Christine, Judy and a few junior assistants. Their offices bulged with calculations, plans, blue-prints and odd pieces of experimental lash-up equipment. Fleming and Bridger had long all-night sessions over wiring circuits and electronic components, and slowly the building filled up with more and more research and design assistants and with draughtsmen and engineers.

Early the following spring a firm of Glasgow contractors appeared on the site and festooned the area with boards saying

MACINTYRE & SONS. A building for the new super-computer, as Fleming's brain-child was called, was put up inside the perimeter but away from the rest of the camp, and lorry-loads of equipment arrived and disappeared inside it.

The permanent staff viewed all this with lively but detached interest and went on with their own projects. Every week or so there would be a roar and a flash from the launching pads as another quarter of a million pounds of tax-payers' money went off into the air. The moorland sheep and cattle would stampede in a half-hearted sort of way, and there would be a few days of intense activity inside the plotting rooms. Apart from that it was as quiet as an undiscovered land and, when the rain lifted, incredibly beautiful.

The junior members of Reinhart's team mixed in happily with the defence scientists and the soldiers guarding them, eating and drinking and going on excursions together and sailing together in small boats on the bay; but Bridger and Fleming walked on their own and were known as the heavenly twins. When they were not either in the computer building or the offices they were usually in one or other of their huts, working. Occasionally Fleming shut himself up with a problem and Bridger took a motor-boat out to the bird island, Thorholm, with a pair of field-glasses.

Reinhart operated from London, paying periodic visits but mostly orbiting round Whitehall, pushing through plans, permits, budgets and the endless reports required by the government. Somehow everything they wanted they got fast and there were few delays. Osborne, Reinhart said modestly, was a past master.

Only Judy was at a loose end. Her office was apart from the others, in the main administrative block, and her living quarters were with the women defence scientists. Fleming, though perfectly amiable, had no time to spend with her; Bridger and Christine went to some lengths to miss her. She managed to keep a general tally on what was going on, and she allowed some of the army officers to take her about, but otherwise there was nothing. During the long winter evenings she took to tapestry and clay modelling and acquired a reputation for being arty, but in reality she was just bored.

When the new computer was nearly finished, Fleming gave her a conducted tour of it. His own attitude was a mixture of deprecation and awe; he could be completely wrong about it, or it could be something unimaginable and uncanny. The chief impression he gave was of fatigue; he was desperately tired now, and tiredly desperate. The machine itself was indeed something. It was so big that instead of being housed in a room, the control room was built inside it.

"We're like Jonah in the belly of the whale," he told her, pointing to the ceiling. "The cooling unit's up there—a helium liquefier. There's a constant flow of liquid helium round the core."

Inside the heavy double fire-doors was an area the size of a ballroom, with a ceiling-high wall of equipment dividing it across the centre. Facing that, and with its back to the doors, was the main control desk, with a sort of glorified typing desk on one side and a printing machine on the other. Both the typing desk and the printer were flanked by associated tape decks and and punch-card equipment. The main lights were not yet working: there was only a single bulb on the control desk and a number of riggers' lamps hanging from the equipment rack. The room was semi-underground and had no windows. It was like a cave of mystery.

"All that," said Fleming, pointing to the wall of equipment facing them, "is the control unit. This is the input console."

He showed her the teletype keyboard, the magnetic tape scanner and the punched-card unit. "He was intended to have some sort of sensory magnetic system, but we've modified it to scan transcript. Easier for mortals with eyes."

"He?"

Fleming looked at her oddly.

"I call him 'he' because he gives me the sense of a mind. Of a person almost."

She had lived so long on the fringe of it that she had grown used to the idea. She had forgotten the shiver that went through her at Bouldershaw Fell when the message first came to them out of space. There had been so many alarms and excursions that the issue had become clouded, and in any case the message itself had been reduced to mundane terms of buildings and wiring and complicated man-made equipment. But standing there beside Fleming, who seemed not only tired but possessed and driven on by some kind of compulsion from outside, it was impossible not to sense an obscure, alien power lurking in the dim room. It merely touched her and passed away. It did not live in her brain as it seemed to live in his, but it made her shiver again.

"And this is the output unit," said Fleming, who did not appear to notice what she had felt. "His normal thought processes are in binary arithmetic, but we make him print out in denary so that we can read it straight off."

The wall of equipment in front of them was broken by a facia of display panels.

"What's that?" asked Judy, pointing to an array of several hundred tiny neon bulbs set in rows between two perspex-sheathed metal plates that stood out at right-angles from the cabinet.

"That's all the control unit. The lamps are simply a progress display device. They show the state of data going through the machine."

"Has any gone through yet?"

"No, not yet."

"You seem sure it will all work."

"I'd never considered it not doing. It would be pointless for them to send a design for something that didn't work." The certainty in his voice was not simply his personal arrogance; there was the effect of something else speaking through him.

"If you understand it right."

"Yes, I understand it. Most of it." He waved a hand at the sheathed metal plates. "I don't quite know what those are for. They're electric terminals with about a thousand volts between them, which is why we put safety covers on. They were in the design and I expect we'll learn how to use them. They're probably some sort of sensing apparatus."

Again, he seemed quite sure of it all, and quite unbaffled by its complexity. It was as if his brain had long been prepared and waiting for it: Judy thought how aching and empty he must have felt the year before when he was talking about a breakthrough and knocking down the railings. Not that he looked any happier now. She remembered that Bridger had said, "John'll never be happy."

Everything else seemed comparatively matter-of-fact as they walked round the room.

"The way it works," said Fleming, "is, you teletype the data in—that's the quickest way we have. The control unit decides what to do. The arithmetic units do the calculating—

calling on the memory storage as they need, and putting new information into memory—and the answer comes out on the printer. The highway ducts are under the floor and the arithmetic units are along the side walls. It's quite a conventional system really, but the conventionality ends there. It has a speed and capacity that we can hardly imagine.

There was complete silence around them. Shining rows of metal cabinets stood on each side of them, hiding their secrets, and the blank face of the control panel stared unseeingly at them in the dim light. Fleming stood casually looking round, seeming as much part of it as he was part of his car when driving.

" He'll look prettier when he's working," he said, and took her round to the area behind the control racks.

This was a large semi-circular room, as dimly lighted as the other, with a huge metal-clad column rising through the centre.

" That's the real guts of it : the memory storage." He opened a panel in the lower wall of the column and shone an inspection lamp inside. " There's a nice little job in molecular electronics for you. The memory is in the core and the core is held in a total vacuum to within a degree or two of absolute zero. That's where the liquid helium comes in."

Judy, peering in, could see a cube of what looked like metal about three foot square sealed in a glass tube and surrounded by cooling ducts. Fleming spoke mechanically, as if giving a lecture.

" Each core is built up of alternate wafers of conducting and non-conducting material half-a-thou. thick, criss-crossed into a honeycomb. That gives you a complete yes-no gate circuit on a spot of metal you can hardly see."

" Is that the equivalent of a brain cell?"

" If you like."

" And how many are there?"

" The core's a three-meter cube. That makes several millions of millions. And there are six cores."

" It's bigger than a human brain."

" Oh yes. Much bigger. And faster. And more efficient."

He closed the door-panel and said no more about it. She tried to imagine how it would really work, but the effort was as far beyond her as the understanding of matter; it was too vast and unfamiliar to visualise. She congratulated him and went away. He looked, for a moment, lonely and haunted but made no attempt to stop her. Then he started checking figures again.

Dennis Bridger was not captivated in the same way. He did his work stolidly and morosely, and made no discernible attempt to follow up his contacts with Intel. Major Quadring and his security people kept a careful eye on him; periodic checks were made on all staff leaving the main gates, to see that they were not taking out documents or other classified material, but Bridger did nothing at all to arouse their suspicion. His only recreation was visiting the off-shore island of Thorholm, from which he would return with gulls' and gannets' eggs and endearing photographs of puffins. Whatever inducement Kaufmann had given him to stay on did not seem to involve him in anything.

Geers regarded the whole team with suspicion. He was never obstructive, but a state of hostility existed between him and them. It was clear he would feel in some way satisfied if the experiment failed. However, as the super-computer neared completion, and the interest of his staff and his superiors in it increased, he took care to identify himself with any possible success. It was he who suggested that there should be a formal, though necessarily private, opening, and the Minister of Science—foiled of his unveiling of Bouldershaw Fell the previous year—allowed himself to be persuaded to cut a ribbon in Scotland. Fleming tried to put off the opening for as long as possible, but it was finally fixed for a day in October, by which time the new computer was due to be programmed and ready to receive its data. General Vandenberg and a couple of dozen Whitehall officials told their secretaries to make notes in their diaries.

Judy, at last, had something to do. There would be no press, but there were arrangements to be made with the various ministries, and plans for the visit to be worked out with Geers's staff. She saw little of Fleming. When she had finished her work she would go for long, solitary walks across the moors in the blustery weather of early autumn.

About a week before the opening, she saw a white yacht standing out to sea. It was a big, ocean-going yacht, a long way off. From the camp, it was hidden behind the island of Thorholm; it could only be seen from further along the coast. Judy noticed it as she walked back by the cliff-top path in the afternoon.

The following afternoon it was still there, and Judy, walking along the path between the cliff edge and the heather, thought she could see the blink of an aldis lamp signalling from it. This in itself would not have made her curious, had she not suddenly heard the sound of a car engine from the moor above her. By instinct, she dodged down behind a gorse bush and waited. It was a powerful but smooth engine that purred expensively as it ticked over.

The next thing Judy noticed was that the signalling had stopped. A moment or two later the engine revved and she could hear a car drive heavily away. After it had gone some distance, she got up and walked to the top of the path. Where it came to the cliff-top, it met a rough cart-track which wound away inland to join the main road in a valley between the hills. A large, shining car was disappearing round the first bend, behind a coppice of firs. Judy stared after it : there was something familiar about it.

She said nothing to Quadring, but went there again next day. There was no yacht and no car. The landscape was empty and silent except for the gulls. The next day it rained, and after that she was too busy with the Minister's visit to go out at all. By tea-time on the day before the opening, she had everything fixed—drivers laid on to collect the party from the station, a landing-crew provided for the Minister's helicopter, drinks and sandwiches in the Director's office, a timetable of the tour agreed with Reinhart and the others. Fleming was surly and withdrawn; Judy herself had a headache.

The sun came out about four o'clock, so she put on a wind-cheater and went out. As she walked along the cliff-path the ground all round her steamed and, far below, the green waves slopped against the rocks in the freshening wind and threw up lace edges of foam that sparkled in the sunlight.

There was no yacht, and again no car where the path met the track at the cliff-top; but there were tyre-marks, recent ones made after the rain. Judy was thinking about this when she became aware of another distant noise. This time it was an outboard motor and it came from the far side of the island, a couple of miles away. Straining her eyes against the sun, she watched the tiny distant shape of a boat edge out from behind the island, making for the bay below the camp at Thorness. It was Bridger's boat, and she could just see one person—presumably Bridger—in it.

She saw no more. There was a whistle and a crack beside her and a splinter of rock fell away from the cliff-face by her head. She did not wait to examine the bullet scar on the rock; she simply ran. Another bullet whistled close to her as she pelted headlong down the path, and then she was round the first turn of the cliff and out of range. She ran as far as she could, walked for a bit and then ran again. Long before she got back to camp the sun had set behind a bank of cloud. The wind rose and blew the day away. She shivered, and her legs were shaking.

She felt safer when she got through the main gates, but terribly lonely. Quadring's office was closed. There was no-one else she could talk to, and she did not want to meet Bridger in the mess. Dusk was falling as she walked between the chalets in the living-quarters, and suddenly she found herself at Fleming's. She could not bear to be outside a moment longer. She knocked once at the door and walked straight in.

Fleming was lying on his bed listening to a recording of Webern on a high-fidelity set he had rigged for himself. Looking up, he saw Judy standing in the doorway, panting, her face flushed, her hair blown about.

" Very spectacular. What's it in aid of?" He was half way through a bottle of Scotch.

Judy shut the door behind her. " John—"

" Well, what?"

" I've been shot at."

" Phui." He put down his glass and swung his feet to the floor.

" I have! Just now, up on the moors."

" You mean whistled at."

" I was standing at the top of the cliff when suddenly a bullet went close past me and smacked into the rock. I jumped back and another one—"

" Some of the brown jobs at target practice. They're all rotten shots." Fleming walked over to the record-player and switched it off. He was quite steady, quite sober in spite of the whisky.

"There was no-one," said Judy. "No-one at all."

"Then they weren't bullets. Here, have a drink and calm yourself down." He foraged for a glass for her.

"They were bullets," Judy insisted. sitting on the bed. "Someone with a telescopic sight."

"You're really in a state, aren't you?" He found a glass, half-filled it and handed it to her. "Why should anyone want to take pot shots at you?"

"There could be reasons."

"Such as?"

Judy looked down into her glass.

"Nothing that makes any sense."

"What were you doing on the cliffs?"

"Just looking at the sea."

"What was on the sea?"

"Doctor's Bridger's boat. Nothing else."

"Why were you so interested in Dennis's boat?"

"I wasn't."

"Are you suggesting that he shot at you?"

"No. It wasn't him." She held the footboard of the bed to stop her hand from trembling. "Can I stay here a bit? Till I get over the shakes."

"Do what you like. And drink that up."

She took a mouthful of the undiluted whisky and felt it stinging her mouth and throat. From the quietness outside came a long low howl, and a piece of guttering on the hut shook.

"What was that?"

"The wind," said Fleming as he stood watching her.

She could feel the spirit moving down, glowing, into her stomach. "I don't like this place."

"Nor do I," he said.

They drank in the silence broken only by the wind moaning round the camp buildings. The sky outside the window was almost dark, with blacker clouds blowing raggedly in from over the sea. She lowered her glass and looked Fleming in the eyes.

"Why does Doctor Bridger go to the island?" She never felt inclined to call Bridger by his first name.

"He goes bird-watching. You know jolly well he goes bird-watching."

"Every evening?"

"Look, when I'm flaked out at the end of the day I go sailing." This was true. Navigating a fourteenfooter was Fleming's one outside activity. Not that he did it very often; and he did it alone, not with the camp sailing club. "Except when I'm really flaked, like now."

He picked up the bottle by its neck and stood frowning, thinking of Dennis Bridger. "He goes snooping on sea-birds."

"Always on the island?"

"That's where they are," he said impatiently. "There's masses of stuff out there—gannets, guillemots, fulmars . . . Have some more of this."

She let him pour some more into her glass. Her head was humming a little.

"I'm sorry I burst in."

"Don't mind me." He rumpled her already tangled hair in his affectionate, unpredatory way. "I can do with a bit of company in this dump. Specially when it's a sweet, sweet girl."

"I'm not in the least sweet."

"Oh?"

"I don't like what I am." Judy looked away from him, down at her glass again. "I don't like what I do."

"That makes two of us." Fleming looked over her head towards the window. "I don't like what I do either."

"I thought you were completely taken up in it?"

"I was, but now it's finished I don't know. I've been trying to get myself sloshed on this, but I can't." He looked down at her in a confused way, not at all as he had done in the computer. "Perhaps you're what I need."

"John—"

"What?"

"Don't trust me too much."

Fleming grinned. "You up to something shady?"

"Not as far as you're concerned."

"I'm glad to hear it." He said, pushing up her chin with his hand. "You've an honest face."

He kissed her forehead lightly, not very seriously.

"No." She turned her head aside. He dropped his hand

and turned away from her, as if his attention had moved to something else. The wind howled again.

"What are you going to do about this shooting?" he asked after a pause.

She shivered in spite of the warmth inside her, and he put a hand on her shoulder.

"Sometimes at night," he said. "I lie and listen to the wind and think about that chap over there."

"What chap?"

He nodded in the direction of the computer, the new computer which he had made.

"He hasn't a body, not an organic body that can breathe and feel like ours. But he's a better brain."

"It's not a person." She pulled Fleming down on to the bed so that they were sitting side by side. She felt, for once, much older than him.

"We don't know what it is, do we?" said Fleming. "Whoever sent ye olde message didn't distribute a design like this for fun. They want us to start something right out of our depth."

"Do you think they know about us?"

"They know there are bound to be other intelligences in the universe. It just happens to be us."

Judy took hold of one of his hands.

"You needn't go further with it than you want."

"I hope not."

"All you're doing is building a computer."

"With a mental capacity way beyond ours."

"Is that really true?"

"A man is a very inefficient thinking machine."

"You're not."

"We all are. All computers based on a biological system are inefficient."

"The biological system suits me," she said. Her speech and vision were beginning to blur. Fleming gave her a short, bear-like hug.

"You're just a sexy piece."

He got up, yawned and stretched and switched on the light. Feeling a sudden loosening of tension, she lolled back on the bed.

"You need a holiday," she told him, slurrily.

" Maybe."

" You've been at it for months now without a break. That thing." She pointed towards the window.

" It had to be ready for his Ministership."

" If it did get out of control, you could always stop it."

" Could we? It was operational over a month ago. Did you know that?"

" No."

" We've been feeding in the order code so that the data can all be in by the time the gentry arrive."

" Did anything happen?"

" Nothing at first, but there was a small part of the order code I ignored. It arranged things so that when you switch on the current the first surge of electricity automatically sets the program working: at its own selected starting point. I deliberately left that out of the design because I didn't want him to have it all his own way, and he was furious."

Judy looked at him sceptically.

" That's nonsense."

" All right, he registered disturbance. Without any warning, before we'd even started putting in data, he started to print out: the missing section of the code. Over and over and over— telling me to put it in. He was very cross." He gazed earnestly into her unbelieving face. " I switched him off for a bit and then started feeding in the data. He was quiet after that. But he was designed to register disturbance. God knows what else he was designed for!"

She lay looking at him, not focusing.

" We shall put the last of the data in to-morrow," he went on. " Then heaven knows what'll happen. We get a message from two hundred light-years away—do you think all it gives us is a handy little ready-reckoner? Well, I don't. Nor do the people who killed Harries and shot at you and are probably tailing Dennis and me."

She started to interrupt him, but thought better of it.

" Remember?" he asked. " Remember I talked about a breakthrough?"

" Distinctly." She smiled.

" The kind of breakthrough you get once in a thousand years. I'll lay you any odds . . ."

He turned to the window and looked out, lost in some unthinkable speculation.

"You could always switch if off."

"Perhaps. Perhaps we could switch it off."

It was pitch black outside, with driving rain, and the wind continued to howl.

"It's dark," he said. He drew the curtain across and turned back to her with the same haunted look in his eyes that she had seen before.

"That makes two of us who are scared," she said.

"I'll see you back to your hut if you like." He looked down at her and smiled. "Or you could spend the night here."

Five

ATOMS

JUDY left him at first light and went back to her own chalet. By midday the first contingent from London had arrived and was being entertained in the mess. She moved between the charcoal-grey suits distributing information sheets and feeling fresh and alive and happy. Fleming was at the computer building with Bridger and Christine, inputting the final section of data. Reinhart and Osborne were closeted with Geers.

Vandenberg, Watling, Mrs. Tate-Allen and the faithful and unspeaking Newby came on the two o'clock train and were met by the two best cars. The Minister was due to arrive by helicopter at three—a typically odd and showy whim which was politely passed over without comment by the rest of the party.

By that time the rain had cleared and a guard of honour was drawn up beside the parade-ground in the middle of the camp. Reinhart and Major Quadring waited with them, Quadring wearing his best battle-dress with clean medal-ribbons, Reinhart clutching a bedraggled plastic mac.

The other guests and hosts assembled in the porch of the new computer building and looked hopefully at the sky. Osborne made whinnying, diplomatic conversation.

"I don't expect you knew the British Isles extended so far north, eh General?" This to Vandenberg, who showed signs of restlessness and potential umbrage. "Eh Geers?"

Geers wore a new suit and stood unyieldingly in front of the others, very much the Director.

"Have they hatched a swan or an ugly duckling?" Mrs. Tate-Allen asked him.

"I wouldn't know. We only have time for practical work."

"Isn't this practical?" Osborne enquired.

Watling said, "I used to fly over here in the war."

"Really?" said Vandenberg, without interest.

"North Atlantic patrols. When I was in Coastal."

But nobody heard him: the helicopter had arrived. It hovered like a flustered bird over the parade-ground and then sank down on its hydraulic legs. Its rotors sliced the air for a minute and then stopped. The door opened, the Right Honourable James Ratcliff climbed down, the guard presented arms, Quadring saluted and Reinhart tripped forward on his dainty feet, shook hands and led the Minister to the assembled company in the porch. Ratcliff looked very well and newly bathed. He shook hands with Geers and beamed and smirked at the rest.

"How do you do, Doctor? It's very good of you to harbour our little piece of equipment in your midst."

Geers was transformed.

"We're honoured, sir, to have work like this," he said with his best smile. "Pure research among us rude mechanicals."

Osborne and Reinhart exchanged glances.

"Shall we go in?" asked Osborne.

"Yes, indeed." The Minister smiled on all. "Hallo Vandenberg, nice of you to come."

Geers stepped forward and grasped the door handle.

"Shall *I*?" He looked challengingly at Reinhart.

"Do," said Reinhart.

"It's this way, Minister." And Geers shepherded them in.

The lights were all working now in the computer room and Geers did the honours of display with some pride. Reinhart and Osborne left him to it and Fleming watched sourly from the control desk. Geers introduced Bridger and Christine and—quite casually—Fleming.

"You know Dr. Fleming, Minister, who designed it."

"The designers are in the constellation of Andromeda," said Fleming. Ratcliff laughed as if this was a very good joke.

"Well, you've done a pretty big job. I see why you all wanted so much money."

The party moved on. Mrs. Tate-Allen was much impressed by the neon lamps; the men in charcoal suits studied blue-painted cabinets of equipment with baffled interest, and Fleming was forced to fall in at the rear with Osborne.

"There's no business like show business."

"It's a compliment in fact," said Osborne. "They entrust it to you: the knowledge, the investment, the power."

"Bigger fools they."

But Osborne did not agree. After they had been round the memory cylinder, the whole group gathered in front of the control desk.

"Well?" said Ratcliff.

Fleming picked up a sheet of figures from the desk.

"These," he said, so quietly that hardly anyone could hear him. "These are the end groups of the data found in the message."

Reinhart repeated it for him, took the paper and explained. "We're now going to pass these in through the input consul and trigger the whole machine off."

He passed the sheet to Christine who sat down at the tele-type machine and started tapping the keys. She looked very deft and pretty: people admired. When she had finished, Fleming and Bridger threw switches and pressed buttons on the control desk and waited. The Minister waited. A steady hum came from the back of the computer, otherwise there was silence. Somebody coughed.

"All right, Dennis?" Fleming asked. Then the display lamps began to flicker.

It was very effective at first. Explanations were given: it showed the progress of the data through the machine; as soon as it had finished its calculations it would print out its finding on that wide roll of paper there. . . .

But nothing happened; an hour later they were still waiting. At five o'clock the Minister climbed unsmiling into his helicopter, rose into the sky and was carried southwards. At six o'clock the remaining visitors drove to the station to catch the evening train for Aberdeen, accompanied by a tight-lipped and crestfallen Reinhart. At eight o'clock Bridger and Christine went off duty.

Fleming stayed on in the empty control-room, listening to the hum of the equipment and gazing at the endlessly flashing panel. As soon as she could, Judy joined him and sat with him at the control desk. He didn't speak, even to swear or complain, and she could think of nothing adequate to say.

The hands of the clock on the wall moved round to ten, and then the lamps on the panel stopped flickering. Fleming sighed and moved to get up to go. Judy touched his sleeve with her finger-tips to suggest some sort of comfort. He turned to kiss her, and as he did so the output printer clattered into life.

Reinhart stopped overnight in Aberdeen, where a Scottish Universities seminar was taking place. The seminar was an excuse; he did not want to spend the rest of the journey face to face with the politely condescending company from London. His one consolation was that he met an old friend, Madeleine Dawnay, professor of chemistry at Edinburgh. She was perhaps the best biochemist in the country, immensely capable and reassuring and with all the charm, her students said, of a test-tube-full of dried skin. They talked for a long time, and then he went off to his hotel bedroom and worried.

In the morning he had a telegram from Thorness: FULL HOUSE. ACES ON KINGS. COME QUICK. FLEMING. He cancelled his plane reservation to London, bought a new railway ticket and set off north-west again, taking Dawnay with him.

"What does it mean?" she asked.

"I hope to heaven it means something's happened. The damn thing cost several million and I thought last night we were going to be the laughing-stock of Whitehall."

He did not know quite why he was taking her. Possibly to give himself some moral support.

When he telephoned the camp from Thorness station to ask for a car and an extra pass, his call was put straight through to Quadring's office.

"Damn scientists," said Quadring to his orderly. "They're in and out as if it were a fairground."

He took the pass the orderly had written and walked down the corridor to Geers's office. In the ordinary way he was a pleasant enough character, but Judy had been in to report the affair of the shooting and he was on edge and tetchy.

"I wonder if you'd sign this, sir?" He put the pass down on Geers's desk.

"Who is it?"

"Someone Professor Reinhart's bringing in."

"Have you checked him?"

"It's a ' her ' actually."

"What's her name?" Geers squinted down at the card through his bifocals.

"Professor Dawnay."

"Dawnay! Madeleine Dawnay?" He looked with new interest. "You don't have to worry about her. I was at Manchester with her, before she moved on."

He smiled reminiscently as he signed the pass. Quadring shuffled uneasily.

"It's not easy keeping track of these Min. of Science bods."

"As long as they stick to their own building." Geers handed the pass back.

"They don't."

"Who doesn't?"

"Bridger for one. He goes out in his boat a lot to the island."

"He's a bird-watcher."

"We think it's something else. My own guess is he takes papers with him."

"Papers?" Geers looked up sharply with a glint of spectacles. "Have you any proof?"

"No."

"Well then—"

"Would it be possible to have him searched at the landing-jetty?"

"Suppose he hadn't got anything?"

"I'd be surprised."

"And we'd look pretty foolish, wouldn't we?" Geers took off his glasses and stared discomfortingly at the major. "And if he was up to something we'd put him on his guard."

"He is up to something."

"Then get some facts to go on."

"I don't see how I can."

"You're responsible for the security of this establishment."

"Yes, sir."

Geers gave it his full attention for a moment.

"What about Miss Adamson?"

Quadring told him.

"Nothing since?"

"Not that we can see, sir."

"Hm." He closed the legs of his spectacles with a snap that dismissed the matter. "If you're going over to the computer building you might give Professor Dawnay her pass."

"I wasn't."

"Then send someone. And give her my regards. In fact, if

they're through at a reasonable hour they might look in for a sherry."

"Very good, sir." Quadring backed gingerly away from the desk.

"And Fleming, I suppose, if he's with them."

"Yes, sir."

He got as far as the door. Geers was looking wistfully at the ceiling, thinking of Madeleine Dawnay.

"I wish we did more primary research ourselves. One gets tired of development work."

Quadring made his escape.

In the end it was Judy who took the pass. Dawnay was in the computer control-room, being shown round by Reinhart and Bridger while Christine tried to raise Fleming on the camp phone. Judy handed over the pass and was introduced.

"Public Relations? Well, I'm glad they let girls do something," said Dawnay in a brisk, male voice. She looked hard but not unkindly at everyone. Reinhart fluttered a little; he seemed unusually nervous.

"What did John want?"

"I don't know," Judy told him. "At least, I don't quite follow it."

"He sent me a telegram."

After a minute Fleming hurried in.

"Ah, there you are."

Reinhart pounced on him.

"What's happened?"

"Are we alone?" Fleming asked, looking coolly at Dawnay.

Reinhart introduced them irritably and fidgeted from one tiny foot to the other while she quizzed Fleming about the computer.

"Madeleine's fully in the picture."

"She's lucky. I wish I were." Fleming fished from his pocket a folded sheet of paper and handed it to the Professor.

"What's this?" Reinhart opened it. Fleming watched him with amusement, like a small boy playing a trick on a grown-up. The paper bore several lines of typed figures.

"When did it print this?" Reinhart asked.

"Last night, after you'd all gone. Judy and I were here."

"You didn't tell me." Bridger edged in reproachfully.

"You'd gone off."

Reinhart frowned at the figures. " It means something to you?"

" Don't you recognise it?"

" Can't say I do."

" Isn't it the relative spacings of the energy levels in the hydrogen atom?"

" Is it?" Reinhart handed the paper to Dawnay.

" You mean," Bridger asked, " it suddenly came out with that?"

" Yes. It could be." Dawnay read slowly through the figures. " They look like the relative frequencies. What an extraordinary thing."

" The whole business is a little out of the ordinary," said Fleming.

Dawnay read through the figures again, and nodded.

" I don't see the point." Judy wondered if she was being unusually obtuse.

" It looks as if someone out there," Dawnay pointed up to the sky, " has gone to a lot of trouble to tell us what we already know about hydrogen."

" If that's really all." Judy looked at Fleming, who said nothing. Madeleine Dawnay turned to Reinhart.

" Bit of a disappointment."

" I'm not disappointed," Fleming said quietly. " It's a starting point. The thing is, do we want to go on?"

" How can you go on?" Dawnay asked.

" Well, hydrogen is the common element of the universe. Yes? So this is a piece of very simple universal information. If we don't recognise it, there's no point in the machine continuing. If we do, then he can proceed to the next question."

" What next question?"

" We don't know yet. But this, I bet you, is the first move in a long, long game of questions and answers." He took the paper from her and handed it to Christine. " Push this into the intake."

" Really?" Christine looked from him to Reinhart.

" Really."

Reinhart remained silent, but something had happened to him; he was no longer dejected and his eyes twinkled and were alert. The rest of them stood in a silent thoughtful group while

Christine sat down to the input teletype and Bridger adjusted settings on the control desk.

"Now," he said. He was even quieter than Fleming, and Judy could not decide whether he was jealous or apprehensive or merely trying, like the others, to work it out.

Christine tapped rapidly at the keyboard and the computer hummed steadily behind its metal panelling. It really did seem to be all around them—massive, impassive and waiting. Dawnay looked at the rows of blue cabinets, the rhythmically oscillating lights with less awe than Judy felt, but with interest.

"Questions and answers—do you believe that?"

"If you were sitting up among the stars, you couldn't ask us directly what we know. But this chap could." Fleming indicated the computer control racks. "If it's designed and programmed to do it for them."

Dawnay turned to Reinhart again.

"If Dr. Fleming's on the right line, you really have something tremendous."

"Fleming has an instinct for it," said Reinhart, watching Christine.

When she had finished typing, nothing happened. Bridger fiddled with the control desk knobs while the others waited. Fleming looked puzzled.

"What's up, Dennis?"

"I don't know."

"You could be wrong," said Judy.

"We haven't been yet."

As Fleming spoke the lamps on the display panel started to flicker, and a moment later the output printer went into action with a clatter. They gathered round it watching the wide white streamer of paper inching up over its roller, covered in lines of figures.

One of the long low cupboards in Geers's office was a cocktail cabinet. The Director stood four glasses on top and produced a bottle of gin from the lower shelf.

"What Reinhart and his people are doing is terribly exciting." He was wearing his second-best suit but his best manner for Dawnay's benefit. "A little set-back yesterday, but I gather it's all right now."

Dawnay, submerged in one of the armchairs, looked up and

caught Reinhart's eye. Geers went on talking as he sprinkled bitters into one of the glasses.

"We've nothing but ironmongery here, really, out in this wilderness. We do a good deal of the country's rocketry, of course, and there's a lot of complex stuff goes into that, but I wouldn't mind changing into some old clothes and getting back to lab. work. Is that pink enough?"

He placed the filled glass on his desk on a level with Dawnay's ear. Its base was tucked into a little paper mat to prevent it from marking the polish.

"Fine, thanks." Dawnay could just see it and reach it without getting up. Geers reached into the cabinet for another bottle

"And sherry for you, Reinhart?" Sherry was poured. "One gets so stuck behind an executive desk. Cheers. . . . Nice to see you again, Madeleine. What have you been up to?"

"D.N.A., chromosomes, the origin of life caper." Dawnay spoke gruffly. She put her glass back on the desk and lit a cigarette, blowing the smoke down her nose like a man. "I've got into a bit of a cul-de-sac. I was just going away to think when I met Ernest."

"Stay and think here." Geers gave her a nice smile and then switched it off. "Where's Fleming got to?"

"He'll be over in a minute," said Reinhart.

"You've a bright boy, though an awkward one." Geers informed him. "In fact you've a bit of an awkward squad altogether, haven't you?"

"We've also got results." Reinhart was unruffled. "It's started printing out."

Geers raised his eyebrows.

"Has it indeed? What's it printing?"

They told him.

"Very odd. Very odd indeed. And what happened when you fed it back?"

"A whole mass of figures came out."

"What are they?"

"No idea. We've been going over them, but so far . . ." Reinhart shrugged.

Fleming walked in with a perfunctory sort of knock.

"This the right party?"

"Come in, come in," said Geers, as if to a promising but gauche student. "Thirsty?"

"When am I not?"

Fleming was carrying the print-out sheets. He threw them down on the desk to take his drink.

"Any joy?" Reinhart asked.

"Not a crumb. There's something wrong with him, or wrong with us."

"Is that the latest?" asked Geers, straightening the papers and bending over them to look. "You'll have to do a lot of analysis on this, won't you? If we can help in any way—"

"It ought to be simple." Fleming was subdued and preoccupied as though he was trying to see something just beyond him. "I'm sure there ought to be something quite easy. Something we'd recognise."

"There was a section here—" Reinhart took the sheets and shuffled through them. "Seems vaguely familiar. Have another look at that lot, Madeleine."

Madeleine looked.

"What sort of thing do you expect?" Geers asked Fleming, as he poured a drink.

"I don't know. I don't know what the game is yet."

"You wouldn't be interested in the carbon atom, would you?" Dawnay looked up out of her chair with a faint smile.

"The carbon atom!"

"It's not expressed the way we'd put it; but, yes, it could be a description of the structure of carbon." She blew smoke out of her nose. "Is that what you meant, Ernest?"

Reinhart and Geers bent over the sheets again.

"I'm a bit rusty, of course," said Geers.

"But it could be, couldn't it?"

"Yes, it could be. I wonder if there's anything else."

"There won't be anything else," Fleming said. He seemed very sure, and no longer preoccupied. "Take it from the beginning. Think of the hydrogen question. He's asking us what form of life we belong to. All these other figures are other possible ways of making living creatures. But we don't know anything about them, because life on this earth is based on the carbon atom."

"Well, it's a theory," said Reinhart. "What do we do now? Feed back the figures relating to carbon?"

"If we want him to know what stuff we're made of. He won't forget."

"Aren't you presupposing an intelligence?" said Geers, who had no time for fancy stuff.

"Look," Fleming turned to him. "The message we picked up did two things. It stipulated a design. it then gave us a lot of basic information to feed into the computer when we'd built it. We didn't know what that information was at the time, but we're beginning to know now. With what was in the original program, and what we tell him, he can learn anything he likes about us. And he can learn to act upon it. If that's not an intelligence, I don't know what is."

"It's a very useful machine," Dawnay said. Fleming turned on her.

"Just because it doesn't have protoplasm, no chemist can imagine it as a thinking agency!"

Dawnay sniffed.

"What are you afraid of, John?" Reinhart asked.

"Its purpose. It hasn't been put here for fun. It hasn't been put here for our benefit."

"You've a neurosis about it," said Dawnay.

"You think so?"

"You've been given a windfall; use it." She appealed to Reinhart. "If you use Dr. Fleming's method and feed back the carbon formula, you may get something else. You may build up to more complicated structures, and you've got a marvellous calculating machine to handle them. That's all it is. Apply it."

"John?" Reinhart turned to Fleming.

"You can count me out."

"Would you like to tackle it, Madeleine?" said the Professor.

"Why don't you?" she asked him.

"It is a long step from astronomy to bio-synthesis. If your university can spare you. . . ."

"We can accommodate you." Geers, when he moved, moved in quickly. "You said you were at a dead end."

Dawnay considered.

"Would you work with me, Dr. Fleming?"

Fleming shook his head. "There's something needs thinking out first—before we start at all."

"I don't think so."

"I've gone as far as I want. Further, in fact, to show I could deliver the goods. But for me the road ends here."

Reinhart opened his mouth to speak, but Fleming turned away.

"All right," Reinhart said. "Will you tackle it, Madeleine?"

They made the rest of the arrangements when Fleming had gone.

Dawnay moved in the following week and set to work on the computer, with Bridger and Christine helping her and Geers now full of enthusiasm and attention. Fleming returned to London and Judy saw nothing of him; being a serving officer tied by oath, she had to stay where she was ordered. In a way it was a relief to be free of their equivocal relationship. After their one night in his chalet she had kept him, as far as possible, at arm's length, for she was torn between the instinct of being in love and the feeling that she did not want him to take her for something other than she was. At least while he was away she did not have to report on him—only on Bridger, and that she minded less.

Bridger gave no clue to any of them. Judy kept away from the moor and Quadring's patrols found nothing. Bridger himself grew steadily more miserable and withdrawn. He worked competently but without enthusiasm, spending his spare time watching the late migrations from the Thorholm nestings.

Autumn darkened into winter. Back in London, Fleming settled down to check the entire message and all his original calculations. Monitoring of the signal went on from Bouldershaw Fell, but it was now only routine. The code was always the same; Fleming could find nothing in all his workings to give him a line on what he feared.

At Thorness Dawnay made better progress.

"The boy was right about one thing," she told Reinhart. "The question and answer business. We fed in the carbon atom figures and immediately it began to print out stuff on the structure of protein molecules."

When she fed that back, it started asking more questions. It offered the formulas of a variety of different structures based on proteins, and it clearly wanted to be given more information about them. Dawnay set her department at Edinburgh to work. Between them they put back into the machine everything they knew about cell formation. By the New Year it had given them the molecular structure of haemoglobin.

"Why haemoglobin?" asked Judy, who had followed her to Edinburgh in an attempt to understand what was happening.

"The haemoglobin in the blood carries the electricity supply to your brain."

"He offered you that as one of a set of alternatives?" Reinhart asked. They had all three met in Dawnay's study in one of the old grey university buildings because she had told them she wanted a Ministry decision.

"Yes," she said. "As before. And we fed that one back."

"So now it knows what our brains run on."

"It knows a great deal more than that by now."

Reinhart stroked his chin with his little fingers.

"Why does it want to?"

"You're under Fleming's influence, aren't you?" Dawnay said reprovingly. "It doesn't 'want to know' anything. It calculates logical responses from information which we give it, and from what it already possesses. Because it's a calculating machine."

"Is that all?" Judy, from what little she knew, shared Reinhart's doubts.

"Let's try to be scientific about it, shall we?" Dawnay said. "Not mystical."

"Professor Reinhart, do you . . . ?"

Reinhart looked uncomfortable. "Fleming would say it wants to know what sort of intelligence it's up against—what sort of computers we are, how big our brains are, how we feed them, what sort of beings we house them in."

"Young Fleming's emotionally disturbed, if you ask me," said Dawnay. She waved her hand towards shelves piled with folders of paper. "We've got so much now we can hardly see daylight, but I've an idea what it's all about, which is why I wanted you. I think it's given us the basic plan of a living cell."

"A what?"

"Not that it's any good to us. We have this huge amount of numbers. It's far too complex for us ever to understand fully."

"Why should it be?"

"Look at the size of it! We can recognise odd bits—odd bits of chromosome structure and so on—but it would take years to analyse it all.

" If that's what you're meant to do."

" What do you mean?"

Reinhart stroked his chin again. His fingers, Judy noticed, had little dimples on them. There was something very comforting and humane about him, even when he was out of his depth in theory.

" I want to talk to Fleming and Osborne," he said.

He got them together, eventually, in Osborne's office. By that time he had all the facts at his fingertips and he wanted action. Fleming looked older and slack, as though the elastic inside him had run down. His face was pouchy and his eyes bloodshot.

Osborne sat back elegantly and listened to Reinhart.

" Professor Dawnay's come up with what appears to be the detailed chromosome structure of a cell."

"A living cell?"

" Yes. It's something we've never known before: the order in which the nucleic acid molecules are arranged."

" So you could actually build one up?"

" If we can use the computer as a control, and if we can make a chemical device to act on the instructions as they come up—in fact, if we can make a D.N.A. synthesiser—then I think we can begin to build living tissue."

" That's what the biologists have been after for years, isn't it?"

" You really want to let it make a living organism?" Fleming asked.

" Dawnay wants to try," said Reinhart. " Fleming doesn't. What do we do?"

" Why don't you?" Osborne asked Fleming quite casually, as though it was a matter of passing interest.

" Because we're being pushed into this by a form of compulsion," said Fleming wearily. " I've been saying that ever since the day we built the damn thing, and I can find nothing to make me think otherwise. Madeleine Dawnay imagines you can just use it as a piece of lab. equipment: she's a cheerful optimist. If she wants to play with D.N.A. synthesis, let her stay in her university and do it. Don't let her use the computer. Or, if you must, at least wipe the memory first."

"Reinhart?" Osborne turned languidly to the Professor. Whatever impression Fleming had made on him did not show.

"I don't know," said Reinhart. "I simply don't know. It comes from an alien intelligence, but—"

"'We can always pull out the plug'?" Fleming quoted for him. "Look, we built it to prove the content of the message. Right? Well, we've done that. We operated it to discover its purpose. Now we know that too."

"Do we?"

"I do! Its' an intellectual fifth column from another world—from another form of existence. It's got the seeds of life in it, and also the seeds of destruction."

"Have you any grounds at all for saying that?" asked Osborne.

"No tangible grounds."

"Then how can we—?"

"All right, go on!" Fleming heaved himself up and made for the door. "Go on and see what happens—but don't come crying to me!"

Six

ALERT

FOR all that, he went to Thorness in the spring—he said, to
visit Judy, but in fact from morbid curiosity. He kept away
from the computer block but Judy and Bridger, separately, told
him what was happening. A new bay added to the building was
filled by Dawnay with elaborate laboratory equipment, including
a chemical synthesiser and an electron microscope. As well as
Christine, she had several post-graduate students of her own at
work on the project, and all the money she could reasonably
need. Reinhart and Osborne between them had got substantial
backing.

"And what about you?" Fleming asked Judy.

They sat on the cliff-top, inside the camp, above the jetty.

"I go round with the seasons." She smiled at him tenderly
but warily. She was shocked by the change in him, by his
blotchiness and general deterioration, and the look of utter
defeat that hung about him. She longed to hold him and to
give herself to him. At the same time she wanted to keep him
away at the distance of their original friendship, which seemed
to her the limit to which she could honourably go so long as
she was acting a part of which she was ashamed. She had even
tried to resign her commission when she heard he was coming
back, but it had not been allowed. She knew too much by now
to be released, and far too much to be able to tell him the truth.

Bridger had stayed in the camp, working all winter, and
had made no suspicious move; but Kaufmann's car had been
seen several times in the neighbourhood and the tall, improbably-
dressed chauffeur had been watching arrivals and departures at
the station and on at least one occasion had telephoned Bridger.
After this Bridger had looked more unhappy than ever and had
taken to having copies of the computer's output retyped for his

own use. Judy had not spotted that, but Quadring had. Nothing had come of it, however. The white yacht had not reappeared, and indeed could hardly have been expected to during a winter of gales and blizzards and wild storm-swept seas. Early in the spring Naval patrols were stepped up and reinforced by helicopters, and the yacht, if it ever had anything to do with it, was scared away. But if security was increasing, so was the value of the information, and there was a general feeling among Judy's superiors that the stakes were rising.

Judy, having nothing to do but watch, had time—as usual—on her hands, and it suited Quadring to have Fleming covered. So she sat on the top of the cliff with him, pretending to be happy to see him and feeling bitterly divided against herself.

"When are you going to hold a press conference?" was his next question.

"I don't know. This year, next year, sometime."

"All this ought to have been referred to the public months ago."

"But if it's a secret?"

"It's a secret because it suits the politicians. That's why it's going the wrong way. Once you take science out of the hands of scientists and hand it over to them, it's doomed." He jerked his shoulder at the compound. "If that lot isn't doomed already."

"What are you going to do about it?" she asked him.

He gazed down at the waves breaking a hundred and fifty feet below them and then turned and grinned at her for the first time in a very long while.

"Take you sailing," he said.

It was one of those early false springs which sometimes come unexpectedly at the beginning of March. The sun shone, a light breeze blew from the south-west and the sea was beautiful. Fleming assumed that Judy had nothing else to do and they sailed every day on the bay and up the coast as far as Greenstone Point and down to the mouth of Gairloch. The water was freezing cold but the sands were warm and in the afternoons they used to beach the boat in any likely-looking cove, splash ashore and lie basking in the sun.

After a few days, Fleming looked healthier. He grew more cheerful and seemed able to forget for hours at a time the cloud that hung over his mind. He obviously sensed that she no longer wanted to be made love to and fairly soon fell back into the role of affectionate and dominating big brother. Judy held her breath and hoped for the best.

Then, one hot and glinting afternoon, they pulled into a tiny bay on the seaward side of the island, Thorholm. The rocks rose sheer behind, reflecting the heat of the sun back on to them as they lay side by side on the sand. All they could see was the blue sky above. The only things to be heard were the heavy, gentle sound of the waves and the calling of sea-birds. After a while Fleming sat up and pulled off his thick sweater.

"You'd better take yours off, too," he told her.

She hesitated, then pulled it off over her head and lay in her shorts and bra, feeling the breeze and sun playing on her body. Fleming took no notice of her at first.

"This is better than computers." She smiled with her eyes shut. "Is this where Bridger comes?"

"Yeah."

"I don't see no birds."

"I can see one." He rolled over and kissed her. She lay unresponsively and he turned away again, leaving a hand on her midriff.

"Why doesn't he go round with you?" she asked.

"He doesn't want to barge in on us."

She scowled up into the sun.

"He doesn't like me."

"It's mutual, isn't it?"

She did not answer. His hand moved down to her thigh.

"Don't, John."

"Signed a pledge for the Girl Guides?" He sounded suddenly cross and peevish.

"I'm not being prissy, only . . ."

"Only what?"

"You don't know me."

"Hell! You don't give me much chance, do you?"

She got up abruptly and looked about her. There was a cleft in the rocks behind them.

"Let's explore."

"If you like."

"Is that a cave there?"

"Yes."

" Let's go and look."

" We're not dressed for it."

" Aren't you formal?" She smiled at him and pulled on her sweater, then threw him his. " Here!"

" They go hellish deep into the cliff. You need caving gear, like pot-holers."

" We won't go far."

" O.K." He hoisted himself to his feet and shook off his bad temper. " Come on."

The cave widened inside and then tapered off as it went deeper into the rock. The floor was sandy at first and strewn with stones. As they went further in they found themselves scrambling over boulders. It was cold and very quiet inside. Fleming brought a torch from the boat and shone it on the rock walls ahead of them; patches of seeping water glittered in its light. After a few dozen yards they came to another chamber with a large pool at the far end. Judy knelt down and gazed into the water.

" There's a piece of cord here."

" What?" Fleming crouched beside her and looked down over the pool's lip. One end of a length of white cord was knotted and held down by a boulder at the edge while the rest of it ran down into the water. Fleming pulled on it: it was quite taut.

" Is it deep?" Judy peered down the beam of the torch but could see nothing but blackness beneath the pool's surface.

" Hold the torch, will you?"

Fleming took both hands to the cord and pulled it slowly up. On the end was a large thermos-type canister weighted with stones. Judy shone the torch on to the lid.

" It's Dennis's!" Fleming exclaimed.

" Dennis Bridger's?"

" Yes. He bought it for picnics. It has that mark like a zig-zag on it."

" Why should he leave it?" Judy spoke more to herself than Fleming.

" I don't know. Better ask him."

Judy opened the lid and felt inside.

" For goodness sake!"

" It's full of papers." She pulled some out and held them under the torch. " Do you recognise them?"

"It's our stuff." Fleming looked at them incredulously. "Copied. We'd better take them back to him."

"No." Judy put the papers back in the flask and fastened it.

"What are you going to do?"

"Leave it where we found it."

"But that's absurd."

"Please, John, I know what I'm doing." She picked up the canister and threw it back into the water, while he watched sulkily, holding the torch.

"What *are* you doing?" he demanded, but she would not tell him.

When they got back to camp they found Reinhart there. He buttonholed Fleming outside the office block.

"Can you spare me a minute. John?"

"I'm not here."

"Look, John," the Professor looked hurt. "We're stuck."

"Good."

"Madeleine's managed a D.N.A. synthesis. Cells have actually formed."

"You must be proud of her."

"Single cells. But they don't live, or only a few minutes."

"Then your luck's in. If they did live they'd be under the control of the machine."

"How?"

"I don't know how. But they'd be no friends of ours."

"A single cell can't do much damage." Judy had never heard Reinhart openly pleading before. "Come anyway."

Fleming stuck his lower lip out obstinately.

"Go on, John." Judy faced round to him. "Or are you afraid they'll bite you?"

Fleming hunched up his shoulders and went with the Professor.

Judy walked straight into Quadring's office and reported.

"Ah," said Quadring. "That makes sense. Where is he now?"

They phoned the computer room, but Bridger had just left.

"Tell the F.S.P. boys to find him and tail him," Quadring told his orderly. "But he's not to see them."

"Very good, sir." The orderly swivelled his chair round to the switchboard.

" Who's on cliff patrol?"

" B Section, sir."

" Tell them to watch the path down to the jetty."

" Are they to stop him?"

" No. They're to let him go out if he wants to, and tell us." Quadring turned to Judy. " His friend phoned him to-day. They must want something urgently to run a risk like that."

" Why should they?"

" Maybe they've a deal on. We listened, of course. It was mostly pretty guarded, but they said something about the new route."

Judy shrugged. This was beyond her. Quadring waited until the orderly had telephoned the field security corporal and gone out to deliver his message to the B Section commander. Then he led Judy over to a wall-map.

" The old route was via the island. Bridger could take stuff there and dump it without having to check out of camp. When needed it could be picked up by the yacht. One of Kaufmann's colleagues probably has an ocean-going job that can anchor well off and send a boat in to rendezvous with Bridger."

" The white one?"

" The one you saw."

" Then that's why—?" It was a long while since the shooting on the moor, but it came back clearly to her as she looked at the map.

"Kaufmann had to have someone to tip off Bridger and keep in touch with the yacht. He used his chauffeur, who used the car."

" And shot at me?"

" It was probably he. It was a silly thing to do, but I expect he thought he could lose the body in the sea."

Judy felt herself turn cold inside her thick sweater.

" And the new route?"

" What with the weather and us, they can't use the yacht any more, so they can't get to the island. Bridger still uses it as a hiding-place, as you've found out, but he'll have to bring the stuff back and smuggle it out of the main gate, which is riskier."

Judy looked out into the cold dusk that was falling on the warmth of the day. Low square roofs of research buildings jutted blackly from the darkening grass of the headland. Lights shone in a few hut windows, and above them the enormous arch of the sky began to dim and disappear. Somewhere Dawnay was working in a lighted underground room, dedicated and unaware of the consequences of what she was doing. Somewhere Fleming was arguing with Reinhart about the future. And somewhere, alone and miserable and perhaps shaking with hidden fear, Bridger was changing into oilskins, fisherman's jersey and wading boots, to go out into the night.

"You'd better put on something thicker," said Quadring. "I'm going too."

It was warm in Dawnay's laboratory. Lights and equipment had been on for weeks and were slowly beating the air-conditioning.

"It smells of biologist." said Fleming as he and Reinhart walked in. Dawnay was peering down the eyepiece of a microscope. She glanced up casually.

"Hallo, Dr. Fleming." She spoke as though he had been out simply for a cup of tea. "It looks a bit like a witch's soup-kitchen, I'm afraid."

"Anything in the broth?" Reinhart asked.

"We've just been preparing a new batch. Like to stop and see?" The microscope had an electronic display tube, like a television screen. "You can watch on there if anything should happen."

"New culture?" asked one of her assistants, fitting a needle to a hypodermic syringe.

"Take some from there, and watch the temperature of your needle."

Dawnay explained her progress to Fleming while the assistant took a small bottle from a refrigerator.

"We do the synthesis round about freezing-point, and they come to life at normal temperature." She seemed perfectly friendly and untouched by what Fleming thought. The assistant pierced the rubber cap of the bottle with the hypodermic needle and drew up some fluid into the syringe.

"What form of life have they?" asked Fleming.

"They're a very simple piece of protoplasm, with a nucleus. What do you want—feelers and heads?"

She took the syringe, squeezed a drop of fluid out on to a slide and clipped the slide on the viewing plate.

" How do they behave?"

" They move about for a bit, then they die. That's the trouble. We probably haven't found the right nutrients yet."

She put her eye to the microscope and focused up. As she moved the slide under the lens they could see individual cells forming—pale discs with a darker centre—and swimming about in the screen for a few seconds. They stopped moving and were obviously dead by the time Dawnay changed to a higher magnification. She pulled the slide out.

" Let's try the other batch." She looked round at them with a tired smile. " This is liable to go on all night."

Soon after midnight Bridger was seen leaving his chalet. The cliff patrol watched him go down the path to the jetty. They did not challenge him, but telephoned through to the guard-room from an old gun emplacement at the top of the path. Quadring and Judy had joined them by the time Bridger pushed out from the jetty. His outboard motor sneezed twice, then spluttered steadily away across the water. There was some moonlight, and they could see the boat moving out over the bay.

" Aren't you going to follow him?" asked Judy.

" No. He'll be back." Quadring called softly to the sentries. " Stay up top and keep out of sight. It may be a long time."

Judy looked out to sea, where the little boat was losing itself among the waves.

The moon went long before dawn, and although they were wearing greatcoats they were bitterly cold.

" Why doesn't he come back?" she asked Quadring.

" Doesn't want to navigate in the dark."

" If he knows we're here . . ."

" Why should he? He's only waiting for a spot of daylight."

At four o'clock the sentries changed. It was still dark. At five the first pearl-pale greyness began to appear in the sky. The night duty cook clanked round with containers of tea. He left one in the guard-room, another at the main gate, another at the computer building.

Dawnay pushed her glasses up on to her forehead and drank noisily.

"Why don't you pack it in, Madeleine?" Reinhart yawned.

"I will soon." She pushed another slide under the lens. There was a tray half-full of used slides on the table beside her, and Fleming sat perched on the corner, disapproving but intrigued.

"Wait." She moved the slide a fraction. "There's one!" On the display tube a cell could be seen forming.

"He's doing better than most," said Reinhart.

"He's getting pretty big." Dawnay switched the magnification. "Look—it's beginning to divide!"

The cell elongated into two lobes which stretched and broke apart, and then each lobe broke again into new cells.

"It's reproducing!" Dawnay leant back and watched the screen. Her face was puckered with fatigue and happiness. "We've made life. We've actually made a reproductive cell. Look—there it goes again . . . How about that, Dr. Fleming?"

Fleming was standing up and watching the screen intently.

"How are you going to stop it?"

"I'm not going to stop it. I want to see what it does."

"It's developing into quite a coherent structure." Reinhart observed.

Fleming clenched his fists upon the table. "Kill it."

"What?" Dawnay looked at him in mild surprise.

"Kill it while you can."

"It's perfectly well under control."

"Is it? Look at the way it's growing." Fleming pointed at the rapidly doubling mass of cells on the screen.

"That's all right. You could grow an amoeba the size of the earth in a week if you could feed it fast enough."

"This isn't an amoeba."

"It's remarkably like one."

"Kill it!" Fleming looked round at their anxious unyielding faces, and then back at the screen. He picked up the heavy container in which the tea had been brought and smashed it down on the viewing plate of the microscope. A clatter of metal and glass rang through the hushed room. The viewing panel went dead.

"You young fool!" Dawnay almost cried.

"John—what are you doing?" Reinhart moved forward

to stop him, but too late. Fleming pulled the splintered remains of the slide out of the microscope, threw them to the floor and ground his heel into them.

"You're mad! All mad! All blind raving mad!" he shouted at them, and ran to the door.

He ran out through the computer room, along the entrance corridor and on to the porch. There he stood for a minute, panting, while the cold air hit him in the face. To come into the open at the pale beginning of day, after a night in the concentration of Dawnay's room, was like waking from a nightmare. He took several gulps of air and strode off across the grass to the headland, trying to clear his brain and his lungs.

In the distance, he could hear an outboard motor.

He changed direction and walked furiously towards the spot where the path from the jetty reached the top of the cliff. The sound of the boat came steadily nearer in the growing light, drawing him like a magnet; but at the cliff-top he stumbled upon Quadring, Judy and two soldiers who were lying in wait on the grass. He drew up short.

"What the devil's going on?" He gazed at them wildly and uncomprehendingly. Quadring stood up, binoculars swinging from his chest.

"Get back. Get away from here."

The motor had stopped. The boat was gliding into the quay below them. Judy started to scramble to her feet, but Quadring motioned her down.

"Go away John, please!" she said in an agonised voice.

"Go away? Go away? What the hell's everyone up to?"

"Be quiet," ordered Quadring. "And keep back from the edge."

"We're waiting for Dennis Bridger," Judy said.

"For Dennis?" He was in a state of shock and only took in slowly what was happening.

"I'd push off," Quadring advised him. "Unless you want to witness his arrest."

"His arrest?" Fleming pivoted slowly from Quadring back to Judy as the meaning dawned on him.

"You *are* all mad!"

"Keep back and keep quiet," said Quadring.

Fleming moved towards the edge of the cliff, but on a nod from Quadring the two soldiers took an elbow each and pulled him back. He stood pinioned between them, frustrated and desperate. Cold sweat trickled down his face, and all he could see was Judy.

" Are *you* in on this?"

" You know what we found." She avoided his eyes.

" *Are* you?"

" Yes," she said, and walked away to stand beside Quadring.

They let Bridger get right to the top of the path, lugging the heavy canister from the cave. As his head came up over the edge, Fleming shouted to him:

" Dennis!"

One of the soldiers clamped his hand over Fleming's mouth, but by that time Bridger had seen them. Before Quadring could get on to him, he dropped the canister and ran.

He ran fast for a man in sea-boots, along the path at the edge of the cliff. Quadring and the soldiers pounded after him. Fleming ran after them, and Judy after him. It was like a stag-hunt in the cold, early light. They could not see where Bridger was going. He got to the end of the headland, and then turned and slipped. His wet rubber boots flailed at the grass at the edge, and then he was over. Five seconds later, he was a broken body on the rocks at the sea's edge.

Fleming joined the soldiers on the cliff-top, looking down. As Judy came up to him he turned away without speaking and walked slowly back towards the camp. He still had a splinter of glass from the microscope in his finger. Stopping for a moment, he pulled it out, and then walked on.

Seven

ANALYSIS

GENERAL Vandenberg by this time had his allied headquarters accommodated in a bomb-proof bunker under the Ministry of Defence. His functions as co-ordinator had gradually expanded until he was now virtual director of local air strategy. However little they liked this, Her Majesty's Government submitted to it in the face of an international situation growing steadily worse: the operations room next to his private office was dominated by a wall map of the world showing traces of an alarming number of orbital satellites of unknown potentiality. As well as the American and Russian vehicles, some of which certainly carried nuclear armament, there was an increasing traffic put up by other powers whose relations with each other and with the West were often near sparking-point. Public morality thinned like the atmosphere as men and machines rose higher, and year by year the uneasy truce which was supposed to control the upper air and the spaces above it came nearer to falling into anarchy.

Vandenberg, through the Ministry of Defence, now had call on all local establishments, including Thorness. He rode gently but with determination, and watched carefully what went on. When he received reports of Bridger's death, he sent for Osborne.

Osborne's position was now very different from what it had been in the early days of Bouldershaw Fell. Far from representing a ministry in the ascendant, he and Ratcliff now had to bow before the wishes of the war men, contriving as best they could to keep some say in their own affairs. Not that Osborne was easily ruffled. He stood before Vandenberg's desk as immaculate and suave as ever.

" Sit down," Vandenberg waved him to a chair. " Rest your feet."

They went over the circumstances of Bridger's death move by move as though they were playing a game of chess; the general probing, and Osborne on the defensive but denying nothing and making no excuses.

"You have to admit," said Vandenberg at the end of it, "your Ministry's snarled it up good and hard."

"That's a matter of opinion."

Vandenberg pushed back his chair and went to look at his wall-map.

"We can't afford to play schools, Osborne. We could use that machine. It's built on military premises, with military aid. We could use it in the public interest."

"What the hell do you think Reinhart's doing?" Osborne was eventually ruffled. "I'm sure your people would like to get your hands on it. I'm sure we all seem anarchistic to you because we haven't got drilled minds. I know there's been a tragedy. But they're doing something vitally important up there."

"And we're not?"

"You can't suddenly stop them in their tracks."

"Your Cabinet would say we can."

"Have you asked them?"

"No. But they would."

"At least—" Osborne calmed down again—"at least let us finish this present project, if we give you certain guarantees."

As soon as he was back in his own office he telephoned Reinhart.

"For heaven's sake patch up some sort of a truce with Geers," he told him.

Reinhart's meeting with the Director was depressingly similar to Osborne's with Vandenberg, but Reinhart was a better strategist than Geers. After two grinding hours they sent for Judy.

"We've got to strengthen the security here, Miss Adamson."

"You don't expect me—?" She broke off.

Geers glinted at her through his spectacles and she turned for understanding to Reinhart.

"My position here would be intolerable. Everyone trusted me, and now I turn out to be a security nark."

"I always knew that," said Reinhart gently. "And Professor Dawnay has guessed. She accepts it."

"Dr. Fleming doesn't."

"He wasn't meant to," said Geers.

"He accepted me as something else."

"Everyone knows you had a job to do," Reinhart looked unhappily at his fingers. "And everyone respects it."

"I don't respect it."

"I beg your pardon?" Geers took off his glasses and blinked at her as if she had gone out of focus. She was trembling.

"I've hated it from the start. It was perfectly clear that everyone here was perfectly trustworthy, except Bridger."

"Even Fleming?"

"Dr. Fleming's worth ten of anyone else I've met! He needs protecting from his own indiscretion, and I've tried to do that. But I will not go on spying on him."

"What does Fleming say?" Reinhart asked.

"He doesn't talk to me since . . ."

"Where is he?" asked Geers.

"Drinking, I suppose."

"Still on that, is he?" Geers raised his eyes to display hopelessness, and the gesture made Judy suddenly, furiously angry.

"What do you expect him to take to, after what's happened? Bingo?" She turned again, with faint hope, to Reinhart. "I've grown very fond of—of all of them. I admire them."

"My dear girl, I'm in no position . . ." Reinhart avoided her eyes. "It's probably as well it is out in the open."

Judy found she was standing to attention. She faced Geers.

"Can I be relieved?"

"No."

"Then may I have a different assignment?"

"No."

"Then may I resign my commission?"

"Not during a state of National Emergency." Geers's eyes, she noticed, were set too close together. They stared straight at her, expressionless with authority. "If it weren't for your very good record, I'd say you were immature for this job. As it is, I think you're merely unsettled by exposure to the scientific mind, especially such an ebullient and irresponsible mind as Fleming's."

"He's not irresponsible."

"No?"

"Not about important things."

"The important things at this establishment are the means of survival. We're under very great pressure."

"To the military, all things are military," said Reinhart icily. He walked across the room and looked out of the window, his little hands clasped uneasily behind his back. "It's a bleak place here, you know. We all feel the strain of it."

For some time after this outburst Geers was unusually agreeable. He did everything he possibly could for Dawnay, rushing through new equipment to replace what Fleming had damaged and generally identifying himself with what she was doing. Reinhart fought hard to retain his foothold and Judy went back to her duty with a sort of glum despair. She even screwed up her courage to see Fleming, but his room was empty and so were the three whisky bottles by his bed. With one exception, he spoke to no-one in the days that followed Bridger's death.

Dawnay had gone straight back to work, with Christine to help her with the relatively simple calculations needed from the computer. Within a week they had another successful synthesis, and they were watching it, late in the evening, in the repaired microscope, when the door of the laboratory was pushed open and Fleming stood unsteadily inside.

Dawnay straightened up and looked at him. He wore no jacket or tie, his shirt was crumpled and dirty and he had seven days' growth of stubble round his jaw. He might have been on the verge of *delirium tremens*.

"What do you want?"

He gave her a glazed stare and swayed a step forward into the room.

"Keep out of here, please."

"I see you've new equipment," he said thickly, with a fatuous twitching smile.

"That's right. Now will you leave us?"

"Bridger's dead." He smiled stupidly at her.

"I know."

"You go on as though nothing had happened." It was difficult to understand what he said. "But he's dead. He won't come back any more."

"We've all heard, Dr. Fleming."

He swayed another pace into the room. "What you doing here?"

"This is private. Will you please go?" She got up and advanced grimly towards him. He stood blinking at her, the smile fading from his face.

"He was my oldest friend. He was a fool, but he was my—"

"Dr. Fleming," she said quietly. "Will you go, or do I call the guards?"

He looked at her for a moment, as if trying to see her through mist, then shrugged and shuffled out. She followed him to the door and locked it behind him.

"We can do without that." she said to Christine.

Fleming found his way back to his hut, took an unfinished bottle of whisky from his desk drawer and poured it down the sink. Then he fell on to his bed and slept for twenty-four hours. The following evening he shaved and bathed and started to pack.

The new experiment grew fantastically. Within a few hours Dawnay had to transfer it from its microscope slide to a small nutrient bath, and the following morning it had to be moved into a larger bath. It continued to double itself during the whole of the day that Fleming slept, and by the evening Dawnay was forced to appeal for help to Geers, who took over the problem with a proprietary air and caused his workshop wing to build a deep, electrically-heated tank with a drip-feed channel into its open top and an inspection window in the middle of its front panel. Towards dawn the new creature was lifted by four assistants from its outgrown bath and placed in the tank.

In its new environment it grew to about the size of a sheep and then stopped. It seemed perfectly healthy and harmless, but it was not pretty.

Reinhart came to a decision that morning and went to see Dawnay. She was in her laboratory still, checking the feed control at the top of the tank. He hovered around until she had finished.

" Is it still alive?"

" And kicking." Apart from looking pale and taut around the eyes and mouth, she showed no sign of tiredness. " A day and a half since it was a smear on a slide: I told you there was no reason an organism shouldn't grow as fast as you like if you can get enough food into it."

" But it's stopped growing now?" Reinhart peered respectfully into the inspection port, through which he could see a dark form moving in the murk of the tank.

" It seems to have a pre-determined size and shape," Dawnay said, picking up a set of X-rays and handing them to him. " There's nothing much to see from there. There's no bone formation. It's like a great jelly, but it's got this eye and some sort of cortex—which looks like a very complicated nerve ganglia."

" No other features?" Reinhart held up the X-rays and squinted at them.

" Possibly some rudimentary attempt at a pair of legs, though you could hardly call them more than a division of tissue."

Reinhart put down the plates and frowned.

" How does it feed?"

" Takes it in through the skin. It lives in nutrient fluid and absorbs straight into its body cells. Very simple, very efficient."

" And the computer?"

Dawnay looked surprised.

" What about the computer?"

" Has it reacted at all?"

" How could it?"

" I don't know." Reinhart frowned at her anxiously. "Has it?"

" No. It's been entirely quiet."

The Professor walked into the computer control room and back again, his head down, his gaze on his neat shoecaps as they twinkled before him. It was as yet early morning and very quiet. He clasped his hands behind him and spoke without looking up at Dawnay.

" I want Fleming back on this."

Dawnay did not answer for a moment, then she said: "It's perfectly under control."

"Whose control?"

"Mine."

He looked up at her with an effort.

"We're on borrowed time, Madeleine. The people here want us out."

"In the middle of this?"

"No. The Ministry have fought for that, but we've got to work as a team and show results."

"Good grief! Aren't those results?" Dawnay pointed a short, bony finger at the tank. "We're in the middle of the biggest thing of the century—we're making life!"

"I know." Reinhart said, shifting uncomfortably from foot to foot. "But where is it taking us?"

"We've a lot to find out."

"And we can't afford any more accidents."

"I can manage."

"You're not on your own, Madeleine." Reinhart spoke with a kind of soft tenseness. "We're all involved in this."

"I can manage," she repeated.

"You can't divorce it from its origin—from the computer."

"Of course I can't. But Christine understands the computer, and I have her."

"She understands the basic arithmetic, but there's a higher logic, or so I think. Only Fleming understands that."

"I'm not having John Fleming reeling in here, breaking up my work and my equipment." Dawnay's voice rose. Reinhart regarded her quietly. He was still tense, but with a determination which had carried him a long way.

"We can't all do what we want entirely." He spoke so brusquely that Dawnay looked at him again in surprise. "I'm still in charge of this programme—just. And I will be so long as we work as a team and make sense. That means having Fleming here."

"Drunk or sober?"

"Good God, Madeleine, if we can't trust each other, who can we trust?"

Dawnay was about to protest, and then stopped.

"All right. So long as he behaves himself and sticks to his own side of the job."

"Thank you, my dear." Reinhart smiled.

When he left the laboratory he went straight to Geers.

"But Fleming has notified me that he's leaving," Geers said. "I've just sent Miss Adamson over to the computer to make sure he doesn't deliver a parting shot."

Fleming, however, was not at the computer. Judy stood in the control room, hesitating, when Dawnay came out to her.

"Hallo. Want to see Cyclops?"

"Why do you call it Cyclops?"

"Because of his physical characteristics." Dawnay seemed completely relaxed. "Don't they educate girls nowadays? Come along, he's in here."

"Must I?"

"Not interested?"

"Yes, but—"

Judy felt dazed. She had not taken in the progress of the experiment. For the past two days she had thought of almost nothing but Fleming and Bridger and her own hopeless position, and so far as she had any image at all of Dawnay's creation, it was microscopic and unrelated to her own life. She followed the older woman through into the laboratory without thinking and without expecting anything.

The tank confused her slightly. It was something she had not reckoned with.

"Look inside," said Dawnay.

Judy looked down in through the open top of the big tank, quite unprepared for what she was going to see. The creature was not unlike an elongated jellyfish, without limbs or tentacles but with a vague sort of bifurcation at one end and an enlargement that might be a head at the other. It floated in liquid, a twitching, quivering mass of protoplasm, its surface greeny-yellow, slimy and glistening. And in the middle of what might be its head was set—huge, lidless and colourless—an eye.

Judy felt violently sick and then panic-stricken. She turned away retching and stared at Dawnay as if she too were something in a nightmare, then she clamped her hand over her mouth and ran out of the room.

She ran straight across the compound to Fleming's hut, flung the door open and went inside.

Fleming was pushing some last things into a hold-all, his cases packed and standing on the floor. He looked across

106

coldly at her as she stood panting and heaving in the doorway.

"Not again," he said.

"John!" She could hardly speak at first. Her head was turning and singing and her throat felt full of phlegm. "John, you must come."

"Come where?" He looked at her with blank hostility. The toll of the past week still showed in his pale skin and the dark pouches under his eyes, but he was calm and kempt and clearly again in full charge of himself. Judy tried to steady her voice.

"To the lab."

"For you?" It was a quiet sneer.

"Not for me. They've made something terrible. A sort of creature."

"Why don't you tell M.I.5?"

"Please." Judy went up to him; she felt completely defenceless but she did not care what he said or did to her. He turned away to go on with his packing. "Please, John! Something horrible's happening. You've got to stop it."

"Don't tell me what to do and what not to do," he said.

"They've got this thing. This monstrous-looking thing with an eye. An eye!"

"That's their problem." He pushed an old sweater into the top of the bag and pulled the strings together to close it.

"John—you're the only one . . ."

He pulled the bag off his bed and brushed past her with it to stack it with his cases. "Who's fault's that?"

Judy took a deep breath.

"I didn't kill Bridger."

"Didn't you? Didn't you put your gang on him?"

"I tried to warn you."

"You tried to fool me! You made love to me—"

"I didn't! Only once. I'm only human. I had a job—"

"You had a filthy job, and you did it marvellously."

"I never spied on you. Bridger was different."

"Dennis Bridger was my oldest friend and my best helper."

"He was betraying you."

"Betraying!" He looked at her briefly and then moved away and started sorting a collection of old bottles and glasses from a cupboard. "Take your official clichés somewhere else.

Half this thing was Dennis's. It was the work of his mind, and mine; it didn't belong to you, or your bosses. If Dennis wanted to sell his own property, good luck to him. What business was it of yours?"

"I told you I didn't like what I had to do. I told you not to trust me. Do you think I haven't . . ."

Judy's voice shook in spite of her.

"Oh, stop snivelling," said Fleming. "And get out."

"I'll get out if you'll go and see Professor Dawnay."

"I'm leaving."

"You can't! They've got this horrible thing." Judy put out a hand and held desperately on to his sleeve, but he shook her off and walked across to the door.

"Good-bye." He turned the handle and opened it.

"You can't walk out now."

"Good-bye," he said quietly, waiting for her to go. She stood for a moment, trying to think of something else to say, and at that moment Reinhart appeared in the doorway.

"Hallo, John." He looked from one to the other of them. "Hallo, Miss Adamson."

She walked out between them without speaking, blinking her eyes to stop herself from crying. Reinhart turned after her as she went, but Fleming shut the door.

"Did you know about that woman?"

"Yes."

Reinhart walked across to the bed and sat down on it. He looked old and tired.

"You couldn't have told me?" Fleming said accusingly.

"No, John, I couldn't."

"Well." Fleming opened drawers and shut them again, to make sure they were empty. "You can hire someone you can trust in my place."

The Professor looked round the room.

"Can I have a drink?" He stroked the tiny fingers of one hand across his forehead to revive himself. The second interview with Geers had not been easy. "What makes you think I don't trust you?"

"Nobody trusts us, do they?" Fleming routed about among the discarded bottles. "Nobody takes a blind bit of notice what we say."

"They take notice of what we do."

108

"Brandy be all right?" Fleming found a drop in the bottom of a flask, and slopped it into a tumbler. "Oh yes, we're very useful mechanics. But when it comes to the meaning of it—having an idea of what it's about—they don't want to know."

He held the glass out.

"Have you a drop of water?" Reinhart asked.

"That we can do."

"And you?" Reinhart nodded to the bottle. Fleming shook his head.

"They think they've just got a convenient windfall," he said, running water from his wash-basin tap. "And when we say this is the beginning of something much bigger they treat us like criminal lunatics. They put their watch-dogs on us—or their watch-bitches."

"There's no need to take it out on the girl." Reinhart took the glass and drank.

"I'm not taking it out on anyone! If they can't see that what we picked up by a sheer fluke is going to change all our lives, then let them find out in their own way. With any luck they'll foul it up and nothing will come of it."

"Something *has* come of it."

"Dawnay's monster?"

"You know about that?"

"It's a sub-program, merely—an extension of the machine." Fleming looked into an empty cupboard, but his attention was beginning to drift. "Dawnay thinks the machine's given her power to create life; but she's wrong. It's given itself the power."

"Then you must stay and control it, John."

"It's not my job." He slammed the cupboard door. "I wish to God I'd never started it!"

"But you did. You have a responsibility."

"To whom? To people who won't listen to me?"

"I listen to you."

"All right." He roamed round the room, picking up oddments and throwing them into the waste-paper basket. "I'll tell you what you're up against: and then I go."

"If you've anything constructive to say—" The drink had put some strength back into Reinhart's voice.

"Look—" Fleming came to rest at the end of the bed and bent over it with his hands on the board at its end, leaning his weight on his arms and concentrating, at last, not on the room,

109

but on what he was saying. "You're all so busy asking 'What?' —'What have we got?', 'What does it do?'—no-one except me asks 'Why?'. Why does an alien intelligence two hundred light-years away take the trouble to start this?"

"We can't tell that, can we?"

"We can make deductions."

"Guesses."

"All right—if you don't want to think it out!"

He straightened up and let his arms flop down to his sides. Reinhart sipped his brandy and waited for him. After a minute Fleming relaxed and grinned at him a little sheepishly.

"You old devil!" He sat down beside the Professor on the bed. "It's a logical intelligence, wherever and whatever it is. It sends out a set of instructions, in absolute terms, which postulate a piece of technology, which we interpret as this computer. Why? Do you think they said: 'Now, here's an interesting piece of technical information. We'll radio it out to the rest of the universe—they might find it useful'?"

"You obviously don't think so."

"Because where there's intelligence, there's will. And where there's will there's ambition. Supposing this was an intelligence which wanted to spread itself?"

"It's as good a theory as the next."

"It's the only *logical* theory!" Fleming banged his fist on his thigh. "What does it do? It puts out a message that can be picked up and interpreted and acted upon by other intelligences. The technique we use doesn't matter, just as it doesn't matter what make of radio set you buy—you get the same programmes. What matters is, we accept their programme: a program which uses arithmetical logic to adapt itself to our conditions, or any other conditions for that matter. It knows the bases of life: it finds out which ours is. It finds out how our brains work, how our bodies are built, how we get our information— we tell it about our nervous system and our sensory organs. So then it makes a creature with a body and a sensory organ—an eye. It's got an eye, hasn't it?"

"Yes."

"It's probably pretty primitive, but it's the next step. Dawnay thinks she's using that machine, but it's using her!"

"The next step to what?" Reinhart asked casually.

"I don't know. Some sort of take-over."

" Of us?"

" That's the only possible point."

Reinhart rose and, walking slowly and thoughtfully across the room, put his empty glass down with the others.

" I don't know, John."

Fleming appeared to understand his uncertainty.

" The first explorers must have seemed harmless enough to the native tribes." He spoke gently. " Kind old missionaries with ridiculous topees, but they finished up as their rulers."

" You may be right." Reinhart smiled at him gratefully; it was like old times, with both of them thinking the same way. " It seems an odd sort of missionary."

" This creature of Dawnay's: what sort of brain has it?" Reinhart shrugged and Fleming went on, " Does it think like us, or does it think like the machine?"

" If it thinks at all."

" If it has an eye, it has nerve-centres—it certainly has a brain. What kind of brain?"

" Probably primitive too."

" Why?" Fleming demanded. " Why shouldn't the machine produce an extension of its own intelligence: a sub-computer that functions the same way, except that it's dependent on an organic body?"

" What would be the value?"

" The value of an organic body? A machine with senses? A machine with an eye?"

" You won't persuade anyone else," said Reinhart.

" You needn't rub that in."

" You'll have to stay with it, John."

" To do what?"

" To control it." Reinhart spoke flatly: he had made the decision some hours before. Fleming shook his head.

" How can we? It's cleverer than we are."

" Is it?"

" I don't want any part of it."

" That would suit it, according to your theory."

" If you don't believe me—"

Reinhart half raised a little hand. " I'm prepared to."

" Then destroy it. That's the only safe thing."

" We'll do that if necessary," Reinhart said, and he walked

to the door as if the matter were settled. Fleming swung round to him.

" Will you? Do you really think you'll be able to? Look what happened when I tried to stop it: Dawnay threw me out. And if you try to they'll throw you out."

" They want to throw me out anyhow."

" They want *what*?" Fleming looked as if he had been hit.

" The powers that be want us all out of the way," Reinhart said. " They just want to know we're breaking up and they'll move in."

" Why, for God's sake?"

" They think they know better how to use it. But as long as we're here, John, we can pull out the plug. And we will, if it comes to it." He looked from Fleming's troubled face to the cases lying on the floor. " You'd better unpack those things."

The meeting between Fleming and Dawnay was electrically charged, but nothing dramatic happened. Fleming was quiet enough, and Dawnay treated him with a kind of tolerant amusement.

" Welcome the wandering boy," she said, and led him off to see the thing in the tank.

The creature floated peacefully in the middle of its nutrient bath; it had found the porthole and spent most of its time gazing out with its one huge lidless eye. Fleming stared back at it, but it gave no sign of registering what it saw.

" Can it communicate?"

" My dear boy," Dawnay spoke as though she were humouring a very young student. " We've hardly had time to learn anything about him."

" It has no vocal chords or anything?"

" No."

" Um." Fleming straightened up and looked in the top of the tank. " It might be a feeble attempt at a man."

"A man? It doesn't look like a man."

Fleming strolled through to the computer room, where Christine was watching the display panel.

"Anything printing out?"

" No. Nothing." Christine looked puzzled. " But there's obviously something going on."

The display lamps were winking steadily: it seemed that the machine was working away by itself without producing results.

For the next two or three days nothing happened, and then Fleming laid a magnetic coil from the machine round the tank. He did not—in fact, he could not—explain why he did it, but immediately the computer display began flashing wildly. Christine ran in from the laboratory.

"Cyclops is terribly excited! He's threshing about in his tank."

They could hear the bumping and slopping of the creature and its fluid from the other room. Fleming disconnected the coil and the bumping stopped. When they reconnected the coil, the creature reacted again, but still nothing came through on the output printer. Reinhart came over to see how they were getting on, and he and Dawnay and Fleming went over the routine once more; but they could make nothing of it.

The next day Fleming got them together again.

"I want to try an experiment," he said.

He walked across to the display panel and stood with his back to it, between the two mysterious terminals which they had never used. After a minute he took the perspex safety-guards off the terminals and stood between them again. Nothing happened.

"Would you stand here a moment?" he asked Reinhart, and moved away to let the Professor take his place. "Mind you don't touch them. There's a thousand volts or more across there."

Reinhart stood quite still with his head between the terminals and his back to the display panel.

"Feel anything?"

"A very slight—" Reinhart paused. "A sort of dizziness."

"Anything else?"

"No."

Reinhart stepped away from the computer.

"All right now?"

"Yes," he said. "I can't feel anything now."

Fleming repeated the experiment with Dawnay, who felt nothing.

"Different people's brains give off different amounts of electrical discharge," she said. "Mine's obviously low, so's Fleming's. Yours must be higher, Ernest, because it induces a leak across the terminals. You try, Christine."

Christine looked frightened.

"It's all right," said Fleming. "Stand with your head between those things, but don't touch them or they'll roast you."

Christine took her place where the others had stood. For a moment it seemed to have no effect on her, then she went rigid, her eyes closed and she fell forward in a dead faint. They caught her and pulled her into a chair, and Dawnay lifted up her eyelids to examine her eyes.

"She'll be all right. She's only fainted."

"What happened?" asked Reinhart. "Did she touch one?"

"No," Fleming said. "All the same, I'd better put the guards back on." He did so, and stood thinking while Dawnay and Reinhart revived Christine, ducking her head between her legs and dabbing her forehead with cold water.

"If there's a regular discharge between those terminals and you introduce the electrical field of a working brain into it . . ."

"Hold on," said Dawnay impatiently. "I think she's coming round."

"Oh, she'll be O.K." Fleming looked thoughtfully at the panel and the two sheathed contacts that stuck out from it. "It'll change the current between them—modulate it. The brain will feel a reaction; there could be some pick-up, it could work both ways."

"What are you talking about?" Reinhart asked.

"I'm talking about these!" Fleming flared up with excitement. "I think I know what they're for. They're a means of inputting and picking up from the machine."

Dawnay looked doubtful. "This is just a neurotic young woman. Probably a good subject for hypnosis."

"Maybe."

Christine came round and blinked.

"Hallo." She smiled at them vaguely. "Did I faint?"

"I'll say you did," said Dawnay. "You must have a hell of an electrical aura."

"Have I?"

Reinhart gave her a glass of water. Fleming turned to her and grinned.

"You've just done a great service to science." He nodded to the terminals. "You'd better keep away from between there."

He turned back to Reinhart.

"The real point is that if you have the right sort of brain—

114

not a human one—one that works in a way designed by the machine—then you have a link. That's how it's meant to communicate. Our way of feeding back questions as answers is terribly clumsy. All this business of printers—"

"Are you saying it can thought-read?" Dawnay asked scornfully.

" I'm saying two brains can communicate electrically if they're of the right sort. If you get your creature and push his head between those terminals—"

" I don't see how we can do that."

" It's what it wants! That's why it's restless—why they're both restless. They want to get in touch. The creature's in the machine's electromagnetic field, and the machine knows the logical possibilities of it. That's what he's been working out, without telling us."

" You can't drag Cyclops out of his nutrient bath," Dawnay said. " He'll die.

" That must have been thought of."

" You could rig up an electro-encephalograph," said Reinhart. " The kind they use for mental analysis. Put a set of electric pads on Cyclops's head and run a co-axial cable from there to the terminals to carry the information. You'll have to put it through a transformer, or you'll electrocute him."

" What does that do?" Dawnay looked at him sceptically.

" It puts the computer in touch with its sub-intelligence," said Fleming.

" To serve what purpose?"

" To serve *its* purpose." He turned away from them and paced up the room. Dawnay waited for Reinhart to speak, but the old man stood obstinately, frowning down at his hands.

" Feeling better now?" he asked Christine.

" Yes, thank you."

" Do you think you could rig up something like that?"

" I think so."

" Dr. Fleming will help you. Won't you, John?"

Fleming stood at the far end of the room, the banks of equipment rising massively behind him.

" If that's what you really want," he said.

" The alternative," said Reinhart, more to Dawnay and himself than to Fleming, " is to pack up and hand over. We haven't much choice, have we?"

Eight

AGONY

JUDY kept as far from Fleming as she could, and when she did see him he was usually with Christine. Everything had changed since Bridger died; even the early burst of spring weather was soon ended, leaving a grey pall of gloom over the camp and over herself. With an additional pang she realised that Christine was likely to take not only her place but Dennis Bridger's as well in Fleming's life, working and thinking with him as she herself had never been able to do. She thought at first that she would not be able to bear it and, going over Geers's head, wrote direct to Whitehall begging to be removed. The only result was another lecture from Geers.

" Your job here has hardly begun, Miss Adamson."

" But the Bridger business is over!"

" Bridger may be, but the business isn't." He seemed quite unaware of her distress. " Intel have had enough to whet their appetite, and now they've lost him they'll be looking for someone else—perhaps one of his friends."

" You think Dr. Fleming would sell out?" she asked scornfully.

"Anyone might, if we let them."

In the event it was Fleming, not Judy, who reported the first move from Intel.

He, Christine and Dawnay had found a way of securing the contact plates of an encephalograph on to what seemed to be the head of Cyclops, and Christine had helped him to link them by cable to the high-voltage terminals of the computer. They added a transformer to the racks below the display panel and ran the circuit through there, so that the current reaching Cyclops had only about the strength of a torch battery. All the same, the effect was alarming. When the first connection was made the creature went completely rigid and the control display lamps of the computer jammed full on. After a little, however, both the creature and the machine appeared to adjust themselves: data processing went on steadily, although nothing was printed out, and Cyclops floated quietly in his tank, gazing out of the port-hole with his single eye.

All this had taken several days, and Christine had been left in charge of the linked control room and laboratory with instructions to call Dawnay and Fleming if anything fresh happened. Dawnay took some hard-earned rest, but Fleming visited the computer building from time to time to check up and to see Christine. He found her increasingly strung-up as days went by, and by the end of a week she had become so nervy that he tackled her about it.

" Look—you know I'm dead scared of this whole business, but I didn't know you were."

" I'm not," she said. They were in the control room, watching the lights flickering steadily on the panel. " But it gives me an odd feeling."

" What does?"

" That business with the terminals, and . . ." She hesitated and glanced nervously towards the other room. " When I'm in there I feel that eye watching me all the time."

" It watches all of us."

" No. Me particularly."

Fleming grinned. " I don't blame it. I look at you myself."

" I thought you were otherwise occupied."

" I was." He half raised his hand to touch her, then changed his mind and walked away to the door. " Take care of yourself."

He walked down the cliff path to the beach, where he could be quiet and alone and think. It was a grey, empty afternoon, the tide was out and the sand lay like dull grey slate between the granite headlands. He wandered out to the sea's edge, head down, hands in pockets, trying to work through in his mind what was going on inside the computer. He walked slowly back to the rocky foreshore, too deep in his thoughts to notice a squat, bald man sitting on a boulder smoking a miniature cigar.

" One moment, sir, please." The guttural voice took him by surprise.

" Who are you?"

The bald man took a card from his breast pocket and held it out.

" I can't read," said Fleming.

The bald man smiled. " You, however, are Dr. Fleming."

" And you?"

" It would mean nothing." The bald man was slightly out of breath.

" How did you get here?"

"Around the headland. You can, at low tide, but it is quite a scramble." He produced a silver case of cigarilloes. " Smoking?"

Fleming ignored it. " What do you want?"

" I come for a walk." He shrugged and put the case back in his pocket. He seemed to be recovering his breath. " You often come here yourself."

" This is private."

" Not the foreshore. In this free country the foreshore is . . ." He shrugged again. " My name is Kaufmann. You have not heard it?"

" No."

" Your friend Herr Doktor Bridger—"

" My friend Bridger is dead!"

" I know. I heard." Kaufmann inhaled his small cigar. " Very sad."

" Did you know Dennis Bridger?" Fleming asked, perplexed and suspicious.

" Oh yes. We had been associated for some time."

" Do you work for—?" The light dawned and he tried to remember the name.

" Intel? Yes."

Kaufmann smiled up at Fleming and blew out a little wraith of smoke. Fleming took his hands from his pockets.

" Get out."

" Excuse?"

" If you're not off this property in five minutes, I shall call the guards."

" No, please." Kaufmann looked hurt. " This was so happy a chance meeting you."

"And so happy for Bridger?"

" No-one was more sorry than I. He was also very useful."

"And very dead." Fleming looked at his wristwatch. " It'll take me five minutes to climb the cliff. When I get to the top I shall tell the guards."

He turned to go, but Kaufmann called him back.

" Dr. Fleming! You have much more lucrative ways of spending the next five minutes. I am not suggesting you do anything underhand."

" That's dandy, isn't it?" said Fleming, keeping his distance.

" We were thinking, rather, you might like to transfer from government service to honourable service with us. I believe you are not too happy here."

" Let's lay this on the line shall we, my herr friend?" Fleming walked back and stood looking down at him. " Maybe I don't love the government, maybe I'm not happy. But even if I hated their guts and I was on my last gasp and there was no-one else in the world to turn to, I'd rather drop dead before I came to you."

Then he turned away and climbed up the cliff path without looking back.

He went straight to Geers's office and found the Director dictating reports into a tape-machine.

" What did you tell him?" asked Geers when Fleming had reported.

" Do you mind!" A look of disgust came over Fleming's face. " It's bad enough keeping it out of the hands of babes and sucklings, without feeding it to sharks."

He left the office wondering why he had bothered; but in fact it was one of the few actions that told in his favour during the coming months.

Patrols were set on the beach, concertina wire was staked down from the headlands into the sea, Quadring's security staff did a comb-out of the surrounding district, and nothing more was heard of Intel for a long time. The experiment in the computer building continued without any tangible result until after Dawnay came back from her holiday; and then, one morning, the computer suddenly started printing-out. Fleming locked himself up in his hut with the print-out, and after about a hundred hours' work he telephoned for Reinhart.

From what he could make out, the computer was asking an entirely new set of questions, all concerning the appearance, dimensions and functions of the body. It was possible, as Fleming said, to reduce any physical form to mathematical terms and this, apparently, was what it was asking for.

"For instance," he told Reinhart and Dawnay when they sat down together to work on it, "it wants to know about hearing. There's a lot here about audio frequencies, and it's obviously asking how we make sounds and how we hear them."

"How could it know about speech?" Dawnay inquired.

"Because its creature can see us using our mouths to communicate and our ears to listen. All these questions arise from your little monster's observation. He can probably feel speech vibrations, too, and now that he's wired to the machine he can transmit his observations to it."

"You assume."

"How else do you account for this?"

"I don't see how we can analyse the whole human structure," Reinhart said.

"We don't have to. He keeps making intelligent guesses, and all we have to do is feed back the ones that are right. It's the old game. I can't think, though, why it hasn't found some quicker method by now. I'm sure it's capable of it. Perhaps the creature hasn't come up to expectations."

"Do you want to try it?" Reinhart asked Dawnay.

"I'll try anything," she said.

So the next stage of the project went forward, while Christine stayed with the computer, taking readings and inputting the results. She seemed all the time in a state of nervous tension, but said nothing.

"Do you want to move over to something else?" Fleming asked her when they were alone together one evening in the computer building.

"No. It fascinates me."

Fleming looked at her pensive and rather beautiful face. He no longer flirted with her as he used to before he was interested, when she was just a girl in the lab. Pushing his hands into his pockets, he turned from her and left the building. When he had gone she walked across the control room to the laboratory bay. It took her an effort to go through into the room where the tank was, and she stood for a moment in the doorway, her face strained, bracing herself. There was no sound except for the steady mains hum of the computer, but when she came within range of the port-hole in the side of the tank the creature began to move about, thumping against the tank walls and slopping fluid out of the open top.

"Steady," she said aloud. "Steady on."

She bent down mechanically and looked in through the port-hole: the eye was there looking steadily back at her, but the creature was becoming more and more agitated, threshing about with the fringes of its body like a jellyfish. Christine passed a hand across her forehead; she was slightly dizzy from bending down, but the eye held her as if mesmerically. She stayed there for a long minute, and then for another, growing incapable of thought. Slowly, as if of its own volition, her right hand moved up the side of the tank and her fingers sought the wire leading in to the encephalograph cable. They touched the wire and tingled as the slight current ran through them.

The moment she touched the wire, the creature grew quiet. It still looked steadfastly at her but no longer moved. The whole building was utterly quiet except for the hum of the computer. She straightened slowly, as if in a trance, still holding the wire. Her fingers ran along it until they touched the sheath of the cable and then closed on that, sliding it through the hollow of her hand. The cable was only loosely rigged; it looped across from the tank to the wall of the laboratory and was slung along the wall from pieces of tape tied to nails at intervals of a few yards. As her hand felt its way along the cable, she walked stiffly across to the wall and along beside it to the doorway to the computer room. Her eyes were open, but fixed and unseeing. The cable disappeared into a hole drilled in the wooden facing of the doorpost and she seemed at a loss when she could follow it no further. Then she raised her other hand and gripped the cable again on the other side of the doorway.

Her right hand dropped and she went through into the other room, holding the cable with her left. She worked her way slowly along the wall to the end of the rack of control equipment, breathing in a deep, laboured way as if asleep and troubled by a dream. At the centre of the racks of equipment the cable ran into the transformer below the control panel. The panel lights flashed steadily with a sort of hypnotic rhythm and her eyes became fixed on them as they had been on the eye of the creature. She stood in front of the panel for a few moments as though she were going to move no further; then, slowly, her left hand let go of the cable. Her right hand lifted again and with the fingers of both she grasped the high tension wires that ran from the transformer up to the two terminals beside her head. These wires were insulated to a point just below the terminals where their cores were bared and clamped on to the jutting-out plates. Her hands moved up them slowly, inch by inch.

Her face was blank and drained and she began to sway as she had done on the day when Fleming first made her stand between the terminal plates. She held on tightly to the wires, her fingers inching slowly up them. Then she touched the bare cores.

It all happened very quickly. Her body twisted as the full voltage of the current ran through it. She began to scream, her legs buckled, her head fell back and she hung from her outstretched arms as if crucified. The lamps on the display panel jammed full on, glaring into her distorted face, and a loud and insistent thumping started from the other room.

It lasted about ten seconds. Then her scream was cut off, there was a loud explosion from the fuse-panel above her, the lights went dead, her fingers uncurled from the naked wire and she fell heavily into a crumpled heap on the floor. For a moment there was silence. The creature stopped thumping and the humming of the computer stopped as if cut with a knife. The alarm bell rang.

The first person on the scene was Judy, who was passing the building when the alarm on the wall of the porch clanged into life. Pushing open the door, she ran wildly down the corridor and into the control room. At first she could see nothing. The strip lights in the ceiling were still on, but the control desk hid the floor in front of the control panel. Then she saw Christine's body and, running forward, knelt down beside it.

" Christine!"

She turned the body over on to its back. Christine's face stared sightlessly up at her and the hands fell limply back on to the floor: they were black and burnt through to the bone. Judy felt for the girl's heart, but it was still.

" Oh God!" she thought. " Why do I always have to be in at the death?"

Reinhart was back in London when he heard the news. When he reported it to Osborne, he got a different response from what he expected; Osborne was certainly worried by it, but he seemed preoccupied with other things and took it as one blow among many. Reinhart was distressed and also puzzled: not only Osborne but everyone else he met, as he moved in and out of Whitehall offices, appeared to have something secret and heavy on their minds. He thought of going to Bouldershaw Fell, which he had not visited for a long time, to try to get away from the feeling of oppression that surrounded him, but he found immediately that the radio-telescope had been put under military control and was firmly sealed off by Ministry of Defence security. This had happened without warning during the past week while he had been at Thorness. He was furious at not being consulted and went to see Osborne, but Osborne was too busy to make appointments.

Christine's post mortem and autopsy reports followed in a few days. The Professor was at least spared the ordeal of explaining to her relatives, for both her parents were dead and she had no other relations in the country. Fleming sent him a short, grim letter saying that no major damage had been done to the computer and that he had a theory about Christine's death. Then there was a longer letter telling him the blown circuit had been repaired and that the computer was working full out, transferring a fantastic amount of information to its memory storage, though what the information was Fleming did not say. Dawnay telephoned him a couple of days later to say the computer had started printing out. A vast mass of figures was pouring out from it, and as far as she and Fleming could tell this was not in the form of questions but of information.

" It's a whole lot more formulae for bio-synthesis," she said. " Fleming thinks it's asking for a new experiment, and I think he's right."

" More monsters?" Reinhart asked into the telephone.

" Possibly. But it's much more complicated this time. It'll be an immense job. We shall need a lot more facilities, I'm afraid, and more money."

He made another attempt to see Osborne and was summoned, to his surprise, to the Ministry of Defence.

Osborne was waiting in Vandenberg's room when he arrived. Vandenberg and Geers were also there: it looked as though they had been talking for some time. Geers's brief case was open on the table and a lot of papers had been splayed out from it and examined. Something harsh and unfriendly about the atmosphere of the room put the Professor on his guard.

"Rest your feet," said Vandenberg automatically, without smiling. There was a small strained pause while everyone waited for someone else to speak, then he added. "I hear you've written off another body."

"It was an accident," said Reinhart.

"Sure, sure. Two accidents."

"The Cabinet have had the results of the enquiry," Osborne said, looking down at the carpet. Geers coughed nervously and started shuffling the papers together.

"Yes?" Reinhart looked at the General and waited.

"I'm sorry, Professor," said Vandenberg.

"For what?"

Osborne looked at him for the first time. "We've got to accept a change of control, a general tightening-up."

"Why?"

"People are starting to ask questions. Soon they'll find you've got this living creature you're experimenting on."

"You mean the R.S.P.C.A.? It's not an animal. It's just a collection of molecules we put together ourselves."

"That isn't going to make them any happier."

"We can't just stop in the middle—" Reinhart looked from one to another of them, trying to fathom what was in their minds. "Dawnay and Fleming are just starting on a new tack."

"We know that," said Geers, tapping the papers he was putting back into his brief case.

"Then—?"

"I'm sorry," said Vandenberg again. "This is the end of your road."

"I don't understand."

Osborne shifted uneasily in his chair. "I've done my best. We all fought as hard as we could."

"Fought whom?"

"The Cabinet are quite firm." Osborne seemed anxious to avoid details. "We've lost our case, Ernest. It's been fought and lost way above our level."

"And now," put in Vandenberg. "you've written off another body."

"That's just an excuse!" Reinhart rose to his small feet and confronted the other man across the desk. "You want us out of it because you want the equipment. You trump up any kind of case—"

Vandenberg sighed. "It's the way it goes. I don't expect you to understand our viewpoint."

"You don't make it easy."

Geers snapped his brief case shut and switched on a small smile.

"The truth is, Reinhart, they want you back at Bouldershaw Fell."

Reinhart regarded him with distaste.

"Bouldershaw Fell? They won't even let me in there."

Geers looked enquiringly at the General, who gave him a nod to go on.

"The Cabinet have taken us into their confidence," he said with an air of importance.

"This is top secret, you understand," said Vandenberg.

"Then perhaps you'd better not tell me." Reinhart stood stiffly, like a small animal at bay.

"You'll have to know," said Geers. "You'll be involved. The Government have sent out a Mayday—an S.O.S. They want you all working on defence."

"Regardless of what we're doing?"

"It's a Cabinet decision." Osborne addressed the carpet. "We've made the best terms we can."

Vandenberg stood up and walked across to the wall-map.

"The western powers are deeply concerned." He also avoided looking at Reinhart. "Because of traces we've been picking up."

"What traces?"

"Notably from your own radio-telescope. It's the only thing we have with high enough definition. It's giving us tracks of a great many vehicles in orbit."

"Terrestrial?" Reinhart looked across at the trajectories traced on the map. "Is that what you're all worried about?"

"Yeah. Someone on the other side of the globe is pushing them up fast, but they're out of range of our early warning screen. The U.N. Space Agency has no line on them, nor has the Western Alliance. No-one has."

Geers finished it for him. "So they want you to handle it."

"But that isn't my field." Reinhart stood firm in front of the desk. "I'm an astronomer."

"What you're doing now is your field?" Vandenberg asked.

" It develops from it—from an astronomical source."

No-one answered him for a moment.

" Well, that's what the Cabinet wants," said Osborne finally.

"And the work at Thorness?"

Vandenberg turned to him. " Your team—what's left of it —will answer to Dr. Geers."

" Geers!"

" I *am* Director of the Station."

" But you don't know the first thing—" Reinhart checked himself.

" I'm a physicist." said Geers. " I was, at least. I expect I can soon brush it up."

Reinhart looked at him contemptuously. " You've always wanted this, haven't you?"

" It's not my choice!" said Geers angrily.

" Gentlemen!" Osborne neighed reprovingly.

Vandenberg moved heavily back to his desk. " Let's not make this a personality problem."

"And Dawnay and Fleming's work?" Reinhart demanded.

" I shan't ditch them," said Geers. " We shall need some of the computer time, but that can be arranged—"

" If you ditch me."

" There's no kind of slur on you, Ernest," Osborne said. "As you'll see from the next Honours' List."

" Oh damn the Honours' List!" Reinhart's small fingers dug into his palms. " What Dawnay and Fleming are at is the most important research project we've ever had in this country. That's all my concern."

Geers looked at him glintingly through his spectacles. " We'll do what we can for them, if they behave themselves."

" There are going to be some changes here, Miss Adamson."

Judy was in Geers's office, facing Dr. Hunter, the Medical Superintendent of the Station. He was a big bony man who looked far more military than medical.

" Professor Dawnay is going to start a new experiment, but not under Professor Reinhart's direction. Reinhart is out of it."

" Then who—?" she left the question in the air. She disliked him and did not wish to be drawn by him.

" I shall be responsible for administering it."

" You?"

Hunter was possibly used to this type of insult; it raised only a small sneer on his large, unsubtle face.

"Of course, I'm only a humble doctor. The ultimate authority will lie with Dr. Geers."

"Supposing Professor Dawnay objects?"

"She doesn't. She's not really interested in how it's organised. What we have to do is put things on a tidy footing for her. Dr. Geers will have the final jurisdiction over the computer and I shall help him with the biological experiments. Now you—" he picked up a paper from the Director's desk—"you were seconded to the Ministry of Science. Well, you can forget that. You're back with us. I shall need you to keep our side of the business secure."

"Professor Dawnay's programme?"

"Yes. I think we are going to achieve a new form of life."

"A new form of life?"

"It takes your breath, doesn't it?"

"What sort of form?"

"We don't know yet, but when we do know we must keep it to ourselves, mustn't we?" He gave her a sort of bedroom leer. "We're privileged to be midwives to a great event."

"And Dr. Fleming?" she asked, looking straight in front of her.

"He's staying on, at the request of the Ministry of Science; but I really don't think there's much left for him to do."

Fleming and Dawnay received the news of Reinhart's removal almost without comment. Dawnay was completely engrossed in what she was doing and Fleming was isolated and solitary. The only person he might have talked to was Judy, and he avoided her. Although he and Dawnay were working closely together, they still mistrusted each other and they never spoke freely about anything except the experiment. Even on that, he found it hard to convince her about any basic thesis.

"I suppose," she said, as they stood by the output printer checking fresh screeds of figures, "I suppose all this is the information Cyclops has been feeding in."

"Some of it. Plus what the machine learnt from Christine when it had her on the hooks."

"What could it learn?"

"Remember I said it must have a quicker way of getting information about us?"

"I remember your being impatient."

"Not only me. In those few seconds before the fuses blew, I should think it got more physiological data than you could work through in a lifetime."

Dawnay gave one of her little dry sniffs and left him to pursue his own thoughts. He picked up a piece of insulated wire and wandered over to the control unit, where he stood in front of the winking display panel, thoughtfully holding one bared end of the wire in each hand. Reaching up to one of the terminals, he hooked an end of the wire over it, then, holding the wire by the insulation, he advanced the other end slowly towards the opposite terminal.

"What are you trying to do?" Dawnay came quickly across the room to him. "You'll arc it."

"I don't think so," said Fleming. He touched the bare end of wire on to the terminal. "You see." There was no more than a tiny spark as the two metal surfaces met.

Fleming dropped the wire and stood for a few seconds, thinking. Then he slowly raised his own hands to the terminals, as Christine had done.

Dawnay stepped forward to stop him. "For heaven's sake!"

"It's all right," Fleming touched the two terminals simultaneously, and nothing happened. He stood there, arms outstretched, grasping the metal plates, while Dawnay watched him with a mixture of scepticism and fear.

"Haven't you had enough death?"

"He has." He lowered his arms. "He's learnt. He didn't know the effect of high voltages on organic tissue until he got Christine up on there. He didn't know it would damage himself, either. But now that he does know he takes precautions. If you try to short across those electrodes, he'll reduce the voltage. Have a go."

"No thanks. I've had enough of your quaint ideas."

Fleming looked at her hard.

"You're not simply up against a piece of equipment, you know. You're up against a brain, and a damn good one." When she did not answer, he walked out.

In spite of the pressure of defence work, Geers did find time and means to help Dawnay. He was the kind of man who fed on activity like a locust; to have a multiplicity of things under his control satisfied the inner craving of his mind and took the place, perhaps, of the creative genius that had eluded him. He arranged for yet more equipment and facilities to be put at her disposal and reported her progress with growing pride. He would do better than Reinhart.

A new laboratory was added to the computer block to house a huge and immensely complicated D.N.A. synthesiser, and during the following weeks newly-designed X-ray crystallographic equipment and chemical synthesis units were installed to manufacture phosphate components, deoxyribose, adenine, thymine, cytosine, tyrosin and other ingredients needed for making D.N.A. molecules, the seeds of life. Within a few months they had a D.N.A. helix of some five billion nucleotide code letters under construction, and by the end of the year they had made a genetic unit of fifty chromosomes, similar to but slightly more than the genetic requirement for man.

Early in February, Dawnay reported the emergence of a living embryo, apparently human.

Hunter hurried over to the lab. building to see it. He passed Fleming as he went through the computer room, but said nothing to him; Fleming had kept to his own side of the business, as he had promised, and made no effort to help with the biochemistry. In the laboratory, Hunter found Dawnay bending over a small oxygen tent, surrounded by equipment and a number of her assistants.

" Is it living?"

" Yes." Dawnay straightened and looked up at him.

" What's it like?"

" It's a baby."

"A human baby?"

" I would say so, though I doubt if Fleming would." She gave a smile of satisfaction. "And it's a girl."

" I can hardly believe—" Hunter peered down into the oxygen tent. " May I look?"

" There's nothing much to see; only a bundle wrapped up."

Under the perspex cover of the tent was something which could have been human, but its body was tightly wrapped in a blanket and its face hidden by a mask. A rubber tube disappeared down by its neck into the blanket.

" Breathing?"

" With help. Pulse and respiration normal. Weight, six and a half pounds. When I first came here, I'd never have believed

. . ." She broke off, suddenly and unexpectedly overtaken by emotion. When she continued, it was in a softer voice. "All the alchemy of making gold come true. Of making life." She tapped the rubber tubing and resumed her usual gruff way of speaking. "We're feeding her intravenously. You may find she's no instinct for normal suckling. You'll have to teach her."

"You've landed us quite a job," said Hunter, not unmoved but anxious already about formal responsibilities.

"I've landed you human life, made by human beings. It took nature two thousand million years to do a job like that: it's taken us fourteen months."

Hunter's official bedside manner returned to him. "Let me be the first to congratulate you."

"You make it sound like a normal birth," said Dawnay, managing to sniff and smile at the same time.

The little creature in the tent seemed to thrive on its intravenous food. It grew approximately half an inch a day, and was obviously not going to go through the usual childhood of a human being. Geers reported to the Director-General of Research at the Ministry of Defence that át the present rate it should reach full adult stature in between three to four months.

Official reaction to the whole event was a mixture of pride and secrecy. The Director-General sent for a full report and classified it in a top-secret category. He passed it on to the Minister of Defence who communicated it, in summary, to an astonished and bewildered Prime Minister. The Cabinet was told in terms of strictest confidence and Ratcliff returned to his office at the Ministry of Science shaken and unsure what to do next. After considering for a long time, he told Osborne who wrote to Fleming calling for an independent report.

Fleming replied in two words: "Kill it!"

In due course he was summoned to Geers's office and asked to account for himself.

"I hardly see," said Geers, his eyes screwed up narrow behind his spectacles, "that this is anything to do with you."

Fleming thumped his fist on the huge desk.

"Am I or am I not still a member of the team?"

"In a sense."

"Then perhaps you'll listen to me. It may look like a human being, but it isn't one. It's an extension of the machine, like the other creature, only more sophisticated."

" Is this theory based on anything?"

" It's based on logic. The other creature was a first shot, a first attempt to produce an organism like us and therefore acceptable to us. This is a better shot, based on more information. I've worked on that information; I know how deliberate it is."

Geers allowed his eyes to open a little. "And having achieved this miracle, you suggest we kill it?"

" If you don't now you'll never be able to. People will come to think of it as human. They'll say we're murdering it. It'll have us—the machine will have us—where it wants us."

"And if we don't choose to take your advice?"

" Then keep it away from the computer."

Geers sat silent for a moment. his spectacles glinting. Then he rose to end the interview.

"You are only here on sufferance, Fleming, and out of courtesy to the Minister of Science. The judgement in this case rests not with you but with me. We shall do what I think best, and we shall do it here."

Nine

ACCELERATION

THE girl, as Geers had predicted, was fully grown by the end of four months. She remained most of the time in an oxygen tent, although she was learning to breathe naturally for increasing periods. By the end of the first month she was off drip feeds and on to a bottle. Beyond this, nothing was done to stimulate her mind and she lay inert as a baby, staring at the ceiling. Geers grew slightly apprehensive as growth continued, but she stopped at five foot seven inches, by which time she was a fully developed young woman.

"Quite a good-looking young woman, too," Hunter said, with a lick of his lips.

Geers allowed no-one but Hunter, Dawnay and their assistants to see her. He sent daily confidential reports to the Ministry of Defence and was visited twice by the Director-General of Research, with whom he made plans for her future. Extreme precautions were taken to keep her existence secret; a day and night guard was mounted on the computer and laboratory block and everyone who had to know was sworn to silence. Apart from Reinhart, whom Osborne told privately, and a handful of senior officials and politicians in London, no-one outside the research team at Thorness knew anything about her.

Fleming, in Geers's opinion, was the most doubtful quantity in the whole group, and Judy was given specific instructions to watch him. They had literally hardly spoken since the previous spring. He had made one surly, half-hearted attempt to apologise but she had cut him short, and since then when they met in the camp they ignored each other. At least, she told herself, she had not been spying on him—the fact that he had dissociated himself from Dawnay's experiment, to which she had been assigned after Bridger's death, had meant he was no longer primarily her concern. Whatever pangs of conscience she had about the past were hidden under the anaesthetic of a sort of listless apathy. But now it was different. Screwing up all her determination, she went to find him in the computer room, her legs feeling curiously flabby beneath her. She handed him her letter of instruction.

"Would you read this?" she said, without any preliminary.

He glanced at it and handed it back to her. "It's on Ministry of Defence paper—*you* read it. I'm choosy what I touch."

"They're concerned about the security of the new creature," she said stiffly, withdrawing in the face of his attack. Fleming laughed.

"It amuses you?" she asked. "I'm to be responsible for its safety."

"And who's to be responsible for yours?"

"John!" Judy's face reddened. "Do we always have to be on opposite sides of the fence?"

"Looks like it, doesn't it?" He said with something between sympathy and indifference. "I'm afraid I don't dig your precious creature."

"It's not mine. I'm doing my job. I'm not your enemy."

"No. You're just the sort of girl who gets pushed about." He looked helplessly around the room. "Oh I've had my say!"

She made a last attempt to reach him. "It seems a long time since we went sailing."

"It *is* a long time."

"We're the same people."

"In a different world." He moved as if he wanted to get away.

"It's the same world, John."

"O.K., you tell them that."

Hunter came past. "We're getting her out."

"Who?" Fleming turned from Judy with relief.

"The little girl—out of her oxygen tent."

"Are we allowed?" asked Judy.

"This is a special occasion—coming-out party." Hunter gave her a stale, sexy smile and walked away into the other room. Fleming looked sourly after him.

"Full-size live monster given away with each packet."

Judy surprised herself by giggling. She felt they were suddenly about a mile closer.

"I detest that man. He's so condescending."

"I hope he kills her," said Fleming. "He's probably a bad enough doctor."

They went through to the laboratory together. Hunter was superintending opening the bottom end of the oxygen tent, watched by Dawnay. Under the tent was a narrow trolley-bed which two assistants drew gently forward. The rest stood round as the bed slid out with the full-grown girl-creature on it: first her feet, covered by a sheet, then her body, also covered. She was lying on her back, and as her face was revealed Judy gave a gasp. It was a strong and beautiful face with high cheek-bones and wide, Baltic features. Her long, pale hair was strewn out on the pillow, her eyes were shut and she was breathing peacefully as if asleep. She looked like a purified, blonde version of Christine.

"It's Christine!" Judy whispered. "Christine."

"It can't be," said Hunter brusquely.

"There is a superficial resemblance," Dawnay admitted.

Hunter cut across her. "We did an autopsy on the other girl. Besides, she was a brunette."

Judy turned to Fleming.

"Is this some horrible kind of practical joke?"

He shook his head. "Don't let it fool you. Don't let it fool any of you. Christine's dead. Christine was only a blueprint."

No-one spoke for a moment while Dawnay took the girl's pulse and stooped down to look at her face. The eyes opened and looked vaguely up at the ceiling.

"What does it mean?" asked Judy. She remembered seeing Christine dead, and yet this was something inescapably like her, living.

"It means," said Fleming, as though answering all of them, "that it took a human being and made a copy. It got a few things wrong—the colour of the hair, for instance—but by and large it did a pretty good job. You can turn the human anatomy into figures, and that's what it did; and then got us to turn them back again."

Hunter looked at Dawnay and signalled to the assistants to wheel the trolley into a neighbouring bay.

"It gave us what we wanted, anyway," said Dawnay.

"Did it? It's the brain that counts: it doesn't matter about the body. It hasn't made a human being—it's made an alien creature that looks like one."

"Dr. Geers has told us your theory," said Hunter, moving away in the wake of the girl on the bed. Dawnay hesitated for a moment before going after them.

"You may be right," she said. "In which case it'll be all the more interesting."

Fleming controlled himself with an obvious effort. "What are you going to do with it?"

"We're going to educate it—her."

Fleming turned and walked out of the laboratory, back to the computer room, with Judy following.

"What's bad about it?" she asked. "Everyone else . . ."

He turned on her. "Whenever a higher intelligence meets a lower one, it destroys it. That's what's bad. Iron Age man destroyed the Stone Age; the Palefaces beat the Indians. Where was Carthage when the Romans were through with it?"

"But is that bad, in the long run?"

"It's bad for us."

"Why should this—?"

"The strong are always ruthless with the weak."

She laid a hand tentatively on his sleeve. "Then the weak had better stick together."

"You should have thought of that earlier," he said.

Judy knew better than to push him further; she went back to her own life, leaving him with his preoccupations and doubts.

There was no early spring that year. The hard grey weather went on to the end of April, matching the grey sunless mood of the camp. Apart from Dawnay's experiment, nothing was going well. Geers's permanent staff and missile development teams worked under strain with no outstanding success; there were more practice firings than ever but nothing really satisfactory came of them. After each abortive attempt the grey wrack of Atlantic cloud settled back on the promontory as if to show that nothing would ever change or ever improve.

Only the girl creature bloomed, like some exotic plant in a hothouse. One bay of Dawnay's laboratories was set up as a nursing block with living quarters for the girl. Here she was waited on and prepared for her part like a princess in a fairy tale. They called her Andromeda, after the place of her origin, and taught her to eat and drink and sit up and move. At first she was slow to learn to use her body—she had, as Dawnay said, none of the normal child's instincts for physical development—but soon it became clear that she could absorb knowledge at a prodigious rate. She never had to be told a fact twice. Once she understood the possibilities of anything she mastered it without hesitation or effort.

It was like this with speech. To begin with she appeared to have no awareness of it: she had never cried as a baby cries, and she had to be taught like a deaf child, by being made conscious of the vibrations of her vocal chords, and their effects. But as soon as she understood the purpose of it she learnt language as fast as it was spelt out to her. Within weeks she was a literate, communicating person.

Within weeks, too, she had learnt to move as a human being, a little stiffly, as if her body was working from instructions and not from its own desire, but gracefully and without any kind of awkwardness. Most of the time she was confined to her own suite, though she was taken every day, when it was not actually raining, out to the moors in a closed car and allowed to walk in the fresh air under armed escort and out of sight of any other eyes from either inside or outside the camp.

She never complained, whatever was done to her. She accepted the medical checks, the teaching, the constant surveillance, as though she had no will or wishes of her own. In fact, she showed no emotions at all except those of hunger before a meal and tiredness at the end of the day, and then it was physical, never mental tiredness. She was always gentle, always submissive, and very beautiful. She behaved, indeed, like someone in a dream.

Geers and Dawnay arranged for her education at a pace which packed the whole of a university syllabus into something which more resembled a summer-school. Once she had grasped the basis of denary arithmetic, she had no further difficulty with mathematics. She might have been a calculating machine; she whipped through figures with the swift logic of a ready-reckoner, and she was never wrong. She seemed capable of holding the most complex progressions in her head without any sense of strain. For the rest, she was filled up with facts like an encyclopaedia. Geers and the teachers who were sent up to Thorness in an endless and academically-impressive procession—not to instruct her directly, for she was too secret, but to guide her instructors — laid out the foundations of a general, unspecialised level of knowledge, so that by the end of her summer-course, and of the summer, she knew as much about the world, in theory, as an intelligent and perceptive school leaver. All she lacked was any sense of human experience or any spontaneous attitude to life. Although she was alert and reasonably communicative, she might just as well have been walking and talking in her sleep, and that, in fact, is the impression which she gave.

"You're right," Dawnay admitted to Fleming. "She hasn't got a brain, she's got a calculator."

"Isn't that the same thing?" He looked across at the slim, fair girl who was sitting reading at the table in what had been made her room. It was one of his rare visits to Dawnay's premises. The laboratory had been gutted and turned into a set of rooms that might have come out of a design brochure, with the girl as one of the fitments.

"She's not fallible," said Dawnay. "She doesn't forget. She never makes a mistake. Already she knows more than most people do."

Fleming frowned. "And you'll go on stuffing information into her until she knows more than you."

"Probably. The people in charge of us have plans for her."

Geers's plan was fairly obvious. The pressing problems of defence machinery remained unsolved in spite of the use they had made of the new computer. The main difficulty was that they did not really know how to use it. They took it out of Fleming's hands for several hours a day, and managed to get a great deal of calculation done very quickly by it; but they had no means of tapping its real potential or of using its immense intellect to solve problems that were not put to it in terms of figures. If, as Fleming considered, the creatures evolved with the machine's help had an affinity with it, then it should be possible to use one of them as an agent. The original monster was obviously incapable of making any communication of human needs to the computer, but the girl was another matter. If she could be used as an intermediary, something very exciting might be done.

The Minister of Defence had no objection to the idea and, although Fleming warned Osborne, as he had warned Geers, Osborne carried no weight with the men in power. Fleming could only stand by and watch the machine's purpose being unwittingly fulfilled by people who would not listen to him. He himself had nothing but a tortuous strand of logic on which to depend. If he was wrong, he was wrong all the way from the beginning, and the way of life was not what he thought. But if he was right they were heading for calamity.

He was, in fact, in the computer-room when Geers and Dawnay first brought the girl in.

"For God's sake!" He looked from Geers to Dawnay in a last, hopeless appeal.

"We've all heard what you think, Fleming," Geers said.

"Then don't let her in."

"If you want to complain, complain to the Ministry." He turned back to the doorway. Dawnay shrugged her shoulders; it seemed to her that Fleming was making a great deal of fuss about nothing.

Geers held the door open as Andromeda came in, escorted by Hunter who walked beside and slightly behind her as though they were characters out of Jane Austen. Andromeda moved stiffly, but was thoroughly wide awake, her face calm, her eyes taking in everything. It was all somehow formal and unreal, as if a minuet were about to begin.

"This is the control-room of the computer," said Geers as she stood looking around her. He sounded like a kind but firm parent. "You remember I told you about it?"

"Why should I forget?"

Although she spoke in a slow stilted way, her voice, like her face, was strong and attractive.

Geers led her across the room. "This is the input unit. The only way we can give information to the computer is by typing it in here. It takes a long time."

"It must do." She examined the keyboard with a sort of calm interest.

"If we want to hold a conversation with it," Geers went on, "the best we can do is select something from the output and feed it back in."

"That is very clumsy," she said slowly.

Dawnay came and stood by her other side. "Cyclops in the other room can input direct by that co-axial cable."

"Is that what you wish me to do?"

138

"We want to find out," said Geers.

The girl looked up and found Fleming staring at her. She had not taken him in before, and gazed back expressionlessly at him.

"Who is that?"

"Doctor Fleming," said Dawnay. "He designed the computer."

The girl walked stiffly across to him and held out her hand.

"How do you do?" She spoke as if repeating a lesson. Fleming ignored her hand and continued staring at her. She looked unblinkingly back at him and, after a minute, dropped her arm.

"You must be a clever man," she said flatly. Fleming laughed. "Why do you do that?"

"What?"

"Laugh—that is the word?"

Fleming shrugged. "People laugh when they're happy and cry when they're sad. Sometimes we laugh when we're unhappy."

"Why?" She went on gazing at his face. "What is happy or sad?"

"They're feelings."

"I do not feel them."

"No. You wouldn't."

"Why do you have them?"

"Because we're imperfect." Fleming returned her stare as though it were a challenge. Geers fidgeted impatiently.

"Is it working all right, Fleming? There's nothing on the display panel."

"Which is the display panel?" she asked, turning away. Geers showed her and she stood looking at the rows of unlit bulbs while Geers and Dawnay explained it, and the use of the terminals, to her.

"We'd like you to stand between them," he said.

She walked deliberately towards the panel, and as she approached it the lamps started to blink. She stopped.

"It's all right," said Dawnay. Geers took the guards from the terminals and urged the girl forward, while Fleming watched, tense, without saying anything. She went reluctantly, her face strained and set. When she reached the panel, she stood there, a terminal a few inches from each side of her head,

139

and the lights began flashing faster. The room was full of the hum of the computer's equipment. Slowly, without being told, she put her hands up towards the plates.

"You're sure it's neutralised?" Geers looked anxiously at Fleming.

"It neutralises itself."

As the girl's hands touched the metal plates, she shivered. She stood with her face blank, as it entranced, and then she let go and swayed back unsteadily. Dawnay and Geers caught her and helped her to a chair.

"Is she all right?" asked Geers.

Dawnay nodded. "But look at that!"

The lights on the panel were all jammed solidly on and the computer hum grew louder than it had been before.

"What's happened?"

"It speaks to me," said the girl. "It knows about me."

"What does it say?" asked Dawnay. "What does it know about you? How does it speak?"

"We . . . we communicate."

Geers looked uncomfortably puzzled. "In figures?"

"You could express it in figures," she said, staring blindly before her. "It would take a very long time to explain."

"And can *you* communicate—?" Dawnay was interrupted by a loud explosion from the next room. The display panel went blank, the hum stopped.

"Whatever's happened?" asked Geers.

Fleming turned without answering him and went quickly through to the first lab. bay, where the creature and its tank were housed. Smoke was rising from the contact wires above the tank. When he pulled them out, the ends were blackened and lumps of charred tissue hung from them. He looked into the tank, and his mouth set into a thin line.

"What's happened to it?" Dawnay hurried in, followed by Geers.

"It's been electrocuted." Fleming dangled the harness in front of her. "There's been another blow-out and it's been killed."

Geers peered into the tank and recoiled in distaste.

"What did you do to the controls?" he demanded.

Fleming threw down the charred remains of the wires. "I did nothing. The computer knows how to adjust its own

140

voltages—it knows how to burn tissue—it knows how to kill."

"But why?" asked Geers.

They all looked, by instinct, to the doorway from the computer-room. The girl was standing there.

"Because it was *her*." Fleming walked across to her grimly, his jaw stuck out. "You've just told it, haven't you? It knows it has a better slave now. It doesn't need that poor creature any more. That's what it said, isn't it?"

She looked levelly back at him. "Yes."

"You see!" He swung round to Geers. "You've got a killer. Bridger may have been an accident; so may Christine, though I'd call it manslaughter. But this was pure, deliberate murder."

"It was only a primitive creature," said Geers.

"And it was redundant!" He turned back to the girl. "Yes?"

"It was in the way," she answered.

"And the next time it could be you who are in the way— or me, or any or all of us!"

She still showed no flicker of expression. "We were only eliminating unwanted material."

"We?"

"The computer and myself." She touched her fingers to her head. Fleming screwed up his eyes.

"You're the same, aren't you? A shared intelligence."

"Yes," she said tonelessly. "I understand—"

"Then understand this!" Fleming's voice rose with excitement and he pushed his face close up to her. "This is a piece of information: it is wrong to murder!"

"Wrong? What is 'wrong'?"

"*You* were talking about killing earlier on," said Geers.

"Oh God!" said Fleming wildly. "Is there no sane person anywhere?"

He stared for a moment more at Andromeda, and then he went, half-running, out of the room.

Bouldershaw Fell looked much as it had done when Reinhart first took Judy to see it. Grass and heather had grown over the builders' scars on the surrounding moor, and black streaks ran down the walls of the buildings where gutters had overflowed in winter storms; but the triple arch was still poised motionless over its great bowl, and inside the main observatory block the equipment and staff continued their quiet, methodical work. Harvey was still in charge of the control desk, the banks of steering and calculating equipment still stood to each side of him, flanking the wide window, and the photographs of stars still hung on the walls, though less fresh and new than they had been.

The only sign of the grim business that preoccupied them all was a huge glazed wall-map of the world on which the tracks of orbital missiles were marked in chinagraph. It betrayed what the outward calm of the place concealed—the anguish and fever with which they watched the threats in the sky above them remorselessly grow and grow. Reinhart referred to it as the Writing on the Wall, and worked day and night with the observatory team, plotting each new trace as it swung into orbit and sending increasingly urgent and sombre reports to Whitehall.

Nearly a hundred of the sinister, unidentified missiles had been tracked during the past months, and their launching area had been defined to within a triangle several hundred miles in extent in the ocean between Manchuria, Vladivostok and the northern island of Japan. None of the neighbouring countries admitted to them. As Vandenberg said, they could belong to any of three of our fellow-members of the United Nations.

Vandenberg paid frequent visits to the telescope and had long and fruitless conferences with Reinhart. All they could really tell from their findings was that these were propelled vehicles launched from about forty degrees north by between a hundred and thirty and a hundred and fifty east, and that they travelled across Russia, Western Europe and the British Isles at a speed of about sixteen thousand miles an hour at a height between three hundred and fifty and four hundred miles. After crossing Britain they mostly passed over the North Atlantic and Greenland and the polar north of Canada, presumably joining up their trajectory in the same area of the North China Sea. Whatever route they took, they were deflected to pass over England or Scotland: they were obviously steerable and obviously aimed very deliberately at this small target. Although nothing certain was known of their size or shape, they emitted a tracking signal and they were clearly large enough to carry a nuclear charge.

"I don't know what the point of them is," Reinhart admitted. He was obsessed by them. However unhappy he was at the way things had gone at Thorness; he was by now fully occupied with this new and terrifying turn of events.

Vandenberg had cogent and reasonable theories. "Their point is that someone in the East wants us to know they have the technical edge on us. They flaunt these over our heads to show the world we've no way of retaliating. A new form of sabre-rattling."

"But why always over this country?"

Vandenberg looked slightly sorry for the Professor. "Because you're small enough—and important enough—to be a kind of hostage. This island's always been a good target."

"Well," Reinhart nodded to the map on the wall. "There's your evidence. Aren't the West going to take it to the Security Council?"

Vandenberg shook his head. "Not until we can negotiate from strength. They'd love us to run squealing to the U.N. and admit our weakness. Then they'd have us. What we need first is some means of defence."

Reinhart looked sceptical. "What are you doing about it?"

"We're going as fast as we can. Geers has a theory—"

"Oh, Geers!"

"Geers has a theory," Vandenberg ignored the interruption, "that if we can work this girl creature in harness with your computer, we may get some pretty quick thinking."

"What *was* my computer," said Reinhart sourly. "I wish you joy."

The night after Vandenberg left, Fleming appeared. Reinhart was working late, trying to fix the origin of ground signals which made the satellites change course in orbit, when he heard the exhaust crackle of Fleming's car outside. It was a little like coming home for Fleming; the familiar room, Harvey at the control desk, the small neat father-figure of the Professor waiting for him. Of the three men, Fleming looked the most worn.

"It seems so sane here." He gazed around the large, neat room. "Calm and clean."

Reinhart smiled. "It's not very sane at the moment."

"Can we talk?"

Reinhart led him over to a couple of easy chairs which had

been set for visitors, with a little table, in a back corner of the observatory.

"I told you on the phone, John, there's nothing I can do. They're going to use the creature as an aid to the computer for Geers's missile work."

"Which is just what it wants."

Reinhart shrugged. "I'm out of it now."

"We're all out of it. I'm only hanging on by the skin of my teeth. All this about being able to pull out the plug—well, we can't any more, can we?" Fleming fiddled nervously with a box of matches he had taken out to light their cigarettes. "It's in control of itself now. It's got its protectors—its allies. If this thing that looks like a woman had arrived by space-ship, it would have been annihilated by now. It would have been recognised for what it was. But because it's been planted in a much subtler way, because it's been given human form, it's accepted on face value. And it's a pretty face. It's no use appealing to Geers or that lot: I've tried. Prof., I'm scared."

"We're all scared," Reinhart said. "The more we find out about the universe the more frightening it is."

"Look." Fleming leaned forward earnestly. "Let's use our heads. That machine—that brain-child of some other world— has written off its own one-eyed monster. It's written off Christine. It'll write me off if I get in its way."

"Then get out of its way," said Reinhart wearily. "If you're in danger get out of its way now."

"Danger!" Fleming snorted. "Do you think I *want* to die in some horrible way, like Dennis Bridger, for the sake of the government or Intel? But I'm only the next on the list. If I'm forced out, or if I'm killed, what comes afterwards?"

"It's a question of what comes first at the moment." Reinhart sounded like a doctor with a hopeless case. "I can't help you, John."

"What about Osborne?"

"He doesn't hold the reins now."

"He could get his Minister to go to the P.M."

"The P.M.?"

"He's paid, isn't he?"

Reinhart shook his head. "You've nothing to show, John."

"I've some arguments."

"I doubt if any of them are in a mood to listen." Reinhart

waved a small hand towards the wall map. "That's what we're worried about at the moment."

"What's that all in aid of?"

Reinhart told him. Fleming sat listening, tense and miserable, his fingers crushing the matchbox out of shape.

"We can't always be in front, can we?" He pushed away the Professor's explanations. "At least we can come to terms with human beings."

"What sort of terms?" Reinhart asked.

"It doesn't matter what sort of terms—compared with what we're likely to be up against. A bomb is a quick death for a civilisation, but the slow subjugation of a planet . . ." his voice trailed away.

The Prime Minister was in his oak-panelled room in the House of Commons. He was a sporty-looking old gentleman with twinkling blue eyes. He sat at the middle of one side of the big table that half-filled the room, listening to the Minister for Defence. Sunlight streamed gently in through the mullioned windows. There was a knock at the door and the Defence Minister frowned; he was a keen young man who did not like being interrupted.

"Ah, here comes the science form." The Prime Minister smiled genially as Ratcliff and Osborne were shown in. "You haven't met Osborne, have you Burdett?"

The Defence Minister rose and shook hands perfunctorily. The Prime Minister motioned them to sit down.

"Isn't it a splendid day, gentlemen? I remember it was like this at Dunkirk time. The sun always seems to smile on national adversity." He turned to Burdett. "Would you bully-off for us, dear boy?"

"It's about Thorness," said Burdett to Ratcliff. "We want to take over the computer altogether—and everything associated with it. It's been agreed in principle, hasn't it? And the P.M. and I think the time has come."

Ratcliff looked at him without love. "You've access to it already."

"We need more than that now, don't we, sir?" Burdett appealed to the Prime Minister.

"We need our new interceptor, gentlemen, and we need it quickly." Behind the amiable, lazy, rather old-world manner lay more than a hint of firmness and grasp of business. "In nine-teen-forty we had Spitfires, but at the moment neither we nor our allies in the West have anything to touch the stuff that's coming over."

"And no prospect of anything," Burdett put in, " by conventional means."

" We could co-operate, couldn't we?" Ratcliff asked Osborne, " in developing something?"

Burdett was not one to waste time. " We can handle it ourselves if we take over your equipment at Thorness entirely, and the girl."

" The creature?" Osborne raised a well-disciplined eyebrow, but the Prime Minister twinkled reassuringly at him.

" Dr. Geers is of the opinion that if we use this curiously derived young lady to interpret our requirements to the computer and to translate its calculations back to us we could solve a lot of our problems very quickly."

" If you can trust it's intentions."

The Prime Minister looked interested. " I don't quite follow you."

" One or two of our people have doubts about its potential," said Ratcliff, more in hope than conviction. No minister likes losing territory, even if he has to use dubious arguments to retain it. The Prime Minister waved him aside.

" Oh yes, I've heard about that."

" Up to now, sir, this creature has been under examination by our team," Osborne said. " Professor Dawnay—"

" Dawnay could stay."

" In a consultative role," Burdett added swiftly.

"And Dr. Fleming?" asked Ratcliff.

The Prime Minister turned again to Burdett. " Fleming would be useful, wouldn't he?"

Burdett frowned. " We shall need complete control and very tight security."

Ratcliff tried his last card. " Do you think she's up to it, this girl?"

" I propose to ask her," said the Prime Minister. He pressed a small bell-push on the table and a young gentleman appeared almost immediately in the doorway. "Ask Dr. Geers to bring his lady-friend in, will you?"

"You've got her here?" Ratcliff looked accusingly at Osborne as though it was his fault.

"Yes, dear boy." The Prime Minister also looked at Osborne, inquiringly. "Is she, er—?"

"She looks quite normal."

The Prime Minister gave a small sigh of relief and rose as the door reopened to admit Geers and Andromeda. "Come in, Dr. Geers. Come along in, my dear."

Andromeda was given the chair facing him. She sat quietly with her head slightly bowed, her hands folded in her lap, like a typist coming for an interview.

"You must find this all rather strange," said the Prime Minister soothingly. She answered in slow, correct sentences.

"Dr. Geers has explained it to me."

"Did he explain why we brought you here?"

"No."

"Burdett?" The Prime Minister handed over the questioning. Ratcliff looked on grumpily while Burdett sat forward on the edge of his chair, rested his elbows on the table, placed his fingers together and looked keenly at Andromeda over them.

"This country—you know about this country?"

"Yes."

"This country is being threatened by orbital missiles."

"We know about orbital missiles."

"We?" Burdett looked at her even more sharply.

She remained as she was, her face empty of expression. "The computer and myself."

"How does the computer know?"

"We share our information."

"That is what we hoped," said the Prime Minister.

Burdett continued. "We have interception missiles—rockets of various kinds—but nothing of the combined speed, range and accuracy to, er . . ." He searched around for the right piece of jargon.

"To hit them?" she asked simply.

"Exactly. We can give you full details of speed, height and course; in fact, we can give you a great deal of data, but we need it translated into practical mechanical terms."

"Is that difficult?"

"For us, yes. What we're after is a highly sophisticated interception weapon that can do its own instantaneous thinking."

" I understand."

" We should like you to work on this with us," the Prime Minister said gently, as if asking a favour of a child. " Dr. Geers will tell you what is needed, and he will give you all facilities for actually designing weapons."

"And Dr. Fleming," added Ratcliff, " can help you with the computer."

Andromeda looked up for the first time.

" We shall not need Dr. Fleming," she said, and something about her calm, measured voice ran like a cold shadow across the sunlight.

After her return from London, Andromeda spent most of her time in the design office, a block or two away from the computer building, preparing data for the machine and sending it over for computation. Sometimes she came to communicate directly with it, with the result that long and complex calculations emerged later from the printer, which she would take away to translate into design terms. The outcome was all and more than Geers could have wished. A new guidance system and new ballistic formulas sprung ready-made from the drawing-board and when tested, they proved to come up to all specifications. The machine and the girl together could get through about a year's development theory in a day. The results were not only elegant but obviously effective. In a very short time it would clearly be possible to construct an entirely new interceptive missile.

During duty hours Andromeda had freedom of movement within the compound and, although she disappeared, under guard, into her own quarters after work, she was soon a familiar figure in the camp. Judy put it about that she was a research senior who had been seconded by the Ministry of Defence.

The following week a communiqué was issued from 10 Downing Street:

" Her Majesty's Government has been aware for some time of the passage of an increasing number of orbital vehicles, possibly missiles, over these islands. Although the vehicles, which are of unknown but terrestrial origin, pass over at great speed and at great height, there is no immediate cause for alarm. Her Majesty's Government points out, however, that they constitute a deliberate infringement of our national

148

air space, and that steps are being taken to intercept and identify them."

Fleming listened to the telecast on the portable receiver in his hut at Thorness. He was no longer responsible for the computer, and Geers had suggested that he might be happier away from it. However, he stayed on, partly out of obstinacy and partly from a sense of impending emergency, watching the progress of Andromeda and the two young operators who had been enlisted to help her with the machine. He made no approaches to her, or to Judy, who continued to hang around with a sort of aimless watchfulness, acting as a liaison between Andromeda and the front office; but after he heard the broadcast he wandered over to the computer block with the vague idea that something ought to be done.

Judy found him sitting brooding on the swivel chair by the control desk. She had not gone near him again since the last snub, but she had watched him with concern and with a feeling of latent affection that had never left her.

She went up to the control desk and stood in front of him. " Why don't you give it up, John?"

" That would please you, wouldn't it?"

" It wouldn't please me, but there's nothing you can do here, eating your heart out."

" It's a nice little three-handed game, isn't it?" He looked sardonically up at her. " I watch her and you watch me."

" You're not doing yourself any good."

" Jealous?" he asked.

She shook her head impatiently. " Don't be absurd."

" They're all so damn sure." He stared reflectively across to the control equipment. " There may be something I've missed, about this—or about her."

Andromeda came in to the computer room while Judy and Fleming were talking. She stood by the doorway holding a wad of papers, waiting until they had finished. She was quiet enough, but there was nothing modest about her. When she spoke to Judy and the others who worked with her she had an air of unquestioned and superior authority. She made no concessions even to Geers; she was perfectly polite but treated them all as intellectual inferiors.

" I wish to speak to Dr. Geers about these, please," she said from the doorway.

"Now?" Judy tried to match her in quiet comtempt.

"Now."

"I'll see if he's free," Judy said, and went out. Andromeda crossed slowly to the control panel, ignoring Fleming; but something prompted him to stop her.

"Happy in your work?"

She turned and looked at him, without speaking. He stretched back in the chair, suddenly alert.

"You're getting quite indispensable, aren't you?" he asked in the tone he had used to Judy.

She looked at him solemnly. She might have been a statue, with her fine carved face, her long hair, and her arms hanging limply down beside her simple, pale dress. "Please be careful what you talk about," she said.

"Is that a threat?"

"Yes." She spoke without emphasis, as if simply stating a fact. Fleming stood up.

"Good grief! I'm not going to—" He stopped himself and smiled. "Perhaps I *have* missed something."

Whatever he had in mind was hidden from her. She turned to walk away.

"Wait a minute!"

"I am busy." But she turned back to him and waited. He walked slowly to her and looked her up and down as though mocking her.

"You want to make something of yourself, if you're going to influence men." She stood still. He lifted a hand to her hair and edged it back from one side of her face. "You should push your hair back, and then we could see what you look like. Very pretty."

She stepped away so that his hand fell from her, but she kept her eyes on him, intrigued and puzzled.

"Or you could wear scent," he said. "Like Judy does."

"Is that what smells?"

He nodded. "Not very exotic. Lavender water or something. But nice."

"I do not understand you." A small frown creased the smooth skin of her forehead. "Nice—nasty. Good—bad. There is no logical distinction."

He still smiled. "Come here."

She hesitated, then took a step towards him. Quietly and deliberately he pinched her arm.

"Ow!" She stepped back with a sudden look of fear in her eyes and rubbed the place where he had hurt her.

"Nice or nasty?" he inquired.

"Nasty."

"Because you were made to register pain." He raised his hand again and she flinched away. "I'm not going to hurt you this time."

She stood rigidly while he stroked her forehead, like a deer being stroked by a child, submissive but ready for flight. His fingers ran down her cheek and on to her bare neck.

"Nasty or nice?"

"Nice." She watched him to see what he would do next.

"You're made to register pleasure. Did you know that?" He withdrew his hand gently and moved away from her. "I doubt if you were intended to, but by giving you human form . . . Human beings don't live by logic."

"So I've noticed!" She was more sure of herself now, as she had been before he started speaking; but he still held all her attention.

"We live through our senses. That's what gives us our instincts, for good or bad—our aesthetic and moral judgements. Without them we'd probably have annihilated ourselves by now."

"You're doing your best, aren't you?" She looked down at her papers with a contemptuous smile. "You are like children, with your missiles and rockets."

"Don't count me in on that."

"No, I don't." She regarded him thoughtfully. "All the same, I am going to save you. It is very simple, really." She made a small gesture to indicate the papers she held.

Judy came in and stood, as Andromeda had done, at the doorway.

"Dr. Geers can see you."

"Thank you." The roles now were changed. In some unspoken way, the three of them stood in a different relationship to each other. Although Fleming still watched Andromeda, she looked back at him with a different kind of awareness.

"Do I smell nasty?" she asked.

He shrugged. "You'll have to find out, won't you?"

She followed Judy out of the building and walked along the concrete path with her to Geers's office. They had nothing to say to each other, and nothing to share except a sort of wary indifference. Judy showed her into Geers's room and left her. The Director was sitting behind his desk, telephoning.

"Yes, we're coming along famously," he was saying. "Only another check and we can start building."

He put down the phone and Andromeda placed her papers on his desk, casually, as though she were bringing him a cup of tea.

"That is all you will need, Dr. Geers," she told him.

Ten

ACHIEVEMENTS

THE new missile was built and tested at Thorness. When it had been fired and recovered, and copies made, the Prime Minister sent Burdett to see Vandenberg.

The General was more than a little worried about the Thorness project. It seemed to him to be going too fast to be sound. Although his chiefs wanted action quickly, he had grave doubts about this piece of foreign technology and wanted it sent for testing to the U.S.A.; but Her Majesty's Government unexpectedly dug its toes in.

Burdett confronted him in the underground ops. room.

" Just for once we have the means to go it alone." The young minister looked very sharp and dapper and keen in his neat blue suit and old school tie. " Of course we shall co-ordinate with you when we come to use it."

Vandenberg grunted. " Can we know *how* you'll use it?"

" We shall make an interception."

" How?"

" Reinhart will give us our target information from Bouldershaw, and Geers's outfit will do the firing."

"And if it fails?"

" It won't fail."

The two men faced each other uncompromisingly: Burdett smooth and smiling, the General solid and tough. After a moment Vandenberg shrugged.

" This has become a very domestic affair all of a sudden."

They left it at that, and Burdett told Geers and Reinhart to go ahead.

At Bouldershaw fresh traces were picked up nearly every day. Harvey sat behind the great window overlooking the Fell and logged them as they went over.

"... *August 12th, 03.50 hrs., G.M.T. Ballistic vehicle number one-one-seven passed overhead on course 2697/451. Height 400 miles. Speed approx. 17,500 miles per hour* ..."

The huge bowl outside, which seemed empty and still under its tall superstructure, was all the time alive and full of the reflection of signals. Every vehicle that came over gave out its own call and could be heard approaching from the other side of the globe. There were electronic scanners in the observatory which showed the path of the targets on a cathode-ray screen, while an automatic plotting and range-finding system was coupled by land-line to Thorness.

At Thorness an array of rockets was set up on the cliff-top; a "first throw" as they called it and two reserves. The three pencil-shaped missiles, with tapering noses and finned tails, stood in a row on their launching pads, glinting silver in the cold, grey light. They were surprisingly small, and very slim and rather beautiful. They looked like arrows strung and ready to fly out from all the heavy and complicated harness of firing. Each one, tanked with fuel and crammed with precise equipment, carried a small nuclear charge in its tapered head.

The ground control was operated through the computer, which in turn was directed by Andromeda and her assistants. Target signals from Bouldershaw were fed in through the control room and instantaneously interpreted and passed on to the interceptor. The flight of interception could be directed to a hair's breadth.

Only Geers and his operational staff were allowed in the control-room at this time. Fleming and Dawnay were given monitoring facilities, as a gesture of courtesy, in another building; Andromeda took over calmly at the computer and Geers fussed anxiously and self-importantly between the launching-site, the computer building and the fire control-room. This was a small operations centre where the mechanics of take-off were supervised. A direct telephone connected him with the Ministry of Defence. Judy was kept busy by Major Quadring, double-checking everyone who came and went.

On the last day of October, Burdett conferred with the Prime Minister, and then picked up a telephone to Geers and Reinhart.

"The next one," he said.

Reinhart and Harvey stood to for thirty-six hours before they detected a new trace. Then, in the early light, they picked up a very faint signal and the automatic linking system was put into action.

The sleepy crew at Thorness pulled themselves together, and Andromeda, who showed no sign of effort, watched as they checked the information through the computer. The optimum launching time came out at once and was communicated to the fire control-centre, and the count-down began. Very soon a trace of the target could be seen on radar screens. There was a screen in the computer-room for Andromeda, another in fire control for Geers, a third in London in the Ministry of Defence Ops. Room, and a master-check at Bouldershaw, watched by Reinhart. At Bouldershaw, too, the signal from the satellite could be heard: a steady *blip-blip-blip-blip* which was amplified and pushed out through the speakers until it filled the observatory.

At Thorness the speakers were carrying the count-down, and launching teams worked briskly round the bases of the rockets on the cliff-top. At zero the "first throw" was to be fired and, if that failed, the second, and, if necessary, the third, with fresh flight calculations made according to their take-off time. Andromeda had held that there was no need for this but the others were all too conscious of human fallibility. Neither Geers nor any of his superiors could afford a fiasco.

The count-down ran out to single figures and to nought. In the grey morning light of the promontory the take-off rockets of the first flight suddenly bloomed red. The air filled with noise, the earth shook, and the tall thin pencil slipped up into the sky. Within a few seconds it was gone beyond the clouds. In the control-rooms, the operations-room and the observatory, anxious faces watched its trace appear on the cathode screens. Only Andromeda seemed unconcerned and confident.

At Bouldershaw, Reinhart, Harvey and their team watched the two traces of target and interceptor slowly converging and heard the *blip-blip-blip* of the satellite ringing louder and clearer in their ears as it approached. Then the traces met and at the same moment the noise stopped.

Reinhart swung round to Harvey and thumped him, wildly and uncharacteristically, on the back.

" We've done it . . . ! "

. . . "A hit!" Geers picked up his telephone for London. Andromeda turned away from her control-room screen as though something quite unimportant were over. In London, Vandenberg turned to his British colleagues in the ops. room.

" Well, what do you know?" he said.

That evening an official statement was made to the press:

" *The Ministry of Defence has announced that an orbital missile has been intercepted by a new British rocket three hundred and seventy miles above this country. The remains of the missile, which is of unknown origin, and of the interceptor, were burnt out on re-entering the earth's atmosphere, but the interception was followed on auto-radar equipment and can, say the Ministry, be verified in minute detail.*"

An almost audible collective sigh of relief rose from Whitehall, accompanied by a glow of self-congratulation. The Cabinet held an unusually happy meeting and within a week the Prime Minister was sending again for Burdett.

The Minister of Defence presented himself neat and smiling, in an aura of confidence and after-shave lotion.

" Any new traces?" asked the Prime Minister.

" Not one."

" Nothing in orbit?"

" Nothing's been over this country, sir, since the interception."

" Good." The Prime Minister mused. " Reinhart was due for a knighthood anyway."

" And Geers?"

" Oh yes. C.B.E. probably."

Burdett prepared for business. " And the computer and it's, er, agent, sir?"

" We might make the young lady a Dame," said the Prime Minister with one of his camouflage twinkles.

" I mean," asked Burdett, " what happens to them? The Ministry of Science want them to revert."

The Prime Minister continued to look amused. " We can't have that, can we?" he said.

" We've a heavy military programme for it."

" Also a heavy economic one."

" What do you mean, sir?"

" I mean," said the Prime Minister seriously, " that if this particular combination can achieve that for us, it can achieve a lot of other things. Of course it must still work on defence, but at the same time it has a very great industrial potential. We want to be rich, you know, as well as strong. The scientists have given us — and I'm very grateful to them — the most advanced thinking instrument in the world. It's going to make it possible for us to leap forward, as a country, in a great many fields. And about time too."

" Are you going to keep it in your own hands, sir?" Burdett spoke with a mixture of irritation and deference.

" Yes. I shall make a statement to the nation in the near future."

" You're not going to make it public?"

" Don't flap, man." The Prime Minister regarded him blandly. " I shall say something about the effects, but the means will remain top secret. That'll be your responsibility."

Burdett nodded. " What can I tell Vandenberg?"

" Tell him to rest his feet. No, you can say to him that we're going to be a great little country again, but we'll continue to co-operate with our allies. With any allies we can get, in fact." He paused for a moment while Burdett waited politely. " I shall go to Thorness myself as soon as I can."

The visit was arranged in a few days — it was obviously priority in the Prime Minister's mind. Judy and Quadring had some difficulty in concealing it from the press, for public curiosity was at its height; but in the end it was laid on with due secrecy and the compound and its inhabitants were quietly and discreetly groomed. Geers had changed distinctly since his success. Confidence was something new to him. It was as though he had taken the chips off his shoulder and put them away. He was brisk but affable, and he not only allowed Dawnay and Fleming access to the computer again but urged them to be on parade for the Prime Minister's tour. He wanted everyone, he said, to have their due.

Fleming had private doubts about this window-dressing but kept them to himself; at least there might be an opportunity to speak. He arrived in the computer building early on the day of the visit, and found Andromeda waiting there alone. She also appeared transformed. Her long hair had been brushed back from her face and, instead of her usual simple frock, she wore a sort of Grecian garment which clung to her breasts and thighs and floated away behind her.

"Phew!" he said. "Something human'll happen to you if you go round like that."

"You mean these clothes?" she asked with faint interest.

"You'll make one hell of an impression, but then you already have. There'll be no holding you now, will there?" he asked sourly. Andromeda glanced at him without replying. "He'll probably ask you to take over Number Ten, and I suppose you think we'll sleep easy in our beds, now we've seen how powerful you are. I suppose you think we're all fools."

"You are not a fool," she said.

"If I weren't a fool, you wouldn't be here now! You shoot down a little bit of metal from the sky—chickenfeed when you know how — and suddenly you're in a commanding position."

"That was intended." She faced him expressionlessly.

"And what's intended next?"

"It depends on the program."

"Yes." He advanced towards her. "You're a slave, aren't you?"

"Why don't you go?" she asked.

"Go?"

"Now. While you can."

"Make me!" He stared at her, hard and hostile, but she turned her head away.

"I may have to," she said. He stood, challenging her to go on, but she would not be drawn. After a few seconds he looked at his watch and grunted.

"I wish this diplomatic circus would come and get it over."

When the Prime Minister did arrive, he was escorted by officials, politicians and Scotland Yard heavies. Geers led him in. They were followed by Burdett and Hunter and by a train of lesser beings, dwindling away to Judy, who came at the end and closed doors behind them. Geers indicated the control-room with a sweep of his arm.

"This is the actual computer, sir."

"Quite incomprehensible to me," said the Prime Minister, as if this were an advantage. He caught sight of Andromeda. "Hallo, young lady. Congratulations."

He walked towards her with his hand outstretched, and she took and shook it stiffly.

"You understand all this?" he asked her. She smiled

politely. "I'm sure you do, and we are all very beholden. It's quite a change for us in this old country to be able to make a show of force. We shall have to take great care of you. Are they looking after you all right?"

"Yes, thank you." The visiting party stood round in a half circle, watching and admiring her, but she said nothing else. Fleming caught Judy's eye and nodded towards the Prime Minister. For a moment she could not think what he wanted, then she understood and edged in beside Geers.

"I don't think the Prime Minister has met Dr. Fleming," she whispered. Geers frowned; his good fellowship seemed to be wearing a little thin in places.

"Good, good." The Prime Minister could think of nothing more to say to Andromeda. He turned back to Geers.

"And where do you keep the rocketry?"

"I'll show you, sir. And I'd like you to see the laboratory." They moved on, leaving Judy standing. "Dr. Fleming—" she tried unsuccessfully, but they did not hear her. Fleming stepped forward.

"Excuse me a moment—"

Geers turned to him with a scowl. "Not now, Fleming."

"But—"

"What does the young man want?" the Prime Minister inquired mildly. Geers switched on a smile.

"Nothing, sir. He doesn't want anything."

The Prime Minister walked on tactfully, and as Fleming moved forward again Hunter laid a hand on his arm.

"For goodness sake!" Hunter hissed.

At the door of the lab. bay Geers turned back.

"You'd better come with us." He spoke to Andromeda, ignoring the others.

"Come along, my dear," said the Prime Minister, standing aside for her. "Brains and beauty first."

The procession filed out into the laboratory, except for Judy.

"Coming?" she asked Fleming, who stood staring after them.

He shook his head. "That was great, wasn't it?"

"I did my best."

"Great."

Judy fidgeted with her handkerchief. "At least you should

have been allowed to speak to him. I suppose he's shrewd, though he looks a bit of an old woman."

" Like another."

" Who?"

" Of Riga." He gave her a faint grin. " Who went for a ride on a tiger. They finished the ride with the lady inside, and a smile on the face of the tiger."

She knew the limerick, and felt irritated. " We're all going for a ride, except you?"

" You know what she said to me just now?"

" No."

He changed his mind and looked away from Judy to the control panel. " I've an idea."

" One I'd understand?"

" Look how beautifully he's ticking over—how sleek and rythmical he is." The computer was working steadily, with a gentle hum and a regular flashing of lights. " Purring away with us inside him. Suppose I pulled out the plug now?"

" They wouldn't let you."

" Or got a crowbar and smashed him up."

" You wouldn't get far with the guards. Anyhow, they'd rebuild it."

He took out a pad and some papers from a drawer in the control desk. " Then we'll have to shake it intellectually, won't we? I've shaken the young lady a bit. Now we'd better start on him." He saw that she was looking at him doubtfully. " Don't worry, you won't have to blow your whistle. Are they coming back this way?"

" No. They'll go out through the lab. entrance."

" Good." He started copying numbers from the sheets on to the pad.

" What is that?"

"A shortened formula for the creature."

"Andromeda?"

" Call her whatever amuses you." He scribbled on. " This is what the machine calls her. Not a formula, really—a naming tag."

" What are you going to do?"

" Re-arrange it slightly."

" You're not going to do any damage?"

160

He laughed at her. "You'd better go on with your conducted tour; this'll take time."

"I shall warn the guards."

"Warn whom you like."

She hesitated, then gave it up and went to rejoin the party. When she had gone he checked the figures and walked over with the pad to the input unit.

"I'll give you something to think about!" he said aloud to the machine, and sat down and started tapping the message in.

He had hardly finished when Andromeda came back.

"I thought you were going to see the rocketry."

She shrugged her shoulders. "It is not interesting."

The lamps on the display panel started to flash faster, and suddenly there was a fantastic clatter from the output unit as the printer began to work furiously.

Andromeda looked up in surprise. "What is happening?"

Fleming went quickly to the printer and read the figures as they were banged out on to the paper.

He smiled. "Your friend seems to have lost his temper."

She crossed the room and looked over his shoulder.

"This is nonsense."

"Exactly."

The printer stopped as suddenly as it had begun, leaving them in silence.

"What have you been doing?" the girl asked. She read the figures through uncomprehendingly. "This doesn't mean anything."

Fleming grinned at her. "No. He's flipped for a moment. I think he's psychologically disturbed."

"What have you done to it?" She started towards the terminals, but he stopped her.

"Come away from there."

She halted uncertainly. "What have you done?"

"Only given him a little information."

Looking around, she saw the pad on top of the input keys. She went slowly over to it and read it.

"That's my name-tag—reversed!"

"Negatived," said Fleming.

"It'll think I'm dead!"

"That's what I meant him to think."

She looked up at him, puzzled. "Why?"

"I thought I'd let him know he couldn't have it all his own way."

"That was very foolish."

"He seems to value you highly," he said scornfully.

She turned away towards the terminals. "I must tell it I'm alive."

"No!" He seized hold of her by the arms.

"I must. It thinks I'm dead, and I must tell it I'm not."

"Then I shall tell it you are. I can play this game until it doesn't know whether it's coming or going."

He let go one arm and picked up the pad from the keyboard.

"Give me that." She pulled her other arm free. "You can't win, you know." She turned away again, and as Fleming moved to stop her she suddenly shouted at him. "Leave me alone! Go away! Go out of here!"

They stood facing each other, both trembling, as if neither could move. Then Fleming took hold of her firmly with both hands and drew her towards him.

He sniffed at her in surprise. "You're wearing scent!"

"Let go of me. I shall call the guards."

Fleming started to laugh. "Open your mouth, then."

She parted her lips and he put a kiss on them. Then he held her at arms' length and examined her.

"Nice or nasty?"

"Leave me alone, please." Her voice was uncertain. She looked at him in a confused way, and then down, but he still held her.

"Who do you belong to?"

"I belong where my brain tells me."

"Then tell it this—" He kissed her again, sensuously but dispassionately, for a long time.

"Don't," she begged, pulling her lips away. He held her close to him and spoke gently.

"Don't you like the taste of lips? Or the taste of food, or the smell and feel of the fresh air outside, or the hills beyond the wire with sunshine and shadows on them and larks singing? And the company of human beings?"

She shook her head slowly. "They're not important."

"Aren't they?" He spoke with his mouth close to her. "They weren't allowed for by whatever disembodied intelligence up there you owe allegiance to, but they're important to organic life, as you'll find out."

"Anything can be allowed for," she said.

"But they weren't in the calculations."

"They can be put in." She looked up at him. "You can't beat us, Dr. Fleming. Stop trying before you get hurt."

He let go of her. "Am I likely to get hurt?"

"Yes."

"Why should you warn me?"

"Because I like you," she said, and he half smiled at her.

"You're talking like a human being."

"Then it's time I stopped. Please go now." He stood obstinately, but there was a note of pleading in her voice that had never been there before, and an expression of unhappiness on her face. "Please . . . Do you want me to be punished?"

"By whom?"

"Who do you think?" She glanced at the computer control racks. Fleming was taken off-guard: this was something he had never thought of.

"Punished? That's a new one." He put the pad of figures in his pocket and went to the door. In the doorway he turned back to deliver a last shot. "Who *do* you belong to?"

She watched him go and then turned reluctantly towards the display panel, and walked slowly, compulsively, up to it. She raised her hands to communicate with the terminals, then hesitated. Her face was strained, but she raised them again and touched the plates. For a moment all that happened was that the lights blinked faster, as the machine digested the information she gave it. Then the voltage meter below the panel suddenly peaked.

Andromeda gave a cry of pain and tried to pull her hands away from the plates, but the current held her fast. The voltage needle dropped, only to swing up again, and she cried out again . . . And then a third time and a fourth and over and over and over . . .

Once more it was Judy who found her. She came in a few minutes later, looking for Fleming, and saw to her horror the girl lying crumpled on the floor, where Christine had been.

"Oh no!" The words jerked out of her, and she ran forward and turned the body over. Andromeda was still alive. She moaned as Judy touched her, and curled away, whimpering quietly and nursing her hands together. Judy raised the blonde head and rested it in her lap and then took the hands and opened them. They were black with burning, except where the red flesh lay bare down to the bone.

Judy let them go gently. "How did it happen?"

Andromeda groaned again and opened her eyes. Judy said to her, "Your hands."

"We can easily mend them." The girl's voice was hardly audible.

"What happened?"

"Something went wrong, that's all."

Judy left her and telephoned Dr. Hunter.

From that moment events moved with almost cataclysmic speed. Hunter put a temporary dressing on Andromeda's hands and tried to persuade her to move into the station's sick bay, but she refused to leave the computer until she had seen Madeleine Dawnay.

"It will be quicker in the end," she told them. Although she was suffering from shock, she went sturdily through Dawnay's papers until she found the section she was looking for. Hunter had given her local shots to ease the pain in her hands, and with these and the bandages she fumbled a good deal, but she pulled out the sheets she wanted and shuffled them across to Dawnay. They were concerned with enzyme production in the D.N.A. formula.

"What do we do with these?" Dawnay looked at them doubtfully.

"Get an isolated tissue formula," said Andromeda, and took the papers back to the computer. She was weak and pale and could hardly walk. Dawnay, Hunter and Judy watched anxiously as she stood again between the terminals and put out her swathed hands; but this time there was no disaster, and after a little the machine started printing out.

"It's an enzyme formula. You can make it up quite easily." She indicated the printer-paper to Dawnay and then turned to Hunter. "I should like to lie down now, please. The enzyme can be applied to my hands on a medicated base when Professor Dawnay has prepared it, but it should be as soon as possible."

She was ill for several days, and Hunter dressed her hands with an ointment containing the formula, when Dawnay had made it up. The healing was miraculous: new tissue—soft natural flesh, not the hard tissue of scarring — filled in the wounds in a matter of hours, and formed a fresh layer of pale pink skin across her palms. By the time she recovered from the effects of the electric shocks, her hands were remade.

Hunter, meanwhile, had reported to Geers and Geers had sent for Fleming. The Director, not yet certain of the outcome of the accident, was sick and thin-lipped with worry, his brief season of fellowship gone.

"So *you* decide to throw it off balance!" He flung the words across his desk at Fleming and pounded his fist on the polished wood. "You don't consult anyone—you're too clever. So clever, the machine goes wrong and damn near kills the girl."

"If you won't even listen to what happened." Fleming's voice rose to match his, but Geers interrupted.

"I know what happened."

"Were you there? She knew she was going to be punished. She should have had me thrown out, she should have wiped out what I'd put into the computer; but she didn't—not soon enough. She hesitated and warned me and let me go, then she went and touched the communication terminals—"

"I thought you'd gone," Geers reminded him.

"Of course I'd gone. I'm telling you what happened inevitably: she let the machine know that she was alive, that it had been given false information, that the source of the information was around and she hadn't stopped it. So it punished her by giving her a series of electric shocks. It knows how to do that now; it learnt on Christine."

The Director listened with thinly disguised impatience. "You're guessing," he said at the end.

"It's not guesswork, Geers. It was bound to happen, only I didn't realise in time."

"Have you your pass?" Geers looked at him glintingly through his spectacles. "To the computer building."

Fleming sniffed and rummaged in his pocket. "You can't fault me on that one. It's quite in order."

He handed it across the desk. Geers took it, examined it, and slowly tore it up.

" What's that in aid of?"

" We can't afford you, Fleming. Not any more."

Fleming banged the desk in his turn. " I'm staying on the station."

" Stay where you like; but your association with the computer is over. I'm sorry."

Geers felt better with Fleming out of the way, and better still when he heard of Andromeda's recovery. He got all the facts he could from Dawnay and Hunter about the enzyme, and then got through on his direct line to Whitehall. The reaction was as he thought. He sent for Andromeda and questioned her and seemed well pleased.

Fleming a year or two back would have hit the bottle, but this time he had no appetite even for that. The same compulsion that had held him to the computer tied him to the compound; even though there was nothing he could now do, no part he could have in the project, he remained on the station, solitary and uncertain and given to long walks and lying on his bed. It was deep winter, but calm and grey, as though something dramatic were being withheld.

About a week after the accident—or punishment, as Fleming thought of it—he was returning from a walk on the moors when he saw an enormous and extravagantly shining car outside Geers's office, and as he passed it a short, square man with a bald head got out.

" Dr. Fleming!" The bald man raised a hand to stop and greet him.

" What are you doing here?"

" I hope you do not mind," said Kaufmann. Fleming looked to see who was around. " Get out," he said.

" Please Herr Docktor, do not be embarrassed." Kaufmann smiled at him. " I am quite official. A.1 at Lloyds. I do not compromise you."

" You didn't compromise Bridger either, I suppose?" Fleming jerked his head towards the main gate. " That's the exit."

Kaufmann smiled again, and pulled out his case of cigarilloes. " Smoking?"

" Slightly," Fleming said, " at the edges. I am not interested in anything you have to offer. Try the next door house."

"I do that." Kaufmann laughed and stuck a small cigar between his teeth before they closed. "I do just that. I stop you, Herr Docktor, to tell you that I shall not bother you any more. I have other means, much better, much more honest."

He smiled again, lit his cigar and walked without hesitation into the vestibule of Geers's office.

Fleming ran over to the security block, but Quadring was out somewhere, and so was Judy. Finally he got hold of Judy on the telephone, but by the time she reached Geers's office, the Director was just showing Kaufmann out. The two men seemed to be on most cordial terms, and Geers was smoking one of the cigarilloes.

"Businesswise," Kaufmann was saying, "the process is immaterial. We are not curious; it is the result, yes?"

"We deal in results here." Geers had his number one smile switched on. He held out a hand. "Auf Wiedersehen."

Judy watched while Kaufmann shook hands and walked back to his car. As the Director turned to go back into his office she said, "Can I speak to you for a minute?"

Geers flicked his smile off. "I'm rather busy."

"This is important. You know who he is?"

"His name is Kaufmann."

"Intel."

"That's right." Geers's fingers itched at the door handle.

"It was Kaufmann whom Dr. Bridger was selling—" Judy started, but Geers cut her short.

"I know all about the Bridger case."

Behind his voice Judy could hear the car driving away. Somehow it made what she felt seem terribly urgent: she had to batter it into him.

"It was Intel. They were taking secrets . . ."

Geers edged into his doorway. "They're not taking secrets from me," he said haughtily.

"But—". She followed him in uninvited, and found Dawnay waiting quietly in the office. She felt suddenly thrown and mumbled an apology to the older woman.

"Don't mind me, dear," said Dawnay neutrally, and strolled away to the far corner of the room. Geers sat back at his desk and looked at Judy with an air of businesslike dismissal.

"We're making a trade agreement."

" With Intel?" The horrifying absurdity of the whole thing crowded in on her: a vision of the piled-up madness of the past months and years. She gaped at him across the polished desk, until she could find words. "I was put on this job because we didn't trust them. Dr. Bridger was hounded to his death—by me among other people—because he . . ."

" The climate's changed."

She looked at his smug, prim face and lost her temper entirely. " Politicians enjoy such convenient weather!"

" That will be enough," Geers snapped.

Dawnay rustled quietly in her corner. " The child's right, you know, and we scientists get a bit jaundiced about it from time to time. We're at the mercy of the elements. *We* can't cheat."

" I'm a scientist too," Geers said pettishly.

" Was." The word slipped out before Judy could stop it. She waited for the explosion, but Geers somehow kept it under control. He went icy.

" It isn't, strictly speaking, your business. What the Government needs now is world markets. When the girl Andromeda burnt her hands, she worked out a synthesis for Professor Dawnay's lab. people. Have you seen her hands?"

" I saw them burnt."

" There's no sign of a burn now. No scar tissue, nothing. Overnight."

"And that's what you're selling to Intel?"

" *Through* Intel. To anyone who needs it."

She tried to think what was wrong with this, and then realised. " Why not through the World Health Organisation?"

" We're not contemplating wholesale charity. We're contemplating a reasonable trade balance."

" So you don't care who you shake hands with?" she asked with disgust. She felt completely reckless now, and turned on Dawnay. "Are you part of this?"

Dawnay hesitated. " The enzyme's not quite in a state to market yet. We need a more refined formula. André—the girl —is preparing the data for computing." They had all got into the habit of calling her André.

" So the whole station's working for Intel?"

" I hope not," said Dawnay, and it sounded as though perhaps she was on her side. Geers cut in.

168

"Look, Madeleine, this is enough."

"Then I won't waste your time." Judy moved to the door. "But I am not part of it, and nor is Dr. Fleming."

"We know how Fleming stands," said Geers sardonically.

"And you know where I stand too," Judy told him, and banged out.

Her instinct was to go straight to Fleming, but she could not quite face the risk of another snub. In fact, it was Dawnay who went to see him, on her way from the office block to the computer at the end of the day. She found him in his chalet, watching the Prime Minister's broadcast on television.

"Come in," he said flatly, and made room for her on the foot of his bed. She looked at the flickering blue screen and tried to believe in the confident, elderly, sportive, civilised face and the slow, drawling voice of the Prime Minister. Fleming sat, and watched and listened with her.

"Not since the halcyon days of Queen Victoria," the disembodied face announced, "has this country held such a clear lead in the fields of industry, technology and—above all—security as that which we now have within our grasp . . ."

She felt her attention wandering. "I'm sorry if I interrupted."

"You didn't." He made a grimace at the television. "Turn the old idiot off."

He rose and switched off the set himself and then mixed her a drink. "Social call?"

"I was just going across to the computer building when I saw a light in your window. Thanks." She took the glass from him.

"Working overtime?" he asked.

She lifted her glass and looked at him over the top of it. "Dr. Fleming, I've said some pretty uncharitable things about you in the past."

"You're not the only one."

"About your attitude."

"I was wrong, wasn't I? The Prime Minister says so. Wrong and out." He spoke more in sorrow than anger, and poured himself a small drink.

"I wonder," said Dawnay. "I'm beginning to wonder."

He did not answer, and she added, "Judy Adamson's beginning to wonder too."

"That'll be a big help," he snorted.

"She put up quite a fight with Geers this afternoon. I must say it made me think." She took a sip and swallowed it slowly, looking quietly across her glass and turning over the position in her mind. "It seems fair enough to make use of what we've got—of what you gave us."

"Don't rub that in."

"And yet I don't know. There's something corrupting about that sort of power. You can see it acting on the folk here, and on the government." She nodded to the television set. "As if perfectly ordinary, sensible people are being possessed by a determination that isn't their own. I think we've both felt it. And yet, it all seems harmless enough."

"Does it?"

She told him about the enzyme production. "It's beneficial. It regenerates cells, simply. It'll effect everything, from skin-grafting to ageing. It'll be the biggest medical aid since antibiotics."

"A godsend to millions."

When she got on to the Intel proposition he hardly reacted.

"Where is it all leading?" she asked. She did not really expect an answer, but she got one.

"A year ago that machine had no power outside its own building, and even there we were in charge of it." He spoke without passion as if reiterating an old truth. "Now it has the whole country dependent on it. What happens next? You heard, didn't you? We shall go ahead, become a major force in the world again, and who's going to be the power behind that throne?"

He indicated the television, as she had done; then he seemed to tire of the conversation. He wandered across to his record-player and switched it on.

"Could you have controlled it?" Dawnay was unwilling to let the subject go.

"Not latterly."

"What could you have done?"

"Fouled it up as much as possible." He began to sort out a record among a pile of L.P.s "It knows that, now it has its creature to inform on me. It had me pushed out. 'You can't win,' she told me."

" She said that?"

Fleming nodded, and Dawnay frowned into her half-empty glass. "I don't know. Perhaps it's inevitable. Perhaps it's evolution."

"Look—" he put down the record and swung round to her. "I can foresee a time when we'll create a higher form of intelligence to which, in the end, we'll hand over. And it'll probably be an inorganic form, like that one. But it'll be something we've created ourselves, and we can design it for our own good, or for good as we understand it. This machine hasn't been programmed for our good; or, if it has, something's gone wrong with it."

She finished her drink. There was possibility in what he said —more than possibility, a sort of sane logic which she had missed lately. As an empirical scientist, she felt there must be some way in which it could be tested.

"Could anyone tell, except you?" she asked.

Fleming shook his head. "None of that lot."

"Could I tell?"

"You?"

"I have access to it."

He immediately lost interest in the record. His face lit up as if she had switched on some circuit inside him. "Yes— why not? We could try a little experiment." He picked up from his table the pad with the negatived name-code on it. "Have you somebody over there can feed this in?"

"André?"

"No. Not her. Whatever you do, don't take her into your confidence."

Dawnay remembered the operator. She took the pad, and Fleming showed her the section to be fed in.

"I'm out of my depth, I'll admit that." she said. Then she put down her glass and went out.

As she walked across the compound, she could hear the beginning of some post-Schoenbergian piece of music from Fleming's chalet; then she was in the computer building and heard nothing but the hum of equipment. André was in the control room, and a young operator. André kept herself even more to herself since the affair of her hands. She haunted the computer block like a pale shadow and seldom left it. She made no attempt to communicate with anyone, and although she was never hostile she was completely withdrawn. She looked with slight interest at Dawnay coming in.

"How's it getting on?" Dawnay asked.

"We have put in all the data," André said. "You should have the formula soon."

Dawnay moved away and joined the operator at the input unit. He was a young man, a very fresh post-graduate, who asked no questions, but did as he was told.

"Input that too, will you?" Dawnay gave him the pad. He rested it above the keyboard and started tapping.

"What is that?" André asked, hearing the sound.

"Something I want calculated." Dawnay kept her away from it, until the display panel suddenly broke out into wild flashing.

"What are you putting in?" André snatched at the pad and read from it. "Where did you get it?"

"That's my business," said Dawnay.

"Why don't you keep out of this?"

"You'd better leave us," Dawnay told the operator. He rose obediently and wandered out of the room. André waited until he had gone.

"I do not wish you any harm." she said then and there was not passion but great strength in her voice. "Why don't you keep out?"

"How dare you talk to me like that?" Dawnay heard herself sounding weak and ridiculous, but she could only answer as it took her. "I created you—I made you."

"*You* made me?" André looked at her with contempt, then crossed to the control panel and put her hands on the terminals. Immediately the display lamps became less agitated, but they continued to flicker so long as the girl stood there, strong and positive like a young goddess. After a minute she moved away and stood looking at Dawnay.

"We are getting rather tired of this—this little joke," she said calmly, as if delivering a message. "Neither you, nor Dr. Fleming, nor anyone else can come between us."

"If you're trying to frighten me—"

"I don't know what you've begun now. I cannot be responsible." Andromeda appeared to be looking through her into a space beyond. The output printer went noisily into action, and Dawnay started at the sound. She followed André over to it, and by the time she got there the message finished. André examined the paper, and then tore it off and gave it to her.

" Your enzyme formula."

" Is that all?" Dawnay felt a sense of relief.

" Isn't that enough for you?" asked André, and watched her go with a set, hostile face.

Dawnay had three assistants working for her at the time: a senior research chemist, a man, and two post-graduate helpers, a boy and a girl. Between them they made a chemical synthesis based on the new formula. It involved a good deal of handling in the laboratory, but none of them worried about it because it had no irritant effect. By the end of a day or two, however, they were all beginning to feel signs of lassitude and wasting. There seemed to be no reason, and they worked on, but by the end of the third day the girl collapsed, and by the following morning Dawnay and the man had keeled over as well.

Hunter packed them off to the sick-bay, where they were soon joined by the boy. Whatever the disease was, it accelerated fast; there was no fever or inflammation, its victims simply degenerated. Cells died, the basic processes of metabolism slowed or stopped, and one after another the four weakened and slid into a state of coma. Hunter was desperate and appealed to Geers, who put a screen of silence round the whole business.

Fleming did not hear details until the fourth day, when Judy broke security to tell him. He immediately phoned Reinhart and asked him to come from Bouldershaw, and he persuaded Judy to find a paper for him. When she gave it to him, he locked himself up in his room with it all night, emerging in the morning grim but satisfied. But by that time the girl assistant was dead.

Eleven

ANTIDOTE

THEY were covering her face when Fleming arrived at the sick bay. The other three lay silent and still in their beds, their faces drawn and as pale as the pillows. Dawnay, in the next cubicle to the girl, was being kept barely alive by blood transfusion. She lay marble-still, like an effigy of some old warrior on a tomb. He stayed looking at her until Hunter joined him.

" What do you want? " Hunter was run ragged, and all rough edges. He gave up the effort to be so much as polite to Fleming.

" It's my fault," said Fleming, looking down at the drained face on the pillow.

Hunter half-laughed. " Humility's a new line for you."

"All right then—it wasn't! " Fleming spun round on him, flaming, and fished a clip of papers out of his pocket. " But I came to give you this."

Hunter took the papers suspiciously. " What is it? "

" The enzyme formula."

" How the devil did you get hold of it? "

Fleming sighed. " Illegally. Like I have to do everything."

" I'll keep it, if you don't mind," said Hunter. He looked at it again. " Why is it crossed through? "

" Because it's wrong." Fleming flicked over the top sheet to show the one underneath. " That's the right formula. You'd better get it made up quickly."

" The right formula? " Hunter looked slightly lost.

" What the computer gave Dawnay had an inversion of what she wanted. It switched negative for positive, as it were, to pay her back for a little game I'd put her up to."

" What game? "

" It gave the anti-enzyme, instead of the enzyme. Instead of a cell regenerative, a cell destructor. Presumably it acts

174

through the skin and they absorbed it while they were working on it." He picked up one of Dawnay's hands that lay limp on the sheet. "There's nothing you can do unless you can make the proper enzyme in time. That's why I've brought you the corrected formula."

"Do you really think . . . ?" Hunter frowned sceptically at the clip of papers, and Fleming, looking up from Dawnay's hand, which he was still holding, regarded him with distaste.

"Don't you want to make your reputation?"

"I want to save lives," said Hunter.

"Then make up the proper formula. It should work as an antidote to the one Dawnay got, in which case it ought to reverse what's happening now. At least you can try it. If not—" He shrugged and laid Dawnay's emaciated hand back on the sheet. "That machine will do anyone's dirty work, so long as it suits it."

Hunter sniffed. "If it's so damn clever, why did it make a mistake like this?

"It didn't. The only mistake it made was it got the wrong person—the wrong people. It was after me, and it didn't care how many people it wrote off in the process. One of your trade agreements with Intel, and it could have been half the world."

He left Hunter scowling at the formula, but obviously obliged to try it.

That afternoon the man died; but the new enzyme had been made up and was administered to the two survivors. Nothing dramatic happened at first but by the evening it was clear that deterioration was slowing. Judy visited the sick-bay after supper, and then began making her way to the main gate to meet Reinhart, who was due on the late train. As she passed the computer block she felt an impulse to go in. There was no operator on duty, and she found André sitting alone at the control desk, gazing in front of her. The accumulated hatred of months, the frustrations of years, suddenly boiled up in Judy.

"Another one has died," she said savagely. André shrugged and Judy felt a terrible urge to hit her. "Professor Dawnay's fighting for her life. And the boy."

"Then they have a chance," the girl said, tonelessly.

"Thanks to Dr. Fleming. Not thanks to you."

"It is not my business."

"You gave Professor Dawnay the formula."

"The machine gave it."

"You gave it together!"

André shrugged her shoulders again. "Dr. Fleming has the antidote. He is intelligent—he can save them."

"You don't care, do you?" Judy's eyes felt hot and dry as she looked at her.

"Why should I care?" asked the girl.

"I hate you." Judy's throat felt dry, too, so that she could hardly speak. She wanted to pick up something heavy and break the girl's skull; but then the telephone rang and she had to go to the main gate to meet Reinhart.

The girl sat quite still for a long time after Judy had gone, gazing at the control panel, and several tears—actual human tears—welled in her eyes and trickled slowly down her cheeks.

Judy took Reinhart straight to Fleming's hut, where they brought him up to date.

"And Madeleine?" the old man asked. He looked tired and uncertain.

"Still alive, thank God," said Fleming. "We may save two of them."

Reinhart seemed to relax a little, and looked less tired. They took his coat, sat him in a chair by the radiator and gave him a drink. He seemed to Judy much older than she had ever known him, and rather pathetic. He was now Sir Ernest, and it was as if the act of knighthood had finally aged him. She could imagine how far in the past his youthful friendship with Dawnay must seem, and could feel him clinging on to her life as though his own were in some way tied to it. He took his drink and tried to think of the next thing to say.

"Have you told Geers yet?"

"What would Geers do?" asked Fleming. "Just be sorry it wasn't me. He'd have me thrown out of the compound, out of the country, if he could. I've been saying since I was in short pants that this thing's malicious but they all love it so. How much more do I have to prove before I convince anyone?"

"You don't have to prove any more to me, John," said Reinhart wearily.

"Well, that's something."

"Or me," Judy said.

"Oh fine, fine. That makes three of us against the entire set-up."

"What did you think I could do?" Reinhart asked.

"I dunno. You've been running half the science in this country for a generation—the good half. Surely someone would listen to you."

"Osborne, perhaps?"

"So long as he didn't get his cuffs dirty." Fleming thought for a moment. "Could he get me back into the computer?"

"Use your head, John. He's answerable to the Establishment."

"Could you get him down here?"

"I could try. What have you in mind?"

"We can fill that in later." said Fleming. Reinhart pulled a rail-air timetable out of his pocket.

"If I go up to London to-morrow—"

"Can't you go to-night?"

"Sir Ernest's tired," said Judy.

Reinhart smiled at her. "You can keep Sir Ernest for garden parties. I shall get a night flight."

"Why can't it wait a few hours?" Judy asked.

"I'm not a young man, Miss Adamson, but I'm not moribund." He pulled himself to his feet. "Give my love to Madeleine, if she's . . ."

"Sure," said Fleming, finding the old man's coat and helping him on with it. Reinhart moved to the door, buttoning himself as he went. Then he remembered something. "By the way, the message has stopped."

Judy looked from him to Fleming. "The message?"

"From up there." Reinhart pointed a finger to the sky. "It's stopped repeating, several weeks ago. Maybe we shall never pick it up again."

"We may have caught the tail end of a long transmission," Fleming said quietly, weighing the implications. "If it wasn't for that fluke at Bouldershaw, we might never have heard it, and none of this would have happened."

"That had crossed my mind," said Reinhart, and gave them another tired smile and went.

Fleming mooched round the room, thinking about what had been said, while Judy waited. They heard Reinhart's car start and drive away, and at the sound of it Fleming came to rest beside Judy and put an arm round her shoulders.

"I'll do whatever you want," she told him. "They can court-martial me if they like."

"O.K., O.K." He took his arm away.

"You can trust me, John."

He looked her full in the face, and she tried with her eyes to make him believe her.

"Yes, well—" he seemed more or less convinced. "I'll tell you what. Get on the blower to London, privately, first thing in the morning. Try to catch Osborne when the Prof.'s with him and tell him he's bringing an extra visitor."

"Who?"

"I don't care who. Garter King at Arms—the President of the Royal Academy—some stuffed shirt from the Ministry. He doesn't have to bring the gent, only his clothes."

"An unstuffed shirt?"

He grinned. "Hat, brief case and rolled umbrella will do. Oh, and an overcoat. Meanwhile you get an extra pass for him. O.K.?"

"I'll try."

"Good girl." He put his arm round her again and kissed her. She enjoyed it and then leant back to ask him, "What are you going to do?"

"I don't know yet." He kissed her once more, then pushed himself away from her. "I'm going to turn in, it's been a hell of a day. You'd better get out of here—I need some sleep."

He grinned again and she squeezed his hand and went out, lightfooted, singing inside herself.

Fleming undressed dreamily, working out plans and fantasies in his mind. He fell into bed, and almost as soon as he turned the light out he was asleep.

After Reinhart's and Judy's departure, the camp was quiet. It was a dark night; clouds were blowing in from the north-east, bringing with them a current of cold air and a prospect of snow, and covering the full moon. But the moon shone through for a few moments at a time, and by its light a slim, pale figure let itself out of a window at the back of the computer block and began to move, ghost-like, across the camp. None of the sentries saw it, let alone recognised it as the girl André, and she made her way stealthily between the huts to Fleming's chalet, her face set and a double-strand coil of insulated wire in her hand.

A little light fell from the window into Fleming's room, for he had drawn back the curtain before he went to bed. He did not stir when the door opened very quietly and André inched in. She was barefoot and very careful, and her hands were sheathed in a pair of thick rubber gloves. After making sure that Fleming slept, she knelt down by the wall beside his bed and inserted the two wires at one end of her coil into a power-point on the skirting, wedged them tight and switched on the current. She held the other end of the coil out from her, the two wires grasped separately between thumb and finger an inch or so down the insulation and the bare live ends extended, and stood up and advanced slowly towards Fleming. The chances of his surviving a full charge were slight, for he was asleep and she could count on being able to keep the contacts on him for long enough to stop his heart.

She made no sound as she moved the ends of the wires towards his eyes. There was no reason why he should wake; but suddenly, for some unknown reason, he did. All he could see was a silhouetted figure standing over him, and more from instinct than reason, he flexed one leg under the bedclothes and kicked out with all his might through his sheet and blanket.

He caught her in the midriff, and she fell back across the room with a sort of sick grunt. He fumbled for his bedlight and switched it on. For a moment it dazzled him; he sat up confused and panting while the girl struggled to her knees, still holding the ends of wire; then, as he took in what was happening, he leapt out of bed, pulled the ends of flex out of the wall-socket and turned to her. But by this time she was on her feet and half-way out of the room.

"No you don't!" He threw himself at the door. She side-stepped and, with her hands behind her, backed across to the table where he had had his supper. For a moment it looked as if she was going to give in; then without warning she lunged out at him with her right hand, and there was a breadknife in it.

"You bitch!" He caught her wrist, twisted the knife out of it and threw her down.

She gasped and lay writhing, holding her wrenched wrist with the other hand and staring up at him, not so much in fury as in desperation. He stooped and picked up the knife keeping his eye on her all the time.

"All right—kill me." There was fear in her face now, and in her voice. "It won't do you any good."

"No?" His own voice was shaking and he was panting hard.

"It'll delay things a little, that's all." She watched intently as he opened a drawer and slid the knife into it. This seemed to encourage her, and she sat up.

"Why do you want me out of the way?" he asked.

"It was the next thing to be done. I warned you."

"Thanks." He shuffled round, buttoning up his pyjamas, pushing his feet into a pair of slippers, calming down.

"Everything you do is predictable." She seemed collected again already. "There's nothing you can think of that won't be countered."

"What's the next thing now?"

"If you go away, go right away and don't interfere—"

He cut across her. "Get up." She looked at him in surprise.

"Get up." He waited while she got to her feet and then pointed to a chair. "Sit down there."

She gave him another puzzled look, and then sat. He went and stood over her.

"Why do you only do what the machine wants?"

"You're such children," she told him. "You think we're slave and master, the machine and me, but we're both slaves. We're containers which you've made, for something you don't understand."

"Do *you?*" asked Fleming.

"I can see the difference between our intelligence and yours. I can see that ours is going to take over and yours is going to die. You think you're the height and crown of things, the last word—" She broke off and massaged her wrist where he had twisted it.

"I don't think that," he said. "Did I hurt you?"

"Not badly. You're more intelligent than most; but not enough—you'll go down with the dinosaurs. They ruled the earth once."

"And you?"

She smiled, and it was the first time he had seen her do so. "I'm the missing link."

"And if we break you?"

"They make another one."

"And if we break the machine?"

" The same."

"And if we destroy you both, and the message and all our work on it, so that there's nothing left? The message has ended— did you know?" She shook her head. Her confirmation of all he feared came flooding in on him, and also the realisation of how to stop it. " Your friends up there have got tired of talking to us. You're on your own now, you and the computer. Suppose we break the pair of you?"

" You'll keep a higher intelligence off the earth, for a while."

" Then that's what we have to do."

She looked up at him steadily. " You can't."

" We can try."

She shook her head again, slowly and as if regretfully. " Go away. Live the sort of life you want to, while you can. You can't do anything else."

" Unless you help me." He returned her look and held it, as he had done before in the computer building. " You're not just a thinking machine, you're made in our likeness."

" No!"

" You have senses—feelings. You're three parts human being, tied by compulsion to something that's set to destroy us. All you have to do, to save us and free yourself, is change the setting." He took her by the shoulders, as if to shake her, but she shrugged his hands off.

" Why should I?"

" Because you want to, three-quarters of you—"

She stood up and moved away from him.

" Three-quarters of me is an accident. Don't you think I suffer enough as it is? Don't you think I get punished for even listening to you?"

" Will you be punished for to-night?"

" Not if you go away." She moved towards the door hesi- tantly, as if expecting him to stop her, but he let her go. " I was sent to kill you."

She was very pale and beautiful, standing in the dark door- way, and she spoke without passion or satisfaction. He looked at her grimly.

" Well, the chips are down," he said.

There was a small lean-to café by Thorness station, and Judy left Fleming there while she met the train from Aberdeen. It was only the following evening: Reinhart had been quick. Fleming went into the little back room which had been reserved for them, and waited. It was a sad and cheerless little room dominated by an old farmhouse table and a set of chairs and walled with dilapidated and badly-painted weatherboards which carried discoloured cola and mineral-water ads. He helped himself to a swig from his pocket-flask. He could hear the rising wind moaning outside, and then the diesel thrumming up from the south. It stopped, palpitating noisily, in the station, and after a minute or two there was a whistle and a hoot on its siren and it drew away, leaving a silence out of which came the sound of the wind again, and of footsteps on the gravel outside the café.

Judy led Reinhart and Osborne into the room. They were all heavily muffled in winter clothes, and Osborne carried a sizeable suitcase.

" It's blowing up for a blizzard, I think," he said, putting the case down. He looked unhappy and thoroughly out of his element. " Can we talk in here?"

" It's all ours," Judy said. " I fixed the man."

"And the duty operator?" asked Reinhart.

" I fixed him too. He knows what to do and he'll keep his mouth shut for us."

Reinhart turned to Fleming. " How is Madeleine Dawnay?"

" She'll pull through. So will the boy. The enzyme works all right."

" Well, thank God for that." Reinhart unbuttoned his coat. He looked no worse for his journey; in fact, the activity seemed to have refreshed him. Osborne appeared to be the most dispirited of them.

" What do you want to do with the computer?" he asked Fleming.

" Try to uncork it, or else—"

" Or else what?"

" That's what we want to find out. It's either deliberately malevolent, or it's snarled up. Either it was programmed to work the way it does, or something's gone wrong with it. I think the first; I always have done."

" You've never been able to prove it."

" What about Dawnay?"

" We need something more tangible than that."

"Osborne will go to the Minister," put in Reinhart. "He'll go to the Prime Minister if necessary. Won't you?"

"If I have evidence," said Osborne.

"I'll give you evidence! It had another go at killing me last night."

"How?"

Fleming told them. "In the end I forced the truth out of her. You ought to try it sometime—you'd believe it then."

"We need something more scientific."

"Then give me a few hours with it." He looked at Judy. "Have you brought me a pass?"

Judy produced three passes from her handbag and handed one to each of them. Fleming read the one she had given him, and grinned.

"So I'm an official of the Ministry? That'll be the day."

"I've forsworn my good name for that," said Osborne unhappily. "It's only for an examination. No direct action."

Fleming stopped grinning. "You want to tie both my hands behind my back?"

"You realise the risk I'm running?" Osborne said.

"Risk! You should have been in my hut last night."

"I wish I had been, then I might be more certain where I stood. This country, young man, depends on that machine—"

"Which I made."

"It means more to us, potentially, than the steam engine, or atomic power, or anything."

"Then it's all the more important—" Fleming began.

"I know! Don't preach at me. Do you think I'd be here at all if I didn't believe it was important and if I didn't value your opinion very highly? But there are ways and ways."

"You know of a better way?"

"Of checking—no. But that's as far as it must go. A man in my position—"

"What is your position?" asked Fleming. "The noblest Roman of them all?"

Osborne sighed. "You have your pass."

"You've got what you asked for, John," said Reinhart.

Fleming picked up the suitcase and put it on the table. He opened it and, taking out a dark smooth-cloth overcoat, a black homberg and a briefcase, dressed himself for the part.

They were all right for a dark night, but they hardly went with his face.

"You look more like a scarecrow than a civil servant," said Reinhart, smiling.

Judy tried not to giggle. "They won't examine you too closely if you're with me."

"You realise you'll be shot for this?" said Fleming affectionately.

"Not unless we're found out."

Osborne did not enjoy the pleasantries; if they were hiding strain in the others, he did not realise it, he had more than enough strain himself.

"Let's get it over, shall we?" He pushed back the cuff of his overcoat to look at his watch.

"We have to wait till it's dark and the day shift have gone off," said Judy.

Fleming burrowed under his coat and brought out the flask. "How about one for the raid?"

It was snowing hard by the time they reached the camp, not a soft fall, but a fury of stinging, frozen particles thrown by a wind from the north. The two sentries outside the computer block had turned up the collars of their greatcoats, although they stood in a little haven of shelter under the porch of the doorway. They peered out, through the white that turned into blackness, at the four approaching figures.

Judy went forward and presented the passes, while the three men hung back.

"Good evening. This is the Ministry party."

"M'am." One of the sentries, with a lance-corporal's stripe on his greatcoat sleeve, saluted and examined the passes.

"Okeydoke," he said, and handed them back.

"Anyone inside?" Judy asked him.

"Only the duty operator."

"We shall only be a few minutes," Reinhart said, coming forward.

The sentries opened the door and stood aside while Judy went in, followed by Reinhart and Osborne with Fleming between them.

"What about the girl?" asked Reinhart, when they were well down the corridor.

"She's not due in to-night," said Judy. "We took care of that."

It was a long corridor, with two right-angle corners in it, and the doors to the computer-room were at the end, well out of sight and sound of the main entrance. When Judy opened one of the doors and led them in, they found the control-room full of light, but empty except for a young man who sat reading at the desk. He stood up as they came in.

"Hallo," he said to Judy. "It went all right?"

It was the very young assistant. He seemed to be enjoying the situation.

"You'd better have your passes." Judy returned Reinhart's and Osborne's to them, and handed Fleming's to the operator. Fleming took off his homberg and stuck it on the boy's head.

"What the top people are wearing."

"You needn't make a pantomime of it," said Osborne, and kept an uneasy eye on the door while the operator was rigged out with Fleming's overcoat and brief case. Even with the collar turned up he was clearly different from the man who came in, but, as Judy said, it was not a night for seeing clearly, and with her to reassure them the sentries would probably do no more than count heads.

As soon as the boy was ready, Osborne opened the door.

"We depend on you to do the right thing," he said to Fleming. "You have a test check?"

Fleming pulled a familiar pad from his pocket and waited for them all to go.

"I'll be back," said Judy. "As soon as I've seen them past the sentries."

Fleming seemed surprised. "You won't, you know."

"I'm sorry," Osborne told him. "It's one of the conditions."

"I don't want anyone—"

"Don't be a fool, John," said Reinhart, and they left him. He went over to the control unit and glared at it, half laughing at himself out of sheer strain, then got down to work at the input unit, tapping in figures from the pad he had brought with him. He had nearly finished it when Judy came back.

"What are you doing?" she asked. She was strung too, in spite of the relief of having got the decoy past the sentries.

"Trying to cook it." He tapped out the last group. "Same old naming-tag lark'll do for a start."

It took the computer a few moments to react, then the display lamps started flashing violently. They waited, listening for the clatter of the printer, but what they heard was footsteps approaching down the corridor. Judy stood rooted and paralysed until Fleming took her arm and pulled her into the darkness of the lab. bay from where they could see through the half-open doorway without being seen. The footsteps came to a stop beyond the far entrance of the control-room. They could see the handle of one of the double doors turn, then the door opened and André stepped in from the corridor.

Judy gave a tiny gasp, which was drowned by the hum of the computer, and Fleming's grip tightened warningly on her arm. From where they stood they could see André close the door and walk slowly forward towards the control racks. The flashing and humming of the machine seemed to puzzle her, and a few feet short of the display panel she stood stock still. She was wearing an old grey anorak with the hood down, and she looked particularly beautiful and uncompromising under the stark lamps; but her face was strained and after a few moments the muscles round her mouth and temples began to work under the mounting tension of her nerves. She moved forward, slowly and reluctantly, towards the panel, and then stopped again, as if she could feel from there a premonition of some violent reaction—as though she knew the signs and yet was magnetised by the machine.

Her face now was glistening with sweat. She took another step forward and raised her hands slowly towards the terminals. Judy, for all her hatred, felt herself aching to go to her, but Fleming held her back. Before their eyes, the girl reached up slowly and fearfully and touched the contact plates.

Her first scream and Judy's rang out together. Fleming clapped his hand over Judy's mouth, but André's screaming went on and on, falling to a whimper as the voltage needle dipped, then rising again when it peaked.

" For God's sake," Judy mouthed into Fleming's hand. She struggled to break away, but he held her until André's cries stopped and the machine, sensing possibly that she no longer responded, let go its grip and she slithered to the floor. Judy tore herself free and ran over to her, but this time there was no groaning, no breathing, no sign of life. The eyes she looked into were glazed and the mouth hung senselessly open.

"I think she's dead," Judy said inadequately.

"What did you expect?" Fleming came up behind her. "You saw the voltage. That was because she hadn't got rid of me—because I was cancelling her out. Poor little devil."

He looked down at the crumpled body in its grey, soiled covering, and his own eyes hardened. "It'll do better next time. It'll produce something we can't get at at all."

"Unless you find what's wrong with it." She turned away and picked up Fleming's pad from the top of the input unit, and offered it him.

He pulled it out of her hand and threw it across the room. "It's too late for that! There's nothing wrong with it." He pointed to the girl's huddled figure. "That's the only answer I need. To-morrow it will ask for another experiment, and to-morrow and to-morrow and to-morrow . . ."

He walked briskly across to the alarm and fuse terminals by the double doors, took the wiring in both hands and pulled. They gave but did not break, so he put a foot against the wall and heaved against it.

"What are you doing?"

"I'm going to finish it. This is the moment, probably the only moment." He tugged again at the wires, and then gave up and reached for a fireman's axe that hung on the wall beside them. Judy ran across to him.

"No!" She seized his arm but he swung her off and with the return movement slashed the axe across the wiring and severed it, then wheeled and looked around the room. The display panel was still blinking fast, and he went across and smashed it with the axe.

"Have you gone mad?" Judy ran after him again and, gripping the axe by the haft, tried to wrest it from him. He twisted it away from her.

"Let go! I told you to stay out of it."

She stared at him and found she hardly knew him: his face was covered in sweat, as the girl's had been, and suffused with anger and determination. She realised now what had been in his mind all the time.

"You always meant to do this."

"If it came to it."

He stood with the axe in his hands, looking speculatively around, and she knew that she had to get to the doors before him; but he beat her to it, and leant with his back against them with the same set expression and the mirthless hint of a grin at the corners of his mouth. She really did think he was mad now. She held out a hand for the axe and spoke as if to a child.

"Please give it to me, John." She winced as he laughed. "You promised."

"I promised nothing." He held on to the shaft tightly with one hand, and with the other locked the door behind him.

"I'll scream," she said.

"Try." He slipped the key into his pocket. "They'll never hear you."

Pushing her aside, he strode through to the memory bay, opened the front of the nearest unit and struck at it. There was a small explosion as the vacuum collapsed.

"John!" She tried to stop him as he made for the next unit.

"I know what I'm doing," he said, opening the front and swinging the axe in. Another small splintering explosion came from the equipment. "Do you think there'll ever be another chance like this? Do you want to go and squeal? If you think I'm doing the wrong thing, go."

He looked straight at her, calmly and sensibly, and dug a hand into his pocket for the key. "Fetch the riot squad if you want to: that's been your favourite occupation. Or has it struck you I might be doing the right thing? That's what Osborne wanted, wasn't it? 'The right thing.'"

He held out the key to her, but for some reason impossible to express she could not take it. He gave her a long chance and then put the key back in his pocket and turned and started on the other units.

"The sentries will hear." Knowing he was not mad after all made her feel committed to him. She stood by the doors and kept watch while he worked his way round the equipment, hacking and smashing and reducing the intricate engineering complex and the millions of cells of electronics to a tangled and shattered waste on the floor, on metal racks and behind the broken facias of cabinets. She could hardly bear to look, but she listened through the splintering and tearing for any sound in the corridor.

Nothing came to interrupt them. The storm of snow outside, unseen and unheard in the buried centre of the building, made its own commotion and hid theirs. Fleming worked methodically at first, but it was an enormous job and he began to go faster and faster as he felt himself tiring, until he was swinging desperately and pulling on his lungs for more breath, almost blinded by the perspiration that ran down from his forehead. He worked all round until he came back to the centre of the control unit, and then he smashed that.

"Take that, you bastard," he half shouted at it. "And that, and that."

He let the axe-head swing down to the floor and leant on the end of the haft to get his breath.

"What'll happen now?" asked Judy.

"They'll try to rebuild it, but they won't know how to."

"They'll have the message."

"It's stopped."

"They'll have the original."

"They won't. They won't have that or the broken code or any of it—because it's in here." He indicated a solid metal door in the wall behind the control desk, then he swung the axe again and went for the hinges. Blow after blow he battered at them, but made no impression. Judy stood by in a trauma of suspence as the ring of metal on metal seemed to shout through the whole building, but no-one heard. After a long time Fleming gave up and leant once more, panting, over his axe. The room was utterly silent now that the computer had stopped, and its stillness went with the motionless body of the girl in the middle of the floor.

"We'll have to get a key," Fleming said. "Where is one?"

"In Major Quadring's duty room."

"But that's—"

She confirmed his fear. "It's always manned," she said. "And the key's kept in a safe."

"There must be another."

"No. That's the only one."

She tried to think of some other possibility but there was none. No one, so far as she knew, not even Geers, had a duplicate. Fleming at first would not believe her, and when he did he went momentarily berserk. He swung up the axe and lashed in fury at the door, over and over again until he could hardly stand, and when at last he gave up and slumped into what had been the control desk chair, he sat for a long while thinking and brooding and trying to find a plan.

"Why the hell didn't you tell me?" he said at last.

"You didn't ask." Judy was trembling from the violence and sense of disaster and only kept control of herself with an effort. "You never asked me. Why didn't you ask me?"

"You'd have stopped me if I had."

She tried to talk sensibly and stop herself shaking. "We'll get it some way. I'll think of some way, perhaps first thing in the morning."

"It'll be too late." He shook his head and stared down past his feet to the body lying on the floor. "'Everything you do is predictable'—that's what she said. 'There's nothing you can think of that won't be countered.' We can't win."

"We'll get it through Osborne or something," Judy said. "But we must get out of here now."

She found the young operator's coat and muffler and put those on him and led him out of the building.

Twelve

ANNIHILATION

IT was very late when they got back to the café. The snow was blowing a blizzard and piling up against the north wall; inside the small back room Reinhart and Osborne, huddled in their coats, were playing a miserable and inattentive game with a portable chess set.

Fleming felt too dazed to make a case for himself. He left Judy to explain and sat hunched on one of the hard farm chairs while Reinhart asked questions and Osborne whinnied at him a long tirade of utter hopelessness and contempt.

"How dare you trick me into this?" The last shreds of his usual urbanity disappeared. For all his Corps Diplomatique training and breeding, he was unbearably distressed. "I only agreed to be party to this in the hope that we might furnish the Minister with a case. But it'll be the end of his career, and of mine."

"And of mine," sighed Reinhart. "Though I think I'd be willing to sacrifice that if the machine's destroyed."

"It isn't destroyed," Osborne objected. "He couldn't even make a job of that. If the original message is intact they can build it again."

"It's my mess," said Fleming. "You can blame me. I'll carry the can."

Osborne neighed scornfully. "That won't keep us out of prison."

"Is that what's worrying you? How about the rebuilt machine and the next creature, and the grip we'll never be able to shake off?"

"Isn't there anything we can do?" asked Judy.

They all looked, with only the faintest of hope, at Reinhart. He went over it with them move by move, like the

191

checking of a calculation, and in the end drew an entire blank. They had no hope of getting a key until morning, and by then Geers would know about it and the whole business would be put in motion again. There was no doubt in their minds now that Fleming's theories were right; what mattered was that he had failed them in action.

"The only thing," said Reinhart, "is for Osborne to go back to London on the first train and when the news breaks look surprised."

"Where am I supposed to have been?" Osborne inquired.

"You came, did a brief inspection, and left. The rest happened after you'd gone, and that's the truth. You wouldn't know anything about it."

"And the ' official ' I took in?"

"He came out with you."

"And who was ' he '?"

"Whoever you can trust. Browbeat or bribe someone to say they came up from London and went back with you. You must clear yourself and keep your influence. We must all clear ourselves if we can. They'll build it again, as John says, and there must be at least one of us who's advice may be taken."

"And who's supposed to have bust the computer?" asked Fleming.

The Professor gave a small smile of satisfaction. "The girl. It can be assumed that she went off the rails and turned against it, and either she was electrocuted in the process or she died of the delayed shock of her punishment, aggravated by the frenzy it drove her into. Or whatever they like to decide. She's dead either way, so she can't deny it."

"You're sure she is?" Osborne asked Fleming.

"Want to inspect the body?"

"Ask me," said Judy, with a bitter sort of sickness. "I see them all die."

"O.K." Fleming roused himself and turned to Reinhart. "What are Judy and I supposed to have been doing?"

The Professor answered him pat. "You weren't there. So far as anyone knows we left the operator in there with Miss Adamson. They left together, and it happened afterwards."

"It won't hold," said Osborne. "There'll be a hell of an enquiry."

" It's the best we can do." Reinhart shivered slightly. " Whatever way you look at it, it's a mess."

They sat in their overcoats around the table, like four figures at a ghostly dinner, waiting for the night to pass and the snow to stop.

" Do you think it'll hold up the trains?" asked Osborne after a while.

Reinhart cocked his head on one side, listening to the beating on the roof. " I shouldn't think so. It sounds as though it's easing off a little." He turned his attention to Fleming. " How about you, John?"

" Judy and I'll go back to the camp in the car. The road was passable when we came up just now."

" Then you'd better go at once," Reinhart said. " Pretend you've been for a joyride and go straight to your rooms. You haven't seen anything or anyone."

" What a night for a joyride!" Fleming stood up wearily and looked from one to the other of them. " I'm sorry. I'm really sorry."

He drove back gropingly through the scudding snow, with Judy wiping the windscreen clear every minute or so, but already the storm was slacking. He left Judy at her chalet and drove round to his own. He was so tired that he did not want to get out of the car. It was an hour or so after midnight and the camp was asleep and deadened by the pall of white. As he opened the door, the inside of his hut looked darker than ever, by contrast with the snow-covered ground outside. He fumbled on the wall for his light switch, and as he touched it another, bandaged, hand fell on his own.

He had a moment of wild panic, then he pushed it off and switched the light on.

André stood there holding one of her bandaged hands in the other and moaning, looking deadly pale and ravaged; but not dead. He stared at her incredulously for a moment, then shut the door and crossed to the window to pull the curtains.

" Sit down and hold out your hands." He took dressings and a tube of ointment from a cupboard and started gently and methodically replacing her rough bandages.

" I thought you couldn't possibly be alive," he said as he worked. " I saw the voltage."

"You saw?" she sat on the bed, holding her hands out to him.

"Yes, I saw."

"Then it was you."

"Me—and an axe." He looked at her pale, burnt-out face. "If I'd thought you'd had any life left in you—"

"You would have finished me too." She said it for him without malice, simply stating a fact. Then she closed her eyes momentarily against a twinge of pain. "I have a stronger heart than—than people. It takes a lot to put me out of action."

"Who did up your hands?"

"I did."

"Who have you told?"

"No one."

"Doesn't anyone know about the computer?"

"I do not think so."

"Why haven't you told them?" He grew more and more puzzled. "Why did you come here?"

"I did not know what would happen—what had happened. When I came round, I could not think of anything at first except the pain in my hands. Then I looked round and saw it all in ruins."

"You could have called the guards."

"I did not know what to do: I had no sort of direction. I felt lost without the computer. You know it is completely out of action?"

"I know."

Her eyes seemed to burn in her pale face. "All I could think of was finding you. And my hands. I bandaged my hands and came here. I said nothing to the guards. And when you were not here, I waited. What is going to happen?"

"They'll rebuild it."

"No!"

"Don't you want that?" he asked in surprise. "How about your 'Higher Purpose'—your higher form of life?"

She did not answer. As he finished tying down the dressing her eyes closed again with pain, and he saw that she was shivering.

"You're ice cold, aren't you?" he said, feeling her forehead. He pulled his eiderdown across the bed and heaped it around her shoulders. "Keep that round you."

"You think they will build it again?"

"Sure to." He found a bottle of whisky and poured two glasses. "Now get that down. They won't have me to help them but they'll have you."

"They would make me do that?" She sipped the whisky and looked at him with burning, anxious eyes.

"You'll need making?"

She almost laughed. "When I saw the computer all smashed I was so glad."

"Glad?" he asked, pausing in his drink.

"I felt free. I felt—"

"Like the Greek Andromeda when Perseus broke her chains?"

She was not sure about this. She handed back her glass. "When the computer was working, I hated it."

"Not you. It was us you hated."

She shook her head. "I hated the machine and everything to do with it."

"Then why—?"

"Why do people behave like they do? Because they feel compelled! Because they are tied by what they think are logical necessities, to their work or their families, or their country. You imagine ties are emotional? The logic you cannot contradict is the tightest bond. I know that." Her voice wavered and became uncertain. "I did what I had to, and now the logic has gone and I do not know what . . . I do not know."

Fleming sat down beside her. "You could have said this before."

"I have said it now." She looked him full in the face. "I have come to you."

"It's too late." Fleming looked down at the lint and strapping on her hands, thinking of the marks she still carried of the machine's will. "Nothing on earth'll stop them rebuilding it."

"But they cannot without the code of the design."

"That still exists."

"You didn't—?" Even if he had doubted her protests

before, there was no doubting the distress in her voice now, or in her eyes.

" I couldn't break open the cabinet and Quadring has the only key."

She fumbled in the pocket of her anorak. " I have one."

" But I was told nobody had."

She pulled the key out, wincing as her bandages caught on the flap of the pocket. " Nobody has, except me, and that was not known here." She held it out to him. " You can go and finish."

It was so easy, and so impossible; here was the one thing he needed above all else, and now he had no means of getting back into the computer block to use it.

" You'll have to go," he said. She shrank back into the eiderdown but he threw it off and took her by the shoulders. " If you really hate it—if you really want to stay free—all you have to do is walk in, unlock the wall cabinet and take out the original message—that's on tape—and my calculations which are on paper, and the program, which is on punched cards. Make a bonfire of all the paper, and when it's going well you can dump the magnetic reels on. That'll wipe them. Then you get out quick."

" I can't."

He shook her, and she groaned a little with pain. " You've got to."

He was alight with excitement, not stopping to think about the consequences to himself or her, or of the fate of all of them now that she was alive, but only of the one essential, immediate thing.

" You can get past the sentries without question. You'll need these to hide your bandages." He took a pair of large driving gauntlets out of his drawer and began to pull them on over her hands.

" No, please!" She shuddered as the gloves touched her bandages, but he still drew them on, very slowly and carefully.

" You can make a bonfire on the floor. I'll give you some matches."

" Don't send me. Don't send me back, please." Her eyes burned in fear and her face, in spite of the whisky, was still white with exhaustion. " I cannot do it."

" You can." He pushed the matches into her pocket and

propelled her gently to the door. He opened it and there before them lay the white ground and the black night. Snow had stopped falling and the wind had dropped. The permanent lights of the camp shone down frostily and the outlines of buildings could just be seen, dark against the ground, with a powdering of white on their roofs. He said, " You can do it."

She hesitated, and he took her arm. After a moment she walked out across the snow towards the computer block. Fleming went with her as far as he dare. When they were nearly in sight of the guards he gave her a little pat on the shoulders.

" Good luck," he said, and went reluctantly back to his hut.

The temperature had dropped and it was icy cold. He found himself shivering, so he shut the door and went to the window and, drawing back the curtains, settled down to watch from there. Until now he had not felt the effort of the past few hours but as he stood there waiting it fell on him in a great wave of tiredness. He longed to lie on his bed and sleep and wake to find that everything was over: he tried to imagine what the girl was doing, to think out the alternatives of what might happen, of what the outcome would be, but his mind would not go beyond the events of the evening and the image of the small pale figure setting out across the snow.

And he could not get warm. He switched on the electric radiator and poured himself another tot of whisky. He wished he had not used it so freely in the past, so that it would have more effect on him now, and he made various resolutions about himself, and about Judy, if they ever came the right way up out of it all. Leaning against the window sill, he waited for what seemed an immense time, looking out into the unbroken stillness of the night.

About three o'clock it began to snow again, not in a gale now, but quietly and steadily, and the lamps that shone all night at odd points about the compound grew blurred behind the white descending flakes. For some time he could not be sure whether it was smoke he saw against the lamplight by the computer building, or merely a blur of snowfall; then he heard an alarm bell ringing, and excited shouts of sentries. Turning up his coat collar, he opened the window, and at once he could hear and see more clearly. It was quite definitely smoke.

His instinct was to run out and see for himself what had happened, to find the girl and hold back any interference with the fire, but he knew there was nothing he could do but rely on the confusion and the dark to give it and her time. With as much smoke as that, the computer-room must be an inferno by now and there was a good chance that nothing would survive, possibly not André herself. He found himself suddenly caught in a cross of emotions: of course he had wanted her gone and out of the way, and yet the idea of sending her to her death had not occurred to him. A part of him wanted her to live, and he felt overwhelmingly responsible for her. The three-quarters of her, or whatever it was, that he could understand was a creature with feelings and fears and emotions that he had helped to create, and now that the cord between her and the intellect that guided her had been cut she was in limbo, and perhaps only he could reach out and save her. If indeed she was not dead.

The camp warning siren suddenly brayed out, lugubrious and menacing, and every light in the compound seemed to come on and dance mistily behind the snowflakes. Beneath the siren wail he could hear motor engines starting up, and the white beam of a searchlight stabbed out abruptly from above the main guard building and began to swing slowly around the camp.

He could imagine the tide of alarm and command rippling like a wave through the establishment: the sentry's phone call to the guard room, the guard commander to Quadring, the duty office to the security patrols, to the fire squad, the perimeter guard, and Quadring to Geers and Geers possibly to London, to a sleeping Minister and to an area commander, fumbling out of bed in his pyjamas to switch on whatever sabotage drill had been laid down.

He strained his eyes to see what was happening behind the light-flecked curtain of snow, and cursed the siren that smothered the other sounds. A fire truck whipped past his hut, clanging and roaring, and its lamps and the beam of the searchlight showed up the silhouettes of other people running—people with greatcoats that they buttoned up as they went, and soldiers with automatic rifles and sub-machine-guns. Another truck went by—a Land Rover with a radar scanner circling on top —and then the lights went and the siren died, leaving a jumble of sounds and snow-hidden movements in the dark. A moment later a second searchlight came on, flooding the open space between the living quarters and the technical area where the computer building was, and into it drove another vehicle, going fast. It was an open jeep, and he could clearly see Quadring sitting beside the driver mouthing into a field telephone. A single figure ran across in front of it and for a split second he thought it was the girl, then he could see that it was Judy, with a coat flung over her shoulders and her dark hair dishevelled round her face. The jeep stopped and Quadring spoke to her briefly, then the driver sent it forward again and Judy crossed behind and ran to Fleming's hut.

She pushed in at the door without knocking and looked round wildly for a moment before she saw him.

" What's happened?" she gasped.

He spoke without turning away from the window. " She's done it. André's done it. That's the code burning."

"André?" She went over to him, not understanding. " But she's dead."

There was no time to explain much, but he told her a little as she stood beside him staring out.

" I thought it was you," she said, only grasping part of it. " Thank God for that anyway."

" What did Quadring say?" he asked.

" Only to wait here for him."

" Has he found her?"

" I don't know. I don't think he's any idea. He was giving orders to the patrols to clear the compound and, if anyone disobeyed, to shoot on sight."

The sounds of shouting and of moving vehicles grew more muffled; whatever was going on was happening at the far side of the camp. The column of smoke from the computer building had swelled and thickened and a tongue of flame flickered up in its centre, clearly visible between the white smudges of the searchlights. Fleming and Judy watched and listened without speaking, then out of the confusion in front of them came the sharp crack of a rifle, followed by another and another.

Fleming stiffened.

" Does that mean they've found her?" asked Judy.

He did not answer. The space in front of the hut was empty now. The searchlight which had swung away moved partly back, throwing a slanting finger of blurred light across it, but at first nothing moved in its beam except the snow falling. Then into this no-man's-land came a small figure, pale and uncertain, stumbling out of the shadows between two buildings.

"André!" Judy whispered.

The girl was half-running, half-staggering, without direction. She made a little rush into the beam of light, stood blinking for a moment, and doubled back. The searchlight crew did not appear to have seen her, but another shot rang out, closer to them, and a bullet whistled away between the buildings.

Judy's fingers clutched on to Fleming's arm. "They'll kill her."

Shaking her off, he turned and ran to the door.

"John! don't go out!"

"I sent her!" He picked up his heavy-duty torch from beside his bed and was gone without looking back. Judy followed him to the doorway, but he was lost at once in the snow-hidden blackness between the huts.

He kept in the lee of the huts for as long as he could, then sprinted across the beam of the light to the darkness on the further side. This time the searchlight crew were on the watch. The white beam swung over with him and dazzled on the buildings beyond, but this only helped him. As he ran he could see the girl slumped against a wall facing him. The snow made heavy going but he managed to keep sprinting until he reached her and, pulling her up by main force, lugged her round the corner into the dark.

At first she did not recognise him, as they leant together panting. He kept her propped up with one arm.

"It's me," he said and, remembering the flask in his pocket, pulled it out and forced what was left of the whisky between her lips. She spluttered and gulped and then, with an effort, managed to stand on her own.

"I did it," she said, and although it was too dark to see her face he knew she was smiling.

"How did you get out?"

"Through a window at the back."

"Shush." He put a finger to her lips and held her to him. In the open space he had just crossed the searchlight wavered to and fro, and a party of men in battle-dress went past at the double, peering from side to side, their guns at the ready. He tried to think what to do next. To go back to his hut was

200

impossible and to hide anywhere else in the camp probably meant that they would be come upon by surprise and be sewn across by a spray of bullets before the men who fired had time to think. Even to give themselves up was probably to court death in the darkness and hysteria of the night. It seemed to him that their only hope was to get clear until daylight came and the search grew less impassioned and more under control.

From where they stood there was only one way of reaching the perimeter fence without crossing the beam of one of the searchlights, and that would take them to the wire above the cliff path that led down to the jetty in the bay. A memory—a very distant memory—came into his mind and filled it, so that all his thoughts turned together to the jetty and a boat. He put his arm firmly round André's waist to support her.

" Come on," he said. He half-led, half-carried her along the snow-covered strips of ground between buildings, zig-zagging from the lee of one to the lee of another, and turning back whenever he heard voices and finding a new way. It seemed impossible that they should not be discovered within minutes, but the falling snow hid them and the snow on the ground muffled the sound of their shoes. André was breathing fast and shallow and obviously could not keep going for very much further, and he remembered that when they got to the cliff they would find the perimeter fence stretched right along—it had been reinforced since Bridger's death and there would certainly be a guard at the gate nearest the path. On the face of it it seemed hopeless, but something buried in his mind urged him to go on and he plodded forward, half blinded with snow, while the girl leant heavily on him and stumbled beside him. Then he remembered what it was he was looking for.

All the pervious day men had been working near the cliff end of the perimeter, clearing the ground for a new building just inside the wire, and they had a bulldozer with them which they left there when they knocked off. It might be too cold to start, but on the other hand it was designed to stand out overnight and still fire in the morning. It was worth trying, if they could get to it.

His own breathing was laboured by the time they reached the last of the buildings, and there was a good fifty yards of open grass to cross before they could reach the dark shape that was the bulldozer. He leant with the girl against the seaward wall and took great gulps of cold air painfully into his lungs. He made no attempt to speak and she seemed not to expect it. Either she trusted him without question or she was too exhausted to think; or both. A mobile patrol went past between them and the wire—an army truck with a searchlight mounted on the cab and the dim figures of a platoon of men in the back—and then the area fell quiet.

"Now!" he said, pointing forward, and hoisting her up, he ran with her across the snow-covered grass. Before they were half-way across she had stumbled twice and for the last twenty yards or so he had to carry her. His head and chest seemed bursting by the time they reached the bulldozer and when he put her down she slithered to the ground with a moan.

He climbed up on to the machine and looked around. Evidently no-one had seen them and he could only hope that, if the motor did start, it would be mistaken for one of the security vehicles.

It did, on the first turn of the starter, and after a few cautious revs he left it to idle over heavily while he climbed down to help the girl up on to it. At first she would not move.

"Come on," he panted at her. "Hurry up. We're on our way."

Her voice came feebly. "Leave me. Don't worry about me."

He lifted her bodily and, without quite knowing how, pushed her up on to a box beside the driver's seat.

"Now hold tight," he said, and made her lean against him. By this time the patrol truck was probably half way round the perimeter and on its way back to them. By this time Quadring had probably been to his hut for Judy and learnt that he and Andromeda were both on the run. By this time the computer room was probably a sodden, smoking mass of ash and embers and the message from a thousand million million miles away, and all that had come out of it, was gone for good. All that was left to do now was to get the girl out of the way; somewhere, somehow to hide and to survive. He straddled the seat, put his foot down on the clutch and let in the gear.

As he eased up the clutch the bulldozer jerked forward and nearly stalled, but he revved it hard and swung it round ponderously towards the fence. Over his shoulder he could see a light approaching, but it was too late to stop. He pressed the accelerator down to the metal footplate and held on while the front of the dozer crunched into the fence. The wire links snapped and tore and went down underneath the tracks, and there was a gap and they were in the middle of it.

He switched off the engine and climbed down, pulling the girl with him. The heavy bulk of the machine stood in the torn fence, plugging it like a cork, and he and André were down in the snow outside. He led her cautiously round towards the edge of the cliff and, bending double, ran for cover behind some bushes that protected the top end of the jetty path. The light from the approaching truck grew brighter and brighter, and from behind the bushes he could see it lighting up the bulldozer. He was too dazzled by the lamp and the snow to see the truck itself, and his fear was that it was the patrol vehicle full of men. Then the light swung away, and the snow cleared for a moment, and he could see that it was the radar van nosing frustrated against the wire with its scanner turning hopelessly round and round above its cab.

He took André by the arm and led her down the cliff path. After the second bend he switched on his torch and went slowly enough for her to keep close behind without help. She had dredged up a little more energy from somewhere and kept with him, holding tightly to his hand. There was no sentry at the bottom of the path and the jetty was dead quiet except for the slop-slop of small waves against its piers. They seemed a thousand miles from the bedlam above them and that, in a way, made it harder to go on.

During the winter all the small boats were hauled ashore and stripped; only the duty boat, a sort of small whaler with an engine amidships, was left afloat and chafed and fretted against the side of the quay. Fleming had used it before, in the summer months when he had wanted to get away and be alone, and knew it with the sort of love-hate a rider might feel about a tough and obstinate old horse. He pushed André into it, freed the fore and aft ropes and fumbled about with his torch for the starting handle. It was not as easy to start as the bulldozer; he cranked until sweat ran down his face with the snow, and began to despair of ever putting life into it. André huddled down under one of the gunwales, while the snow fell on them and melted to join the water slapping about in the bilge. She asked no questions as he churned away, panting and swearing, at the rusty handle, but from time to time she made little moaning sounds. He said nothing, but went on turning until, after a series of coughs, the engine started.

He let it run idle for a while, with the boat vibrating and the exhaust plop-plop-plopping just above the water, and then engaged the shaft and opened the throttle. The jetty disappeared immediately, and they were alone on the empty blackness of the water. Fleming had never been on the sea in snow before. It was marvellously calm. The flakes eddied down around them, melting as they touched the surface. It actually seemed warmer so long as they were in the shelter of the bay.

There was a small compass in front of the wheel—which was like the steering-wheel of a very old car—and Fleming steered with one hand while, with the other, he held the torch to shine on the compass face. He knew the bearing of the island without having to think, and roughly the amount to allow for a drift of current. In this calm sea he could guess the speed of the boat and by checking his watch every few minutes he could make an approximate calculation of the distance. He had done it so often before that he reckoned he had a good chance of making a landfall blind. He only hoped he would be able to hear the waves splashing against the rocks of the island a length or so before they came upon them.

He called to André to go into the bow and watch out, but she did not answer at first. He dared not leave the wheel or compass for a moment.

" If you can get forward, do," he called again, " and keep a look out."

He saw her edging her way slowly towards the bow.

" It won't be long now," he said, with more hope than he felt.

The boat plodded steadily on for ten, fifteen, thirty minutes. When they got further out they ran into a slight swell, and dipped and wallowed a little, but the snow stopped and the night seemed a few shades less dark. Fleming wondered if they were far enough from the cliff to be a trace on someone's radar screen, and he wondered, too, what was going on behind them at the camp, and what lay ahead of them in the empty dark. His eyes ached, and his head and his back—in fact every part of him— and he had to think constantly of the girl's burnt and throbbing hands in order to feel better about himself.

After about forty minutes she called back to him. He eased
the throttle and let the boat glide towards a darker shape that
lay in front, and then spun the wheel so that they were running
alongside the smooth rock-face of the island. They went on very
slowly, almost feeling their way, and listening for the sound of
breakers ahead of them until, some ten minutes later, the rock
wall sloped away and they could hear the gentle splash of waves
on a beach.

Fleming ran the boat aground and carried the girl through
bitter knee-high water to the sand. There was a definite light-
ness in the sky now, not dawn but possibly the moon, and he
could recognise the narrow sandy cove as the one he had found
with Judy that early spring afternoon so long ago when they
had discovered Bridger's papers in the cave. It was a sad but at
the same time a comforting memory; he felt, in an irrational
way, that he could hold his own here.

He looked around for somewhere to rest. It was too cold
to risk sleeping in the open, even if they could, so he led the
way into the cave-mouth and along the tunnel he had explored
with Judy. He could no longer hold on to André, but he went
ahead slowly and talked back over his shoulder to encourage her.

" I feel like Orpheus," he said to himself. " I'm getting my
legends mixed—it was Perseus earlier on."

He felt light-headed and slightly dizzy with fatigue, and
mistook his way twice in the dark tunnels. He was looking for
the tall chamber where they had found the pool, for he remembered it had a sandy floor where they could rest; but after a
while he realised he had gone the wrong way. He turned,
swinging his torch round, to tell André. But she was no longer
behind him.

In sudden panic, he ran stumbling back the way he had come,
calling her name and flashing the torch from side to side of the
tunnel. His voice echoed back to him eerily, and that was all
the sound there was except for his shoes on the boulders. At
the cliff entrance he stopped and turned back again. This was
absurd, he told himself, for they had not gone very far. For
the first time he felt resentment against the girl, which was quite
illogical; but logic was having less and less concern for him.
As he went down the tunnel again he noticed that there were
more branches than he had remembered: it seemed to be a part
of the sly madness of the place that they should multiply

silently in the dark. He explored some of them but had to retrace his steps, for they became, in one way or another, impassable; and then, suddenly, he found himself in the high chamber that he had missed.

He stood and called again and swung his torch slowly from side to side. Surely, he decided, she must be here: she could not have gone much further, exhausted, in darkness. He swung the beam of his torch to the sandy floor and saw her footmarks. The prints led him to the middle of the cave, and there he stopped short while a shiver of horror ran from his scalp right down his body. The last imprint was in the slime on the rocks by the side of the pool, and floating at the edge of the water was one of his gauntlets. Nothing more.

He never found anything more. They had taught her so much, he thought grimly, but they had never taught her to swim. He was stricken by a great pang of sorrow and remorse; he spent the next hour in a morbid and hopeless examination of the cave, and then went wearily back to the beach where he propped himself between two rocks until dawn. He had no fear of sleeping; he had a greater, half-delirious fear of something unspeakable coming out of the tunnel mouth—something unquenchable from a thousand million million miles away—something that had spoken to him first on a dark night such as this.

Nothing came, and after the first hour or so of daylight a naval launch swept in from seaward. He made no attempt to move, even after the launch reached the island, and the crew found him staring out over the ever-changing pattern of the sea.

Andromeda
Breakthrough

1

OUTLOOK UNSETTLED

THE alarm signal buzzed quietly but insistently above Captain Pennington's head, a discreet echo of the bell jangling outside the guard room across the parade ground of the headquarters unit No. 173 Marine Commando.

Pennington groped for the bedlight switch and sat up. He stared uncomprehendingly at the vibrating clapper arm. In every officer's room were these little buzzers. They were painted red; they existed for No. 1 alert. It was accepted that a No. 1 would in reality mean only one thing: notification of the seven minutes the ballistics people had worked out as the breathing space before World War Three came and went.

Captain Pennington heaved himself out of bed. He was conscious of running feet as the Marine Commandos observed their long-taught procedure. The bedside phone rang as he was struggling into his denims.

"Major Quadring," came the abrupt, clipped voice. "Sorry about the panic measures. Orders from Whitehall. It's not the big thing, so ease up. But it's bad enough. Thorness. Major fire. Probably sabotage. Can't be sure that the trouble isn't sea-borne. Hence the S.O.S. to your boys."

"Thorness!" Pennington repeated. "But that's the king-pin of ——."

"Exactly. Save your mental reactions till later. Get over here within an hour. Four groups, with amphibians and frogmen, of course. I'll be at the gates to get you through. Tell your men not to fool around. The guards here won't be waiting to ask questions."

The phone clicked dead. Pennington checked his assault kit and ran from the officers' barrack hut into a night of soft-falling snow. He could make out shadowy figures of the men already standing to by their trucks and amphibious vehicles, the engines ticking over. Not a light showed.

"Right," he called loudly through the darkness. "You'll be glad to know that this isn't it. Nor is it just a dummy run. Some real bother at the rocket station down at Thorness. I know no more than you, though we're going because there's probably a sea job to do. You can, of course, use headlights. I'll set the rate; we ought to average fifty. Keep the inter-com channel open till I order otherwise. Carry on!"

A Land Rover wheeled round and stopped beside him. He got in. Orders snapped out and the Marines got aboard their trucks. Pennington nodded to his driver and they roared through the gates.

They had a forty-five mile run from their base to the lonely promontory nosing into the Atlantic on which Thorness had been built as the nerve centre of Britain's rocket testing range. The whole area had been cleared of civilians, and the twisting, undulating road straightened and levelled for the articulated rocket carriers and fuel tankers. Pennington made the trip in precisely 55 minutes.

The main gates between the barbed-wire-festooned chain link fencing were shut. Guards with automatic guns stood under the floodlights. Dobermann Pincher dogs sat, immovable and alert, beside them. At the sound of the convoy Major Quadring came out of the concrete guard post with an N.C.O. Quadring was a lithe officer of middle-age, smartly dressed and unruffled. After a glimpse at the Commando identity marks on Pennington's vehicle he gave orders for the gates to be opened.

"Pull into the parking bay to the left," he said as Pennington jumped down. "Tell your chaps to relax, but to remain with the vehicles. Then come on in here. I'll put you in the picture. Over a cup of char—laced, of course."

Beyond the floodlights at the entrance, a double necklace of lamps edging the main road of the camp strung away into the misty night. The snow had stopped and what had fallen was melting into slush, so that the ground was dark, and the shapes of the camp buildings were dark, too, except where emergency lights were shining at windows.

Faintly inside the compound there was another smudge of light, where mobile lamps were trained on the main computer building, and a heavier pall—which was smoke—hung, smelling sulphurous, among the mist. Quadring led Pennington across the concrete into the guard hut.

Only in the light of the unshaded bulb of the guard room was it evident that Quadring was a worried man. His face was grey with fatigue and strain, and he tipped an over-liberal portion of rum into his own mug of tea.

"I'm sorry about a sortie on a night like this to this God-forsaken place. I think Whitehall and Highland Zone overdid it a bit with that No. 1 alarm and excursion, but then I'm only a simple soldier. They know better than I what's involved, though even to my un-technical mind this is a bloody business."

He refused Pennington's offer of a cigarette and began ramming tobacco into a blackened pipe. "The sea mist has closed in like a blanket down on the coastline. You drop from the station right into cotton wool. Not a damned inch in front of your nose. It'll lift with dawn, probably with rain or sleet. I tell you, it's a nice place.

"Someone or something attacked this place about four hours ago, and destroyed its brain. Which means, if my job here is as vital as they tell me, that old Lady Britannia is stripped of power, wealth, and about everything the politicians were banking on."

Pennington looked at him sceptically. "Frankly sir, you're over-dramatising things, aren't you? I mean, everyone knows Thorness is a rocket testing base, and where they run the computers which made those I.B.M. interceptions such a wow. Surely the machines aren't unique. The Yanks and the rest of N.A.T.O. . . ."

"The machines were unique," Quadring answered. "If you commandeered every computer in commercial or Government use in the country they wouldn't amount to more than a cash register compared with the scientific toy that's now a tangled mess of valves and wires and smouldering insulation. Nor does the rocket side matter all that much."

Pennington drained his rum and tea, easing himself on the hard wooden chair. "Of course, I've heard some pretty bizarre accounts of the sidelines here," he said with a grin. "It's pub gossip. That sort of thing was bound to start rumours."

"But nothing as good as the truth," Quadring said. "I've had an okay from G.D.1 to put you vaguely in the picture. Your

211

boozing pals in the bar parlour haven't burbled anything about the Dawnay Experiment in their cups, have they?"

"The Dawnay Experiment?" Pennington repeated. "No sir."

"I'd never have believed my security was so good," the Major grinned.

He re-lit his pipe and sucked gratefully at it a while.

"This Dawnay woman's a sort of de-sexed biochemical genius from Edinburgh, though I admit I found her a pleasant person before she fell ill, through some infection from her own work, poor old girl. And so far as I can understand it, the computer helped her to synthesise chromosomes, which you no doubt learned when you were told about the birds and the bees being the seeds of life.

"She obviously hadn't much of a clue as to what it was all about, beyond the fact that the formulae spewed from the computer made sense. But the upshot was a human embryo."

"Human?"

"That's what they say. I agree it's a nice point. It grew like fun—or rather she did, for the organs of sex were there—and in four months she was 5 ft. 7 ins. tall and weighed 123 lb. The report is good on pointless and harmless facts."

Pennington tried to look amused. "Was this zombie, robot or whatever she was still in some sort of enlarged test tube, fixed in a clamp, or what?"

"Not a zombie by any means," Quadring retorted. "They called her human, because she looked human, behaved like a human, had human intelligence and human physical abilities. Though not, I gather, human instincts or emotions until she was taught them. In fact a rather pretty girl. I know. I've met her dozens of times."

"The people who know about all this and have to look after her must have a feeling of revulsion," Pennington said thoughtfully. "I mean a thing produced in a lab . . ."

"Don't kid yourself, and don't just take my word for it. Everyone accepts her as an attractive girl. But a very special girl. Dawnay built her, but she was only the artisan. The design came from the computer, and it saw to it that she was tailor-made for its purpose. She absorbs knowledge from the computer, and the machine needs her to programme it, or rather, did do so."

"Did?"

"She's gone."

"You mean she's disappeared?"

Quadring looked into the dark congealed mess in the bowl of his pipe. "That's exactly what I do mean."

Pennington laughed, a little too loudly. "Perhaps she didn't exist! I mean, I don't think one can really believe in a manufactured human being with a mental rapport with a computer."

"We service types aren't paid to think," said Quadring. "Right now, our job is to find her, and whoever destroyed the computer. It could hardly have been an outside job. It was done too expertly and quickly. The building was burning nicely by the time the patrols called me and had bashed through the locked doors and plied their extinguishers. Anyway, there wasn't a lot of point. The computer had been well and truly damaged with an axe before the arson. Security checks have told us one thing so far: the girl—she's called Andre, after Andromeda, the star or whatever it is that's alleged to have transmitted the dope for the computer—is missing, along with a scientist named John Fleming."

"Anything known about him?"

"He's marked with a query on the files. Nothing definite. But he's the usual sort of bright young genius who thinks he knows better than the Establishment. The story is that he'd fallen for the girl. And she sort of depended on him for advice the computer didn't or wouldn't give. They were certainly always together—at work and off it."

"So they might be together now?"

"Exactly. At first light, if the mist clears, you and your boys start looking. Some half-asleep guard down at the jetty thinks he saw a man and a woman get in a boat and head out to sea just before the alarm siren started."

"They could have landed anywhere along the coast by now," Pennington said.

"Not in that boat. It's known it hadn't more than a gallon of petrol. It's just a little outboard effort for pottering along the promontory to check the defences. They'd make one of the islets off the coast, no farther."

"What about a rendezvous out at sea?"

Quadring glanced at his companion. "A snatch by our old friend a Foreign Power?" He shrugged. "It could be. The Navy got the alarm along with you. Destroyers and aircraft by now will have started combing the Western approaches and away up North for too innocent-looking fishing trawlers and blatantly neutral tramps. But our radar watch would have picked up anything bigger than a rowing boat.

"My bet is they'll find nothing. Maybe you won't either. But with this sort of weather a little open boat isn't exactly healthy. The island makes the best of some poor bets."

Quadring stood up and looked through the window. "Time to get moving," he said. "And I've a tricky report to write on my incompetence to date."

There was an almost imperceptible lifting of the blackness of the sky when Pennington walked across to the parking lot. The men were smoking and talking in undertones. Pennington told them briefly that a couple of suspected saboteurs, a man and a girl, were believed to have escaped by boat either to land farther up the coast or on one of the islands in the vicinity.

"They're wanted alive—not dead," he finished. "So no rough stuff. They're not believed to be armed, and there's no real reason why they should be unpleasant. The girl is—er—a particularly vital witness. We'll get down to the jetty and arrange sweep and search routine from there."

They had to hang around at the water's edge for another half hour for daylight. The mist began slowly to lift like a vast curtain, exposing first the grey sullen sea and then, a couple of miles out, the lower slopes of the nearest island with patches of snow still smudged against the northern sides.

Their landing was an anti-climax. Pennington was in the leading amphibian when he saw the figure of a man standing motionless on the shingle beach of the island. He didn't move when the vehicle lumbered out of the water and pulled up beside him.

"My name's Fleming," he muttered. "I expected you."

He was a tallish, well-built man in his early thirties with a handsome but haggard face. His hair was wet and matted with sand, and his clothes torn and muddy. He stood quite still, as if exhausted.

"You must consider yourself under arrest," Pennington said. "And the girl who came with you?"

Fleming continued to stare out to sea. "I lost contact with her when I was looking for shelter. She wandered off. There are footmarks. They end at a cave entrance. There's a deep pool inside."

"She—she's killed herself?" Pennington demanded, mystified.

Fleming rounded on him. "They killed her. The whole damned circus which used her." He became calmer. "She was hurt, badly hurt. If she slipped into that water she wouldn't have had a chance. Her hands—well, her hands were—."

"We'll dive in the pool; drag it," said Pennington.

Fleming looked at him with something like pity. "You do that," he said. "Your bosses will demand their pound of flesh, drowned if they can't have it alive."

Pennington called to a Marine. "Take Dr. Fleming back to the mainland. Hand him over to Major Quadring. Tell the Major we're staying here to search the island."

The direct line between Thorness and the Ministry of Science in Whitehall had been busy since the news of the disaster to the computer had been flashed to the duty officer just after midnight.

The Minister himself had arrived at his office at the unheard-of hour of 9 a.m. He used a side door in case some observant reporter got the idea of a crisis. Rather to his annoyance, he found his Personal and Private Secretary, Brian Fothergill, already there, looking his usual calm and elegant self.

"Good morning, Minister," he said affably. "A nasty morning. The roads were quite icy."

"To hell with the icy roads," the Minister muttered pettishly. "What I want is some information about this Thorness business. Defence woke me at five. I didn't worry the P.M. for an hour. He took it badly, very badly. He's arranging a Cabinet for eleven. We must have useful material for him, Fothergill. If not a solution. I suppose we're still in as much of a fog as that bloody place in the Highland mists."

Fothergill delicately laid a neatly typed sheet of quarto on the Minister's desk. "Not completely, sir," he murmured, "as you will gather from this precis of the position. It's a preliminary, of course, all that I've been able to compile in the"—he glanced at his wafer-thin wrist watch—"seventy-five minutes since I inaugurated an investigation."

"For God's sake," snapped the Minister irritably, "drop that ghastly jargon. What you mean is that you've been nagging everyone for something to put down here. I hope you got the whole crew out of their beds."

The Minister read quickly through the report. "Good, good," he nodded, "as far as it goes. Which actually means bad, bad. Not your fault, Brian," he added hurriedly. "You are to be congratulated on the energy with which you have gone round in circles. But there are features of interest."

He re-read the report.

"The computer's gone. The girl's gone. The months of recording of the Andromeda equations by the radio-telescope at Bouldershaw Fell have gone. Somebody named Fleming whom I recall as an untidy and self-opinionated upstart has gone too. He gave me the impression when I met him that he drank. Which probably means he womanises too. I suspect that there's the usual tawdry sexual undercurrent in this debacle. However, that's a matter for M.I.6 and their confreres at the Yard. They must find them. More interesting is this note that our colleague Osborne visited Thorness yesterday evening."

He looked up and glanced blandly at Fothergill. "Where is Osborne? Missing, I presume?"

Fothergill permitted himself a moment's hesitation before he replied. "No, sir, I have located him. He caught the overnight sleeper which arrived at Euston half an hour ago. I took it upon myself to request his immediate presence here in your name."

"Quite right. And I'll put him through the hoop. These civil servants in the permanent jobs think themselves unanswerable to anyone." The Minister cleared his throat. He realised he was infringing convention in openly criticising the Department's Permanent Under Secretary to a junior.

"That will be all, Fothergill, for the moment. Show Osborne in as soon as he arrives. And don't let me be late for that 11 o'clock Cabinet. I shall need you at 10.30 to take my memorandum."

Fothergill faded noiselessly away. The Minister had time to ascertain a few more facts before Osborne was announced. As a senior civil servant the Under Secretary was permitted, even encouraged, to keep in personal contact with the Thorness project. But why this visit on the previous day? And why, as the Thorness guard room record book showed, had he signed in a visitor, name not given?

The thought of some espionage scandal directly affecting the

Ministry of Science built up his fury to a zenith by the time Osborne entered immediately after he had knocked.

The Minister glowered at him. "Who was this chap you took to Thorness with you?" he asked without preamble.

"An assistant," Osborne answered shortly.

The Minister was determined to keep his temper if he could. "Why did you take him?" he demanded. "What did you need an assistant for on this nocturnal visit?"

Osborne seemed to discover something of tremendous interest on the Minister's desk. "It is essential for him to be in the picture," he murmured.

The Minister got up from his chair and crossed to the window. He felt uneasy at the calmness of this man, and knew that there would be little chance of getting at the truth unless he could disturb his calm. Right now the only person in danger of losing his temper was himself.

"He didn't leave a bomb, I suppose?"

He knew it was the wrong approach. Whatever unethical views Osborne might hold, he wasn't the kind to help in violence. "All right, of course he didn't," he went on hastily. "But you know what this means, don't you?"

He moved from the window and confronted Osborne. "We've lost our national capital, all of it. The computer's gone. The girl's gone. Even the original message which the Bouldershaw telescope picked up has gone. There's no chance of starting again. From being a first class power, with the know-how for unassailable defence plus all the potential for industrial supremacy we're now relegated to a second-rate power; third-rate in fact."

Osborne turned his gaze from the desk and looked mildly at his inquisitor. His silence infuriated the Minister still more.

"Once in a million years," he pointed out, "or probably longer, a planet gets a Christmas present from another planet. And what does some dam' fool do? They go and burn it."

Once again he crossed to the window and looked down on the traffic in Whitehall.

"Were they fools?"

Osborne's comment was not more than a murmured question.

"We'll be back on American aid by the end of the year," the Minister retorted.

"At least America's a boss you can understand," Osborne suggested. "This Andromeda information we had to take on its face value. The results seemed splendid. But who understood what it was all about? From somewhere in that dying and half-dead spiral nebula of Andromeda comes a briefing that makes no sense to anyone but a computer—and a freak girl; and maybe one honest-to-God human scientist."

"You mean Fleming," the Minister said.

Osborne ignored him. "Given that an intelligence in some recess of space sends us a stream of technical data which enables us obediently to make an anthromorphic creature to run its machine, who's honestly going to believe that the whole business is for our benefit and not theirs?"

The Minister lighted a cigarette. He could not help but be a little impressed with the argument. "Is that what Fleming thought?" he asked.

"That it was an attempted take-over? Yes. I'm not saying he did blow the computer to pieces, but if he did I for one don't blame him. I thank God it didn't fall into anyone else's hands."

The Minister was a simple-minded man. He disliked arguments about ethics. People were better off when they only did what they were told. "My country right or wrong, my mother drunk or sober" was a motto he had heard when he was a boy. He thought it rather good.

"Whose side are you on, Osborne?"

Osborne gave him a bland smile. "The losing one, usually, Minister."

His chief snorted in disgust. "I had hoped you would have had something useful to contribute. I was wrong. Perhaps Geers has bestirred himself enough to discover what the hell's been going on at the place he's supposed to be the director of."

The Minister switched on his intercom and told a secretary to get Thorness on the line. Osborne took it as a gesture of dismissal. He walked slowly from the office. He was privately rather surprised that he was still a free man. Never before in his precisely-planned and sedate career as a civil servant had he allowed his feelings to colour his sense of duty. Yet, in view of what had happened, he felt no regret whatever. He had, in fact, helped Fleming, and he was only concerned that no one should be able to prove it.

As he returned down the corridor to his own office he permitted himself a smile of amusement at a mental picture of Geers on this morning of crisis.

Geers was a careerist. As Director of Thorness he was the fair-haired glory boy of the Ministries of Defence and Science. He had adroitly swung over to enthusiasm for the Dawnay Experiment after several days of obstinate obstruction in favour of rocketry. Geers was a man who knew which side his bread was buttered. He had virtually achieved the pleasurable miracle of having it buttered on both sides.

But away up in Scotland Geers was now presenting the picture of a victimised and harassed autocrat. Despite the frantic messages to his quarters during the night he had dressed as slowly and as carefully as usual, his shirt collar uncomfortably stiff and his tie pulled tight into a small neat knot. But the impression of dignified pomposity which he considered essential for a key man in the nation's scientific technocracy was marred by the hunted look in his tired eyes behind their glasses, the black sheen of an inadequate shave, and the nervous tautness of his mouth.

He sat at his vast stainless steel desk, bereft of papers, but festooned with telephones, and glared at the visitors he had summoned—Fleming and Dawnay.

Madeleine Dawnay sat in the one easy chair near the window. Her rather mannish face was parchment yellow and her eyes were dull with fatigue and illness. She had pulled her dressing gown tightly round her emaciated body, missing the even warmth of the sick bay. Gratefully she sipped from a cup of coffee Geers' secretary had brought her.

Her eyes moved thoughtfully from Geers to Fleming, who lolled against the office partition. She said nothing, despite the glance of appeal Geers made to her.

"I've got the whole of Whitehall round my neck," Geers said plaintively. "The Minister of Defence is on the blower every five minutes, and half the senior staff at Science are badgering me, and I don't even know what happened."

Dawnay put her coffee carefully on the window sill. The slight physical action seemed an effort. "I don't know what's happened either," she said quietly.

"Osborne arrived at the station just after ten. With someone else. The public relations girl took them to the computer room. God knows why, but then I'm only the Director here. Afterwards, when Osborne and his guest had booked out, the duty operator locked up for the night."

"And Osborne went back to London?" Fleming looked better now; he had had a shave and a bath, and his usual casual slacks and wool shirt and sweater were at least moderately clean. He seemed now more despondent than tired, but there were strain marks around his eyes and at the corners of his mouth.

"Yes," said Geers. "No one else went in to the computer block after that, except the girl, Andromeda. After she'd been there some time the guard corporal thought he smelt burning. He went into the main control room and found the place a perfect shambles and full of smoke."

"And where was Andre?" Dawnay asked.

"Got out through the emergency exit, according to the corporal. Anyway, she or someone dropped a glove. A man's glove."

He turned and looked at Fleming, suddenly displaying a leather gauntlet taken from the desk drawer. "Yours."

Fleming did not trouble to look.

"So you know it all," Geers said. "Only two people know, you and the girl. The girl's dead."

Fleming nodded. With maddening slowness he repeated: "The girl's dead. So that's that."

"Not quite," said Geers angrily. "You have some questions to answer. You're the only person, Fleming, who wanted the computer destroyed. You always have. I can tell you that your security file is full of instances when you've shot off your mouth about it. In that I'm glad to say you're unique. Others have a better sense of loyalty, more vision."

Dawnay protested. "I think some of us were beginning to have doubts."

Geers turned and stared at her unbelievingly. He was about to speak when the intercom buzzed.

"Major Quadring is here, sir," came his secretary's voice. "He has the Marine Commando report on the island search."

"Right," Geers told her. "I'll see him in his office."

He rose and crossed to the door. "You're to stay here, Fleming," he ordered. Less brusquely he told Dawnay that he would try not to keep her much longer.

When the door closed Fleming moved across the office and stood close to Dawnay, looking out of the window.

"He's no business to drag you into all this," he said. "You're not well enough yet."

She laughed shortly. "I'm all right. I'm a tough old bird. I must be, or I wouldn't be here. But tell me, John, what really happened? You did it, didn't you?"

He kept on looking out of the window. "You don't want to be saddled with this."

"I don't," she agreed, "but as I'm involved whether I like it or not I'll just say that you can trust me if you want to trust anyone. Osborne must have smuggled you in. Then you and the girl destroyed it."

"The girl's dead."

There was a break in his voice which surprised her. In her experience John Fleming easily got emotional about principles, ideals, wrongs. But seldom about people.

"Anyway," she said quietly. "There's no one, no one, to give evidence against you."

Before he could answer Geers returned. He was grim but pleased with himself. Major Quadring had brought useful information.

Deliberately he took time to seat himself at his desk before he spoke.

"Right, Fleming; right," he barked.

"Right what?" enquired Fleming lazily.

"What happened when you got to the island?"

Fleming ambled around the desk. "Why ask me when obviously the snoops have told you? But I'll confirm what they have undoubtedly said. We got into the caves and I lost her. They're big caves. We had no torch. She blundered into a dead-end with a deep pool. That was it. Poor bloody kid."

Dawnay noted the break in his voice again. "I thought you held Andre wasn't human," she observed.

"Human enough to drown."

"Are you sure she fell in?" Geers asked suspiciously.

"Of course I'm sure," Fleming snapped. "Quadring told you that they'd found the bandages off her hands, didn't he? Or was that one bit of his smug little report he forgot to give? Or were those jolly Marines so dumb they didn't think them worth picking up?"

Geers studied Fleming in silence, taking his time so that he could be certain of noting any reaction. "I have news for you,

Fleming, if it is news in your case. They've both dived and dragged the pool. There's no body."

There was no doubt about Fleming's surprise. "She must be in there," he shouted. "I traced her into that part of the caves. They've not dragged properly. There's no other way out. I searched thoroughly."

"So Quadring says," Geers murmured. His briskness had gone. He had hoped to bluster a confession from Fleming. But Fleming was obviously dumbfounded.

"She can't get off the island, and as it's been under constant survey since daylight that means she's somewhere in the caves. I'm going to look for myself. It's the only way to get things done in this damned situation."

"I'll take you," said Fleming firmly.

"No, that won't do," Geers retorted. "You're under arrest."

"Only on your instructions."

"Let him," Dawnay interrupted. "He knows the place. He wants to find Andre far more even than you."

With bad grace Geers agreed and the two men went off to get into warm clothes and seaboots.

Fleming was authorised to draw torches and a high-pressure lamp, and to fuel an outboard motor boat. Within half an hour they were crossing the two miles of angry water to the island. Neither said a word on the trip. Geers sat hunched in the middle of the boat staring at the silhouette of the rocky islet rising out of the mist. Fleming sat at the stern holding the tiller.

He beached the boat on the shingle right opposite the mouth of the cave.

Geers waded through the surf while Fleming heaved the boat clear of deep water. They clambered through the steep shingle at high tide mark and moved to the mouth of the cave. Gulls wheeled and called at this invasion of their private kingdom but the silence inside the cavern made a weird contrast to the screaming birds and the rhythmic hiss of the breaking waves.

"Sure this is the way you came?" Geers asked, moving cautiously forward in the wavering light of the lamp and Fleming's torch.

"Sure," grunted Fleming. "You automatically memorise this sort of thing just to make sure you don't forget the way out." He directed his beam of torchlight along a narrow sloping passage which curved to the right. "That's the way to the chamber with the pool. You can see the Commando's footsteps in the sand."

Geers began to move forward, shining the lamp on the disturbed sand. He stopped abruptly when he sensed that Fleming was not following. "Where are you going?" he called.

Fleming was moving to the left. "I'm taking a look down this passage. There's another pool in here too."

"You think they dragged the wrong one?" Geers asked.

"No. Even Quadring and that Marine Officer aren't that stupid."

Geers turned back. "I don't know what your idea is, but I'm coming to see. We'll look at the other pool afterwards."

The passage dropped steeply, and the aperture became smaller. Fleming crouched low and moved steadily ahead. Geers, trying to keep up with him, caught his boot on a boulder and fell headlong. He grunted with pain as a jagged rock caught his shoulder.

Fleming turned and shone his torch on him. "Hurt yourself? It's tricky if you haven't done much caving. Wait here while I take a look at the pool. I won't be long."

Geers got up awkwardly and took a few steps back to the wider part of the passage. Fleming's footsteps echoed softly but clearly along the cave walls, getting fainter and fainter.

For a full minute there was the cold, dead silence of a lifeless world. Then, to his right in the direction of the main cavern, came the hard, clear sound of a stone moving across the rock face. It dropped with a dull plop into water. Geers froze into immobility, instinctively holding his breath. Another stone fell into the water, and then the rasp of several pebbles.

Geers' reaction was a mixture of excitement and fear. The fear won. He dared not move by himself. He yelled for Fleming.

His voice was a falsetto, and the urgency brought Fleming back as fast as he could clamber up the slope.

"Hi!" he said. "What's up?"

"Didn't you hear anything? Find anything?" Geers demanded.

"It's a deep pool, like the other. I think it's just behind the rock face of the main cavern. When you get deep pools like these in cave holes they are sometimes connected at the base —like a U tube. What goes in one may come out of the other."

"But nothing has?"

Fleming shook his head.

"No, but a body could be caught at the bottom. They'd better drag the second pool as well."

Geers shivered, though it was not as cold in the cave as outside. "Not a nice death, even for a creature," he muttered. More loudly he asked, "Did you throw stones into the pool?"

Fleming shone his torch on the other's face. "No," he answered. "Why do you ask?"

At that moment there again came the faint noise of moving pebbles. In the echoing and re-echoing of the tiniest sound it was almost impossible to identify the direction of the noise.

"There it is again. The noise. Stones moving," whispered Geers.

"Dislodged by me, and still not settled. It always happens."

Geers wasn't satisfied. He moved a step or so along the right hand passage, the light from his lamp swinging along the sides of the pool cavern. The rocks were wet and grey, with here and there pyrites glistening as the light caught them.

Fleming also switched on his torch and the beam reached right across the pool where the rock face curved gently into a rounded surface at the edge of the water. In a recess the light caught and held a blob of white.

"What is it?" whispered Geers, clutching at his companion's arm.

Fleming shook off Geers' hand and moved forward. The torch beam probed into the crevice.

"What is it?" Geers repeated urgently.

"Her, of course. Give me a hand to get her out."

Fleming eased forward, cautiously seeking a foothold on the slimy rock. Geers did not follow.

"At least play the light so I can see," Fleming shouted angrily.

When he reached Andre he thought she was dead. Her dress was saturated and clinging to her body. She felt stone cold as Fleming put his hands under the waist and shoulders to half-lift half-drag her back.

Difficult as the job was, he realised how little she weighed, how fragile this man-made *femina sapiens* was.

Gently he laid her on the dry sand at Geers' feet, leaning against the rock face while he gasped for air. Geers stood transfixed.

"Is she . . . ?" he whispered, placing the lamp on the ground so it illuminated the girl's face. She looked like the death-figure of a young goddess, slim and fair and palely beautiful.

Fleming squatted down and pulled up an eyelid. The blue iris seemed sightless. There was no visible contraction as the light caught it. He groped on the ice-cold wrist for the sign of pulsation. There was a tremor of movement. He could not be sure whether it was in his own fingers or proof that Andre still lived.

"I'm not a doctor, so I can't be sure. But I think there's a flicker. She once said she had a better constructed heart than humans."

Fleming once more put his hands under her shoulders and pulled her to a sitting position. When the upper part of her body was upright her head fell forward. And she moaned.

"She is alive," shouted Geers exultantly.

"Just." With his free hand Fleming fumbled in his jacket pocket and pulled out a flask.

"Try a drop of the hard stuff, duckie," he said. With his teeth he unscrewed the cap.

"You shouldn't force her to drink alcohol. It's a fallacy that——."

"To hell with your boy scouts' first aid rules! Here, my sweet," he murmured to the girl, "it's the real McCoy."

He let a few drops of whisky seep through Andre's pale, clenched lips.

Not daring to move, both men waited for the reaction. It came gradually. The lips relaxed and parted a little. The tongue tip emerged and moved across them.

Fleming gently brushed the matted blonde hair from her face. He was rewarded by a momentary flickering of the eyelids.

"That's it," he murmured close to her ear. "Now try to swallow a mouthful." He forced the mouth of the flask between her lips and against her teeth, tipping in a spoonful of spirit.

Andre gulped, spluttered and then swallowed it. Fleming could feel her body relaxing against his encircling arm.

"How did she get here?" Geers demanded.

"There must be a syphon between the two pools. She'd sink on one side and come up on the other. God knows how she managed to hang on the side and pull herself up. Not with those injuries."

He nodded towards Andre's hands, lying close together in her lap. They were grotesquely swollen and discoloured, the bloated whiteness of the back and knuckles contrasting horribly with the seared flesh of the fingers where the computer had burnt them.

Geers shuddered. "Can we carry her out of here?" he asked doubtfully. "We must get her to the mainland as soon as we can. Then perhaps we'll find out the truth about this business."

The impatience in Geers' tone infuriated Fleming. "Give it a rest, can't you? The girl's half dead and all you can think of is putting her in thumbscrews."

He believed that Andre half understood what was being said. Her body tautened in his arms and she made a pathetic attempt to shift away.

Awkwardly Fleming struggled out of his duffle coat without releasing his hold on her and draped it around her shoulders. "You're okay," he reassured her. "It's all over now. We'll go away for a nice long holiday. You know who I am, don't you?"

Her clouded eyes opened wider and stared at his face. She nodded almost imperceptibly.

He felt ridiculously pleased. "Fine! I'm going to lift you up. Keep your hands just where they are and they won't get rubbed. Here we go!"

Geers made no attempt to help. He watched Fleming grasp Andre and lift her like a baby, shifting the weight until he had her held securely, her head against his shoulder.

Satisfied that they were leaving at last, Geers bent down to pick up the torch. Fleming was just behind him. With a quick shove from his boot he sent Geers sprawling. Then he kicked the lamp away. There was a tinkle of glass as it hit the rock face and the light went out.

Fleming laughed aloud. "Hold tight, darling, we're taking off," he whispered to Andre. Half crouching to avoid bumping the cave roof, he loped ahead helped by the fitful, jerking light from his own torch. Geers' wails of fright and fury echoed behind him.

Fleming reached the cave entrance with no more than one bad bump on his shoulder. There was a stretch of thirty yards to the boat. He noted with satisfaction that the tide had turned and the stern was already afloat.

He was wading in deep water before Geers stumbled from

the cave entrance, bawling Fleming's name and alternately threatening punishment and appealing for him to wait.

Fleming lowered Andre into the bottom of the boat. She groaned pitifully as her hand struck a rowlock.

Fleming crouched over the motor. If only the damned thing would fire first time. Outboard engines were temperamental until they got heated up. He forced himself methodically to check choke and fuel control before he wrenched at the starter cord. He whipped it out with all his strength. The engine fired with a staccato burst of noise, spluttered, and then settled in to a steady rhythm.

With a kick over the side that filled his boot with sea water Fleming pushed off stern first. A couple of yards and there was room to veer. He gave the engine full throttle and the boat swung seawards. Geers was standing impotently up to his knees in water, shaking his arms and burbling incoherent imprecations. Fleming didn't trouble to turn round to look at him.

The sea was pretty calm while the island protected it from the ocean swell. He grabbed the chance to check the petrol reserve and to wrap his coat more tightly around Andre. She was either asleep or had lapsed into unconsciousness again.

The boat moved crabwise because of the current running through the narrows between the island and the mainland. On this course he was merely making a return trip right up to the jetty at Thorness.

The headlong flight had been without much reason. His objective had simply been to get Andre away from Geers and all that he represented in cold, efficient care and ruthless questioning.

Now he had time to think up a plan. But not much time. The sea was getting perceptibly rougher. They were hitting a swell. Foam frothed here and there on the crescents of the heaving water ahead. He made up his mind.

He turned the rudder to port and headed straight into the current. Emergency made his memory crystal clear. He could see this grey, misty waste of angry water as it was in the rare calm of a summer's day. He remembered the haphazard pattern of shoals, rocks and islets which had made the area forbidden territory to any sailor except a few crab fishermen even before the Admiralty cordoned it off as a rocket range.

Fleming was not unduly worried about crashing the boat. It

wasn't capable of more than ten knots and was as manoeuvrable as a coracle. Though the half-hearted light of a winter's day was already lessening he felt sure that the noise of breaking waves and the swirl of foam would give him all the warning he needed of danger.

What he wanted was something a bit larger than a collection of rocks where maybe a long-deserted crofter's cottage or bird-watcher's eyrie existed. Such places were built to resist wind and cold; they were as strong as the rocks from which they were made. They would give him a breathing space while he thought out the next move. Not for the first time in his life he half-regretted acting precipitately.

A flurry of sleet hit him in the face. The gust of wind which accompanied it shook the boat, and a little water burst over the side, wetting Andre's face. She cried out and lifted her hand to brush away her matted hair. The touch of her hand on her forehead made her moan again.

Fleming opened the throttle still more. There was no point in conserving petrol. He had got to get her out of the boat before the storm grew worse or before nightfall. He wasn't certain which would come first.

For a full hour he sped northwards, straining his eyes and ears for a sign of land. There was nothing but the howl of the increasing wind and the expanse of the spume-flecked sea. Then, unmistakably, he heard the uneven roar of water crashing on to rocks and shingle. The sea became less broken, turning into a sullen, greenish swell. Beyond the broken mist a dark grey bulk loomed up—much darker than the twilight grey of the sky.

He throttled down and veered to starboard. With the currents and sporadic gale-force winds he had no real idea where he was. He had no intention, even now, of landing on the mainland, right into the arms of some official or meek and law-abiding citizen.

He steered a course a generous forty feet from the breaking waves. He tried to tell himself that he recognised the coast as one of the islands he had visited for recreation back in the summer, but he knew it was just self-persuasion. In such conditions all these islands looked much the same. All he could be certain of was that it was an island, a small one. Many gulls, disturbed by the noise of the boat as they settled down to roost for the night, wheeled around, with their piteous calling. Gulls preferred islands.

The rock face sloped abruptly downwards at the point where the boat veered round until it was almost east of the land. Where the rocks met the water was a tiny beach, or rather a steep stretch of rounded stones, not more than twenty feet wide.

Without hesitation Fleming steered straight for it, running the boat half out of the water. There was a vicious jerk and the sound of tearing timber. The lower section of the boat had been stove in.

Fleming jumped over the side, feeling for a foothold. Then he caught hold of Andre and lifted her out. He laid her gently down on the stones above the water line and returned to the boat. He manhandled it round until it pointed seawards. Water was gurgling in fast. Tying the tiller midway, he set the throttle at full. The boat shot crazily away, the nose already down and the thrashing screw almost out of the water. He did not wait to see the boat go under; he lifted Andre once more and clambered as fast as he could to the higher ground beyond the stones.

There was a distinct track where the ground provided some shallow soil where coarse grass and stunted heather struggled to live.

Fleming was not surprised about this. He had expected it. For just at the moment the boat had swung towards the beach he had seen a dull yellow light a few hundred yards behind and above the landfall.

From the track the light had shape. It was a narrow vertical chink between some patterned curtains.

He did not care who lived there. Coastguard, radar operator, rocket trajectory observer, recluse. The main thing was to get warmth and help for the girl. She was now as lifeless in his arms as when he had first grabbed hold of her at the edge of the cavern pool.

2

COLD FRONT

THE Azaran Embassy was easily identified in the long row of Edwardian houses whose bed-sitter occupants liked to claim that they lived in Belgravia, while in fact the postal number was Pimlico. It was noticeable because its decaying and crumbling stucco had been repaired and given a coat of glossy cream paint. It also displayed a gaudy flag and a highly polished brass name-plate.

The interior was luxurious. The Ambassador's study was furnished with that refinement of taste and air of luxury possible only when money hardly matters. And Azaran, over the past few years, had floated to superficial and temporary prosperity on the small lake of oil British geologists had tapped beneath the desert.

Colonel Salim, Azaran's accredited representative to the Court of St. James's, had been the military strong man of his country's revolution. He had worked hard to make himself indispensable to the idealist whom fate and intrigue had made President, and his reward had been the best diplomatic post the President could offer. As a matter of fact, Azaran did not bother about the status of embassy in any other European country, but Britain, for the time being, was master of Azaran's economy.

Salim enjoyed living in the West more than he enjoyed switching from force to diplomacy. He was a hard man and something of a genuine idealist, but he had forgotten his religious precepts sufficiently to enjoy alcohol and he had tempered his fierce racial beliefs enough to develop a taste for Western women. Much more, he had been impressed with the practical uses to which Europeans put their wealth. In his country, wealth had to be gaudily displayed. But in the West it was exploited to buy something infinitely more desirable: power.

It was the prospect of unlimited power which kept Salim restlessly walking around his study on this grey winter's evening. He was getting rather soft with good living and a desk job. Fat was growing at his hips and in the jowl of his swarthy, handsome face. But he was still reasonably young. It was not merely vanity which told him that he was still impressive.

He turned eagerly when a manservant entered and announced, with a bow, that a Herr Kaufman wished to see him.

"Show him in," Salim ordered. Quickly he sat down at his desk and opened a file of papers.

The servant returned with the visitor. Kaufman was tall, and rigidly erect. Salim recognised him as a soldier; probably a Nazi junior ex-officer or N.C.O., possibly in a crack S.S. regiment. Salim did not mind that. There had been the occasion, back in 1943, when he had confidently assured Rommel's emissary that, when the time was ripe, he would bring the Azaran army over to the German side.

"Herr Kaufman," he exclaimed, extending his hand. "Take a pew." He was rather proud of his mastery of the English vernacular. It inspired a friendly attitude he had found.

Kaufman bowed slightly from the waist and smiled. His light blue eyes, enlarged by the thick lenses of his rimless gold spectacles, were appraising everything on the desk and around the room.

He continued smiling as he deferentially murmured that he had been ordered by his superiors to wait on the Ambassador.

"By Intel," nodded Salim. "What else were you told?"

Kaufman stared back unblinkingly. "Nothing else, your excellency."

Salim offered him a box of heavily chased silver. "Smoke?"

The other withdrew a case from his inner breast pocket. "These, if you don't mind." He selected a small, almost black cheroot and lit it.

Salim got up and walked across the room to a table where some photographs of Azaran were displayed.

"Interested in archaeology, Herr Kaufman?" he asked. "We are particularly rich in relics: Greek temples, Roman arenas, Turkish mosques, Crusader's castles, British anti-tank traps. They've all had a go at us." He turned and eyed Kaufman. "And now Intel. Your employers are taking a deep interest in my small and harmless little country."

Kaufman puffed out a cloud of smoke. It eddied over Salim, who made a gesture of distaste. "And if my employers are indeed keeping their commercial information up to date? As routine, of course. Is this important to you?"

Salim lowered his voice. "It's not unheard of for business interests to finance a breakaway state. And we propose to break with the British oil interests, Herr Kaufman. Their field has not been a very exciting one. We believe you will have more to offer than oil."

Kaufman thoughtfully shook the ash from his cigarello. "Our collateral?" he enquired.

Salim rubbed his hands together. "Let's be frank. You're a trading organisation. Probably the biggest commercial undertaking ever known. Just what cartels and groups are involved no Western government has been able to discover. Holding companies, secret understandings, private agreements, patent monopolies, offices registered in small and tolerant countries. But why need I tell you all this? You know it. You also know that with the Common Market and the increasing tendency for Governments to co-operate, the Intel organisation will find it harder to pursue its private way. Nobody very much likes such a successful enterprise."

"This may be true," Kaufman agreed.

"Your registered offices are in Switzerland," Salim went on. "I read with interest the other day that both the Canton and Federal Governments are getting impatient over income tax matters. They hint at laws enforcing investigation of accounts and so forth. Your directors seem usually to meet in Vienna, capital of a tolerant and non-committed country. But Austria would not, could not, afford to ignore pressure from her powerful neighbours. You are, in fact, an organisation without a home."

Kaufman seemed unimpressed. "We have offices in at least sixty countries. And influence in as many."

"The offices are merely trading posts, innocuous and politically negligible. Your influence is in jeopardy."

Salim crossed to the map of the Middle East which was spread across half the rear wall of the study. "That little area painted red is my country. It could be the home sweet home for the headquarters of Intel. No interference. In return just some expert help for our own plans."

Once more Salim sat down. "What do you know of Thorness?"

Kaufman pondered for a moment.

"Thorness?" he repeated, as if the word meant nothing.

Salim made a gesture of impatience. "I have information that you have long been in touch with the British Government's experimental station at Thorness. Unofficially, of course. I believe that you could even explain an unfortunate fatality to one of the scientists there, named Bridger, but no matter. I mention it to show that I am not without knowledge of your current activities."

"They are no longer current," growled Kaufman. "The station has been virtually destroyed. The computer and everything associated with it were blown up and burned. That, at any rate, is what I have so far ascertained."

"Blown up?"

"That is correct."

Salim was non-plussed. His Court of St. James's manners disappeared as he waved away the cloud of Kaufman's cigar smoke. It was as if some latent violence in him had exploded.

"Please refrain from burning those filthy things in here. If you wish, go to the toilet and smoke there."

His visitor obediently stubbed out his cigarello. He seemed impervious to insults. "No thank you," said Kaufman after he had carefully extinguished all the burning remains. "But if you wish the interview to end . . . ?"

Salim glanced at the file on his table. Everything had suddenly changed and what was expected of him now was something which he understood. Action. He re-read the copy of the appreciation of the situation he had dictated a few days earlier. A smile hovered round his mouth. The gods might after all be working in their mysterious way for his benefit, even with this Thorness debacle.

"There's a Professor Madeleine Dawnay at the station," he said. "I am offering her a post with our Government's biological research department immediately. And there's a Dr. John Fleming."

"A difficult person, Herr Doctor Fleming," muttered Kaufman. "It would not surprise me if he was involved in this tragedy for the British economy."

"Indeed," said Salim thoughtfully. "Anyway, you will agree

that he has a brilliant mind. I am informed that in fact he was the man who supervised the construction of the computer."

"That is true," agreed Kaufman. "Fleming has an astute and imaginative mind. He is disliked by most of his colleagues."

"But the Government of Azaran would like him," Salim murmured. He was quite calm again, almost silky. He smiled at Kaufman. "Indeed, it is my belief that my President would confirm his offer to Intel only on the understanding that it was a package deal, as they like to say over here; the package including Fleming. As a loyal employee of Intel, you have some ideas?"

Kaufman withdrew his cigarello case, thought better of it, and carefully replaced it in his pocket. "It would be difficult, costly," he muttered. "If my theory about sabotage is correct Herr Fleming will already be under arrest."

"Your directors undoubtedly prefer facts to theories," Salim observed. "Perhaps you should return to Scotland and continue your investigations. Phone me regularly to report progress. Guardedly, of course. Remember I am a diplomat."

Kaufman stood up, bowed stiffly, and took his leave. "You may rely on me, your excellency," he said.

As he neared the cottage Fleming moved more cautiously. Anxious as he was to get Andre under shelter he had no intention of walking straight into the arms of the enemy. He shifted off the narrow track and approached through the unkempt garden at the side.

It was a typical crofter's home of the Western Isles—ugly, squat, but solid. Wooden shutters suggested a cosiness inside. It was a broken shutter which had allowed the lamp light to stream out.

Fleming sidled up to the window. The tattered cretonne had been carelessly pulled across the tiny panes. Inside he could see a man sitting at a table. His pale, ascetic face had a simple youthfulness about it which was denied by his shock of greying hair and the criss-cross lines around his eyes. Fleming judged him to be in his forties or maybe fifties. The polo-necked sweater he wore was good but very old. His expressive hands were gesticulating, his long fingers grasping a pencil which he waved in the air in a to-and-fro rhythm, and he was talking, evidently to himself.

Fleming pressed his face closer to the glass to look around the rest of the room. It was a jumble of old, heavy furniture, and there were books everywhere. But there was no one else. The unpainted door on the far side was shut tight. Fleming felt satisfied that this was a reasonably safe refuge. He knocked loudly on the heavy oaken door.

A chair scraped on bare boards and a rather high-pitched bleating voice asked who was there. The door remained closed.

"Let us in, please," Fleming bawled as loud as he could. "It's urgent!"

A bolt moved protestingly in its runners. There was the click of a latch and the door opened a couple of inches.

"Who are you? What do you want?" A grey eye peered into the gloom.

Fleming pushed the door with his shoulder. "Just let us in first, uncle," he said. "Explanations later."

The man let the door swing open. He stood aside as Fleming strode in. He peered suspiciously but hopelessly at the unconscious girl in Fleming's arms.

"You're not a nephew of mine," he said uncertainly. "And I'm nearly sure I've never met the young lady."

He shut the door with a little fatuous, old-maidish gesture of resignation.

"No," agreed Fleming, crossing to the stone fireplace where a peat fire smoked sullenly but warmly. "Uncle's an old runic greeting." He laid Andre gently on a sofa drawn close to the fireplace.

The man's eyes lighted up with interest. "Runic, you say? I've never——" His voice tailed away.

Fleming removed his soaking coat, and threw it on a vast and half-collapsing easy chair. "Can we stay for a bit?" he asked.

The man hovered around helplessly. "I suppose so," he said without enthusiasm. "Where have you come from?"

Fleming was occupied in removing Andre's coat, pulling gently at the sleeves so as not to touch her hands. "The sea," he said shortly. "By boat. It's gone now. Smashed, I hope."

The man poked at the logs, sending up a cascade of sparks. "I must confess I find you difficult to understand," he observed.

Fleming straightened up and grinned. "I'm sorry. We're a bit flaked. Tough weather for a sea trip."

The other man was looking at Andre. He sort of shivered as he saw the shapeless, purplish flesh around her fingers.

"What has happened to your friend's hands?" he enquired diffidently, as if ashamed of ungracious curiosity.

"She burnt them. Touched some high voltage wiring. You haven't anything hot, have you? Soup?"

"Only out of a tin." The man drew a deep breath, ashamed of his attitude. "I'll get it. You must forgive me," he went on, smiling almost boyishly. "It's just you were so unexpected. My name's Preen. Adrian Preen. I—er—write." He glanced longingly at the table with the sheets of large, scrawling writing. "I'll get the soup." He went through the rear door, closing it carefully behind him.

Andre shuddered, moaned, and opened her eyes. Fleming knelt down beside her. "How do you feel?" he whispered.

Her eyes were vacant, but she was able to turn her head and look at him. She even smiled. "I'm better now," she murmured. "My hands throb. What has happened?"

"We're running away," he said, caressing her hair. "We started running two nights ago when we bust up the computer. Remember?"

She frowned and shook her head. "Computer? What computer? I can't remember anything."

"It'll come back," he assured her. "Don't worry your head about it." He got up and crossed to the table, glancing at the manuscript. "Sir Gawain and the Green Knight," he read aloud. "This is a rum do. I hoped for a shepherd, but we've found a sheep. Wonder how he manages to make a living with this stuff?"

He was interrupted by the click of the latch and he stood away from the table. Preen returned with a couple of steaming bowls on a tray. He grabbed a stool and placed the tray on it alongside Andre. "Condensed tomato, I'm afraid," he said apologetically.

"That'll be fine," Fleming said. He took a spoon and began feeding Andre, who sipped hungrily at the thick, red liquid. "What's the name of this island?" Fleming went on to Preen. "Soay?"

"It's just off Soay and very much smaller."

"Then you're on your own?"

Preen nodded. "And at your mercy." Hastily he apologised. "That was crude of me. But you were a surprise, you know.

236

Anyway, I'll leave you and your friend to enjoy the soup. Might I enquire your name?"

"Fleming, John Fleming." He did not volunteer Andre's.

"I ask only out of courtesy," said Preen mildly. "Since I'm your host. You'll have to stay here, naturally. There's nowhere else to go. That's why I chose this island."

"But why isn't really answered, is it?" Fleming suggested.

Preen hesitated, looking embarrassed. "I came because it's safe, or comparatively so. I used to protest against the Bomb and so forth, but I got tired of exposing lunacy and decided it was more sensible to opt out."

Fleming gulped down the last of his own soup. "That makes three of us," he grinned. "But when the bombs drop and you're the last oasis of life and learning how are you going to ward off the pirates, all frightened, starving, and full of radiation sickness?"

With an air of conspiratorial triumph Preen walked over to a heavy old chest which served as a window seat. From it he removed a short automatic rifle.

"Splendid," laughed Fleming. "We'll sleep safe tonight. I take it that we can all doss down somehow and get some sleep? It's been a busy day."

Preen showed unexpected resources. He had his own bed in the shelf alcove beside the fire. From another cupboard he produced heavy wool rugs. Andre was tucked in, the fire was made up, and Fleming wrapped himself up and lay down on the floor beside the sofa. Preen shot the bolts on the door and turned out the paraffin lamp. Fleming vaguely heard the indeterminate noises of his host undressing and going to bed before a sleep of utter exhaustion swept over his brain and body.

It had been three hours before the continued absence of Geers and Fleming aroused misgivings, and a Marine Commando launch went to the islet to investigate.

By the time action could be taken to locate the fugitives night had fallen and the weather had become almost impossible.

Geers, ill with his miserable wait on the island and sick with apprehension about the repercussions in London, sat at his desk drinking a hot toddy and blusteringly ordering Quadring and Pennington to do something. But he could not put off for very long the unpleasant task of phoning Whitehall with news of the latest debacle.

The Minister of Science took the call himself. He remained completely silent while Geers babbled on about the bad luck of the whole business in general and the unforgivable treachery of Fleming in particular. The great man's silky comments before he hung up were worse than the most sarcastic reprimand.

"Most unfortunate," he said softly. "You have my complete sympathy in a situation where you seemed to be surrounded by incompetents and traitors. You may leave it to me to put the best construction on it to the Old Man. He's unusually disturbed about all this, which is so uncharacteristic. Not going to Chequers. Staying at No. 10. And you know how he loathes the place since it's been done up. I do hope I can get his P.A. Such an excellent buffer when the P.M.'s in one of his captious moods. Well, good-bye. Keep in touch."

The Minister did get the P.A. He could be more forthright with him. "Just had a call from Thorness, Willie," he said. "They found the girl, and then the bloody fools promptly lost her. Now Fleming appears to have abducted her. So romantic, isn't it? Geers has bawled futile orders to every R.A.F. and Navy station from Carlisle to Scapa. I suppose masses of ships and planes and little men with radar sets are now rushing about like mad. Met. reports Gale Force 9, and storms of both the moisturised and electrical variety. The pursuers won't have much luck, and I don't feel this is a situation where praying for miracles would be listened to. But officially, Willie, I'm asking that you'll tell the Old Man that we're leaving no stone unturned, exploring every avenue. You know, the usual pap. Oh, I've decided to send Osborne back to Thorness so we get some coherent facts, and also to broach something else that's cropped up. He put up a bit of a black so he'll be all the more anxious to please. He's a sound chap at heart."

Osborne was sent for in the early hours of the morning and despatched to Thorness at first light by air. He was in Geers' office by noon. The Director had grabbed a few hours' sleep on a make-shift bed in the night duty officer's room. For the first time in his life he was conscious of looking dishevelled and grubby. He had disliked Osborne from the start. The fact that the man was still entrusted with a job which was nothing less than a check-up on his own efficiency made him dislike him still more.

"No news from the searchers, of course," questioned Osborne, taking a chair without invitation.

Geers shook his head. "We'll just have to wait and hope. It's my fault," he mumbled. "I should never——"

"It doesn't really matter whose fault it is," said Osborne kindly. "It's happened. How's Madeleine Dawnay?"

Geers looked at him suspiciously, wondering about this new topic. "Much better," he replied. "The electrical burns she got from the computer weren't in themselves particularly bad. It was using that damned enzyme formulated from the machine. Or rather some error her morons made in compounding it. Fortunately Madeleine had the mental power to check it and see the mistake. From then it was easy: a miracle cure which will revolutionise our burns units and indeed all plastic surgery. One last priceless benefit from that machine the vandals have smashed."

"I'm glad—about Madeleine, I mean," said Osborne. He paused thoughtfully. "There's nothing more for her to do here, is there? Now the computer's wrecked?"

Geers shrugged. "Nothing much left for any of us," he said. "I wonder where the devil Quadring's got to? He should have some news of what's happening. Good or bad."

Osborne ignored this. "We've had a request for her from the Azaran Government."

"Who?"

"From Colonel Salim, in fact. The Azarani ambassador."

"No, I mean who have they asked for?"

"Dawnay, whom we've been talking about," said Osborne impatiently. "A formal request passed to us last night via the Foreign Office. They want a bio-chemist."

"What the hell for?" Geers demanded. Then, resignedly: "It's up to her, if she wants to go. I've other things to worry about."

"Ask her," Osborne replied. "And either you or she can phone the Ministry. Don't defer a decision too long. These little oil states love protocol. Mustn't suggest discourtesy by ignoring their enquiry."

"All right," grunted Geers.

The phone rang and he snatched it from the cradle. He listened to the brief message and then replaced the receiver, smiling with relief and satisfaction.

"They've located some wreckage. Splintered wood and so on. Registration number on one piece. It's the boat Fleming took; no doubt of that. No sign of bodies so far. Take some time for them to come up, of course. They hadn't a hope in hell." There was no tinge of regret in his voice. Geers was not mourning the presumed death of two colleagues.

"Whereabouts was the wreckage?" Osborne enquired.

Geers glanced at some figures he had jotted on his memo pad during the phone call. "They give Victor Sugar 7458 as the approximation." He went to the wall map of the Thorness rocket lanes and prodded with a finger at a spot on the grid lines.

"About there. A little south from Barra and east from South Uist. Shoal water. Only someone as crazy as Fleming would have risked it in such bad visibility. But the Navy will go on looking, just as a routine formality."

The two men sat in silence for a time. "I'll see if the canteen can manage some lunch," said Osborne. Geers nodded. He made no move to accompany him.

It was a day of abnormally high temperature for so early in the year. The air was saturated with moisture and the mist turned to a steady rain over the land. Out at sea visibility went from bad to worse. Even for Western Scotland, the weather was breaking every kind of record. Fleming normally ignored the climate, but now he found it oddly in tune with the melodrama of the crisis at Thorness.

Clambering around the island, he heard the occasional impatient whoop-whoop of a destroyer's siren and the regular throb of dieseled launches cruising slowly. Once or twice raucous voices cursed cheerily as the search parties tried to find some humour in their boring, pointless task.

He had told Preen he needed exercise and would collect firewood. He had said nothing about the possibility of a major search for Andre and himself. Preen was patently anxious not to enquire too closely into what the whole escape was about, though Fleming suspected that a man who had been a C.N.D. marcher would not have ignored Thorness or the possibility that a man and a girl fleeing for their lives on a winter's evening might be connected with the place and with nefarious reasons for getting away from it.

But Fleming was not really worried about Preen. The streak

of anarchy in the man's make-up practically guaranteed that he would not pompously blether about a citizen's duty and so forth. By almost fantastic good fortune they had found a well-nigh perfect ally.

Fleming was far more preoccupied about Andre. He suspected that even her formulated constitution, free from the defects of heredity which were the birth-wrong of every human being, could not battle against the poisonous sepsis in her hands. Somehow he would have to get skilled help for her.

All that day the patrol boats cruised off the island. Late in the afternoon the mist thinned sufficiently for a couple of R.A.F. helicopters to nose around. Fleming was outside when he heard them. Alarmed, he ran back to the cottage. He grabbed a couple of green logs which were smoking on the fire and doused them in a rainwater butt at the back door.

"The choppers may sweep over here," he explained quickly to Preen. "Though I doubt it; a bit tricky to mess around in lousy visibility at zero feet with this hunk of granite in the way. Still, there's no future in arousing their curiosity with a smoking chimney."

Preen mumbled something incoherent and retired to the ingle nook with an obscure volume of Middle English texts to annotate. He had done his best to suppress his misgivings about the continued presence of his visitors, but he left Fleming in no doubt that he would be glad when they were gone.

Andre was sitting placidly on the sofa. She had gone out with Fleming after the makeshift lunch Preen had devised and walked a few steps. The effort had quickly tired her, and she seemed afraid of the loneliness. Fleming carried her back to the cottage.

He was getting more and more worried about her; not only was she physically exhausted and in severe pain but her mind seemed to be more or less a blank. He had noted how she seemed to be unable to make any spontaneous effort except for the basic ones of walking, drinking and eating.

Preen had rustled up some boiled sweets and when he had offered her the tin she had simply stared at it, not recognizing their purpose. Fleming had put one in his own mouth and sucked it noisily before she got the idea.

Now, with one ear alert for the sound of the helicopters, Fleming sat beside her, his arm protectively along the back of the sofa and his hand touching her shoulders. "What do you remember of all that's happened?" he asked gently.

She gave him the look of a bewildered child. "It's all jumbled," she murmured. "I ran. Then I fell. In water."

She tried to clasp her hands and drew in her breath sharply at the stab of agony.

Fleming got up, rummaging on the mantelshelf above the half-dead fire for some scissors Preen kept there among a conglomeration of useful articles. "I don't think these rags I put round your hands last night were a very good idea. There's a lot of suppuration. I'll have to cut them away."

With almost feminine gentleness he began to cut into the material, trying to ease it off. He bent over her hands so she could not see them, and he talked quickly to help her ignore the pain.

"Before the running—you remember nothing?" he asked.

She spoke hesitantly, not only because she was searching for memories but in the effort to prevent herself crying out at the throbbing darts of agony. "There was a camp, a kind of camp, with low concrete buildings and huts. We were there, and lots of other people."

Fleming had got most of the matted linen off one hand. What was revealed wasn't pretty. "The machine?" he asked. "Do you remember a machine?"

"Yes," she said, nodding to herself. "It was big and grey. There was always a low hum, and often a lot of clicking. Those were the figures emerging. Everything was in numbers." She frowned and her mouth puckered, as if she was going to cry with frustration. "It's the numbers I can't remember."

"Good," said Fleming. "We can get along without the numbers. They don't mean anything any more to you or anyone. Those numbers were evil; they——"

He stopped abruptly. The bandage on the other hand had come away easily—too easily. A whole crust of matter came with it. Underneath there wasn't pink, healing flesh, but the ominous purple of necrosis. He could not recognise gangrene, but he had some idea about septicaemia. He bared Andre's arm past her elbow. The sleeve of her dress could not be pushed further up. The arm was swollen, and the main artery stood out dark on the white skin.

"Preen," he said quietly. "Just come over and look at this, will you?"

Their host unwillingly laid down his book and walked across. He glanced down and then abruptly shut his eyes, swaying a little with nausea.

"My dear!" he whispered, "how can you stand it?"

Fleming got up and took Preen across the room to the window. It was quiet outside, with the familiar mist eddying back in whorls from the sea. No helicopter engine marred the silence.

"I hate asking you for another favour," he said, "but could I borrow your boat?"

"Why?" Preen demanded suspiciously. "Where do you want to go with it?"

"To the mainland."

"It isn't seaworthy enough."

"All right, to Skye then," said Fleming impatiently. "I could arrange a meeting on Skye."

"You want to find a doctor, I suppose? Bring him here? That poor girl's hand. . . ." He swallowed down another surge of nausea.

"Not a doctor, something better. I'll not bring anyone here; I promise you."

Preen rather sullenly agreed to loan the boat. Once the decision was made he was anxious for Fleming to go. The sooner he went the sooner he'd be back. And then perhaps he could see some possibility of getting rid of his visitors so that he could be left alone in peace.

He accompanied Fleming down to the little beach where his launch was kept under the shelter of a leaning rock. A jerry-can of petrol stood close by. While they prepared the boat for sea Preen tried to apologise once more for his attitude. He said he would do his best to look after the girl.

"Fine," said Fleming with more optimism than he actually felt. "I shouldn't be gone more than twenty-four hours at the very most. Now, if you can brief me on the course for Skye."

Preen gave a landsman's vague instructions. "The current and what wind there is are always north-west. If you keep heading that way you'll pick up the light buoys at the entry to Loch Harport in under half an hour. I always beach at the end of the loch, where there's a little hamlet with a general shop."

"How far from there to Portree?"

"Over the hills not above ten miles; much longer if you manage to go by road, but you might get a lift in daylight."

Fleming glanced at his watch. "I'll walk," he said. "My torch still has plenty of life in it. Should make it well before dawn."

He did. He hung around the outskirts of the little town until people were moving around and it was safe to go to the airport without attracting attention. He got a snack there after checking that the next flight for Oban wasn't due to take off for half an hour.

Then he went to a phone booth. Thorness was an unlisted number and the local exchange was manually operated. He thought he noticed a hesitancy when the operator repeated the number and asked what number he was calling from. It was a risk he had to take. Unless the local police were very quick off the mark and unless Quadring was even quicker in alerting them he'd be away on the plane before anything happened.

He knew, of course, that calls to Thorness were monitored at the station as a matter of routine. In the present crisis this was doubly certain. He had to hope that the tapping was just the usual tape recording for checking later, and not some super snoop who sat in a cubicle eavesdropping on everyone.

Rather to his surprise the call went through in under a minute. He recognised the P.B.X. operator at the station.

"Professor Dawnay," he murmured as quietly as he could. "Professor Madeleine Dawnay. Sick quarters."

"She may be in her room. I'll check."

The operator's voice was in the usual impersonal and efficient tone. Fleming listened closely for any tell-tale click of an extension coming into circuit. There was none.

"Dawnay."

He was surprised how mannish her voice sounded as she gave her name. But he recognised her all right.

"How are you, Madeleine?" he asked.

He heard her intake of breath, and half-speak exclamation his name. It was no more than the J sound. She repressed it instantly. Fleming smiled.

"I phoned to say I hope you're in the pink as it leaves me at present," he said lightly. More slowly and distinctly he went on, "but I'm worried about one health matter. What does one do for burns? You are so expert on them. Not for me, you understand."

For a second or two he thought she had hung up. But eventually she said quietly. "Where?"

"Oban. Solo by B.E.A. I shan't have too much time before I must catch a return plane."

"You're a fool," she said calmly. "But as soon as I can. In the airport building."

His flight took barely twenty minutes. He had to wait nearly an hour before Dawnay arrived. He saw her get out of a taxi while he stood looking out of the window in the men's lavatory. He noticed a second car behind hers, and he waited to see who alighted from it. There were three passengers: a middle-aged couple and a small boy, with a couple of suitcases. So that was all right. She hadn't been followed.

He walked leisurely into the foyer and studied a travel poster. "You're mad to come," he heard her whisper behind him. "But I've got the stuff."

He half turned round and nodded to a hot drink machine in a deserted corner. They walked over to it.

"Tea, coffee, or cocoa?" he asked, handing her a drinking carton, while he fished in his pocket for coins.

"It all tastes the same," she smiled. She took the carton and at the same time passed a little white cardboard box to him. He slipped it in his pocket before he pushed the coin into the slot.

"Thanks," he said. "It's the healing enzyme this time, I hope. Not the one that nearly polished you off."

Dawnay sipped her drink and made a wry face. "They call it coffee. . . . Yes, this lot is all right, I'll guarantee that. It's the original formula the computer gave when she was burned the first time. You remember how perfectly it worked. Sepsis overcome in hours; renewal of the nerve fibrils and lymphatics complete in under three days. How is she?"

Fleming got himself a drink. "Not too bad, except for her hands. I must get back. I don't want a dead girl on the premises."

She glanced at him, amused. "So you think of her as a girl now, do you? But you were mad to come here," she repeated. "I don't know exactly what's doing back at the station, but the search is certainly still on."

He glanced at his watch. "Got to be going," he apologised.

"And thanks for the stuff. Talking about madness, you're pretty crazy to be doing this for me; I'm an enemy, or didn't you know?"

"No, I didn't," she answered. "As for doing it for you, I'm doing it for her. She's mine too, don't forget. I made her!"

They walked together towards the departure bay when the public address system announced the flight for Skye and Lewis.

"I don't expect I'll be seeing you again," she said. "I've been offered a new job. No point in staying at Thorness now this Andromeda project is over. It should be quite an experience, new faces, new tasks."

"Where?" he asked.

"In the Middle East, one of those places all sand and oil, but little else."

Fleming wasn't particularly interested. "Best of luck," he said vaguely. He impulsively bent down and kissed her on the cheek. She seemed girlishly pleased.

Fleming passed through the doors to the airport apron. There seemed to be only four or five other passengers—all entirely innocent looking.

He was unaware of a middle-aged man, discreet in black homburg and tweed overcoat, who had been standing beside the magazine kiosk, reading the *Times*. He lowered the paper when Fleming handed his ticket to the B.E.A. girl for checking. Once Fleming had passed from the building the man hurried towards the road exit. The chauffeur in the car parked there immediately started the engine . . .

GALE WARNING

FLEMING did not get back to the island until late that evening. He had to wait until darkness before he dared launch the boat which he had heaved up on to the shingle in a small inlet of the loch. The rain poured down remorselessly all the way back, but he was in high spirits and drove the little boat full out. The speed wasn't much, but the noise was considerable. He was so excited about getting back that he did not care whether any search vessels were around to hear him and investigate.

He burst into the cottage with a yell of greeting. Preen was sitting talking to Andre. Her appearance alarmed Fleming. Her face, even in the lamplight, was almost putty coloured. But at the sight of him she stood up and stumbled across to him, throwing herself against him, her arms held high to protect her swollen hands.

"Easy, easy," he whispered to her, clasping her gently. "I've got the repair kit. You'll soon be okay." Over her head he grinned at Preen. "Everything in order. Not arrested or even questioned. And I didn't tell anyone about you!"

Preen was visibly relieved. "I'll get you something to eat while you do whatever you can with her hands . . . An ointment, is it?"

"I suppose you could call it that," Fleming agreed, helping Andre to the sofa. "But a special kind. The only good thing I know of that came out of our inter-galactial tuition. But the less you know about that the better, in case your honest soul should ever be taxed by our lords and masters. You can take it from me that your forebodings about a pretty corpse are over."

He took the little box from his pocket. "Enzymes—a glorious little ferment of living cells, all ready and willing to build anew."

Preen shook his head, bewildered. He went to the kitchen

and opened yet another tin of soup. Fleming began immediately on the treatment.

The almost transparent jelly-like material spread quickly when it came in contact with Andre's unnaturally hot, mutilated flesh.

She watched him carefully, without any vestige of a memory that it was she who had programmed the computer to produce the formula, or had interpreted the stream of figures on the output recorders.

Fleming removed her shoes and carefully tucked a blanket around her, placing her hands on a folded towel. "Sleep if you can, my pretty," he murmured. "The pain will ease, slowly but steadily. And in the morning. No pain. You'll see!"

She wriggled lower on the sofa and smiled at him like a trusting child. Obediently she closed her eyes.

All the way back to Thorness, Madeleine Dawnay brooded on the offer of a job in Azaran. Essentially a lonely woman, she had aways immersed herself in work as an anodyne for the subconscious unhappiness she felt about her lack of sociability and attractiveness. Her synthesis of living cells, culminating in the development of a female organism which vied with, and in some ways surpassed, natural womanhood had been a triumph which she believed justified her life and held out entrancing promise for the future.

Then came the burns she suffered from the computer and the terrible mistake in the compounding of the healing enzyme formula so that the injections destroyed instead of constructed. Not only did this experience show her the dangers of believing that the half-understood equations from the computer were benign and valuable, but the hovering of death had frightened her more than she would have believed possible.

It was wonderful, of course, to discover that the fault in the enzyme had been entirely in human minds, and that the formula was literally the gift of life. But there remained the nagging suspicion that John Fleming was right. The intelligence which actuated the computer was not impersonal and objective. It had its own purposes, and they did not seem to include the welfare of man.

In any case all the work was over. The glittering prospect of building a scientific technocracy for Britain had evaporated in the smoke from the computer building. She even felt relieved that the great binary code which had reached them out of space, and on which it was all built, had gone up too. She would be glad to get away from it all, to return to ordinary research.

Azaran appealed to her idealism and her curiosity. Here was a little country, temporarily and superficially wealthy on its subterranean El Dorado of oil, but poverty-stricken in the basic needs of fertile land and adequate food for its people.

As soon as she got back to Thorness, she asked for leave to visit the Foreign Office and set off at once for London.

The minor official in the Middle East Department was inclined to dismiss Azaran as a comic opera state. He described the President as a man of dying fire. The revolution which had put him in power and ousted the dynastic ruler just after the war had been a bloodless affair of little international consequence. The President had hastily assured the British oil interests that he would maintain all agreements provided some slight adjustment of the royalty arrangement could be made. This was done after the usual haggling. The President had announced that the revenue would be used to improve the lot of his people.

The desert would blossom through irrigation. Schools would be built. Roads would open up trade. Hospitals would stamp out the diseases which killed one child in five and cut the expectation of life to 32 years. The schools, the roads, and the hospitals had gone up. But the desert remained desert, and now the oil was giving out.

"There's water," the official went on; "a French company sank artesian wells. To the north there's a subterranean lake with more water than the oil deposits to the south. Trouble is the surface. Not even sand; mostly stones and rock. You can irrigate it but it won't grow crops."

"The erosion of several thousand years can't be put right with a bit of water," said Dawnay quietly. "There'd be no official objection to my going?"

"None," the official said, "so far as the F.O. is concerned, that is. We're anxious to maintain our friendly relations with these people. They're a small nation, but any friends are valuable nowadays. The terms of your engagement are naturally not officially our pidgin. You'd be interviewed by Colonel Salim, the ambassador here. He's a slippery customer, though probably it's largely Arab love of intrigue. Anyway, he's probably just the go-between for the President."

Dawnay left the interview, her mind made up. She would take the job if the terms were reasonable. A taxi deposited her at the Azaran Embassy fifteen minutes later.

She was ushered into Salim's office without delay. Rather to her surprise, he seemed to know all about her career and he discussed her work with considerable intelligence. More or less as an afterthought he mentioned the salary. It was fantastically large and he heard her slight gasp.

"By British standards the income is high," he smiled, "but this is Azaran, and one commodity we have in plenty at present is money. The Europeans—doctors, engineers and so on—who work for us need some compensation for absence from their homeland and the fact that of necessity the job is not for life. In your case we had in mind a contract for five years, renewable by mutual arrangement.

"But it's the work which would interest you. We are an ancient nation stepping late into the twentieth century, Miss Dawnay. Eighty per cent. of our food has to be imported. We need to have a programme of vision and scientific validity to make our country as fertile as it is rich." He hesitated. "For reasons that will become clear shortly this will become more and more vital for our future, even for our very existence."

Dawnay hardly heard his final words. The old excitement about a problem of nature which challenged the ingenuity of the mind had taken hold of her.

"Colonel Salim," she said quietly, "I'll be proud to help. I am free to go as soon as you wish." She smiled a little ruefully. "As you may know from what seems to be a comprehensive survey of my background, I have no private ties, no relatives, to hold me here. And for reasons I can't go into, my recent work is now completed."

Salim gave her a large, warm smile. "I shall telephone my President immediately," he said. "I know he will be deeply grateful. Meantime, there are the usual international formalities to be seen to—inoculations, vaccination, passport, and so forth. Shall we say the day after tomorrow—about 10 a.m.—to complete the arrangements? I can then discuss the actual time of your departure."

Dawnay agreed. The decision made, she was anxious to be

gone. She telephoned Thorness and had her batwoman pack her few belongings and put the cases on the train. Ruefully she told herself that apart from a mass of books in her old room at Edinburgh University she owned nothing else in the world. Nor was there a close friend to whom she had to say goodbye.

She went shopping the following morning, getting a Knightsbridge department store to fit her out with tropical kit. She reduced the salesgirl to despair by approving the first offer of everything she was shown. It was all done in a couple of hours. The store agreed to deliver the purchases, packed in cases, to London Airport when instructed.

Next morning she found a doctor and had her inoculations. They made her a little feverish and she rested in her hotel room that afternoon and evening. Promptly at 10 a.m. on the following day she presented herself at the Azaran Embassy.

Salim greeted her courteously, but he was ill at ease, half listening to a powerful short-wave radio from which, amid considerable static, a stream of Arabic spluttered quietly.

"Splendid, Professor Dawnay," he said eventually, after glancing cursorily at the passport and inoculation certificates. "Here are your visa and air tickets. I have provisionally booked you on the 9.45 flight the day after tomorrow. Will that be suitable?"

Before she could reply he sprang up, rushing to the radio and turning up the volume. He listened attentively for a couple of minutes and then snapped off the switch.

"That was the announcement of our freedom," he said dreamily.

"But you *are* free!" Dawnay looked at him in surprise.

He turned to her. "Political freedom is a matter of paper and ideals. Real freedom is a matter of business. We have at last broken off our ties with your country; we have renounced all our oil and trade agreements." He indicated the radio. "That is what you heard." He smiled at her again. "You can see why we need the right people to help us. I shall be returning to Azaran myself as soon as diplomatic affairs are cleared up here. We want to remain on friendly terms with Britain; with all countries. But we need to be independent in the best sense of the word. So you will help us!"

Dawnay felt slightly disturbed at this sudden turn of events. Throughout her career she had studiously avoided politics, be-

251

lieving that scientists were above party and national factions, their duty being to the welfare of mankind. "I hope I can do something," she murmured politely.

Salim did not appear to be listening. He began frowning over the documents she had handed to him. "No yellow fever inoculation?" he queried. "Surely you were notified that it's necessary?"

"I don't think so," she replied. "But I can have it done today."

He stood up and smiled ingratiatingly. "I can do better than that. It so happens that the embassy doctor is here this morning."

He pressed a switch on his intercom. "Ask Miss Gamboul if she can manage another yellow fever inoculation," he told a secretary.

There was a pause and then a man's voice replied that Miss Gamboul could do so.

Again the sense of misgiving prodded Dawnay's brain. For a moment she could not identify the reason. Then she found it. A woman doctor was not usually described as Miss. She dismissed the suspicion as trivial, putting it down to Salim's imcomplete knowledge of English.

While they awaited the doctor's arrival he came round and leaned against the desk, close to Dawnay. "Tell me about a colleague of yours, a Dr. John Fleming. I believe he worked with you at that Scottish research station. Is he still there?"

"I can't say," she answered shortly.

"I heard one report that he was dead."

"I'm afraid I can't tell you anything about him." Her tone was all he needed to tell him that Fleming was alive, but he did not react to it. He looked up instead at the opening door.

"Ah, Miss Gamboul!"

A woman in a white coat had entered without knocking. She was dark-haired and rather attractive and—one could put it no closer than that—somewhere in her thirties. She had a flawless skin, and a good brow above fine dark eyes; but she did not look in the least like a doctor. Even in her white coat she gave an impression of sensuousness and haute couture; Dawnay felt sure that she was more used to being called Mademoiselle than Miss.

And yet there was a surprising degree of professional intelligence and seriousness in her face. Dawnay did not like the hardness in her eyes nor the thin red-pencilled line of her mouth, but most of all Dawnay did not like people to be enigmatic. She noticed that the nails on the hand which clutched a napkin-covered white dish from which the base of a hypodermic protruded were varnished bright red and the ends were pointed. Dawnay glanced automatically at her own stubby, close-cut nails. Neither doctors nor scientists, she felt, should allow themselves such unhygienic luxuries as long nails and lacquer.

"Now, Professor Dawnay, which arm would you like punctured?" Her voice was business-like; she had a strong French accent, Dawnay realised with satisfaction.

Stifling her instant dislike of the woman, she said she would prefer to be injected in the right arm. She removed her coat and pushed up the sleeve of her blouse.

Mademoiselle Gamboul dabbed her upper arm with a wad of spirit-soaked cotton wool. Dawnay looked away when the needle went in. It was badly done and the clumsy jab made her wince.

Salim had not moved away. He watched the inoculation as if fascinated. He began to talk rapidly. "You'll have every facility for your work when you get to our capital, which is called Baleb. We have recently completed building the laboratories. Anything you need——"

His voice seemed to thicken, and his swarthy face, looking down at her still bared arm, became hazy.

She tried to fight off the sense of dizziness.

"Can—can I have a glass of water?" she faltered. "I can't be as fit yet as I thought . . ."

Her head slumped forward. She felt the hardness of the rim of a glass pressed against her lips and she drank some water. Her vision cleared a little, and she saw the red fingernails around the glass.

From an immeasurable distance, yet clear and menacing, came Salim's voice again.

"Now, where is Dr. Fleming? If you know, you will tell us every detail. Now, I repeat, where is he?"

As if it were some other woman talking, Dawnay heard herself meticulously describing her meeting at Oban airport. Word for word she repeated her conversation with John as if she were reading from a play script. Her memory was crystal clear. And she could not stop until she had explained every detail of the meeting.

Salim laughed. "So that is how a truth drug works." He looked at Dawnay with interest.

Janine Gamboul nodded. "Sodium amytal. It'll work off in five or ten minutes. She'll remember nothing. Tell her she fainted with the yellow fever injection or whatever it was. And see you get her on that plane."

She took off her white coat, revealing a dress which had indeed come from Paris, and a good deal of herself as well. Although she was no longer a girl, the skin of her throat and the upper curves of her bosom looked as young and smooth as her face. She seemed completely relaxed and at ease. She perched on a corner of the table and looked at Salim with a mixture of malice and amusement as she lit a cigarette and slowly and delicately inhaled and exhaled. Salim watched her with something like admiration until she spoke again. "Repeat what you've heard to our man Kaufman," she told him without any effort at grace. "He is unimaginative but resourceful. Tell him that speed is vital. And this girl Fleming has with him. The one he got the medicament for. Tell Kaufman to bring her too."

"But she is nothing," protested Salim. "The man's mistress, one presumes. What do we need with her? We can supply reliable girls once Fleming's out in Baleb. They'll help to keep him happy."

"Nevertheless," said Gamboul, "we will have her."

Salim obediently lifted the receiver of the telephone. It took some time to locate Kaufman. The hotel where he had reported he was staying said that their guest was out tramping; the receptionist volunteered the information that Mr. Kaufman was a great one for the open air and the rolling hills of Scotland. Salim cut her short and grunted that he would ring again. He had no wish to leave his number.

When eventually he got through and Kaufman's guttural voice answered the extension to his bedroom Salim talked rapidly. "We have reliable news. An island off an island near an island." He stopped, aware of the ridiculousness of his words. "A moment, I have written down the names of these places of which I have never before heard. Ah yes, there is a place called Skye?"

"Of course," grunted Kaufman. "I have been. Our friend was seen taking a plane there. But no information."

"And near this Skye is Soay." Kaufman opened a map and located the word which he could pronounce no better than the Ambassador.

"Good, you have it," said Salim. "Near this Soay there is perhaps a smaller island?"

"I'll need a more detailed map," came Kaufman's voice. "I know there are several. We had better end this call, I think. You may leave things to me."

"I hope so. I have done my part. Now it is up to you." Salim replaced the phone. Kaufman folded up the map and considered.

First he made his plans for a discreet survey of the off-shore islands around Skye. He put in a couple of calls to Glasgow to enrol some assistants whose co-operation for adequate reward had been tested on some previous matters. Then he moved to Portree. There he hired a powerful little launch on the pretext of photographing sea birds. The well-paid owner did not question Kaufman's statement that he specialised in taking flash-light photos by night of their roosting habits. Bird watchers were all queer—but profitable.

The lonely peace of Preen's island pushed time into the background. Fleming mentally noted the fact that it took two days for Andre's hands to start building new flesh; on the third there was no need for bandages.

Life by then had settled down into a rather pointless round of waking, preparing scratch meals from Preen's store of canned and dehydrated food laid down in quantities literally to outlast a war, arguing over a game of chess, and gently helping Andre's memory to re-discover the threads of life.

There was little opportunity to go out even to check the fish nets Preen had laid down in rocky inlets, but one still, misty day Andromeda went down alone to the small beach and when she came back to the croft she was looking puzzled.

"The mist is going back into the sea," she said in her slow, vacant way.

Fleming did not believe her and she never had an opportunity of proving it, for the weather changed again to an interminable frenzy of storm and gale. There seemed to be no end to the restlessness of the sky and sea. When they listened in on Preen's transistor the forecast invariably included gale warnings, and the weather was so wild throughout the northern hemisphere that it was usually mentioned in the news bulletins. Andre continued to look vacant and confused and began to grow a little clumsy.

But there was a sense of impregnable security within the cottage while the wind howled and battered outside. The tension which Fleming had felt at first whenever the door rattled violently or something banged outside had eased to a pleasant fatalistic calm.

Consequently he was quite unprepared one night when, as he was quietly playing chess with Preen and Andre was half-lying on the sofa staring at nothing, the door cracked loudly and immediately burst open. He sprang to his feet, knocking over the chessboard. Three men were grouped in the doorway. They were thickset, brutal and wild-looking. The water streamed from their oilskins and their tousled heads.

The tallest of them took a step inside, jerking his head to the other two to back him up. He never took his eyes off Fleming, so that he did not see Preen open the chest, grabbing his automatic rifle from inside it.

"Get out! Get out of here!" Preen bleated, prancing from side to side. His anger at this new invasion of his isolation made him oblivious of danger.

Fleming had moved back to protect Andre. She clung close to him, watching wide-eyed. "Better do what the gentleman says," Fleming advised the intruders.

The leading man stepped backwards, bumping into the two behind him. They half-stumbled as they hit the doorposts. Suddenly the leader dug into his oilskin pocket. In a flash he was pointing the snout of a Luger at Preen.

"Look out!" yelled Fleming.

Without taking aim, Preen fired a burst. Five or six explosions of high velocity bullets reverberated round the room. Glass from the window tinkled on the floor. The man with the gun collapsed without a sound, his mouth agape, his eyes still fixed straight ahead. One of the others screamed like a child and staggered drunkenly into the darkness, collapsing outside. The third simply fled, his footsteps crashing along the stony track to the sea.

Preen had dropped the gun at the force of the recoil. But he started to charge after the third intruder, his mouth working in frenzy of anger. "Hold it, Preen," Fleming yelled. "Don't go outside. There may be more."

Preen did not seem to hear. He was still in the light from the open door when a gun barked from the darkness. Preen stopped dead in his tracks, spun round, and fell to his knees, groaning.

"Take this," said Fleming, picking up the rifle and thrusting it into Andre's hands. "If you see anyone, point it at him and pull this." He crooked her finger round the trigger.

Then, crouching low, he ran outside and sprawled beside Preen. He waited for a moment for bullets to come spurting out of the dark at him, but nothing happened. All he could hear was Preen's agonised breathing. "All right," he said, "you're not dead. I'll get you inside and patch you up."

He started dragging him towards the door. He paused while he heaved the body on the path out of the way. The man was quite dead, like the one outside the cottage. He motioned Andre to put down the gun and she helped him to get Preen on to the couch.

Fleming dragged the other body out over the step and then shut the door. The bolt was useless but the catch still held. He paused to get his breath before he examined Preen.

Blood was spreading through his sweater below the armpit. Fleming cut the material away and pulled the shirt aside. The blood was not spurting. But there was a neat hole at the side of the chest and another more ragged one below the shoulder blade where the bullet had come out.

No blood was coming from Preen's mouth, so Fleming felt sure that the lung had not been pierced; the worst was a chipped or broken rib.

"You're not badly hurt, Adrian," he said. "I'll put on a pad to staunch the bleeding; and then we'll use the old magic treatment. Just leave it to your old Professor!"

He made Preen as comfortable as possible, talking optimistically about the enzyme. His optimism seemed to convince the watching, worried Andre, though he himself did not really believe in it. The little which was left after Andre's treatment would doubtless tackle sepsis and re-create the surface skin. It could not deal with splintered or broken bone, nor with any internal injury.

He resigned himself to the fact that in the morning he would have to go over to Skye and get a doctor. And he would have to let the police know that a couple of corpses were lying around.

Meantime there was the puzzle of who the thugs were. When Preen fell asleep and Andre was dozing in the easy chair he cautiously crept outside and looked over the dead men with the aid of a flashlight. They looked even uglier in death than they had in life. Both carried wallets, but the contents were money only; no driving licence, no envelopes or letters. The absence of identifying items was in itself suspicious. His mind went back to the time he and Bridger had been shot at when they had taken a day off from building the computer. Bridger had clearly known what the attack was all about, and badgered by Fleming he had impatiently snapped out the word "Intel", regretting it as if he had said too much.

It had seemed ridiculous at the time to link a secretive but perfectly legitimate world-wide trading cartel with gunmen lurking on a Scottish moor. But after Bridger's murder the word had always had a sinister flavour in Fleming's mind.

That a commercial enterprise should use strong-arm tactics to obtain secrets of the kind Thorness could provide did not really surprise Fleming once he had accepted the situation. It was in accord with his conception of the rat race of individuals and nations to amass wealth and exert power. That was why he did not find it difficult to accept a theory that Intel was behind this abortive attack, though the motive remained a mystery. If the information they had obtained from Bridger had been even superficially right the brains behind Intel must be aware that the individuals counted for nothing without the machine they served. Not even Andre could provide saleable information.

Not even Andre——. Fleming very rarely displayed fear, but like any intelligent man he often felt it. He felt it now, and Andre was the reason. One of the assailants had got away. He would no doubt be back sometime with reinforcements, and they would come prepared for a shooting battle. He had no wish to die himself; but he dreaded far more the plan Intel might have for the girl. It was another reason why he would get help.

He took Preen's boat for Skye at dawn. He phoned for a doctor from the first house he found with a telephone, explaining that the patient was suffering from a shot wound and adding that there were also two corpses to be picked up. The doctor informed the police before he set out. By then Fleming was well on the way back.

Fleming had the mischievous pleasure of shouting out, "I'll come quietly!" as a boat-load of police arrived at the cottage door later in the day.

It was all very sedate and polite. They treated Andre and him with deference, hardly knowing what it was all about. They let him remain beside Preen until the doctor had made his examination and reported that there was little wrong, but an x-ray would be needed to check for bone injuries. Fleming noted with amusement that the doctor could not get his eyes off the tiny circles of young healthy flesh already growing around the bullet wounds.

"And this happened only last night?" he kept muttering.

They were taken down to a police launch where Preen was laid in the stern, comfortably wrapped in blankets. A constable was left behind to watch over the two bodies, which would be picked up later when the C.I.D. from Inverness had made their usual on-the-spot checks.

Fleming and Andre said goodbye to Preen when they disembarked on Skye. Their involuntary host seemed almost distraught at the parting. "You must come again," he said.

"If we ever get out of the Tower, we certainly will," Fleming grinned.

Expressing soft Highland apologies, the station police sergeant said that he would have to put his prisoners in a cell when they got to Portree.

"It's forbye a murder case, ye'll be understanding," he said. "But it'll be the Inspector to decide on a charge, if there's to be one. I'm going to permit the young lady to be with you. I'll have your word of no trouble, sir?"

"Of course," said Fleming. "We're grateful for your hospitality."

They had to wait in the cells for a couple of hours. The sergeant's wife sent in two steaming plates of mutton stew. Both ate ravenously. It was good to eat a proper meal after Preen's diet of soup and vegetables.

Then Quadring arrived. He was smiling. But not with any touch of triumph. He seemed relieved to see them both alive and well.

"You've given us one hell of a chase, Fleming," he said. "You are all right, my dear?" he added, looking hard at Andre. "Well, as you may imagine, your bosses are very excited at the way you've both turned up, particularly Dr. Geers. I'm afraid I have instructions to take you to London right away. There'll be a Transport Command plane touching down presently."

"I expected that," Fleming replied. "But I hope you'll get your sleuthing powers working on just who the gentlemen were who visited us last night."

"Any ideas?" Quadring asked.

Fleming hesitated. "Nothing definite," he answered.

The failure of Intel's attempt to kidnap Fleming and Andre had caused consternation as much as anger in Kaufman's mind. He had learned to be completely unprincipled in the service of whoever paid him, but he had a distaste for personal violence. He had tried to explain this to a war crimes court back in 1947 when he sat in the dock along with the riff-raff from one of the minor camps. He had vehemently protested that he had never laid a hand on a single Jew or gipsy prisoner; his only connexion with the extermination section had been to supply them with his carefully tabulated lists of outworked and over-age prisoners. The court had been obtuse; they had sentenced him to seven years, reduced by his perfect behaviour to five.

The charming man who had then offered him a confidential post with Intel had been the first person to appreciate the virtues of Herr Kaufman's life. "We like to use men like you," he had said.

And now he had badly let down these considerate and generous employers. Two men shot dead and a third getting out of the country as fast as he could. His frantic report over the phone to Salim had not been an experience he would like repeated. Unkind things had been said; even threats. Salim had appeared to be repeating the words of someone else in the room, judging from the way he constantly paused. Finally Kaufman had been told to be at Oban airport and await a caller. A director of Intel coming from Vienna. Kaufman had never previously met any executive above district manager.

Nervously he hung around the airport building. An hour passed, then another. Beads of sweat glistened on his close-cropped head despite the coldness of the day. He wanted to run away. But he knew he dared not. For one thing it would be disobedience of orders; for another he was Intel's employee for life; there had been so many things he had done on their behalf which were in the crime dossiers of the police of a dozen countries. . . .

"So you are here. . . ."

It was a woman's voice. Kaufman spun around and saw Janine Gamboul. He grinned with relief. So they were going to use the old trick of feminine allure to get hold of Fleming.

But he had to be cautious. "Excuse?" he said gutturally. "You are . . . ?"

She ignored his question. "You are Kaufman. Where is Fleming?"

"But Colonel Salim said a director from Vienna. . . ." Kaufman mumbled.

She cut him short. "So naturally you imagined a man."

"You are . . . ?" he stuttered. Then he was all deference and politeness. "I am sorry, I did not realise."

"I repeat, where is Dr. Fleming? Or have you frightened him off?"

"He is at the same place. The little island. It was not my fault. Two men were killed. And I am not a gunman."

She walked towards the airport café, not troubling to see whether he followed. He rushed ahead to open the door for her. When they were seated at a table in a quiet corner she lighted a cigarette and drew in a deep lungful of smoke.

"We shall arrange things better this time," she murmured. "We must have Fleming quickly. Nothing is more vital."

"May I ask why?" he muttered.

She gazed at him with impatient contempt. "To help us with some equipment. He has some special knowledge we need." She gave him a cold smile. "It's really the result of your commendable activities on behalf of the company. Stupid you may be, but you are loyal and energetic. I think you should have been told before."

She dropped her voice to a murmur. "When we heard that a message had been received from space you recall that you were told to make contact with Dr. Denis Bridger, Fleming's partner.

You did well, Kaufman. From Bridger you got the specification for making a computer to interpret the message."

"Nothing ever came of it," said Kaufman mournfully. "Bridger—er—got himself killed."

"So you think nothing came of it?" she laughed. "We have been building a copy of that computer; in Azaran. Only now we need a little expert advice. Salim has got Professor Dawnay, but she was only indirectly involved. She'll possibly be useful. But Fleming will be essential."

Kaufman felt relieved. Even happy. He ventured to light a cigarello.

"So you see, Herr Kaufman," Janine Gamboul finished, stubbing out her cigarette, "this time there must be no mistake in enrolling Doctor Fleming on our staff."

4

SQUALL LINES

THE attendants in the Palais des Nations at Geneva told one another that there had not been such a smoothly running international conference for years. Russians nodded cheerfully as their interpreters repeated the heart-felt views of an American delegate. Even the French were inviting ideas for co-operative effort. In fact, the whole thing was almost boring.

The reason was that the subject under discussion was the weather. Everyone could agree that it was undeniably bad. As gales blew indiscriminately over East and West, and abnormally heavy rainfall was prevalent throughout the Northern hemisphere, no sensitive nationalist could find an excuse for blaming his neighbour.

A few nations, imaginative enough to realise that weather control was within the realms of possibility, had sent scientists as well as meteorologists to Geneva in the hopes of getting some agreement about methods and policy before haphazard experiments began. Britain was among them. That was why the Ministry of Science had despatched Osborne as an *ex officio* delegate.

Osborne had gone, disturbed in mind. Despite inter-departmental briefs which had been circulated to draw attention to climatic phenomena for which there was no precedent, this weather conference seemed really of just academic interest—one of those United Nations' activities which kept a lot of people happy and did no one any harm. Osborne wondered whether the trip had been arranged as a preliminary to a transfer to some innocuous department like Met. as the result of the suspicions of his complicity in the Thorness business.

The Minister had been remarkably considerate about the whole thing. Security officers were still interviewing personnel, and Osborne's assistant had become very nervous and timid. Osborne had brightly insisted that if they both stuck to the story that the assistant had accompanied him to Thorness on that momentous night all would be well. It was perfectly normal for a senior official to go around with his P.A. Rather unwillingly the assistant agreed to stick to his story. Osborne suspected that real pressure by the sleuths, or the simpler method of putting the young man on oath, would exact the truth. It was another reason why he would have preferred to remain in Whitehall to watch for a weakening of his assistant's resolution and to give moral support.

Once in Geneva, he decided to make the best of it. Whatever foulness the winter was producing elsewhere, in the Alps it just meant more than the usual amount of snow. Heavy night falls were followed by brilliant sunshine with clockwork regularity. The lake lay ice-blue in the brightness; the famous fountain spurted high in the sky, its spray in rainbow colours. The clean, snow-cleared streets were alive with delegates and their relatives enjoying themselves between sessions.

When he looked through the tall windows of the rooftop café at this pleasant scene he thoroughly regretted the time spent in the close and over-heated conference room. But Professor Neilson's paper had not been without interest. These Americans certainly got down to bedrock when there was a problem to be solved.

Osborne had left before the discussion began—with its inevitable pointless questions which were really statements. He was lazily watching his café filtre drip into the glass when a woman approached his table. She was not young, but looked intelligent and pleasant.

"Mr. Osborne?" Her accent was American.

Osborne stood up. "Yes," he answered. "I don't think I know—."

She smiled. "I'm Professor Neilson's wife." They shook hands and Osborne pulled out the adjoining chair. She sat down.

"I'm afraid you've missed your husband's paper," he began. "He's just finished reading it. Everyone was most impressed. He'll be out soon; the discussion should be almost over."

She did not seem to be heeding what he said. "Mr. Osborne," she said quietly, "I think my husband would like to talk to you. Not about the conference." She glanced towards the door where a crowd of delegates were moving around the foyer. "If you could possibly wait till he comes. I'd rather let him tell you what it's about."

"Of course," Osborne said. "Meantime, may I order you something?"

She nodded. "Some coffee, please."

When Neilson arrived he looked round carefully, then sat down and addressed himself without any preamble to Osborne.

"I suppose my wife has left it to me to tell you. I badly want to talk. I'll come to the point. How much do you know about an outfit called Intel?"

Osborne took time to decide on his answer. "They're a big international trading consortium. Very big."

"Sure," agreed Neilson, "they're big. The thing is: are they reputable?"

"I don't really know," Osborne said cautiously.

"Mr. Osborne," said Mrs. Neilson. "This morning we had a cable from our son. We haven't seen him for two years. All the cable said was 'Will meet you at the café Nicole in Geneva one evening this week, Intel permitting' It's the first clue that he was even alive we've gotten since the Christmas before last."

"But you knew more or less where he was and what he was doing?" Osborne suggested.

Neilson gave a short laugh. "He went after a job in Vienna two years back. A postcard said he was okay and not to worry. That's all."

"What sort of job?" Osborne asked.

"Well, I guess that as he graduated from the Massachusetts Institute with a Ph.D. in electronics, it'd be a job in that line."

"I believe Intel have an office here, or certainly in Zurich. Have you enquired?"

"Of course," Mrs. Neilson replied. "They said they knew nothing about the staffs at the firm's offices outside Switzerland. That's why I persuaded my husband to ask you for information."

"But why?" Osborne demanded.

"Because you're a friend of a friend of my son's," Neilson said. "John Fleming. Jan brought him home a couple of times when Fleming came to the Institute on an exchange set-up with the Cavendish Laboratory at Cambridge. They were great buddies. And, of course, we know Fleming became a key man in your Ministry's programme."

"I don't think there's anything I can do to help you," said Osborne woodenly. "We've lost touch with Professor Fleming. . . ." He paused, embarrassed, and then went on hurriedly, "but I'm not returning to London till the day after tomorrow. Perhaps I could meet your son? If he says in his cable that he's coming this week it must mean either this evening or tomorrow."

The Neilsons were grateful. They invited him to have dinner with them at the café that evening, and, if Jan didn't turn up then, the following evening as well.

That evening Mrs. Neilson insisted on going to the café by seven. "I'll sit in the front part," she told her husband; "then he'll be sure to see me. We can go into the dining room later."

She ordered a kirsch and was taking the first sip when he materialised out of the dusk and sat down beside her without speaking; a pale, serious young man, very much on edge. She was shocked by the way he had aged and got so lean; and by how nervous he seemed. He kissed her on the cheek, but he pulled his hand away when she tried to clasp it.

"Please don't make us conspicuous, Mom," he muttered. "I'm sorry if that hurts you. But—well, you see, I've good reasons." He stubbed out a half-smoked cigarette.

"Surely, son," his mother said, trying to smile. "I understand. But at least you're here. I can look at you. It's been so long."

The love in her eyes hurt him. "Mom," he began, hunching towards her across the table. "I've got to talk, and I may not have much time. You see, I'm on the run. No," he tried to smile, "I'm not a criminal. The shoe's on the other foot. The crooks are after me."

He paused when a waiter came for his order. He sent the man away for a large Scotch, and then started to talk, hurriedly and a little incoherently, as if time was running out.

Soon Neilson arrived with Osborne. The two men had met just outside the café. Neilson greeted his son with delight, thumping him on the back and grinning happily. "We'll celebrate this with the biggest steak the Swiss can think up. And champagne." He remembered Osborne was standing quietly beside them.

"My apologies, Osborne," he said. "I'd like you to meet my son . . . Jan, Mr. Osborne is a friend of Professor Fleming."

Osborne had just extended his hand when a youth with a flashgun and a cumbersome plate camera came up.

"Professor Neilson," he shouted at them. "Un moment, s'il vous plait. A picture, please. For the American press."

He bustled around, pushing all four into positions he wanted for the photograph. Jan he had standing between his seated mother and father, Osborne well to one side. Satisfied, he backed towards the café entrance, peering into the range-finder.

"Bon!" he exclaimed. The flash momentarily blinded everyone with its burst of white light.

Simultaneously Jan fell sideways against his father, moaning. The photographer disappeared into the street, and a gentleman who had been reading a newspaper at a table beside the door put on his hat, slid something black and shiny into the breast pocket of his overcoat and walked quite unhurriedly after the photographer.

The Neilsons were bent over their son, but Osborne had seen the careful and methodical movements of the man near the door. He had seen what that black thing shoved inside the coat was, noticing the squat round cylinder of a silencer on the muzzle of the gun. He loped through the door—in time to see a Citroen, its number plate covered in frozen slush, pick up photographer and gunman and cruise away along the lakeside road which led to Vevey and the frontier.

He returned to the Neilsons. "It's no good," he said gently. "They got away."

The Neilsons took no notice. They were isolated by their grief as they awkwardly nursed the body of their dead son, one on each side.

Mrs. Neilson looked helplessly at her husband. "He—he told me he feared this," she moaned. "They've been hunting him for months. They kept him prisoner before that, but he escaped. They made him work."

"Who did?" her husband exclaimed. "Where could he have been imprisoned?"

She began caressing Jan's hair, touching his eyelids. "He said it was in a country called Azaran."

In a discreet house on the outskirts of Berne, Kaufman was compiling the details of the report he had to send his employers.

The gunman stood at the side of the bureau desk, eyeing the bundle of American dollars which he had earned.

"So the pictureman was late," Kaufman said; "he will be reprimanded in due course. But you are sure you killed the Neilson boy before he could talk?"

"He wouldn't talk much after he was hit," the gunman laughed. "But he talked plenty before. To his mother. And she can talk to her husband—and to some Englishman the old man brought with him. He was introduced to the boy as Osborne."

Kaufman sighed. "Osborne. It would have to be. All this killing. I dislike it. One death—and you have to organise another. So it goes on."

He pushed the money to the corner of the desk. The gunman stuck it inside his coat, a cushion for the revolver which lay there.

"Get out of the country right away," Kaufman told him. "As for me, I shall have to return to England."

Andre and Fleming were flown to the R.A.F. station at Northolt to avoid publicity problems at London Airport. A Government car awaited them on the apron and they were driven straight to the Ministry of Science.

The Minister had decided to handle the interview personally, with Geers sitting in to brief him on the technical side. He had a foreboding about questions in the House some time or other about this business if the secret leaked, and he had no intention of having to admit inefficiency. He was also a just man, which was why he had called a solicitor from the Attorney General's office to sit in and watch over the normal rights of a British citizen. His worried mind found a touch of humour there. Was the girl a British citizen? She had no birth certificate; no parents. So far as Somerset House was concerned she did not exist. It was an interesting point if this affair ever came to a legal trial. He fervently hoped it wouldn't.

The Minister greeted his visitors coldly. But he went out of his way to stress that this was in no sense a trial; it was an informal enquiry.

Fleming, untidy and doing his best to disguise the strain he felt, laughed sardonically. "Very informal," he said. "I noticed the informally dressed plain clothes nark hanging around the door just in case I might make a run for it. Ah, and my dear Geers is here as well."

The Minister ignored him and turned to Andre. "Sit down, my dear," he said gently. "You must be very tired. But this is unfortunately necessary."

He sat at his desk and re-read the brief report of the preliminary questioning Quadring had sent by tele-type.

"I'm informed that you are suffering from amnesia," he began, and motioned to Geers.

Geers rose from his chair to the Minister's right and confronted the girl. "Andromeda," he said harshly. "Surely you haven't forgotten the factors involved in the synthesis of living tissue? Do you really mean to tell us you know nothing about the fact that one of the formulae obtained from the computer on which you worked enabled Professor Dawnay to construct living matter in the laboratory? And that the outcome of that work was you yourself?"

Andre looked back at him, wide-eyed but quite calm, with the placidity of a child. She slowly shook her head.

Geers' face flushed with frustration and anger. "You're not going to insist that you can't remember your work with the computer?"

The solicitor coughed discreetly. "I think that is enough, Dr. Geers," he said mildly. To Andre he murmured, "Don't worry to answer all these questions just now."

"I agree," said the Minister, glaring at Geers. "The girl's unfit and distraught. Perhaps we can have her history properly explained to her in a calmer atmosphere."

Fleming strode forward to the desk. "That's the last thing!" he shouted.

The Minister looked at him coldly. "I beg your pardon."

Hurriedly the solicitor interposed. "I think that my professional advice would be that this lady must testify once she is medically fit and has been properly informed of the past. Her evidence would, of course, have to be before a properly constituted Board of Enquiry."

"I could brief her," Geers said eagerly.

The Minister looked at him with hardly concealed distaste. "I would have preferred Osborne if circumstances had been different. In any case, he cannot be brought back from Geneva until tomorrow." He smiled at Andre. "Perhaps you'll wait in the ante-room while we talk to Dr. Fleming?"

Fleming crossed to the door and opened it. He smiled reassuringly at her as she went out.

"Now, Dr. Fleming, why did you abduct this woman?" The Minister's gentle tone had changed.

"That's beside the point," Fleming retorted truculently.

"Then what is the point?"

"That the message from the Andromeda nebulae, and all that derived from it, was evil." Deliberately he forced himself to speak calmly and quietly. "It was sent by a superior intelligence that would subjugate us, and would have, if necessary, destroyed us."

"And because you thought that, you destroyed the computer." The Minister's tone was grim, though the inflexion suggested he was posing a question rather than making a statement. "Yet you seem to be ready to do anything to protect the girl who worked it. Your contention surely involves her in your condemnation."

"The girl is nothing without the computer. The will, the memory, the knowedge—they were all in the machine. You can see there's something lacking in her now that the computer no longer exists—thank God. Something missing in her character. Ask Geers; he knows what she was like . . ."

The Minister ignored the invitation. He had no intention of getting involved in by-ways of ethics when he believed the issue was far simpler.

"I put it to you, Dr. Fleming, that you destroyed the computer and you abducted the girl because she might have told us what happened."

"I took her because she needed to be protected from the people around her." Fleming looked at Geers.

The Minister picked up a sheet of paper tucked into the bulky file before him. "Perhaps you'd care to comment on the fact that Mr. Osborne's assistant, the man supposed to have accompanied him to Thorness on the night of the fire, admitted when questioned late this afternoon that he did not go there."

"You'll have to ask Osborne who he did take, won't you?" said Fleming.

"We shall," the Minister glowered. "In the meantime, Dr. Fleming, you must consider yourself under surveillance. To avoid the necessity of formal arrest and indictment at Bow Street, with all the unpleasant sensationalism affecting both ourselves and you and the girl, I hope you will co-operate sensibly. I cannot force you to be our guest without a charge. But we can arrange very pleasant accommodation."

"So Magna Carta still operates?" said Fleming sarcastically. "If I insist on being arrested, on what grounds could you cook up a charge?"

"Defence Regulations," murmured the solicitor. "The relevant Acts would be——"

"Spare me the details," Fleming interrupted. "I'll come quietly. And where is this—er—hotel for unwelcome guests of the Government?"

"Not too far away," said the Minister vaguely. "It will do you good, or at least the girl will benefit. A glimpse of more spacious days of the kind one pays 2s. 6d. on Sundays to inspect. I'm afraid I can't be more specific than that. The army's been using part of it ever since 1942. It would be best, I think, if you went there right away and both got a good night's rest. You may see things more clearly, even sensibly, in the morning."

The car journey took a couple of hours. Even Fleming could find no fault with the accommodation or service. Someone used to this sort of thing had arranged for every comfort—drinks, clean clothes, books, baths, everything. Andre was as lavishly provided. Fleming was, however, not over-enamoured with the solid-looking maidservants who hovered around. Their white overalls did not disguise their regulation hair styles and their khaki nylon stockings and sturdy black shoes. Fleming had never approved of women in the armed services.

But he found the clumsiness of the 6 ft. waiter who served their excellent dinner amusing. There was something about a policeman which could never be disguised, not even when he was a member of the Special Branch.

Otherwise they were left to themselves in the days that followed. They could walk as much as they liked around the vast parkland. Fleming noticed that Andre seemed to be growing increasingly vacant and that she stumbled quite often even on the smooth grass. He also noted that the chain link fence was the usual Government type, precisely like that round Thorness. The old gatehouse at the entrance to the main drive had been visibly transformed into a guard room. The guard carried an automatic rifle.

One afternoon Andre was taken away. Geers had arrived and wanted to talk with her. She spent many hours of the ensuing day with the scientist. He did his work well. Andre emerged thoughtful though still curiously unmoved. She told Fleming that she accepted that all Geers had said was true, but it was like the life outline of some other person. It struck no strong chord in her own memory, although she realised that she had been involved in the destruction of the computer.

"What will they do to us?" she asked when they sat in the lounge, idly watching some inanity on T.V. late that evening.

Fleming was quiet for a time, marvelling that the moronic woman simpering at the camera had just won a spin dryer for confirming that the Amazon was a large river. "I imagine they'll wait until poor old Osborne joins us here," he said eventually. "Then they'll have a trial in camera. He and I will be beheaded at the Tower, Osborne a perfect gentleman to the very end. As for you"—he found he could not go on, and they sat without speaking for a long while in the flickering half-light of the telly.

Suddenly there were footsteps outside, heavy ones, on the parquet flooring.

"Who's that?" Andre asked. Both had grown accustomed to the flannel-footed silence of the minions who watched over them.

"Could be Osborne," Fleming suggested. "It's about time he joined the party. Nice if they let us all spend our last days together."

But it wasn't Osborne. It was Kaufman. He was dressed in an over-long black overcoat. In one hand he held a black homburg, in the other a briefcase. He was momentarily taken aback at the sight of Fleming and Andre.

"Excuse please," he murmured, shutting the door quietly. "I had expected to meet Mr. Osborne. . . ." He nervously licked his lips and then put on a big smile. "I was informed he was due here this evening. Instead I have the honour of greeting Dr. Fleming." He advanced, podgy hand outstretched.

"Mein frend Kaufman," mimicked Fleming, ignoring the handshake. "How did you flannel your way into this place?"

Kaufman drew himself up. "I am representing Mr. Osborne's

lawyer. It is all so difficult, this matter. But now I have the good luck. I meet you."

He peered myopically through his spectacles at Andre, still sitting in her easy chair. "And this is the famous young lady!" He crossed to her, bowed, and took her hand, brushing the back of it with his lips.

"You see, my dear, how charming these Viennese are," said Fleming.

Kaufman scowled. "I do not come from Vienna, but from Dusseldorf, mein liebe Doktor!"

"It's not so long since you were taking pot shots at your liebe doctor," Fleming pointed out. "Not you, of course. You get other people to pull triggers and make uncomfortable trips to small private islands."

Kaufman seemed genuinely embarrassed. "I am not a free agent," he said. "I do not act as I would wish."

"Only as your bosses in Intel wish."

There was something unexpectedly sad and bitter in Kaufman's answer. "Some of us are not lucky enough to do the things we would choose."

Fleming nodded. "Why did they send you after us?"

"You have something my directors want." Kaufman was restless. He tip-toed to the window and pulled aside the heavy chintz curtains. Momentarily light swept over his face from moving lamps. At the same time there was the quiet throb of an idling engine and the faint swish of wheels braking on gravel.

"Your client, Mr. Osborne, maybe," suggested Fleming.

Kaufman shook his head. "Mr. Osborne is supposed to be already in this house. No, Dr. Fleming, this is a van. It will stop round the back, in the stable yard." His voice grew clipped and stern. "Now, please, you will both come with me." He partially drew the curtains and pushed open the long, low window.

"Don't take any notice of what he says," Fleming muttered quietly to Andre. "Just go on sitting there."

"Please," beseeched Kaufman. "Last week I have a young man shot dead. A nice young man. I did not even know him. I do not like such things."

There was some noise outside and a trench-coated figure sprang lightly over the sill. He was a thin, sallow-faced youngster hardly out of his teens. His narrowed eyes darted round the room. The gun in his hand was held rock-steady.

"Come on," he ordered in a small morose voice, "it's bloody cold and wet hanging around out there. Let's get going."

Kaufman moved behind the gunman. "We wish to have you alive, Herr Doktor," he said, "but we should be prepared to stretch a point with the young lady." The man in the trench coat pointed the revolver towards Andre. There was a studied movement of his thumb as he spun the bullet chamber. Fleming knew it was a crude theatrical gesture, but a purposeful one. He beckoned to Andre. With her hand in his they crossed to the window.

Kaufman climbed through the window first, turning to help Andre. The gunman brought up the rear, his pistol close to Fleming's back, but suddenly whirled round as he heard the door into the lounge opening. The others were already on the terrace. Fleming stopped dead and looked back.

Osborne was standing in the doorway, gaping at the gunman. Just behind him was a soldier, wearing the scarlet armband of the Military Police.

"What the dickens, Who the devil . . . ?" Osborne managed to say as the soldier pushed him roughly out of the way. But it was too late. The gunman fired—once. Osborne crashed back against the door from the impact of the bullet. The gunman leaped to the window and fired again wildly as he clambered through. The bullet missed the soldier, who had started to rush forward, but sent him sprawling for cover.

From where he lay he blew his whistle for aid, while Osborne collapsed slowly to the ground with his left hand clasped to his right shoulder and a frozen look of surprise on his face.

"What a damned ridiculous thing to happen," he said slowly and distinctly, and then slumped forward.

Outside, in the darkness and the gusty rain, unseen hands grabbed Fleming and Andre. They were picked up bodily and pushed into the back of a van. The rear doors were slammed shut, and the engine started. Then with a scream of protesting tyres the van shot away, rocking so violently that it was impossible for Fleming to get to his feet. The vehicle gathered more speed on the long straight drive to the gates. Fleming heard confused shouts as they roared past the guardroom and on to the highway. Time after time they almost overturned as the driver took sharp turns at full speed, the sideways skids forcing

274

Andre and Fleming to lie flat, bracing their feet against the steel sides.

After a while they settled down to a fast, steady speed. Fleming guessed that they were on a motorway. He cursed the fact that he had no watch, but he estimated that this stretch lasted for half an hour—say forty miles since they had started.

The van slowed, swerved to the right and again there came bursts of speed alternating with abrupt turns. The bumpiness suggested a badly made road or lane.

Gingerly he stood up and with the aid of the futile flame from his cigarette lighter looked quickly round the van. He knew it was just a gesture. The interior was solid metal. The door was secured by the usual lock bars from the outside. There was no aperture beyond a small wire-meshed peep hole at the front near the driver. This was covered.

The van slowed down to a crawl, cruising slowly over uneven ground. It began to bump badly and the tyres made no more noise. They were obviously on grass. Then the van stopped.

There was a pause before the rear doors were opened. Rain was pouring down. Kaufman stood there smiling in the glimmer of a shaded flash light held by someone to the rear. Beside Kaufman stood the gunman.

"Well, Doctor," said Kaufman, "will you be so good as to get out; the young lady as well?"

Taking his time, Fleming jumped down. He lifted Andre out. "Your friend has rubbed out the perfectly harmless Osborne," he told Kaufman. "I wouldn't say that we're harmless, so what's your programme in our case? And where are we?"

"On a disused airfield of our great American allies," Kaufman said. "The runways are enormous and still excellent. We are saving you the unpleasantness of a trial and imprisonment for sabotage. I am sure your Government consider you a traitor." He removed his glasses and cleaned off the globules of rain. "No more time for talking." He seemed almost regretful. "The plane must leave immediately. Come!"

The gunman moved behind Fleming, and Kaufman led the way. Soon Fleming could see the wet, shining surface of an aircraft fuselage.

"Welcome aboard madame—and you, sir," said a woman's voice.

Fleming laughed at the madness of it. The girl at the top of the aircraft's steps was neatly dressed in a dark blue uniform. She was the usual type of air stewardess, trim, neat, and pretty. In the glowing red of the night emergency lights in the cabin Fleming saw that she was oriental. Swiftly she directed her guests to a couple of seats forward, helping them to fasten their safety belts. She completely ignored the man with the gun, who went to the seat across the gangway and sat there, half turned towards them, the gun still in his hands.

Kaufman disappeared through the crew door. The starter motor whirred. First one engine whined, then a second.

"Jets!" muttered Fleming to himself. "Trust Intel to do things properly. No expense spared."

There was no run-up of power. The jets were given full throttle with the brakes on; they sighed down from their crescendo, and then began to whine once more. The aircraft moved smoothly down the runway.

As soon as they were airborne they climbed steeply. The pilot obviously intended to get well clear of the commercial air lanes with their inquisitive radar controls. Soon they were through the clouds and bathed in cold moonlight. Fleming estimated from the stars he could identify that they were heading in a southerly direction.

When Kaufman emerged from the cabin he confirmed this. "We have just crossed the English coast," he beamed. "We are now over international waters. All is well. I suggest you try to get some sleep after the hostess has served refreshments. We shall be landing in about four hours in North Africa."

"Whereabouts in North Africa?" Fleming enquired.

"Of no importance," said the German. "Just for refuelling. The major part of the journey follows. To Azaran."

5

SUNNY AND WARM

DAYLIGHT came long before the aircraft slowly lost height and crossed the Azaran frontier. Fleming, gloomily looking through the aircraft window, found nothing to arouse his interest. The brown-grey land, flat and interminably dreary, stretched towards the horizon where low hills drew an uneven contour. Now and then he saw a blur of dust where a camel train moved along the dark threads which marked the age-old desert tracks. Apart from a few ragged shaped blobs of lighter contours, the pattern of a few miserable houses round a water hole, the place seemed lifeless.

The jet's whine sunk to a hum and the port wing dipped. Below Fleming saw the discs of the top of oil tanks, and not far from them the tracery of derricks. The ground slid closer and a town came into focus, its white buildings brilliant in the morning sun. The aircraft swung the other way, and the horizon dropped past Fleming's window. When the machine levelled off he just had time to note a long grey building, flat roofed and modern. It stood isolated some five miles from the town.

The jet engines picked up power, eased, and faded. They were landing.

A soft heat struck their faces like a muffled blow when they emerged from the cabin. Arab soldiers, in battledress and American-style steel helmets, lounged around with sten guns at the ready. An ancient British limousine, the camouflage paint peeling from its body, drew up beside the aircraft. Kaufman, sweating profusely, hustled Fleming and Andre into the rear seat. He himself sat beside the army driver.

A good concrete road led straight into the town. As soon as they reached the slummy outskirts, where huts roofed with battered corrugated iron clashed obscenely with decrepit but still lovely houses of traditional Arabic architecture the road widened into a badly maintained highway, packed with people. Women, veiled and graceful, led donkeys half hidden under huge panniers. Some men were in Arab costume, but most wore cheap, shabby Western clothes.

The Azaran flag hung from every building. Here and there loud speakers blared oriental music, the discord heightened by distortion. The driver went full tilt into the mob, his hand continually on the horn ring. Past the huge market place, where hundreds were standing around, aimless yet animated, the car swung through the narrow entrance to a large house. Two sentries looked poker faced at the car's passengers as the driver carefully steered the car into the cool, shady courtyard round which the house was built.

Kaufman alighted and spoke some words to an Arab in a neat Western-style suit. Then he disappeared through a doorless entrance. The Arab came across to the car and in careful English ordered Andre and Fleming to follow him. He took them across the courtyard, up some stone steps and through a beautifully ornamented door.

"Wait here, please," he said. He closed the door behind him.

Fleming strolled round the room. It was small but high ceilinged. A series of narrow slits, fitted with modern glass, allowed panels of sunlight to pattern the stone floor. Persian carpets hung on the walls. There were comfortable modern chairs as well as fragile little oriental tables. On one of the latter stood a brass tray with a silver jug and tiny cups. Fleming picked up the jug. It was hot; the aroma of coffee smelt good. He poured some of the thick, syrupy liquid into the cups and handed one to Andre.

"What is this place?" she asked as she sipped the coffee.

Fleming took off his sports jacket and unbuttoned his shirt. "A very hot country," he grinned. "A place called Azaran which seems to be small but likely to be notorious. This is doubtless some pasha's desirable residence. Unless it's Kaufman's."

"He is not a bad man," said Andre.

Fleming glanced at her with surprise. "You sense that? Basically you're right, I'm sure. The trouble is the hard veneer stuck on that lovely, harmless soul of his."

But Andre's attention had drifted away again.

There was a rustle of the hangings in the far corner of the room. Janine Gamboul came towards them. She was wearing a silk sheath dress and managed to look both cool and eye-catching.

"Doctor Fleming?" she murmured, pausing in front of him, unsmiling.

"Who are you?" Fleming asked rudely.

"My name is Gamboul," she answered, turning from him and studying Andre.

"The lady of the house?" he asked.

She did not take her eyes off Andre. "This is the home of Colonel Salim, a member of the Azaran Government. He could not come himself. He is extremely busy. Today is the anniversary of Azaran's independence, and this year the celebrations have a special meaning because the Government has terminated the oil agreements. In case of interference the frontier has been closed."

"A great day, as you say," Fleming said. "And this Salim had us brought here?"

She turned then and looked him over slowly. "I—that is to say, we—had you brought."

"I see. And you—singular or plural—are the flowers-by-wire service, the great Intel?"

"I represent Intel," she said coldly. She looked once more at Andre. "And you are—"

"A colleague," Fleming said quickly.

Janine Gamboul let the ghost of a smile play round her sensuous lips. "You are——?" She asked Andre again.

"We are what is popularly known as 'just friends', in the rather old fashioned and more exact sense of the term," Fleming said. "Her name is Andre. Just Andre."

"Please sit down, ma petite," she said pleasantly to Andre. "I hope you're not too tired from your journey; that you were well treated."

"Not particularly," Fleming answered for her.

"I'm sorry," she said formally. "We brought you here because we think we can help each other. You're on the run from the British Government. They won't get you here, this is a closed country. No extradition."

"That's your version of helping us. Now suppose you explain how we're to be forced to help you?"

She was saved from losing her temper by the arrival of Salim. The ex-Ambassador was in a perfectly tailored uniform, with two rows of medals on his breast. He clearly found life very good indeed.

"Ah, Dr. Fleming," he exclaimed, flashing his white teeth and extending his hand. Fleming turned his back on him. Not put out at all, Salim went to Andre. "And you are Miss——"

"Andre," Janine said.

"Just——?"

Gamboul shrugged. "Si. So the loquacious Dr. Fleming says."

Salim took Andre's hand in both of his. "I'm charmed," he murmured admiringly.

Andre smiled a little. "How do you do," she said politely.

Salim released her hands and threw himself in a chair, stretching his long legs in their immaculately polished boots. "Well, to explanations. Dr. Fleming, we are now a new country. Except for our oil we are under-developed. Not since two thousand years ago, when we were a province with our own rights under the old Persian Empire of Xerxes, have we been anything but a slave state of other people. We need help now we are independent."

"You go about hiring help in a curious way," said Fleming.

Salim waved his hand expressively. "How else could we have got you? The Intel organisation has sunk a great deal of capital here, in the form of industrial and research developments. As the host government we shall benefit. We have engaged a great many progressive and brilliant people—scientists."

"Collected in the same way?" Fleming enquired.

"In different ways. Once they are here they find it worth while. We treat them well. They don't usually wish to give it up."

"Do they have any option?"

"Let us have a drink," Janine Gamboul interrupted. Salim nodded and pulled a bell cord.

"You're a physicist, Dr. Fleming, and a mathematician specialising in cryrogenics," she went on.

"Sometimes," Fleming agreed.

Salim motioned to the manservant who brought a bottle-laden tray to put it down. "What will you have, Janine?" he asked. "We had another young scientist working here—Neilson. . . . What would the young lady and you like to drink? Whisky, or something soft?"

"This is very un-Moslem of you," said Fleming with a small smile.

Salim turned to him slowly and seriously. "I am a modern man," he said without affectation and turned away.

"In that case," said Fleming, "Andre would like some fruit juice if it isn't laced. I'll have a Scotch, neat." Fleming regarded his impassive back. "So Jan Neilson was here? I suppose your intelligence service knows that Jan, Denis Bridger and I were at the Massachusetts Institute of Technology for a spell? It all begins to fit. . . ."

Salim handed Andre and Fleming their drinks. He busied himself with two glasses for Gamboul and himself. "We thought a lot of Neilson; he was very brilliant." His voice was detached, as if he were quoting a hand-out.

"But dead?" Fleming asked.

Salim turned again and stared calmly at him. "Neilson did all the real organisation of our main research project. But he failed to complete it. Even if he had stayed I think he was in a blind alley." He looked thoughtfully at the ice bobbing about in his glass. "So, of course, we had to find a better man."

"To do what?" Fleming found his hand was shaking with anger and fear.

Salim came close to him. "You worked on the Thorness computer. We have one."

"What sort?" Fleming asked, dreading the answer.

Gamboul gave a short laugh. "You ought to know, Dr. Fleming. Your late colleague, Denis Bridger, provided the design. Your other late colleague Neilson built it."

Fleming fought to keep calm. "I suppose you don't really know what you've got hold of," he said at last. "I'll give you the best advice I can: blow it up."

"As you blew up the other?" Gamboul's eyes were dancing with amused triumph. "I'm afraid you won't have the same chance here."

"How do you know that we, that I——"

She waited before she answered, savouring the pleasure of the impact to come. "Professor Dawnay told us."

"Dawnay!" Fleming could only stare at her.

"She came here of her own free will," Salim interposed. "With you and the lady professor we feel we have the needful set-up. The computer Neilson built is to be the basis of all the technology Mam'selle Gamboul's organisation has placed here."

He crossed to the window slit and peered out. The noise of

the crowd was an incoherent accompaniment to the still booming public address system. "Those people out there are emerging from a long sleep," he said with sincerity. "You're a liberal-minded man, Fleming. You will help them to awake and take their place in the modern world."

"Where is Madeleine Dawnay?" Fleming demanded.

"At the Intel research station," Salim explained, "where you will be taken. It is very comfortable, up to the best oil company standards. We may be poor, but we are not barbarians." He drew himself up proudly. "But I must nevertheless point out that you are in no position to refuse to co-operate." He looked thoughtfully at Andre, sitting quietly, complete puzzlement on her face, as she glanced from Salim to Fleming and back again. "We will keep the young lady here to ensure your co-operation."

Fleming sprang to his feet. "No!"

Salim hesitated. He looked towards Gamboul, who nodded. "All right," he said. "We'll leave the young lady with you."

Janine Gamboul put down her empty glass. "We have talked long enough. I'll take them to the research station," she told Salim. "My car is waiting."

When Fleming, his hand on Andre's elbow, passed through the swing doors of the computer building which Gamboul held open, he stopped almost as if he had been hit in the stomach.

The hall was uncannily like that at Thorness, except that the khaki-clad armed guard inside had a swarthy face instead of the cheerful ruddiness of the sentries he had got to know so well in Scotland.

The air was the same—the cool lifelessness of air-conditioning. Through the grey painted door to the computer section the similarity was accentuated. Here was the heavy, indefinable smell of electricity, the pervading hum of a myriad active circuits, the inhuman personality of a room built entirely of control panels.

And there, down two steps it stood—the familiar rectangular mass of steel panelling with its control desk and cathode ray screens.

He moved forward slowly, still holding Andre's elbow. Several young Arabs were working on the machine. In an odd, outlandish way they reminded him of the British technicians he had supervised two years back at Thorness. They were even talking to one another in English—as if it were the natural language for science.

Gamboul called one of them.

"This is Abu Zeki," she said. "Dr. Fleming."

Abu Zeki's eyes gleamed with pleasure. He seemed a sensitive and likeable young man, with delicate Arab features and a crew-cut which gave him a curiously beat-generation look. He too was obviously "a modern man". "How do you do sir?" he said. "I've heard much about you, of course. I am to be your senior assistant. I hope I shall be of use; anyway I can pass on your instructions to the staff." He looked proudly along the control panel of the computer. "We are going to do great things with this."

"You believe that, do you?" Fleming said quietly.

"I'll show you around," Gamboul interrupted, and led them along the endless bays of wiring.

She knew her way remarkably well. She accurately identified every section of the huge machine, though Fleming noted that it was the second-hand knowledge of the layman who was concerned with what things did rather than how they did them. The layout was slightly different from what he had built at Thorness, but the input, the output and the huge memory circuits were basically the same.

They returned to the wide gangway in front of the control unit. "Construction was completed some time back. It was fully programmed. But nothing happened. That is why we need you. It presents no problems to you so far as operation is concerned?"

"Probably not," Fleming admitted. "The layout is superficially different. But in essence it is identical." He gave a mirthless laugh. "It should be. It has been built from instructions in the same message. You know what happened to the Thorness job?"

Gamboul shrugged her shoulders. "We're not interested in what went wrong there. We want this one to go right. We want to build up a centre of production unsurpassed in the world and free from interference, political or otherwise. This machine is to be Intel's brain."

Fleming felt mesmerised by the baleful quietness. He dreaded to see once again the ominous section which made this computer unlike any other man-made brain—the heavy brass terminals nestling in their plastic insulation guards.

He turned to Abu, standing deferentially nearby. "Where is your high voltage output?"

Janine Gamboul looked at him suspiciously. "Why do you ask? What is its purpose?"

"There are two high tension leads extraneous to your control panel. Or there should be."

Abu nodded. "There were, yes," he agreed. "We led them into the end compartment. We did not understand their purpose." He led them down the passageway and slid the grey panel on its smooth runners. Fleming stared at the harmless looking metal shapes. Hateful memories crowded into his brain. He turned to Andre, but to his relief she seemed quiet and unstirred by interest.

"Dr. Neilson considered they were for sensory communication with the memory circuits," Abu said. "So that the operator could have direct contact with the computer's positive calculator relays. He worked out that it should be done visually through this display." He nodded towards a battery of aluminium-sprayed cathode ray screens which were ranged above the terminals.

"I remember!"

Fleming turned at the sound of Andre's voice.

Her eyes were alight with excitement. Fleming felt suddenly sick. Things seemed to be moving remorselessly and inevitably beyond control.

He moved close to her. "You know what this is?" he whispered. "It's what we were running away from."

She did not turn to him. She seemed transported and her eyes remained on the control panel. "Don't be afraid," she murmured. Fleming could not decide to whom she was talking.

He whipped round on Gamboul. "Just blow the whole thing up. Now."

She looked at Andre, and then at Fleming. She began to smile, not concealing her contempt. "Destroy it?" she exclaimed. "We shall control it." Her tone changed. "Now I will show you to your quarters. They are very comfortable. Your old colleague is most anxious to meet you once more—Professor Dawnay."

She led them from the computer building into the cruel heat outside. A soldier immediately came forward and in obedience to a few words in Arabic from Gamboul, escorted Fleming and Andre to a row of bungalows shaded by a few palm trees. Andre was still dazed and walked without speaking.

Madeleine Dawnay was sitting in a deck chair on a tiny, browned patch of grass. Her face was already tanned though she looked gaunt and thin in her tropical clothes. She greeted them both with unaffected joy.

"My dear," she said taking both of Andre's hands in hers, "I'm so happy to see you. Your maidservant has been told exactly how to look after you." She turned to John. "So you're here."

He did not offer any greeting. "I'm here because I was hijacked," he said quietly. "I shan't try to get out yet awhile because of what I've just been shown. But as for you, Madeleine, I'm damned if I can see how you can voluntarily work for this lot."

Dawnay refused to be offended. "It's no use sticking labels on them, my dear. The circumstances are so different. I must say I was alarmed at first. I suspect Salim drugged me in London. I don't know why."

"To find out where I was. You were the only person I told, and they turned up immediately."

She was deeply upset. "I'm sorry," she said miserably, "I'd no idea."

"How did they get you?" Fleming asked.

"By asking me nicely. They've got a most interesting agricultural problem. They want to be self-supporting with food. They've tried all the usual ways of fertilising barren land. But they realise they need a really new, wholly scientific conception. I hope—I think—I can help."

Her unquestioning faith in the goodness of science had always worried him. Their easy comradeship had been strained when she had seen no risks in the first success with her life-synthesis experiments. She was caught in the same unbalanced enthusiasm now.

"Madeleine," he said gently, "if we can't get away from this place without finishing up abruptly dead then surely I can at least warn———"

She looked at Andre, sitting quietly near them, dreaming in the comforting dappled shade from the palm trees. "Who can you warn, John?" she asked. "Who'll listen to you now that they know what you did back at Thorness?"

"So we just stay here and do the thing's filthy work?" he asked bitterly.

She frowned. "My work isn't dirty. I'm trying to help ordinary, mortal people, a good many of them starving at this moment. Salim may be ruthless, but his motives are good. He wants to do something for his country."

Fleming reached for a cigarette box which an orderly had silently placed on a table at the side of his chair, along with some iced fruit. The service, as Gamboul had promised, was very good. He lit a cigarette and then thoughtfully watched the smoke spiralling from the glowing end. "There's one possibility," he said at last. "I can probably get the circuitry right pretty easily. Neilson obviously did a fairly good job, and young Abu Zeki knows his stuff. The computer will work, but it'll depend partially on the information we feed into it. If I make it think I'm for it. . . ."

He paused to sip his drink. "That was my mistake last time. I attacked it, and I couldn't really win. But if I inform its memory circuits that they—Intel and Co.—are really against it, its logical processes will come up with something to defeat them."

"Perhaps by destroying them—and the whole country?" Dawnay suggested.

Fleming nodded. "That would be better than the alternative. Which would be that it would lay down the law wholesale through Gamboul, Salim and the rest of the crooks they're working for."

Dawnay looked thoughtfully across at Andre, who had relaxed in a day-dreaming half sleep. She looked very lovely and feminine.

"And the girl?" she asked.

"I've stopped thinking of her as anyone from, well, outside this planet. She's a virtually normal piece of human chemistry. The danger is when the machine gets her and uses her. I want to stop that whatever else I do or don't do. I've grown rather fond of her."

"Don't sound so sad about it!" Dawnay laughed.

He glanced to make sure that Andre was not trying to listen. "There's more to it than that. Her co-ordination's going. She spends too much time like she is now. And when she moves around it's jerky, like a mild spastic case. I thought at first it was shock or the after effects of her experience, physical after effects of her injuries. But it's getting worse. There's something wrong with the way she was made."

"You mean I made a mistake. . . ."

286

"Not necessarily you," he reassured her. "Something wrong with the programming for the calculations."

He stopped talking. Andre opened her eyes, stretched lazily, and sat up. "What gorgeous sunshine," she said smiling.

She walked, rather jerkily, out of the shade and began to look around. Fleming and Dawnay saw her move near the doors to the computer building. The sentry, lolling against the wall, stepped forward, thought better of it, and let her pass inside.

Fleming jumped up out of his chair. "Why don't they stop her?"

He started to move away, but Dawnay put out a hand to stop him.

"She'll be all right."

"With *that*?" Fleming asked her. "You're mad."

"I'm not mad. Leave her there."

Reluctantly Fleming stayed. They waited tense and alert as the minutes ticked by.

Abruptly the vague vibrationary hum which came all the time from the building grew louder, and there was a rhythmic clicking.

"What the hell's that?" shouted Fleming, jumping to his feet.

Dawnay's exclamation, "It's the computer, it's working," was needless. Both of them rushed across to the swing doors and down the corridor.

Abu Zeki came running towards them.

"What's happened?" Fleming asked.

"I can't say, Dr. Fleming," Abu replied. "The young woman came in, stood looking around, and then sat down before the control panel in the sensory bay."

Fleming pushed past him. The master screen was quivering with wavy bands of light; crazy geometrical patterns shifted across, faded, and changed their shapes.

Seated in the chair at the panel was Andre.

"Andre," Fleming called, pausing in the face of some force which he did not understand but which seemed to paralyse his legs. She did not turn. "Andromeda," he yelled.

Very slowly she turned her head. Her pale face was glowing with joy.

"It speaks to me!" she cried. "It speaks!"

"Oh my God," Fleming groaned.

Abu coughed. "I must go and inform Mam'selle Gamboul of what has happened," he said.

6

CYCLONE

FLEMING watched with misgiving the tranformation which came over Andre. The lethargy and almost childlike innocence disappeared. She was alert and avid for activity; yet she seemed unexcited. Fleming knew that the change was due to the computer, yet this was a different Andre from the robot of Thorness —the changes were indefinable but nevertheless they were there.

He was a little comforted by the frankness and trust which she showed towards him. He thought about it all night, alternately lying on his narrow, comfortable bed and then pacing about the small, neat, air-conditioned room which had been allotted him. By the morning he had made a decision. If he was to cancel out the evil which he felt in the machine he must somehow trick it into working in the way he wanted. This he had already decided to do—it was his only possible ally against his hosts. But he could not trick it if it was working through Andre; he could not trick her. He had to gamble on making an ally of her too. In the morning he told her all he felt about it.

When he had finished she laughed almost gaily. "It is very easy," she insisted. "We must tell it what to do."

He did not share her confidence. "I can't see how it's a practical policy."

She became thoughtful. "I think the facts are these. All the real complexity is in the calculating and memory sections. The memory is enormous. But when a calculation has been made it has to be presented for assessment in a very simple form."

"You mean like a company's brief balance sheet summarises all the complex activities of a year's trading?"

She nodded. "I expect so. But if the balance is weighted——"

"I get it!" he interrupted. "The decision circuits act like the shareholders reading that balance sheet. On the basis of what they read into it they decide future company policy." He frowned. "But I'm dead sure that our balance sheet, produced by the computer's memory section, is nicely tricked up via the programme formulated by the original message, the stuff from Andromeda. So the decision circuits will execute its orders, not ours."

"Unless we change them."

He got up and paced around the room. "Our changes would just be deletions. The result would be a glorified adding machine. Neither enemy nor ally. There'd be no sense of purpose."

"But it could be given our purpose," she said urgently. "One that we communicated to it. Or at least, one I communicated. I can do it, John."

"I suspect you can. That's why I've tried to keep you away from it."

"You can't," she said quietly. "It is the reason why—I'm here." She stretched her hand and brushed it against his. "If you want to use the computer you'll have to trust me."

He turned to look at her, his eyes searching into hers. "I think I'll go for a stroll around the compound," he said abruptly. "You get some rest. You aren't fit yet. And don't think too much about all this."

He went past the sentry and paced up and down the sandy waste ground which lay around the buildings. Then he made for Dawnay's quarters.

Madeleine was surrounded by maps of the country, making notes of the geological factors. She seemed glad to abandon her work and gossip.

He told her of Andre's confidence and how he believed that she was just deceiving herself; the computer would dominate her as before.

She regarded him thoughtfully. "I don't think so, John," she said. "At least, not unless you drive her back under its spell. If you're hostile and suspicious you'll alienate her. You've built up ties between the two of you—ordinary human emotional ties. Those are strong influences."

He looked away. "What I want to know, Madeleine, is what's happening to her—physically?"

"What you've seen for yourself. Some sort of deterioration of muscle control. I'll have her examined if you like. But if, as I suspect, it's some motor deficiency in her nervous system there's nothing we can do about it."

"Oh my God," he said harshly. "The poor kid." He was silent for a moment. "It may be part of the programme which planned her: to chuck her aside when her job's over."

"There's the possibility that it's my fault," Dawnay said. "I made her—seemingly with built-in deterioration." She controlled herself and smiled. "Really you have no choice, John. You'll have to trust her as she has trusted you over these past weeks. Let her alter the computer in the way she plans and let her work with it." She hurriedly bent over her maps so he could not see her uncharacteristic tears. "From what I've seen of her muscular movements it won't be for very long. Let her final days be happy and useful. She may even get you out of here."

Fleming went to see Andre in her quarters—another small, neat air-conditioned room like his. She was sitting eating a meal off a tray. He was as appalled by the way she talked about her work as by the difficulty she found in conveying food to her mouth; but he was relieved that her speech had not so far become disjointed. The deterioration was not affecting her vocal muscles nor, thank God, her brain.

When she had eaten he took her arm and they walked the short distance to the computer building. Despite the fact that they were on a smooth path she stumbled once or twice.

Once before the computer console she seemed to regain all her powers. Automatically she took control and the computer immediately came to life, the clicking of relays providing an accompaniment to the ceaseless sullen hum. Oscillographs were soon pulsating and the main screen portraying a coherent pattern.

Fleming stood in the background with Abu Zeki, watching Andre seated at the console, her head tilted to watch the screen above her. At last, satisfied, she swivelled round on her chair and smiled triumphantly.

"It is done," she said. "The computer is fully operational."

Abu turned to Fleming incredulously. "This girl, Dr. Fleming. She has done this? Just in a matter of minutes?"

Fleming took him back to the duty office. He sat down at the desk. "I'm going to ask you to accept that what I'm telling you now are facts," he began. "The girl can communicate with the computer, picking up the electro-magnetic waves and inter-preting them, re-transmitting her orders in the same way." He paused. "You don't believe me, of course?"

"Perhaps I must believe; but I do not understand," Abu con-fessed. Fleming liked the young Arab scientist. There was hon-esty, inherent decency, about him. He believed that the man could be an ally. He told him that Andre was a man-fabricated being, constructed in order to forge a link with the computer, even if that had not been the intention of her human mentors.

Abu listened attentively, but he politely protested that the method of communication between her and the machine was still inexplicable.

"Look," Fleming said, "we have eyes and ears and noses be-cause they're the best instruments for picking up information in our sort of world. But they're not the only ones even ordinary humans like you and I have. There are senses we haven't de-veloped and senses we've let atrophy. The girl has another sense we haven't—and that's what she is using. To give information to the machine and to receive it."

"How will she use it?" Abu asked.

Fleming shrugged. "God knows, Abu Zeki, God alone knows."

Both men started at a slight sound by the door. They had not noticed that Andre had come quietly into the office.

"How do you want me to use it?" she demanded.

She did not wait for their answer. With hesitant steps, growing quicker as she progressed, she returned to the sensory console.

Abu, when he had time to digest the information Fleming had given him, was immediately anxious to use it. A young man like thousands of others in Azaran, he had been more fortunate than most in that his father had worked on the oil plant. The company had provided educational facilities for the workers' children. Abu had grabbed the opportunity. An imaginative English teacher had realised the boy's potentialities, helping him with spare time tuition.

When Abu was sixteen the new regime had emerged and the idealistic President had announced a state scholarship pro-gramme. Abu Zeki had been among the first twenty youths selected. He had emerged the only real success of the scheme.

Naturally Abu was grateful. He was also patriotic. The chance to work on the construction of a computer which surpassed any in the world had thrilled him. The presence of Europeans to direct his activities had not seemed anything but reasonable. He had been told that Intel was sponsoring the enterprise. What Intel was he neither knew nor cared. The basic fact was that this was an Azaranian project to better the country. Abu believed that not only was his own career rosy with promise but that he was working to ensure that life for his baby son would be even more wonderful.

He had been in despair when the computer failed to work, feeling that he was somehow to blame since Neilson had disappeared. Now, all that was in the past. In co-operation with this cynical yet likeable Englishman and his girl friend, the product of some weird and wonderful scientific gimmickry, he could repay the trust his President had put in him.

From the files in the records office Abu took several sheets of calculations. They had been passed over to him by Dawnay for processing by the computer. There had been nothing to do but file them until it was operational.

He mentioned what they were to Fleming.

"Give them to the girl," Fleming said wearily. "Let her feed the data in her own way."

Abu gave Andre the sheets of figures and busied himself in the office. He went through blue prints and circuit diagrams. His brain did not register any detail. He was forcing himself to do something while he listened anxiously to the rapid clicking of the machine.

It was twenty minutes before the output printer motor whirred and the circuit light glowed red. From the slot the print began to emerge, jerking slowly to the left and then abruptly to the right as line after line of equations was typed.

Abu stood mesmerised, reading the figures on the jerking paper. The motor sighed to silence and the circuit light went out. The calculations were complete. He tore off the paper and rushed to Fleming in the records office.

"Some of Professor Dawnay's calculations," Abu said. "This is the result of handing the project to Miss Andre. It's quite extraordinary!"

He crossed to another filing cabinet, a locked one. He withdrew a bulky file of papers, sorted through them, and went off to talk to Andre. By the time he returned the output printer was beginning to work again.

Fleming, still lounging at the desk, occupied with his thoughts, looked up lazily. "More stuff," he said. "What is it?"

Abu kept his back to Fleming. "I'm afraid I'm not allowed to tell you, Dr. Fleming."

"Look!" Fleming paused, trying to curb his anger. "What am I supposed to be here? In charge, or what?"

"I'm sorry," Abu said with sincerity. "But I have my orders."

Fleming looked at him levelly. "What have you given it?" he asked again. But Abu stared back at him with gentle obstinacy.

"It is work which Mam'selle Gamboul wishes done. I am not at liberty to discuss it."

"Then I'll stop it."

"I'm afraid you won't, Dr. Fleming."

Abu nodded towards the nearest sentry, who was watching them with a sour, bored interest. Fleming turned on his heel and stalked out.

Outside the office another sentry was leaning against the pillar, shading himself from the glaring sun. The soldier abruptly stepped forward and snapped to attention.

Fleming glanced across the compound and saw Janine Gamboul walking beside an elderly bearded man and talking quickly and brightly. Abu came out and stood beside him.

"Who's that with the glamorous Gamboul?" Fleming asked.

"That is our President." Abu's eyes were alight with pride. "He must have been visiting Professor Dawnay's laboratory. Her assistant told me that she's working on something quite new: a protective membrane to prevent water evaporating from the soil, but letting the oxygen and nitrogen molecules through so the land could breathe. It's a marvellous idea. It will make the desert blossom."

"And no doubt about to take a leap forward." Fleming nodded to the record sheets from the computer which Abu still held.

"I wonder if the President will be coming here," said Abu hopefully.

But the President did not visit them. He glanced across to

the computer. Gamboul said something. He nodded and disappeared into the headquarters building.

The afternoon siesta had put the town to sleep when Gamboul drove to Salim's residence. She found him taking his ease on the stone balcony, looking out over the quiet square and the acres of shabby roofs with a few minarets which made a dun-coloured pattern into the shimmering haze. He was in uniform, as he liked to be.

She threw down her wide-brimmed hat and crossed to the table where bottles and a bowl of ice stood.

Salim did not trouble to get up. "Been doing your duty?" he murmured.

"I've taken the old fool round the establishment," she answered, busy mixing her drink. "That will keep him quiet for a bit. He was most impressed with the Dawnay woman. Naturally,"—she gave a brittle laugh—"I didn't take him into the computer building, though he asked what was happening there." She sipped her drink, frowning as Salim made no effort to offer her a chair. "I'm going inside; it's cooler, and there may be somewhere to sit."

He heaved himself to his feet and followed her through the bead screen to the spacious room he used as an office. Across one wall was a detailed map of Azaran. Little flags of various colours were pinned here and there. Gamboul glanced at it with lazy curiosity and then stretched herself on a sofa. She was growing tired of Salim.

He came close, looking at her body in its thin and too tight dress. "Who's this girl you had brought over with Fleming?" he demanded.

Gamboul hunched her shoulders. "I don't know. Abu says she is highly intelligent. Kaufman's report merely says she was connected with the Thorness computer. They used quite a number of females up there. Dawnay for example. Kaufman thinks the girl was connected with the destruction of the machine and Fleming's shielding her. Presumably they're lovers."

Salim was disturbed. "Have her watched closely," he ordered. "We don't want to risk sabotage. And you'd better get out of Fleming who she is. I'm sure you could manage that."

She smiled at him, running her hand down her hip and

thigh. "I don't think I fancy Dr. Fleming." As if the subject bored her she got up and crossed to the map.

"What is all this playing around with little flags?"

Salim stuck his thumbs in his belt and stood solid and sure in front of the map. "The flags mark troops I can rely on. Roughly, an infantry battalion here, in Baleb, and a squadron of armoured cars. Some motorised units on the frontiers and the main army barracks at Quattara. Also the majority of the air force units."

"To do what?" she asked.

"To support me. Us." He corrected himself. "The computer must be safe. It belongs to Intel, and Intel holds the concession from the President. And I am not yet the President."

Gamboul studied his face. "Is that what you want?" she asked.

Salim returned to the balcony to look over the city. His eyes lifted to the lovely old palace which stood on a slight eminence to the right. "The President is a soft man," he murmured. "A tired man. He fought for independence, but now he thinks he can rest. He could be influenced—by any liberal-minded bumbler."

Gamboul was close beside him, her body touching his. "Like the Dawnay woman?" she suggested.

"Dawnay?" The idea seemed new to him and of no consequence. "Anyone could persuade him to interfere with your work, and then you and I would lose control. We must prepare for that eventuality. Why do you think I came back?"

"You're planning a coup d'etat!" she said, surprise and admiration in her expression. "And I didn't know."

He turned and put his hands on her shoulders. "You're with me, aren't you, Janine?"

She leaned forward until her body was pressed hard against him. "I thought you knew," she whispered. "When will it be?"

He looked out across her shoulder to the rooftops. "For Arabs time is a servant. When the time is right I shall act. Perhaps two days; a week. Not more."

At Fleming's insistent request Madeleine Dawnay asked for a doctor to come and see Andre. The efficient and smooth-running staff organisation of Intel said that they would have a neurologist in the compound within twenty-four hours.

He arrived the following morning. He was an Arab, who diffidently mentioned to Dawnay that he held a degree in neurosurgery from the Radcliffe Infirmary at Oxford and had continued his studies at Johns Hopkins.

His examination of Andre was long and thorough and Dawnay was impressed.

She answered the knock on the door of the neat little sick bay and found Fleming outside. "You can't see her yet," she said, coming out to join him on the verandah. "The doctor's still busy. Taking a lumbar puncture for a spinal fluid check. But his preliminary diagnosis is much the same as ours. Her muscular system's going more and more wrong. Maybe some gland has packed up, or her nerve set-up is different from ours, needing a blood nutrient that was there when she was built but is now depleted."

"You mean it wasn't in the blueprint?" he suggested.

Dawnay shrugged. "It isn't being made now," she said shortly.

"Could we synthesise it?"

"I wouldn't know where to start. Back home I might get advice and help. . . ."

"So what happens?" he asked harshly.

"She'll lose the use of her muscles progressively. It'll show in her limbs most obviously, but one day it'll be the pectoral muscles and then the heart." She turned to look at the closed door. "That's what the doctor is explaining to her now. I asked him to." Her calmness broke quite suddenly. "I made her! I made her to suffer this!"

He gripped her arm. "Madeleine. You didn't do it deliberately. And what about me? Who started it all with the design of the computer? Who prevented her dying more or less peacefully in that cave?"

Dawnay did not respond. She went on staring at the closed door. Presently the doctor came out. He looked across at the two of them, and then away as he crossed to the visitors' block.

"She ought to be properly nursed; sent away," Fleming said.

Dawnay gave a mirthless laugh. "You can see them allowing her to leave here. She's produced my crop formula. They know how useful that will be. There will be other things for her to do for them."

"There is another thing, already," said Fleming, remembering what Abu Zeki had told him at the computer.

"What?"

"I don't know exactly," he said thoughtfully. "I only hope what I think it is is wrong."

As if to contradict him, six jet fighters abruptly screamed across the sky, climbing fast from the airfield. They watched the machines become dots in the blueness of the shimmering canopy of sky. Dawnay wiped her face. "I'd better talk to the doctor, John. You have a word with Andre. Be gentle with her."

He knocked softly on Andre's door, waiting for an answer, almost dreading to go in. A pretty little Arab nurse came and opened the door, silently standing aside to permit him to enter.

Andre was sitting beside the austere iron bedstead, wearing a housecoat. The brightly coloured flowers of the pattern accentuated her extreme pallor. She was leaning back with her head turned sideways so that her long fair hair hung across her cheek. Fleming guessed that she had been crying.

The nurse brought a small, hard chair, and Fleming sat down. "Andre; Andromeda," he murmured. "There may be some answer." He saw the hair move as she gave a slight shake of the head. "We've done so much together," he insisted.

He put his fingers gently on her chin and pulled her face round. She reacted weakly, jerking away and covering her face with her hands. "Don't!" she begged. "Do you think I want to die? That it's nice to know I'm doing what you want? To end existence just like you ended the existence of the other computer?"

The words hurt him badly. "It's not what I want," he said, trying to keep his voice under control. "I'm frightened for you. And sorry for what I've done. I want to get you away from here, and all it means."

"Away?" she repeated, wonderingly. "But why? I've done what Dawnay asked; she has her data. And I've done what you asked; I've changed the computer's decision circuits . . ."

Her voice tailed away. Fleming felt a stab of real alarm; he knew that she had been on the point of saying more.

He went closer to her. "What else have you done, Andre? What else? At least be honest with me."

Her manner changed. She moved her head, pushed the hair from her face. She tried to smile at him. "I have seen what is the purpose of the message from out there."

He fought down the feeling of primitive terror that was

297

sending the blood pounding in his temples. "You've what?" he whispered.

"It's hard to explain," she said uneasily. "I'm a bad translator. But I know it's all right. We must put ourselves in the hands of the people who will protect us."

He let the words sink in, grappling with the fact that once again he had lost a battle. In his over-confidence he had believed he had persuaded Andre to do as he believed right, to make the computer her slave. But she was quietly stating that she wanted to serve "people who would protect us". People, she called them—this intelligence across the time-space of the universe—as if they were her brothers.

Before he could find words she sat up, smiling and confident despite the difficulty of the physical movement.

"Now I have seen the message I understand," she said. "You are frightened because you know only that the computer can have power over us; not why it has."

"You are what I'm frightened of," he said. "Now the computer's been doctored, the only way the message can enforce its will is through you. That's why I want you to get away from it! Live while you can, peacefully!"

She shook her head. "You think it's evil," she protested. "It isn't. It's giving us a solution, a power. If you are to survive you need that power. All that is happening in the country is only a symptom of what's happening all over the world. It's unimportant. We can take it all out of their hands and use as we want!"

He marvelled at her faith and feared her assurance; it was as if she pitied his limited imagination.

Abruptly she fell back on the sofa. The enthusiasm was spent; all it left was a frail, rather timorous young girl. "It drains me," she whispered. "It takes all my strength. It will kill me even quicker than you thought."

"Then leave it alone!"

She passed her forearm wearily over her head and gripped the back of the head rest. "I can't," she said. "I've something to do before I die. But I can't do it alone." Her lower lip trembled and she began to cry.

He crouched down and put his arm protectively around her waist. "If I'm to help; if I'm to trust you, you must tell me. In words—simple words—what is the real core of the message?"

For a time she lay with her eyes closed. Fleming did not interrupt her reverie. Then she gave a slight shudder and tried to move. He helped her sit up.

"You must take me to the console," she said. "I don't think I can explain in words. But I can show you."

He helped her to stand and held her by the arm as she walked with jerky, staggering steps the short distance to the computer building. Once inside, she seemed as usual to draw on hidden strength. She needed no assistance to sit before the sensory panel. Almost instantly the machine began operating, the master screen producing the familiar pattern of wave forms which the output printer translated into figures.

Fleming stood behind her as she gazed enthralled at the interminable pattern. "It's the high speed information between the equation groups which contains the real message," she said. "It tells about the planet from which the data came."

Fleming watched the screen. He could identify the wave forms which were the electronic versions of figures, but the occasional surges of angular blobs of light which intervened were meaningless to him. He had always imagined them to be the normal pick-up by the sensitive selenium cells of stray currents in the machine's framework.

"What does all this gibberish tell you?" he asked.

Andre's eyes never left the screen while she began to explain. "That it has been through all this. It knows what must happen, what has happened in other planets where intelligences have only developed as far as yours. You endlessly repeat a pattern until it wipes itself out."

"Or the world gets too hot and does the job for us?" he suggested.

Andre nodded. "Life of a biological creature begins very simply." She talked slowly as if paraphrasing a complicated mass of information. "But after a few thousand centuries it all becomes so complicated that the human animal can no longer cope. One crack—a war perhaps—and the whole fabric crashes down. Millions are killed or die off. Very few survive."

"Who start again," he finished for her.

She swung round to look straight at him. "In about one hundred and thirty years from now there will be a war. Your civilisation will be destroyed. It's all exactly predictable. So can the period before recovery be calculated. Just over a thousand years. The cycle will then repeat itself. Unless something better happens."

"As has happened on some planet in Andromeda?"

"Yes," she replied. "The species changed, adapted itself in time. Now it can intervene for earth people."

He had to take his eyes off her; off the dazzling, ever-faster moving patterns on the screen. He felt sick at the way she talked about "earth people" as if she was some alien creature.

He walked down the aisle, the whole length of the computer, and back again. Its cloying warmth reached out to him despite the air conditioning. Then he made his decision.

"All right," he said firmly. "Let's try to learn from it. Let's discover what we can and then tell people so they can decide what they think best."

She made a gesture of impatience. "That's not enough," she said. "We've got to take power. That's how we're meant to use the message to help us. Not to destroy the people here but to help them, and in the end they will hand the power over to us. It's all been calculated."

The simple directness of her faith exasperated him because he knew it was an emotion too strong for him to destroy. Nevertheless, he determined to fight it.

"Every dictator in history has argued like that—to force people into actions for their own good," he said. "And I'm supposed to think that it will be all right if we help impose the will coming from somewhere in Andromeda through Intel or these people in Azaran or any other dirty little power-drunk agency you choose. It's ridiculous!"

"That's only the means," she said. "What's important is the end."

He crashed his fist on the console desk, making her flinch. "No," he shouted. "I fought it before at Thorness, and I fought you at first—because the world must be free to make its own mistakes or save itself." He looked at her with a mixture of remorse and fury. "That's why I trusted you to handle this."

"I only did what was logical."

"I should have left you—left you to die," he whispered.

She turned back to the console. The screen had darkened, its aluminium coating grey and lifeless. "I shall die very soon anyway," she said.

All his fears for her returned and he could only stand in silence with his hand on her shoulder. Neither of them moved.

Then he heard the printer in the output bay tapping rapidly once more.

He strode across and read the figures appearing on the steadily emerging roll. The equations were terribly familiar, taking him back to an afternoon at Thorness more than two years before.

Mesmerised, he read the stream of figures which continued to emerge. He sensed that Andre had come across and was standing beside him.

"What is this?" he demanded.

"Basic calculations for a missile interceptor," she said in a matter-of-fact voice. "Surely you remember the Thorness project? There are a few minor modifications in this one."

He whirled on her. "Why have you programmed the machine for this?"

"Abu Zeki wanted the calculations," she said. "They need means of defence. It's all part of the plan."

He ripped the paper from the ejector and crumpled it in his hand. "For God's sake, stop," he begged her. "I didn't save you to work for them, to obey every filthy order they give you. You still have freedom to choose what you'll do."

She made some reply, but the roar of jet engines screaming at high speed over the building drowned her words.

"What?" he said when the racket had died away.

"I said it's too late," she repeated. "I have chosen. It's already started."

Fleming turned away from her and walked quickly down the corridor to the main doors. The pallid heat struck him in the face as he ran into the open space clear of the buildings.

The compound gates were closed. A light tank stood in front of them. On the main road a convoy of army lorries was roaring at high speed towards Baleb.

Slowly he returned to the residential area, hoping to find Dawnay. He badly needed some kind of normality among all this madness.

Dawnay wasn't in her room, and he went to her laboratory. A white-overalled Arab girl assistant was bending over a microscope.

"Professor Dawnay?" she said in answer to his enquiry. "She is not here. She went to see the President half an hour ago," she added calmly. "Now there is revolution."

7

STORM CENTRE

MADELEINE DAWNAY'S visit to the President was an impulsive action, resulting from an argument with Kaufman. The German was constantly roaming around the establishment, keeping himself informed of any tit-bit of information which might help to ingratiate himself with his superiors. Although all senior staff were in theory employees of the Azaranian Government, in practice it was Intel which made the decisions. Consequently Kaufman, as the senior Intel representative regularly available, was regarded as a liaison officer by the directors.

Dawnay's bio-chemical experiments had progressed far enough for field-testing. Study of the terrain suggested that a coastal area near the Persian Gulf would be a good one. But she wanted to analyse the tidal strip to ascertain what effect wind and sea had had on the soil. On one of Kaufman's visits to her laboratory she asked for him to arrange transport for her to make a series of trips, imagining it would be a routine matter.

The German immediately became suspicious. He demanded to know the reason, and her natural retort that he would not understand seemed to anger him.

But Dawnay could be very obstinate when she chose. She insisted that if she was to carry out her work the arrangements must be made. Kaufman muttered that he would have to get a government permit.

"Fine," Dawnay said. "You can jump in your car and get it right away, can't you?"

He frowned. "At this moment, almost impossible."

This was more than Dawnay was inclined to take. She removed her overall and picked up her sun hat. "If you enjoy putting up ridiculous obstacles then I'll see the President myself."

"I wouldn't count too much on the President," he said, "but

302

by all means go if you want." He went to the reception desk to call her a staff car. When it came he opened the door for her with a studied flourish.

On the short journey to the Presidential palace Dawnay's anger seethed and she reminded herself of Fleming's pessimistic views on the whole set-up. She determined to discuss more than a trip to the coast with the President. After all, she told herself, he was head of State and if a challenge came Intel could no more win than mammoth oil companies in half a dozen little states had been able to do.

The streets seemed very empty, although this did not particularly arouse her interest. She had visited the capital so rarely that she had no means of comparison.

The car slowed at the palace gates until it was waved on by a lounging sentry. The man showed no interest in it. Dawnay alighted and passed through the doorless portico.

A bearded Arab in native costume bowed and put his hands to his forehead in greeting. The palace was beautiful and very old, unspoiled by any attempt to repair the crescent arches or the filigree stonework with plaster.

A little incongruously, the old Arab picked up a house telephone fixed to the wall behind a pillar. After some murmured words he returned to Dawnay and said in halting English that his master would see her.

A little negro boy tripped down the stairs, greeted her with a dazzling smile and in his soft soprano voice asked her to follow him. They went to the first floor and along a labyrinth of passages, silent with age-long peace. The boy knocked on big double doors and threw them open.

The President advanced towards Dawnay, his hand extended. His creased face, she thought, was that of a very old man—older than she knew he actually was. But his eyes were bright and intelligent, and he was meticulously neat and tidy, his beard trimmed short, and his large sensitive fingers soft and gentle when they shook hands. The jarring note was his Western dress —an old-fashioned though well-cut tweed jacket and breeches of the kind English aristocrats wore on week-ends fifty years before. Dawnay envisaged some London tailor carefully repeating a bespoke order originally given in the spacious age of pre-1914.

His courtesy was as genteely old-fashioned as his appearance.

Delighted to be entertaining an English lady, he explained that he had been looking through his film slides and hoped she would be interested in seeing some of them.

"Photography is my hobby," he said. "A way to have mementoes of my country—its people, its valuable archaeological and historical features, and of course the improvements which, with Allah's help, I have been able to make."

The negro boy was already standing beside the projector. At a nod from his master he switched off the ceiling lights and began the screening. Dawnay hid her impatience and made polite and appropriate remarks as her host carefully explained each picture. The show ended at last. The boy switched on the lights and was told to leave.

The President took a chair facing her and folded his arms in his lap. "And now, why did you want to see me?" he asked.

Urgently Dawnay recited the words she had been rehearsing to herself as she watched the slides. She hoped she was cogent, objective, and fair. She told him of the origin of the computer design, of the bio-chemical experiments which culminated in the creation of the girl, and finally of the reasons why Fleming had contrived the destruction of the machine in Scotland.

The President was quiet for some moments when she had finished. "I have only your word for all this," he said quietly. "It is, as you will understand, somewhat difficult to accept, or, perhaps I should say, understand."

"I'm sorry it can't be made more clear, your excellency. We don't understand a great deal of it ourselves. Dr. Fleming has always suspected its purpose."

"And do you?"

She pondered on her reply. "I think there are right ways and wrong ways of using it," she eventually said.

He darted a glance at her. "And we are using it in the wrong way?"

"Not you, but Intel."

"We are in their hands," he sighed, like a weary old man. "This is a difficult time."

He stood up and crossed to the window, pulling the heavy draperies aside and letting an almost blinding shaft of sunlight into the dim room. For a time he looked out on the city which dropped away below the palace. "When one is in my position, a government has to show results or it does not survive. Intel gives results."

He returned to the middle of the room but remained standing. "I am a moderate," he smiled. "There are factions here which are fiery, youthful, impatient. They are also powerful. I need all the help I can get to retain the people's loyalty."

The door had opened, and the little negro boy had appeared. In his hand he held a telephone. He plugged it into a wall jack and then stood before the President, holding the instrument free of the cradle. The President took the phone and listened. He said a few words in Arabic and then gave the phone back to the boy.

He walked across the room and stood once more before the window. A soft thud, a long way off, sent a tiny vibration through the old building. It was followed by the harsh reverberation of automatic fire. The President pulled the curtain back across the window and looked at his guest.

"I do not think, Professor, that I shall be in a position to help you. The telephone call was from Colonel Salim, an efficient and ambitious officer." He paused to listen to the distant rumble of heavy engines and the racket of caterpillar tracks which rapidly grew in volume on the roadway below the palace. "That, I imagine, is the proof of what he told me."

Only half understanding, Dawnay stood up and hesitantly moved to the door, thanking him for his patience in listening. She remembered too late that she had not asked for a permit to visit the coast.

"Goodbye, Professor," the old man said. He did not look at her. He had sat down, very erect, very still, in an old-fashioned high backed chair. Dawnay had the impression of a king who had only his dignity left to sustain him.

The negro boy was standing in the passage outside. His eyes were big with fear or perhaps excitement. He almost ran in his anxiety to escort her to the courtyard.

The car she had come in had gone. Instead, two soldiers came across and stood on either side of her. They motioned with their guns that she was to wait near the doorway. Presently an army scout car came to a halt beyond the portico. The soldiers jerked their heads to show she was to enter it.

A young officer saluted her. "We take you back, Miss," he said in halting English.

The driver had frequently to pull out of the way as mobile columns roared towards Baleb. There were a few half-tracks and some light tanks. Their crews were in war kit but they were standing in their vehicles. They obviously did not expect serious shooting.

The gates to the Intel compound were open but an armoured car was stationed outside, and there were groups of helmeted troops everywhere. Dawnay was driven straight to her quarters, where more guards were patrolling. The young officer who had accompanied her indicated courteously but firmly that she was to remain in her room until further orders.

The military coup organised by Salim had been based on three actions—to close all frontier roads and ports, take over control of the capital, and to secure the Intel establishment. The Intel action, was, of course, a formality, thanks to Janine Gamboul.

The first clue Fleming had as to what was happening came from Abu Zeki. The two men had quarrelled for the second time. Abu had proudly told Fleming that the destruction of the missile equation sheets had been futile because the punched master tape was intact. He had gone on to boast of the power and might his country would have with the defence devices the computer could design.

"Already we are grasping that power. Even now Colonel Salim's troops are taking over our protection."

"From the President?" Fleming asked.

"The President's a tired, senile old man. He's finished."

"And Intel?"

"They're taking over with Intel," Abu Zeki replied. He saw Fleming glance towards the empty sensory bay. "If you're looking for the girl she's not in the building. She is in our custody."

Fleming hurried from the building and ran across to the residential area. Two armed guards stood before the door of Andre's quarters. He tried to push between them but they did not budge.

"They'll not let you in; I'm afraid they no longer trust you, Dr. Fleming," said a familiar voice.

He wheeled round. Kaufman was walking slowly towards him, grinning. "Anyway, the girl is not here," the German went on.

"She is being cared for. Meanwhile Mademoiselle Gamboul wishes to see you."

"Where?" Fleming grunted. "And when?"

Kaufman's smile disappeared. "Now," he said. "You will come with me." He led the way to his car.

They drove to Salim's house. There were no soldiers there and no servants met them as they went upstairs. Kaufman opened a door and motioned to Fleming to enter. The door closed and he was left alone.

He walked round the familiar room where he had first met Salim, and then wandered out on the balcony. It was a few moments before he moved to the far end where some cane furniture stood around a table. On the table were bottles of whisky and glasses. He felt he needed a drink.

His approach to the table took him past a sun screen and alongside a chaise-longue. He let out an involuntary shocked gasp.

Janine Gamboul was sprawled on her side, her head drooped over the edge and her arm hanging limply to the floor. Her face looked pale as wax, except for the red line of her lipstick and the dark pencilling of her eyebrows, and her eyes were half open and glazed.

Fleming's immediate reaction was that she was dead. He bent down and put his hand under her head, lifting it back on to the chaise-longue. She moaned.

Then, as he pulled her arm against her body he saw the glass on the floor. He sniffed it: it smelt of whisky.

He was just about to leave her when she opened her eyes fully and laughed. She hauled herself up with difficulty into a half-sitting position and waved clumsily at him.

"You thought I was dead?" she giggled. "I'm not, as you see. I told Kaufman to ask you here. I wanted to talk." With studied effort she put her feet on the ground and stood unsteadily. "Lemme get you a drink." She staggered the few paces to the table.

She slopped some whisky into two glasses and then gaped around. "No syphon," she muttered thickly. "Been drinking it neat, but you like soda—yes? Salim must have it in his room." She managed to pick up the two glasses and waveringly started for the door from the balcony. Fleming stood motionless, watching her.

She stopped and half turned. "What are you looking at me like that for?" she said thickly. Then, with an arch smile, "It's no use getting ideas about me; not till I've learned more about the other woman, your woman. . . ."

She started off once more, putting the two glasses down on a heavy sideboard while she swayed over the cupboard beneath. There were two syphons there but apparently it was too great an effort to lift one out. Instead she bent down with the glasses in turn and squirted in the soda. Fleming, who had moved no nearer than the doorway, did not see how deliberately and accurately she half-filled one glass from each.

She was humming a little French love song as she swayed towards him. She gave him one glass, and fell into an easy chair with the other.

"Tell me all about your girl friend," she murmured, looking at him over her drink.

"Hasn't Abu Zeki told you all you need to know?" he said sullenly.

She giggled. "Oh, something quite fantastic. So absurd that of course I believe it—and want to know more. A votre santé!" She raised her glass.

Fleming hesitated and then sipped his drink. The bite of the whisky on his palate made him feel better. He decided to play along for a little while. She was still acting drunkenly, her speech slurred and her body limp. It made her more attractive than usual.

"What have you against us?" she asked. "The smell of commerce? The dirt that's supposed to stick to money?"

"Partly," he grunted.

"We haven't such a bad record in this country," she continued. "There was nothing here till we came. Now that Salim's taken over we can progress still more." Her eyes were bright with excitement. "Perhaps we shall become fabulous and great, like medieval Venice or the East India Company. Anyway soon no one will be able to compete with us. The whole world will be at our feet."

"Or at hers," he observed, sipping again from his glass.

She leaned forward. "Hers?" she repeated. "Why don't you tell me about her? There is something she alone knows? Something she will do?"

Her eyes were fixed on him, unblinking, malevolent. He had

a ridiculous feeling that she was mesmerising him. To break it he looked away and gulped the rest of the whisky. As he put the glass down he knew the drink had been drugged. His legs felt weak and he couldn't stop his mind wandering purposelessly into vagaries about the past. He groped for a chair he couldn't properly see and slumped in it.

Immediately Gamboul was across and standing over him.

"Now you'll tell me," she ordered.

He talked hesitantly at first, sentences unfinished, subjects trivial and unconnected; but by the end of half an hour she had learned the whole story.

She sat looking at the half-conscious Fleming sprawled awkwardly in his chair for a long time after the questioning. She wondered if this enigmatic but highly desirable Englishman had somehow outwitted her and faked his reaction to the truth drug. She dismissed the idea as absurd; she knew all there was to know about its effects.

She picked up the house phone on Salim's cleared desk and gave an order for Fleming to be taken back to his quarters. For herself she called for a car to be brought round.

Twenty minutes later she arrived at Andre's quarters. The door was open and only one guard was near. She asked him in Arabic where the white girl was, and the man answered that she had come out and gone to the building opposite. Frightened, he added that they had not been ordered to use force to prevent her moving within the station.

Gamboul went to the computer building. Abu Zeki was not there; only two guards walked ceaselessly up and down the main corridor. She saw Andre sitting quietly before the sensory screen in the communication section.

"What are you doing here?" Gamboul asked suspiciously.

Andre smiled at her. "I am waiting," she said tonelessly. "For you. You are the logical choice." She looked intently at the darkened screen. "What have you forced Dr. Fleming to tell you?"

"You—you know about that?" Gamboul exclaimed.

Andre nodded. "It is all predictable. No doubt you could not believe all he said. But I will show you. Sit beside me. Do not be frightened. There is no need."

Gamboul pulled across a chair. Andre gave her a reassuring nod and then placed her hands on the sensory controls. The

309

screen produced a dot of light which expanded and faded. Then came a vague, misty imagery in half-tones.

"What is that?" Gamboul whispered.

Andre's voice was flat and mechanical. "Watch," she said. "I will explain. It is where the message comes from. Soon you will know what has been calculated for you to do."

Far into the night the two women sat before the screen, the frail, slight figure of Andre taut and somehow proud; Gamboul, motionless, transfixed, as her eyes tried to assimilate the strange figurations which hovered, cleared and grew misty on the screen, while her brain absorbed the low murmur of Andre's interpretation.

Abu Zeki was the only person, apart from the uninterested guards, who saw them there. Recognising Gamboul, he turned away. The woman intimidated him, and he disliked her. In any event, he had heard of her intimacy with Colonel Salim. It would not be wise to get involved with the new dictator's mistress.

He went to his quarters and lay on his bed. He knew he would not be able to sleep properly, the time was too momentous. He thought happily about the brave new world that had been born at the moment the state radio announced the change of government. Yet there was a niggling premonition of disaster at the back of his mind. He recognised that this was the result of his talk with Fleming. He liked Fleming; liked the way he saw through the trappings of a problem to the heart of it. Abu wanted to learn to be like that.

Deliberately he forced his mind to shift to pleasanter things —his wife, his baby son. But it was no good. The low hum of the computer seemed to permeate the very air. He dozed off. . . .

The hum. So it was still operating. He sat up and looked at his watch. The luminous hands showed 3.30. If the women were still there they had been working for at least eight hours.

He got up. Already the eastern sky had a pinkish tinge. He ran across the compound to the computer block. A guard, asleep on his feet, started with fright. Abu identified himself and the man lolled back against the wall.

Inside the block the lights were bright, and the air was heavy and warm after the sharpness of the night air from the desert. Abu crept forward slowly. The two women were still there, staring at the screen. Andre's voice was so low that he could not make out what she was saying even when he stopped a few feet behind them.

"Mm'selle Gamboul," he said. "What is happening? Miss Andre, it is I—Abu Zeki."

For all the notice they took he might have been a voiceless ghost. He felt a prickle of fear and crept quietly away.

Outside he stopped and breathed deeply the fresh, lovely air. He felt better and it cleared his mind. He realised what he must do next.

He ran to Fleming's quarters. A guard outside, wide awake, barred his way. The soldier called over his shoulder and the door opened. Kaufman came out.

"I must see Dr. Fleming," Abu said.

Kaufman grunted that he could come in. Fleming was sprawled, fully clothed, on his bed. A couple of chairs facing each other showed where Kaufman had been resting while watching him.

Abu shook Fleming roughly by the shoulder. "Doctor Fleming," he begged, "you must come right away!"

Fleming groaned, opened his eyes, and screwed up his face. "What time is it?" he mumbled.

"Nearly four."

Fleming sat up with a start. He fought off a bout of dizziness.

"The doctor has had a little drug," Kaufman explained. "He will be all right presently."

Fleming got gingerly to his feet. "What's the matter, Abu?" he asked, ignoring the German.

"I do not understand what is happening," Abu said: "Mm'selle Gamboul came to the computer yesterday evening. She was with the girl. I went to bed. They are still there—in the communication unit. I spoke to them, but they took no notice. They did not seem to know I was with them. They were watching the display tube."

Fleming ran his fingers through his hair. "Oh my God! I should have guessed." He crossed to the door. Kaufman moved in front of it, his plump hand round the handle.

"I have orders," he said uneasily.

Fleming braced himself for a show-down. Hastily Abu intervened. "He must come," he shouted at Kaufman; "he is needed for the computer."

Kaufman looked doubtfully from one to the other. He was

bewildered. The computer was everything. His job was above all else to serve it.

"If he must, he must," he grumbled. "But I will escort you," he said to Fleming. "My orders are to watch you."

"Hold my bloody hand if you want," snarled Fleming; "but for God's sake let's go." He turned to Abu. "Go and wake Professor Dawnay," he ordered. "Tell her to come over to the computer block right away."

The air and the short walk did him good. The fuzziness in his brain cleared and he soon felt he had proper control of his limbs. He slammed through the swing doors and loped towards the computer section. Immediately a guard pointed his automatic rifle at him. Kaufman took a step to one side.

Fleming stopped, the muzzle against his chest. Down the lighted corridor he could see Gamboul rising from her chair. A different Gamboul. She was meekly listening to something Andre was saying. Then she nodded and came towards them.

Kaufman moved behind Fleming and gripped his arms, pinioning them against his body. Gamboul passed them all as if they did not exist. Her head was tilted back and there was a vague smile on her lips.

Fleming struggled to free himself. "Stop her," he yelled. "For God's sake don't let her get out of here."

He struggled violently, but Kaufman held him. "You will stay with me!"

Gamboul had passed through the entrance hall and there was the sound of her car moving off before Madeleine Dawnay came hurrying in.

Kaufman released his grip on Fleming and nodded to the guard. "They may pass."

Fleming ran to the console and bent over Andre. She glanced at him and then leaned back, lost in reverie. Dawnay came up. She was alarmed at the death-like pallor of the girl.

"What is it, John?" she asked. "What's happened?"

Fleming grasped the back of the swivel chair and pulled Andre round so that she could not avoid his gaze.

"What have you done?" he whispered.

She smiled serenely. "What had to be done," she murmured. "Mademoiselle Gamboul knows what to do." Her lip curled almost contemptuously. "She was not afraid when I showed her the meaning."

Suddenly her strength and assurance left her and she crumpled up like a sick, helpless child.

Dawnay bent over her. "She's desperately ill, John," she said gently. "Let's get her to the sick bay."

Fleming snapped an order to Kaufman. Frightened and servile, the German came forward, lifting Andre by the shoulders while Fleming took her feet. They carried her to the sick bay, where Dawnay ordered them outside while she and the nurse got the girl to bed.

Kaufman tried to talk to Fleming, anxious for reassurance; he sensed that he was somehow involved in a disaster and would be blamed for it. Fleming ignored him and the German walked away disconsolately.

When Dawnay came out she drew Fleming away from the door. "She's weak, terribly weak," she whispered, "as if she'd been making some enormous effort. But she's falling asleep. The nurse will tell us if there's any change. Come across to my room and I'll make some coffee."

While the percolator was heating Dawnay asked if there was any news from outside. "Colonel Salim's taken over completely, I suppose?"

"I don't know much," said Fleming wearily. "I was drugged last night—by the Gamboul woman. Made me tell her about Andre. Probably the same drug as they used on you in London. Afterwards she must have come straight here to the computer and found Andre waiting for her."

"But why?" Dawnay demanded.

Fleming sighed. "The computer has selected Gamboul as the boss. I thought it would choose Salim, but this is cleverer. Through her the machine will take power."

"How?"

"I don't know. Somehow the machine communicated to her what Andre couldn't put into words for me. I suppose it managed to give Gamboul the sort of appalling, momentary flash of revelation saints and prophets are said to have. It's all so damnably logical and inevitable. Like Andre's always saying, the whole thing's predictable."

The coffee was bubbling. Dawnay poured out two cups and handed one to Fleming. "I've never had quite this feeling before," she said. "Of everything closing in."

He laughed shortly. "You know I have. And I also proved

313

that appealing to someone, Osborne for instance, or taking destructive action, didn't really help." He stirred his coffee violently, splashing it in the saucer. "Now the computer's won, the whole thing's out of our hands—for good. We're finished."

Appropriately, as if for effect, a gust of wind moaned across the compound and scratched grittily against the outside walls. Dawnay went to shut the door while sand spattered against the window.

She stopped, seeing Abu Zeki running across to them. He stood panting when he arrived, getting his breath. "Dr. Fleming," he got out at last. "Colonel Salim is dead."

Fleming nodded, as if he felt no surprise. "And all his army stooges?"

Abu licked his lips. "I don't know," he said. "I don't really understand. The army guards have gone from here. There are just the Intel wardens and orderlies. But they are now armed. I cannot understand."

Fleming stood up and stared out of the door. "I'll tell you what's happened," he said. "Gamboul's taken control. She either had Salim murdered or did it herself. She is perfectly capable of killing, even if an exterior force didn't tell her to. There can't be hitches in this plan, so if Salim's coup has failed it isn't a mishap but a stage in the general scheme. What about the old man?"

"The President, you mean?" Abu asked. "He is still in his palace. The message announcing Colonel Salim's death came from him, personally."

Another gust of wind swept through the compound. Fleming bent his head as sand stung his eyes. He turned and shut the door. "The President will be the lady's front man. She'll pull the strings and he'll twitch. We'll all be her puppets soon."

Dawnay slowly drained the last of her coffee. "John," she said thoughtfully, "it's very strange."

"Strange? What's strange about it? Gamboul's doing just what she's compelled to do. Part of the programme."

She shook her head impatiently. "I don't mean the political thing. But the wind. Here it doesn't normally blow like this, not at this time of the year."

"Doesn't it?" he answered absent-mindedly. "A nice reminder of Thorness. The weather was hell when Andre and I were hiding up on that island."

314

"Yes," she agreed. "Conditions were abnormal there as well. I think I'll do some work in the lab." She looked already pre-occupied, as if she were working. "I wish I could get those sea samples I wanted."

"Lucky to have something to do," Fleming said. "I don't feel anxious to report as an obedient serf to that electronic dictator across the way." He looked at Abu. "But someone had better be there, Abu. Go over and hang around for instructions. I've no doubt Gamboul will be sending her Teutonic stooge with some orders."

Fleming wandered back to his own quarters. The wind still blew, sweeping momentarily stinging gusts of sand and then subsiding as quickly as it had come.

He glanced at his watch. It was early, just after 6.30. He switched on his short-wave radio, tuned to the B.B.C. Middle East service. He wondered how long they'd be left with even this one-way link with anywhere else.

The static was bad, the voice from London fading and distorting so that it was sometimes inaudible.

". . . No further news has come in about the situation in Azaran. The frontiers remain closed, and during the night the government station at Baleb has merely continued to re-transmit the President's announcement that a military junta has been set up . . ."

The spluttering drowned the bulletin for a few minutes. When it eased the newsreader was saying ". . . similar conditions are reported from all over Western Europe and from countries bordering the Mediterranean. Gales of unusual force are being recorded as far afield as the East coast of Africa, in the vicinity of Aden, and from weather stations in Iceland and Newfoundland."

Fleming switched off the set. He found it almost natural that the world's weather should have gone mad at a time when the world itself was moving irrevocably to a crisis.

FORECAST

O n the following day Janine Gamboul summoned Kaufman to her office. Instead of one of her usual chic frocks she was wearing a plain tailored suit, but he noticed at once that there was something else different about her; she had a dedicated and, at the same time, unnaturally exalted air.

She did not look up from her desk when Kaufman entered, and he stood stiffly at attention a little distance away from her.

When she had finished writing, she glanced up at him coldly, not inviting him to sit down.

"The situation is perfectly quiet," she said in decisive tones. "I suggest you inform your department of this fact, together with a report of what happened. Explain that we are in control and will remain so."

"And Colonel Salim," he asked diffidently, "what shall I say about him? He was well regarded by the Vienna office."

She shrugged. "Tell them the facts. That I—that he was shot because he was in the way. He was a petty nationalist and if he had got power he would have used the computer for his own stupid little ends. You can explain that?"

She dismissed the matter and picked up the sheet of paper on which she had been writing. "This morning the President is giving audience to his Council. Poor little man. He's very bewildered, and frightened. But he realises that he must co-operate. He is perfectly amenable, particularly since Salim was dealt with. He will ensure the loyalty of all these old men of the government. You will attend the meeting to represent Intel. I have outlined proposals so far as we are involved." She handed him a document.

Kaufman took it and read it slowly. Occasionally he nodded,

as if pleased. "I have always done my best," he murmured. "You may rely on me in the future."

"Good," she said, with a gesture of dismissal. "Now go to the palace and instruct the President's secretary."

The councillors were seated around the Presidential dais: a dozen proud, elderly Arabs in traditional dress. True to their race they concealed whatever emotions they felt as the President, with a kind of tired dignity, gave them a carefully doctored version of what had happened and told them that he himself was taking personal control. The traitor Salim, the way of his death unexplained, was to be buried without military honours; all officers who had taken part in the revolt were already suspended and would be court-martialled. The troops and all civil branches of the Government would be answerable only to the President's personal edict. In due course there would be elections, but in the meantime the existing Parliament would not be called into session.

At a nod from the President these edicts were translated by his secretary into English, out of courtesy to Kaufman.

One Councillor half rose to his feet. "And who will the President be responsible to?" he demanded, deliberately speaking in English and glaring at Kaufman.

"To himself," Kaufman answered sharply.

The President remained impassive, and the Councillor sat down, muttering into his beard.

"Gentlemen," said Kaufman, rising proudly to his feet. "The President, and therefore the country, can rely on a continuance of help on an increasing scale by the mercantile consortium, Intel, which I represent. To further the welfare of Azaran without interference, it is the wish of my superiors that the country should not renew diplomatic relations with other nations."

The words were translated and caused a low hubbub of conversation.

"You should say more about the kind of help you are to give," said the President uneasily.

Kaufman beamed. "The Cosortium is producing new instruments of defence and technical value. It will shortly be making available a new process, perfected in our laboratories here, to turn the desert into fertile agricultural land."

He waited while the secretary translated, and a wizened old Arab whispered urgently to the secretary.

"The Sheik Azi ben Ardu wishes to know what the process is."

"It is a spray," said Kaufman shortly. "In a short while it will be demonstrated."

The Councillor who had asked the question about Presidential reponsibility glowered at Kaufman. "And the wind that has come out of season and blows our soil away, what can your laboratories do for that?"

Kaufman had no prepared answer. He looked to the President for help.

"What can they do?" the President replied mildly. "The wind is the servant of Allah. We must not question it."

Fleming had never been under any illusion about his situation. He knew that he was virtually a prisoner, but only on this first morning of the new regime did he feel the reality of it. There was no work he wanted to do, or could be persuaded to do, knowing what it would be. There was no one to talk to; even Abu had disappeared into the executive building in answer to a summons from Gamboul. Guards were patrolling everywhere. Before breakfast they had forbidden Fleming to approach the sick quarters where Andre lay. The best he had managed was to insist on seeing the nurse who had come out and reported that her patient was a little worse, but was sleeping.

He sat a long time over a late breakfast, ignoring the coarse brown bread, fruit and olives they always served, and drinking cup after cup of sweet, thick coffee.

Then he strolled across to Dawnay's laboratory. The guards eyed him suspiciously but did not prevent him from entering the building.

Dawnay was busy at a laboratory bench. She greeted him absent-mindedly and did not react very much to his worried talk about Andre.

"There's nothing we can do for her," she muttered. She paused and then picked up one of a row of large test tubes.

"I'd like you to look at these, John," she said.

He glanced at the one in her hand. It was full of a semi-transparent, greyish fluid which clung to the glass when she shook it. The other tubes seemed to be identical.

"What are they?" he asked.

"Sea water samples they got for me." She gave a short laugh. "I must admit that Intel are efficient. They wouldn't let me go and take my own specimens, but they did much more than I asked. Not only are these from the Persian Gulf, which I wanted, but they've had samples flown in from the Mediterranean and Indian Ocean and even the Western Atlantic. So that there should be samples from other areas for comparison, I suppose."

"And is there anything to compare?" he asked.

She shook the tube vigorously. The fluid inside went completely opaque.

"See?" she said. "Now, normal sea water should be like this one. You'll see it's clear." She handed him another test tube.

Fleming picked up some of the other tubes. They all went opaque when he shook them. "Sure Kaufman didn't fool you and get them all from the same place?" he grinned.

She shook her head. "Not he. He got his orders from Intel, not from me. You know what he's like. If they told him to fetch water from the Antarctic he'd get it. But I want you to watch what happens when this milky sea water mixes with the clear sample."

She took a clean test tube, poured in some of the clear water and then added two minute drops of the opaque fluid. The milky droplets dissolved and disappeared. Dawnay clamped the tube in a holder with a light reflector behind it.

"Now watch," she said.

Slowly the water clouded near the bottom of the tube; the cloudiness spread upwards until the water was as opaque as the others.

"I wonder how the fish like it," murmured Fleming. "Any idea what it is?"

"A bacterium," she said. "Come over here."

He followed her to the table where she switched on a light and focused a microscope. "Look at this slide," she told him.

Fleming peered into the microscope, adjusted the focus, and gave a low whistle. A globular organism was palpitating; as he watched, it divided and swelled. Thirty seconds later the division was repeated. He straightened up from the microscope. "Know where it comes from?"

Dawnay made no reply. She picked up a slide from a small cabinet and slid it into a second microscope. "This one's dead. It conforms to no bacterium group I've heard of. It's a very simple organism, as you'll see if you look at this one which I've stained. It doesn't appear to have more than one remarkable property—the ability to reproduce fantastically. If it wasn't shut in the test tubes——." She hesitated. "If it had the whole ocean in which to breed. . . ." Again she stopped.

Fleming walked back to the bench, thoughtfully looking at the neatly labelled test tubes. "The areas marked on these specimens," he said, "rather coincide with those I keep hearing in the B.B.C. shipping forecasts and weather reports—storms, gales, and so forth."

"Yes," she agreed, "and one of them we know quite well. A very rich mixture."

She lifted a test tube labelled "Minch" gingerly, as if she were half afraid of it. "The channel between Scotland and the Hebrides."

"With Thorness on the east side," he finished for her. "So what?"

"It must have all started somewhere," she said. "In the originating area it would have a higher density of bacteria than the more newly infected zones."

He stared at her. "You've no proof for saying that this one from the Minch. . . ."

She shook her head. "No. All these samples were populated to capacity when I got them. There's no telling the percentage of bacteria when they were drawn from the sea. To make a proper check I'd have to get accurate and localised storm centre reports and then make on-the-spot checks of sea water samples in the same zones. There just might emerge a correlation between these little beasts and the weather."

"Or again you might not," he said with a rather badly-contrived heartiness. "Look here, Madeleine, we don't want to get too imaginative or maudlin about all this. Collate the data, sift out the facts, draw the inferences—that's the routine. And incarcerated here we haven't got a chance of doing much, though I guess you can do a break-up on the bacterial structure.

"But it's pretty obvious, the smart way they got you all this ocean, that Intel have some notions along your lines—that the weather is more than naturally upset. My guess is that you can put in a chit for samples from here to Timbuktu, or at least wherever there's a bit of sea, and the resourceful Kaufman will send off his minions with their little buckets and bottles to get them for you. All you can do to inject some sense and order into the sources you need is for us to glue our ears to the B.B.C. bulletins."

They agreed that one or other of them should try to listen in to every bulletin and weather report, making notes of the areas mentioned.

There was no dearth of information. The midday bulletin gave priority to weather news. The first hurricanes ever recorded in Britain had caused death and destruction on a major scale from Penzance to Wick. The electric grid had broken down because of smashed pylons. Huge areas of Lancashire and East Anglia were flooded. The Air Ministry could hold out no hope of improvement. The barometric pressure remained the lowest ever known outside tropical areas.

Fleming and Dawnay heard that bulletin together. Neither had any need to write down the details, and neither felt inclined to talk about it. But when a boisterous gust of wind abruptly surged in from the desert, whirling up little spirals of sand and making a clatter as open doors banged and windows crashed, they both felt the burden of something sinister with more force than the distant wavering voice from London had caused. The wind was hot and dry, but Dawnay shivered as it buffeted her.

Fleming moved the tuning dial on the short-wave set, searching for more news. Words, music, and more words flicked in and faded—meaningless to occidental ears. Then he found what he was looking for: the Voice of America.

A beat record clamoured abruptly to its close and the announcer came on with his station identification. The news which followed had no political significance. As in London, ideologies and flag-waving had been shelved. The news was solely of the weather.

"The United States Weather Bureau," said the newsreader, "today gave warning of further gales approaching the Eastern seaboard of the United States. They are expected to be on a similar scale to those which swept across Western Europe during the night. American scientists are speaking of a shift of world weather patterns comparable to those at the beginning of the Ice Age. . . ."

Fleming snapped off the switch. Dawnay got up. "I'll be in the lab if you have any ideas," she said.

More or less deliberately they avoided one another in the next couple of days. They both felt completely helpless, but they listened meticulously to every bulletin, noting down the areas where the storms were worst.

The wind scale figures were the best guide. On the third morning, after the early morning bulletin had reported more havoc in Britain, the Netherlands, France and Spain, Fleming went back to Dawnay's lab. He was impressed by what she had been doing. One end of the laboratory had been cleared. A huge map of the Northern hemisphere had been pinned up on the wall. Coloured pins were dotted about it, thickest in a strip from Gibraltar to the Orkneys, with a big cluster east of the Hebrides.

"Hello, John," she greeted him. "You see, a pattern's emerging all right. And that's not all." She beckoned him across to a long bench against the wall on which several dozen test tubes stood in a long row.

"Kaufman hasn't had time to get all the samples I asked for, of course, but ten more arrived late last night. From off-shore spots in Britain. I told him that all samples were to be boiled as soon as possible after they were taken. This bug is killed at 100 degrees Fahrenheit; that way there wasn't any chance of a bacterial increase during transit."

She stubbed a finger on one test tube. "That's the thickest. It comes from the coast of Obanshire. The evidence is circumstantial of course, but I think we must accept it. I've arranged for Andre to be brought here this morning."

Fleming started. "But she's sick," he protested. "She can't help."

"She is sick, and getting sicker," Dawnay answered. "That's why we must see her quickly. Please, John, you know I'm not callous—but she must help if she can and I believe it's possible."

Fleming sighed. "You're the boss. But I don't like it."

A nurse pushed Andre to the laboratory in a wheel chair. Fleming managed a welcoming smile as he clasped her hands. It was not easy; she looked desperately fragile and her eyes stared out of her drawn, pale face.

He was appalled by how much she had deteriorated since he had last been allowed to see her.

The nurse made her comfortable and then Dawnay explained the situation, showing her the test tubes and pointing out that the most opaque sample came from the Minch.

"What is the Minch?" Andre asked.

"The channel off Thorness, where all this started," Dawnay said harshly.

"It is impossible. It does not make sense. It has nothing to do with the message." She looked from Dawnay to Fleming, bewildered and wary. "The message has a different plan."

Dawnay snorted. "There won't be any different plan if this engulfs us. Think, girl; think!"

"There is nothing about it in the computer," Andre insisted.

Fleming took a step forward. "Not now, maybe," he said thoughtfully. "But there's something vaguely familiar about this bug. I'm sure there is. How far have you got with your analysis, Madeleine?"

Dawnay said nothing, but went to her desk and picked up a file. "As far as I've got has been coded in binary. Is that of any help?" she asked.

He took the file, walked to the window, and sat on the sill while he studied the figures. He laid the file aside. "It confirms my hunch, memory, or whatever it is. It reads terribly like something I already know."

"Then it's something you started," Andre interrupted.

He looked round in surprise. "That I started?"

"At Thorness. That's why this machine has no memory of it." She paused and lay back, as if trying to summon up some strength. "How many times did you try to destroy the other computer before you succeeded?" she asked.

"Several."

"After one of those times the computer decided to hit back. With this bacterium." Her eyes became cold and hostile, giving Fleming an empty feeling of despair. "You have a great force sent to help you and you turn it against you. You won't listen to me. You won't listen to anyone. You condemn your whole race because you won't accept. There is nothing you can do now. It will engulf you!"

There was a sort of inhuman resignation in her tone. Fleming turned away, making for the door. He felt sick to his soul.

For a day or so afterwards he avoided everyone. Intel had provided its internees with a first class library and subscriptions had been taken out for the world's technical journals. He read in a desultory sort of way, his brain hardly registering the information. The journals were all back numbers; interference with communications since the storm cycle had increased had cut off all but essential supplies, although some Intel transports still plied between Azaran and Europe.

He heard the hum from the computer and guessed that the thing had drawn Andre to it, no doubt on orders from Gamboul. He could imagine what the machine was working on—rocket interceptors of the kind that had been its first official triumph at Thorness. There was a ghastly this-is-where-I-came-in flavour about the whole thing. He wondered a little how the formulae were being handled once the output printer had produced the equations. Without proper interpretation they were just gibberish even for skilled electronic engineers. But, of course, there was Abu Zeki. Fleming readily accepted that the young man was as good as any highly-paid boffin in his particular line of country; it wasn't surprising really. The Arabs had invented the whole basis of mathematics as modern civilisation knew it.

Fleming pondered a lot on Abu, not just Abu the first-rate product of a technological age, but Abu the man. He was innately decent, kindly and blessed with imagination. His patriotism was fiery and nationalistic, but he did not let his emotions completely stifle his reasoning.

Fleming swung off the bed where he had been sprawling, his mind made up, and picked up his room telephone. In a losing battle one ally was better than none at all. He would ask Abu to fix some time when they could talk without interruption.

The operator told him Dr. Abu Zeki was in the computer block. Fleming had no wish to go there and see Andre slowly dying as the machine sucked the last use out of her. He asked to be put through, not caring that the call would probably be monitored.

"Hello, Abu. Fleming. I wondered, with the week-end coming up, whether we could have a chat? Maybe I could meet your family? I'm afraid my tame guard would probably have to come too."

"Why yes, Dr. Fleming, I'd be honoured to be your host." Abu sounded guarded. "It will be good for you to meet the ordinary people of Azaran. My home is very simple, I'm afraid, but you will be welcome. Please stay overnight."

They fixed a time to leave on Saturday at midday, when Abu was off duty till Monday morning. Deliberately Fleming phoned through to Kaufman's office to request permission for a social visit. The German was out but a secretary took the details. The pass was brought to Fleming's quarters that evening. No one queried the reason.

Abu was the proud possesser of a little Italian car, and his home was only twenty-five miles from the Intel station. But, as he explained while they sped along the highway past the airport, his contract demanded that he live on the site except at week-ends.

"My wife doesn't like that, but she has her mother with her," Abu went on. "With the baby to look after, Saturday soon comes round."

It was as though he were talking about Surbiton, Surrey, or White Plains, New York. But the similarity soon ended.

The road petered out into a wide track of rolled stones and then to a little more than a sandy track. Abu dropped his speed when the little car laboured with its unaccustomed load of three men. The guard, sitting in the occasional seat at the back, cursed in Arabic about the bumps, but he seemed glad to be away from the compound, even though the wind sent sand whirling grittily into the car.

The track began to wind with a gradual gradient. The terrain became more stony. Ahead the low range of mountains, rocky hills really, grew more defined despite the sporadic sandstorm. Fleming had often looked at them because of their fascinating, ever-changing colours at different times of the day. In early morning they were pink, changing to white when the sun climbed higher. By midday they were always blurred by heat haze; in the evening they towered black and vast.

Abu pointed to a small collection of rectangular, flat-roofed dwellings lying on a tiny plateau immediately below a fault in the range.

"That is my village," he said, "or at least the one where I have made my home. People have lived here since long before your Christ. Look!"

Fleming followed the direction of Abu's glance. The rock face bore traces of enormous bas-reliefs—formalised animals and serried ranks of bearded warriors. None was perfect, rock falls jagging into the sculpture.

"Persian," Abu explained. "English archaeologists were here many years ago; more recently the Americans. All have gone now, of course. What they were really interested in was the temple. You'll see it round the next bend."

Dwarfed by the rock face, the temple was just a ruin, a few pillars still standing amid a mass of rubble. Abu said that the pillars were Roman, but the site had yielded remains of several civilisations and religions—Assyrian, Persian, and a few tablets of Egyptian origin. "As you know, Azaran has been a vassal of many empires," Abu said. "Now of none!"

He bumped off the track and down what was little more than a donkey path. His wife was standing outside the tiny house, a pretty woman, little more than a girl. Although she wore Arab costume she was unveiled.

She lowered her eyes when Abu introduced Fleming, but her welcome was warm, and in perfect English. "Lemka was at Cairo University, among the first girl students under Colonel Nasser's new scheme," Abu said proudly.

"You are hot," Lemka said to Fleming. "Please come inside out of the terrible wind. It is cooler. Perhaps you will have some of our wine." She glanced towards the car and saw the soldier leaning against the shady side of the vehicle.

"What is the man doing?" she asked, clutching her husband's arm. "You are now under guard?"

"He is an escort for Dr. Fleming," Abu told her, but she was not completely satisfied.

"There is much trouble in the city?" she asked. "On the radio they say so little. Just that the coup is over and all is peace again. Is it so?"

"Yes," Abu said. "Everything is normal. Now get us something to drink and then see about a meal. I have told my friend he will have to take what the English call pot luck."

Lemka passed through the curtained opening to the tiny kitchen at the rear.

"My wife is Christian," Abu said; "that is why she is not so effacing as most Arab wives."

"But you are Moslem?" Fleming asked. "Yours is a Moslem name."

"I'm a scientist," he retorted. "And I am also for my country."

Fleming eased himself down on the low backless settee. "And I'm for the whole human race—more or less. Look, Abu, you didn't believe me about the computer, did you? Well, now believe me about the girl."

Lemka returned with a jug of wine and some glasses. She

poured some out and handed a glass to Fleming. The wine was sweet and thin, but refreshing.

"It's a pretty simple set-up," Fleming began, not caring that Lemka was listening. "Intel built the computer and employed you to help operate it. As you know, after Neilson got away it wouldn't work, so they hi-jacked me and I brought the girl. Intel's aim was to get a technical edge on all their competitors and a well-protected base from which to operate. Hence the missile designs you've been working on. Your President was agreeable to the arrangements. This suited the intelligence behind the computer. But it didn't suit Salim. He was an intelligent and ambitious man. He wanted to have absolute control of the whole set-up."

"He was a patriot," said Abu defiantly.

Fleming shrugged. "He certainly wasn't a man to play second fiddle to another influence. Andromeda knew it, or at least she learned it from the computer which could calculate such an eventuality. So Andre made the decision: to put the power into the hands of Intel, in fact. Our handsome boss was shown the message, or part of it, and had the meaning of it explained to her by Andre the night they were together in the computer."

"And that could influence her?" Abu was doubtful.

"Influence her?" Fleming retorted. "Obsess her completely. She had Salim killed or probably shot him herself. She's a convert who suddenly saw a vision. It made her fanatical."

"Like St. Paul?"

Both men started. They had forgotten Lemka. "But how could a vision be put into words?" she asked.

"St. Paul managed it," Fleming suggested.

"He only described it in your Bible," Abu said. "He couldn't pass it on as he really knew it."

"You're right," Fleming agreed. "You can't pass such things on, but you can impose them. That was the intention of the computer, then of Andromeda, and now of Gamboul. You can also describe the inferences. I myself have had a glimpse of that description."

Abu thoughtfully examined his empty glass. "You believe what you say? How would you describe this vision?"

"It says that mankind goes round by a long road, and it may

be too long. We may destroy ourselves before we take the next step."

"But if we can have the help of a higher intelligence and avoid that mistake," Abu protested.

"It's the handshake of death. The friend who knows better than you what's good for you." Fleming pointed towards the tiny window, at the vista of desert they had crossed in the car.

"You've heard of the Pax Romana," he said, "the calm of desolation the Roman legions left after they had forced their idea of right on the barbarians. That's the sort of peace you're working for, Abu my friend. Personally I'd rather we muddled our way along."

"And destroy ourselves?"

"No!" Fleming shouted. "If anything destroys us it will be something sent from outside. Via the computer."

"You have no proof," said Abu obstinately.

Lemka looked from one man to the other. "You should know when a man is right," she told her husband. "And help him."

Abu glared at her but she held his gaze, and slowly he smiled. Awkwardly he slid his hand into hers. "I will try," he said quietly. He turned to Fleming. "On Monday, Doctor, I will seek an interview with Mm'selle Gamboul."

Fleming thanked him, doubting whether this futile little manoeuvre would make any difference. With an effort he stirred himself. "Fine," he said. "We'll work out the sort of thing to say, to appeal to her conscience, if any. But all this is unfair on your wife. It's the week-end."

The friendship between the two men grew warmer in the few hours away from the strain of the Intel establishment. Abu took Fleming exploring among the temple ruins on the Sunday morning. They had to cut the visit short because the wind was much stronger than on the previous day, bringing small but dangerous cascades of stones and rocks from the precipitous heights behind the temple. Fleming explained Dawnay's and his theory about the origin of the abnormal weather. Abu could accept this because he had seen some of the results of the computer's calculations on the sea water bacteria. He promised to try to explain it to Gamboul.

The two men and the guard drove back to the station at dawn on Monday, choosing an early start because they had already learned that sunrise and sunset brought a short period of calm. As they zig-zagged down the mountainside towards the plain they heard a roaring in the distance and saw a sudden rush of flame up into the sky.

Abu applied for an interview with Gamboul as soon as he went on duty. He was told to report to the executive suite at 11.

She greeted him almost effusively. "Well, Dr. Zeki," she said. "You'll be the first here to know that this morning we tested the missile prototype. It was a complete success. We are now as good as Britain in that field." She smiled expectantly. "And you have other good things on the way for us?"

"Yes, Mm'selle," he said. "But I wish to ask your permission to speak on another matter."

"What is it you want?" she asked, her friendliness vanished, quickly replaced by suspicion.

"I come on behalf of Dr. Fleming. He thinks that the weather conditions in Europe and America, and even here, arise in some way from the computer. From the message." He stopped, momentarily intimidated by her look of implacable hostility. "Dr. Fleming would like permission for Professor Dawnay to contact the International Weather Bureau."

"No!" She banged her fist on the desk like a man. "What he says is nonsense."

"But if the message. . . ."

"I know the message! What it tells us to do is perfectly clear. And the weather is not part of the mission the message has given to us."

Abu shifted a little. "If you would just see Dr. Fleming——" he began.

She half shouted her answer at him. "He doesn't interest me. He has nothing to say which interests me. Do you understand?"

Abu backed to the door. "Thank you, Mm'selle," he muttered.

When the door closed Gamboul bent over the inter-com microphone on her desk. The red switch was already depressed.

"Herr Kaufman," she called quietly. "You heard what Doctor Abu Zeki had to say? Good! You will have him watched now, all the time."

DEPRESSION

OSBORNE stared out of the carriage window at the sprawl of South London. His left arm was still in a sling to take the strain off the pectoral muscle which Kaufman's gunman had shot through. Otherwise he was very little hurt, and the wound itself was healing rapidly.

If he had had a miraculous escape, so had London. Damage from the previous night's hurricane was not as great as he had feared, so far as he could see from the slowly moving train. T.V. aerials were bent grotesquely and a lot of roofs had gaping holes where chimney stacks had toppled. He was jammed against the glass by the pressure of the other standing passengers. The journey from his home at Orpington had taken more than two hours already. He could not complain the train was late; it was unscheduled. With the power lines out of action only diesel trains from the coast were getting through. His train eased forward in stops and starts, passed from section to section by manual signalling.

Being a cautious man, he had started out early, knowing that after a night like the past one travel would be difficult. But he was beginning to worry. The Ministry meeting was scheduled for 10.30. The others, living around Whitehall, would doubtless be there on time.

The train stopped for ten minutes south of the river. Osborne saw Battersea power station, as vast and solid as ever, the usual plume of white smoke from the stack whipped away by the still boisterous wind. Almost imperceptibly they started again, and kept going. The electric signalling system was working here and they swung over the points and cruised gently into Charing Cross. Hastily scrawled notices gave warnings about falling glass from the roof; they were ignored by the rush of exasperated commuters making for the exits.

Out in the Strand life seemed fairly normal. A hoarding had blown down, but traffic was moving, though slowly. The centre of Trafalgar Square was roped off. Nelson still looked across London from his column, but presumably the authorities were taking precautions.

Osborne turned into Whitehall. A barricade or two where windows had been blown out, nothing more. Big Ben stood unharmed, its clock proclaiming that it was 10.21. Osborne quickened his steps. He would be just in time after all.

The Minister was already in his office when he arrived. He grunted a perfunctory greeting and returned to his reading. "Neilson sent a message he'd be on time," he said without looking up.

The American arrived a moment later. Osborne cut short his attempt at a cheerful greeting at the sight of the black band on Neilson's arm. The man looked older; the death of his son had hit him hard.

Without preliminaries the Minister opened the meeting. "No time or reason for formalities," he said. "Professor Neilson wants your help, Osborne." He paused and gave a quizzical look. "As Neilson's in the picture as regards your position over the Thorness debacle, you won't mind my referring to it. To put your mind at rest, the enquiry's shelved. It's pretty pointless with the two main witnesses, Fleming and the girl, missing. So put that business out of your mind for the time being. This is what you might call a national emergency. An international commission's being set up under Professor Neilson, and we want someone to run the secretariat."

"Preferably you," said Neilson. The words were unnaturally hoarse and loud.

Osborne turned to him. "You're feeling it too, are you?" he asked. "The breathing?"

Neilson nodded. "It's pretty general, and worse in the hills."

"They're evacuating the Highlands," said the Minister. "We haven't announced it yet, but it's all part of a general pattern. The air at any altitude is getting too thin to be able to breathe."

Neilson got up and walked to a table where a weather map had been spread out, held in position by drawing pins. "The Alps and the Pyrenees are now depopulated," he said. "Would you just come over here, Minister, and you, Osborne? I can show you what we've so far ascertained."

The two men stood on either side of the American. "The atmospheric pressure's falling rapidly all around here"—he swept his hand in a wide curve from the Shetlands to Brittany— "as well as in all spots where we have weather ships or Navy vessels able to make careful checks. In other words, the pressure's lowest over the sea in the Northern Atlantic and into the Mediterranean. The indications are slighter in the Indian Ocean and the Pacific, but they are there. Naturally, air rushes from the land masses to compensate, and so you have your storms and this thin atmosphere."

"What do you want me to do?" Osborne asked.

"If you're fit enough?" interposed the Minister. "Not getting any trouble from your injury?"

"I'm all right, Minister."

"Good," said Neilson. "Now, as you can imagine, the data I've been able to collect is too vague, too sporadic. We want all the news we can get, properly collated, and then rationalised. That takes some organising."

The Minister moved to Osborne and put his hand on his shoulder. "With this regrettable sabotage business hanging over you, the security people are rather agin your continuing to have access to—well, you understand, old boy? But we can second you to this weather job and faces are saved all round. Specious but practical."

Osborne gave a wry smile. Before he could say anything, Neilson began explaining what he wanted. "We've got to work back through the weather records for the past month or six weeks. Your Air Ministry has got out some preliminary data. There's no doubt in my mind that this abnormally low pressure began in one area."

The Minister returned to the map. "And I expect you can guess where that was, Osborne," he said. "It was here." He stabbed with his index finger into a cluster of spirals. Beside his finger point the dotted lines of the prohibited maritime area fanned westwards—the Thorness rocket testing range. Osborne felt no surprise. There was a sort of inevitablity about the whole thing.

"So now you have some idea of the channels into which your work may lead," said the Minister resignedly. "But I would impress on you that you must remain objective. For a good while your work must be organising a reporting system from all countries. The U.N. people in New York have pushed through a general agreement for co-operation with the committee. You'll get no niet's or non's."

A mass of wind surged against the building, the modern steel windows protesting but not rattling. It died away as suddenly as it had come. Somewhere in the street glass was tinkling. "The great thing is speed," said the Minister.

For the rest of the day Osborne and Neilson worked on setting up an organisation. Largely it was a matter of instructing clerical staff and setting up communications. The Meteorological people at Bracknell would service the information. They installed a radio link. Land lines were no longer reliable.

Before the spring night had fallen the wind began to increase again. There was every sign of a far worse storm even than during the previous night. Osborne gave up all idea of going home.

Neilson went off to his hotel to get some dinner and Osborne was left alone. He took time off to relax and think. The way every nation, large and small, had signified its eagerness to co-operate had been encouraging and stimulating. One tiny blank appeared in the long list of countries listed as willing to help. Osborne felt it peculiar that in the face of such danger from a natural phenomenon internal politics should be so jealously regarded in Azaran.

He picked up the phone and asked for the communications duty officer in the Middle East Section at the Foreign Office. The phone was answered immediately, but it was difficult to hear. The air had chosen that moment to whirl itself into a frenzy. Osborne had to shout his request, the effort making him gasp for breath.

Equally laboured came the reply: "We'll try, sir, but things are difficult. Line communications have gone to hell, and radio is no more reliable. We'll be lucky to get any message out of this building tonight, let alone overseas. And as you know, sir, there's been an upheaval there. Azaran's officially sealed itself off." A crash drowned out the rest of the words. "Window's just blown in," came the voice. "God, what a night!"

It was mid-afternoon when Fleming heaved himself off his bed and went to his shower. Lethargy was insidiously enveloping him, making it possible to lie for hours doing nothing, sometimes hardly thinking. He had not really imagined that Abu would have any success in getting him an interview with Gamboul, any more than he had a definite idea of what he could say to her if he got the chance. Yet, in the frustration of his existence, he had played a sort of game ever since Abu had gone, pretending that the next ten minutes, or the ten minutes after those, would bring a summons.

It hadn't come, of course. Showered and refreshed in body, if not in mind, he made his way to the computer building. Andre was seated at the console, Kaufman close by. She looked desperately ill. Fleming hesitated beside her, but she took no notice of him and he moved away along the corridor.

The output printer was working and Abu was studying the figures emerging.

"I could do nothing," murmured the Arab, without looking up. "I'm suspected now."

Fleming bent down as if to read the figures. "I don't think there's anything any of us can do—except warn people."

Abu tore off the newly completed sheet and stood up. "Go to my home this evening," he whispered. "Give the guards a slip. I can't come. I'm being watched. Lemka will tell you."

Before Fleming could question him further Abu had walked quickly away to the filing office. Fleming watched his retreating back thoughtfully.

Dawnay came from the other end of the corridor. "I saw Abu Zeki all conspiratorial with you through the glass doors," she said, "so I held back. What was it all about?"

"I don't know," Fleming admitted. "A trap perhaps; he had a session with La Gamboul this morning. Or it may be a wild goose chase. But we may as well go down fighting. And what happy tidings have you got?"

"I know what the little beast is."

"What is it?"

"An artificially synthesised bacterium. If we knew how it acts we'd have an idea of what we're up against."

"Can Andre . . . ?" He hesitated.

Dawnay gave a rueful smile. "I tried. She says the computer can't help. It knows nothing about the bacterium."

They walked towards the door, to get away from a guard who had paused near them. "I'm reduced to straw-clutching," he continued. "So I'll try walking into our friend Abu's trap if that's what it is."

She clutched at his arm. "Be careful, John," she begged. "With you gone——."

"I always turn up," he grinned.

Getting away from the compound wasn't easy. Fleming had to wait until nightfall, and he was not too certain of the place where Abu said he had left his car. But he was helped by the weather. The wind, after sporadic bursts of boisterousness throughout the day, was developing into a major gale. The guards had all sought shelter against pillars and walls from the stinging sand.

His eyes adjusted to the moonless darkness after he had walked from the main compound into the service area. Abu's car was parked among several others. The ignition key was in position as Abu had promised. He drove away, not too fast, in case the speed aroused some hidden sentry.

Following the route was tricky. He wished he had taken more careful note of landmarks on the week-end trip. Twice he ran off the track during a particularly violent gust of wind when dense clouds of sand hit him, but the rear-engined Italian car was ideal for the terrain. He got to Abu's house in a couple of hours.

The door opened an inch when he knocked. He identified himself and Lemka told him to come in quickly.

An old woman in Arab costume was sitting in one corner. She pulled her veil over the lower part of her face but her eyes were friendly. On her lap she nursed a baby.

Fleming looked at the child. "Your son?" he asked Lemka.

"Yes; Jan," she said proudly. "Dr. Neilson was his godfather. You have children?"

"No." He felt awkward with this very direct young woman.

"You would like some coffee?" Lemka said. She spoke to her mother in Arabic. The woman laid the child down in its cot and went to the kitchen.

"What's all this about?" Fleming asked when they had both sat down, Lemka beside the cot which she gently rocked. "Abu couldn't tell me anything."

"I made him ask you to come," Lemka said quietly. "You see, I have a cousin who is radio navigator of Intel's air transports. He's on the Europe run."

"They're still flying there?"

She nodded. "It's difficult, but they get through. It would help if you could get in touch with English scientists? My cousin is not allowed to carry messages. All crews are searched before take-off. But he has promised me he will try."

Fleming became thoughtful. It all seemed like a trap. "Why should he?" he asked.

Lemka's mother came in with the coffee, poured out two cups and stole silently away, squatting on the floor in the far corner. Lemka glanced at her, then at the baby. "He'd do it for me, for his family; for our little Jan."

It was something simple, human—the sort of human value which shone out in this nightmare world. Fleming believed her.

"He's going to London; fine. What could he take? A letter?"

She nodded. "It is dangerous, you understand. People are locked up for such things. Even shot."

"Thank you," was all Fleming could find to say. "I will ask Professor Dawnay what the message could usefully include." He stood up to go.

Lemka came beside him. "What is going to happen?" she whispered.

He drew the curtain back from the tiny window. Sheltered by the precipitous hill, the air was clear of sand and the stars sprinkled the black vault of the sky with myriad pinpoints of light.

"There are two things," he said half to himself. "First, the intelligence out there in Andromeda that sent the message wanted to make contact with whatever forms of life it could find anywhere in the galaxy—in a sort of evangelical way." He looked down at Lemka and smiled. "Remember how we mentioned St. Paul?"

Lemka nodded.

"The intelligence is a sort of missionary in space," he continued. "When it finds life which responds, it converts it; takes it over. It's tried before, maybe, over several million years on different worlds—maybe with success—and now it's tried here, through the girl Andromeda, for what she calls our own good. That's one thing."

"And the other?"

"Where it finds an intellect hostile to it, it destroys it and possibly substitutes something else. That's what's happening

now, because we fought. Or rather, because I fought. And lost."
His voice faltered. "That's why, Lemka, you might say that I've
condemned the whole human race."

"Not yet," she whispered.

"No," he agreed, "not quite yet. There's just a chance that
Professor Dawnay will have something for your cousin."

It was early morning when Fleming got back to the compound. He simply drove openly through the main gates under
the flood lamps, waving cheerfully to the sentry. The man
grinned back. It was clear that so far as the Western people
were concerned the guards were instructed to stop them getting
out, not to prevent them coming in.

Fleming waited till the working day had begun before he
went to see Dawnay. Whatever they put in the message it had to
be terse, factual and conveying something more than an appeal
for help.

Abu Zeki was in the laboratory with Dawnay. He looked relieved to see Fleming but said nothing.

Dawnay was bending over a big tank she had had installed
below the low long window. The glass top was screwed down.
Several rubber tubes and wires passed through seals in the top.
They were connected to recording instruments, one of which
Fleming recognised as a barograph. In the bottom were two or
three inches of an opaque fluid.

She greeted him perfunctorily. "No luck with Andre," she
said, busy with notes on the instrument recordings. "She was
trying to be helpful, I think, but she hasn't the will to do much.
Still, I got some of the data I wanted, thanks to Abu."

"Found anything?" Fleming asked.

"Not much. I now know what it does." She removed a test
tube clamped vertically with its mouth over one of the tubes
from the tank. "It absorbs nitrogen. You'd find less than 3 per
cent. in this sample from the air just above the water surface. It
also takes up some oxygen, not much—but see for yourself."

She turned to a filing cabinet and withdrew an untidy sheaf
of papers. "Just glance over those formulae, will you, John? Tell
me if you've seen anything like them before."

He studied the data in silence. "I said it looked familiar. It
still does." He handed the papers back.

"It's another synthesis," she murmured.

He was really alarmed. "Not another one starting?" he exclaimed.

"No," she reassured him. "We worked back to this a long way. Yesterday evening I was on familiar stuff. It came out of the computer at Thorness—oh, it must have been more than a year ago, when I began the D.N.A. synthesis."

"It's part of that?" he asked in a low voice. "Part of the programme which constructed the girl?"

"No. It came up quite separately," Dawnay was firm about it. "I based an experiment on it; one had to at that stage when we were still groping in the dark, really." She moved to the tank and looked with despair down at the opaque, sullen fluid at the bottom.

"I actually made some of these bacteria."

"What happened to them?"

She answered with an obvious effort. "They seemed harmless, pointless. Another failure. I kept them in a whole range of cultures for a week. They did not die, but they did not develop. Just multiplied. So the tubes were washed out and sterilised."

He started towards her. "Don't you realise . . . ?"

"Of course I do," she said sharply. "The bacteria went down the sink, into the drain, from the drain to the sewer, and into the sea."

"Which is precisely what that bloody machine intended should happen! But an ounce or so is the most it can have been. It can't have spread the way it has."

"Not impossible," she said. "I've tried to fix the date more or less exactly when I abandoned that line of research. It's an academic point really. But I'm certain it is a year ago at least. With this tank fixed up I have been able to calculate the rate of growth. It's fantastic. No virus or bacteria so far known has a rate even comparable to it. And now the build-up's greater. You can envisage the sort of progression now that it's invaded all the main oceans."

"How long," he asked, "will it take . . . ?"

She looked up at him. "Possibly another year. Probably less. All sea water will then reach maximum saturation."

Fleming studied the wall-graph which recorded hour by hour the nitrogen content in the air of the tank. "It does nothing but absorb nitrogen and some oxygen?" he asked.

"Not so far as I've discovered," she replied. "But the sea normally absorbs nitrogen very, very slowly. Plankton and so on. Any artificial fertiliser manufacturing plant takes out in a week as much as the sea absorbs in a year. It hasn't mattered. There's plenty. But this bacteria could easily absorb all the nitrogen in the world's atmosphere. That's what's happening now. It's bringing down air pressure. In the end there'll be no nitrogen and therefore no plants. When the pressure really drops off the scale there won't be any way for us to absorb oxygen, and then there'll be no more animals."

"Unless——," Fleming began.

"There's no unless."

Fleming glanced at Abu Zeki, standing quiet and expectant in the background. "Madeleine," he said, "thanks to Abu there's a chance of us getting a letter to London."

She showed little interest. "To say what?" she demanded.

"What it is."

"There's no point." She shrugged. "But all right, if you wish. It will be a gesture, though it's too late." She bent once more over the tank, staring down into the fluid. "The girl was right," she muttered. "The computer made life. This time it's made death. So far as we're concerned that's Finis—down in that water."

"We'll write, all the same," Fleming insisted. "Lemka's cousin is ready to take the risk. Keep it short but put in every fact you know." His voice was decisive. It stirred Dawnay a little out of her despair.

"All right, John," she agreed.

Abu smiled. "I'll wait till the note is ready, Professor," he told Dawnay. "I'll go into town for a meal. It's my normal practice. My cousin goes to the same café."

Fleming moved to the door. "Good luck, both of you," he said with forced cheerfulness. "Maybe we can all meet back here later this evening?"

He strode out into the hot wind, making for his own quarters. He was glad to be by himself. It was difficult for him to play the role of optimist. And he wanted time to think. He always thought best by himself, with a bottle of Scotch by his side.

He sent an orderly to the commissariat for a new bottle. The boy returned in five minutes. Intel did not stint the creature comforts, the mental and spiritual dope, for its prisoners.

He skipped dinner and so he was a little drunk when he returned to the laboratory. The wind was as wild as ever, and it was already dark. There had not even been the usual brief twilight. Abu was already there with Dawnay. "I saw my cousin," he told Fleming. "He took the note. I don't know, of course, how he got on at the airport, but I heard the transport take off on schedule. Just on an hour back."

Fleming thanked him. "It may not get through; it may be ignored at the other end, and even if it isn't we don't know what they can do if they study it and accept the truth of it. It would take a lot of swallowing." He flexed his arms. "So we're still really on our own. Which means we need the girl. Go across to sick quarters, Abu, and tell the nurse to bring her over."

"Now?" Abu asked doubtfully.

"Now," Fleming repeated. "Kaufman has her dragged out whenever they want a computing job done. The nurse has to obey, poor lass."

"What do you propose to do with her?" Dawnay asked disapprovingly.

"Use her as an ally."

"She won't play. Anyway, she's too weak."

"She'll have to try, won't she? She's the only thing we've got. If the computer at Thorness made a bacterium there must be an anti-bacterium. I'm not expert in your line, Madeleine, but surely that's a basic fact of biology?"

"Do you happen to know of this bug which will conveniently act in the opposite direction?" she asked.

"The computer must." He waved away her sarcasm. "I realise it's not the same computer, but it managed to reconstruct the formula for the original one, or at least we and Andre made it work. We can do it again, for an antidote."

Before Dawnay could reply Abu returned. He held the door open while the nurse brought Andre inside in her wheelchair. Fleming was accustomed to see the girl a little weaker, a little more wraithlike, every time he saw her. But he had not got used to the way she now glared at him, her eyes smouldering with resentment.

"All right, nurse," he said without looking at Andre, "leave her. We'll call you when it's time to take her back."

The girl stood her ground. "She should not be here, sir; I had just got her to sleep."

Abu interposed. "Please be sure it's all right."

The nurse patted the rug round Andre's legs and reluctantly left. When the door had closed Andre asked what they wanted her for; she did little more than whisper, even that was jerky and hard to understand.

"We need another formula from the computer," Fleming explained. "Another bacterium or perhaps a virus. It's got to kill the first one and then work the other way round. It would have to release nitrogen held in the water."

"And it would have to breed faster than the first one," Dawnay added. "It would be another tricky piece of bio-snythesis, another life-creating process. For that I need a formula."

Andre had listened with almost horrifying intensity, looking from one to the other, hanging on every word.

"But why?" she protested.

Fleming lost his temper. "For God's sake!" he shouted. Dawnay uttered a word of warning and with difficulty he calmed down. Then, crouching beside Andre, he slowly and patiently explained how the existing bacteria were changing the world's weather and making it impossible to breathe, the preliminary to complete destruction of all life. "So we need just one small bug to start breeding on an even greater scale to counteract it," he finished.

Once more she shook her head. "It is not possible," she whispered.

"Look," he said urgently, "if you can come up with one sort you can come up with another—and save us all."

Her big eyes looked back into his. Imperceptibly they softened, the hostility lessening. "Save you?" she managed to say aloud. "What about me?" She tried to move her hands over her breasts and touch her face. The effort was too much and she lay back.

"If you had the strength—you'd try." It was Dawnay who was begging her now.

"I don't know." She shook her head weakly. "It would take too long."

Fleming looked over Andre's head at Dawnay. "Would it?" he muttered.

Involuntarily Dawnay glanced at the girl. "I don't know," she said. "She's . . ." She got a grip on herself. "If you mean would I take too long with the actual lab work, that's another matter. There are still twenty-four hours in however many days we've got left, and I don't like sleeping much."

Both of them looked at Andre again. They were two people willing her to obey, to do the seemingly impossible. The ghost of a smile flickered over her mouth, and she nodded.

Fleming turned to Abu. "Get the nurse to take her back," he said. "She's the only ally we've got, poor kid. Tell the nurse to have her ready for duty at the computer at 9 tomorrow morning. Try to explain that we're not sadists. Tell her how necessary it is. Frighten her a bit if you like by hinting how she'll also die if she fails us."

Abu's persuasion—or intimidation—worked. The nurse obediently wheeled Andre into the computer block shortly after nine the next morning. The girl said her patient was too weak to move, and she would have to use the wheelchair to work while interpreting the screen.

Only Fleming was present. Dawnay felt too little hope to be able to bear to watch, and Abu remained in the main office so that he could report any approach by Kaufman or the mysteriously silent Gamboul. One of the things which would have been disquieting, if Fleming had not been so preoccupied with a greater problem, was the way Intel seemed to be leaving them to their own devices.

Andre put her hands unsteadily on the sensory controls. The computer had hummed to activity as soon as she entered the building. But the screen brightened very slowly. Its imagery was blurred, and even when Fleming pulled the curtains over the windows across the hall the pattern was almost indistinguishable. He watched Andre raise her head to the screen; he saw how she seemed to be gripping the controls as if they yielded some supply of strength. Her effort to concentrate was pathetic. Presently she relaxed her hold. Her body slumped and her head bowed to her breast. She began to talk thickly, sobs shaking her shoulders.

Fleming bent over her. "I can't follow them," he heard her say. "Take me away from it." And then she added, as if to herself, "I don't want to die."

The nurse came forward, pushing Fleming away. "She has done enough; too much, you must not ask. . . ." Abruptly she grasped the chair and wheeled Andre away from the screen.

Fleming refused to move out of the way. "Andre," he said quietly, "none of us wants to die, but we all will, unless some miracle starts sucking the air back out of the sea."

She raised her head with an effort. "You will die together.

I'll die alone." He put out his hand to comfort her, touching hers. She moved her arm away. "Don't touch me," she whispered. "I must seem horrible to you."

"No!" he said urgently. "You have always seemed beautiful to me. Ever since . . . ever since we ran away from Thorness. But try to think, please! Only you can help us now. I don't even know what this is doing. Is the power still with Gamboul?"

He indicated the mass of the computer ranged all around him and she nodded her head. "Then why does she never come here?" he demanded.

Andre remained quiet, gathering her strength. "There is no need. She has seen the message. The computer has set her on a path. She will not turn back. Nor will she come here. She needs no more. I could not show her anything. I can hardly see it any more." Her eyes looked askance towards the blank screen. "I will come back when I have rested."

Without asking permission, the nurse started to push the chair away. Fleming did not stop her this time. He watched them disappear through the exit doors and for a full minute he remained where he was, in the heavy silence of the deserted building.

Suddenly he jumped. The output printer was working. It clicked rapidly, then stopped. Once more it started. This time the keys moved slowly but they kept on. He went to the section and took hold of the short length of paper already typed.

"Pretty ropey," he decided as he looked through it, "but some sort of biological data, all right."

He went to tell Dawnay. It was a triviality in itself—this preliminary analysis. But in its inference it was tremendous. It showed that after all Andre would help, and maybe Dawnay could still achieve a miracle—if they had time.

As he stepped out of doors the fury of the wind swept over him, making him stagger. He began panting, and there was no help in the gulps of air he took. With head down and body leaning into a dry, suffocating gale, he plodded through the swirling sand to the laboratory doors. His zest and optimism had gone. Time was something they couldn't buy.

Three thousand miles away dawn was breaking over London —a London stricken with disaster. A few tin-hatted policemen stood in the middle of the wider streets well away from the buildings. The jangle of an ambulance bell occasionally pene-

343

trated the howling of the wind. Lights burned weakly on the first floor of the Ministry of Science building from the few windows which had not been blown out and boarded.

The grey light of early morning accentuated the weariness of the four men sitting around the littered table. For several hours they had not contributed a constructive idea. Discussion had really become argument, the futile criticism of over-exhausted men.

Neilson, normally reticent and co-operative, had given way to exasperation when Osborne and the Prime Minister's secretary launched into an interminable argument about departmental responsibility and finance for the expanded activity agreed upon the previous evening.

"You have a wonderful talent here," observed Neilson, "for plodding through routine while the heavens are falling."

"We're tired, Professor Neilson," said the Minister sharply. "We can only do what we feel is best."

"I'm sorry," Neilson said.

The Prime Minister's secretary reached for a cigarette, found the packet empty, and hurled it into a corner. "There's no power over half the country, and the rest is under water, or snowed up or blown down. People are dying faster than the army can bury them. If you could only give us some sort of forecast how long it's going on. . . ."

Neilson was on the point of answering when a secretary came in, tip-toeing to Osborne.

"Something urgent for you, sir," he said. "Brought by a despatch rider from London airport."

Osborne took the buff-coloured envelope and slit it open. With deliberate slowness he unfolded the flimsy paper, and read it.

At last he looked up. "It's from Azaran," he said, "from Madeleine Dawnay." He handed it to the Minister.

"You two had better see this together," the Minister said to Neilson and the Prime Minister's secretary. "It will save time. The Cabinet must be informed right away, of course." He waited impatiently while the two men read the note. "Any proposals, Neilson?" he asked.

Neilson nodded. "Can you get me to Azaran—today?" he demanded.

10

VORTEX

THE four-engined aircraft cruised to the apron, slewed round and stopped. Electric trolleys moved forward to unload the cargo. The crew, tired from a non-stop flight from London during which they had never topped 6,000 feet and had been buffeted for seven hours without respite, clambered down the ladder and made their way to the flight office. A uniformed Arab and a bullet-headed European greeted them perfunctorily as the Captain handed over the aircraft papers. The European flicked through them and passed them to the Arab, and then extended his pudgy hand for the crew's personal documents. He let the Captain go through immediately, but when he looked up at the next two men standing before him he referred again to the papers in his hand.

"Who is this?" he asked in German. The two air crew members looked blankly at him. He repeated his question in halting Arabic.

Yusel, Lemka's cousin, the younger of the two, smiled ingratiatingly. "My second navigator. He not understand Arabic or the language you use first."

The Intel man scowled. "I've not been notified of any change in crew plans. Why are you carrying a second navigator?"

Yusel explained. "For route familiarisation. We have to fly so low; no air pressure up top."

Not really satisfied, the Intel man re-read the documents. When he could find no fault in them, he threw them across the desk. Yusel picked them up and led his companion into the crew room where they got out of their flying kit. His companion was Neilson.

"That's the worst over," Yusel told him. "Now I'll take you

to my cousin's house. It'll be quite safe. Her husband, Doctor Abu Zeki, will contact you as soon as he can."

Neilson nodded. "The sooner the better."

Yusel drove him to Abu's home and then returned to Baleb. It was late afternoon when he got to the café, and he had to wait an hour before his cousin arrived. When he did come Abu Zeki had the furtive air of a man who knows he is watched. Quietly, over two bottles of locally-made Azarani Cola, Yusel told him about Neilson's arrival.

"He wants to see Doctor Fleming and Professor Dawnay," he finished.

Abu Zeki glanced anxiously around the bare little café.

"I don't know if they can both get away," he said. "But I will tell them."

As soon as he heard that Neilson senior was safely in the country, Fleming decided to throw caution to the winds and go and see him. He told Dawnay to be ready to leave as soon as it was dark, if she was willing to take the risk.

The weather helped them. A violent storm broke with nightfall, sheet lightning illuminating the sky and short bursts of rain lashing the buildings and swirling sand. The guards crept, frightened and shivering, into any shelter they could find. Fleming and Dawnay plodded through the cascades of rain without once being challenged.

The drive was appalling, Abu's little car slithering in the thick scum of mud on the desert sand. But the rain had been local. After forty minutes they were driving on dry terrain, the storm providing an accompaniment of reverberating thunder and almost continuous flashes of lightning.

Fleming felt a sense of quite unreasonable relief when Lemka opened the door and he saw Neilson standing behind her. The American's wordless greeting, the way he gripped his hand, was absurdly reassuring.

To Dawnay, Neilson was someone who signified a gleam of hope that she had refused to admit existed, but she was still not sure why he had come. They both sat quietly, suppressing their excitement, while the big calm man ate his way methodically through a bunch of grapes and told them what had been happening in London. They learnt for the first time how Osborne had survived the shooting at their country-house prison, how Neilson had been called in to "head a probe into this weather thing," as he put it, and how they also had put two and two together and traced the source to Thorness. And how they had then come to a dead stop until they had received the message from Dawnay.

"Is there really any hope?" he asked her.

"About as much as a grain of sand in a desert."

She pushed aside the little tray on which Lemka had set Neilson's supper and spread out the bundle of papers she had crammed into the waistband of her skirt.

She impatiently flattened out the creases. "These are most of the figures for the D.N.A. helix," she began. "The computer has worked out what I think you'll agree is a feasible analysis. So far as I can judge, it's a potential bacterium. But the molecular structure is one thing. Getting the components and synthesising them another, but it might, possibly, produce the anti-bacterium we need."

Neilson studied the figures. "And this is the work of the machine Jan built?"

She nodded.

"I can't help wondering . . ." A tremor made his words tail off.

Fleming was sitting beside the cot, absent-mindedly revolving a toy suspended for the child's amusement. "What would have happened if your son had stayed," he finished.

Neilson turned to him. "They shot him in cold blood," he said. "In front of our eyes. If I could find the man. . . ."

"I can't tell you who pulled the trigger," Fleming said. "But I know who told him to. A man named Kaufman, who is 'looking after' us here."

"I should like to meet him," said Neilson.

"Maybe you will."

Dawnay began gathering the papers together. "At least your son's death was quick," she said with compassion. "Which is more than ours will be. Unless these work." She stuffed the papers back in her skirt band. "There's a lot more to come if only the girl can get it for us."

"How is she?" Neilson asked.

Dawnay looked down at the baby; the child was wide awake, smiling at the sight of so many faces around him. "She was an artificial sort of life," she muttered. "Not like . . ." She turned abruptly away from the baby. "There's some constituent lacking in her blood; something I didn't know about and something the computer didn't allow for."

"Can't she get some help from the machine for herself?" Neilson asked.

"No time," Fleming replied. "She might have done, I suppose, but there was this anti-bacterium job. She elected to work on it. . . ."

Neilson eyed Fleming speculatively. "That was a hard decision," he said.

Fleming paused to light a cigarette. He inhaled deeply. "Yes," he said at last. "It was a hard thing, as you say."

Fleming rose and turned away from the others. He crossed to the window and stared out into the night. Hastily, to ease the tension, Dawnay began asking if Neilson wanted copies of the computer data. Neilson shook his head. He explained that the only practical thing would be a test tube of the anti-bacterium. "If the girl can complete the analysis," he started, but Fleming interrupted.

"Shush!" They stared at him. "Lemka's coming."

Lemka, who had been keeping watch on the road, came running across the courtyard to the house. They could hear her sandals on the rough paving.

"We're watched all the time," Dawnay said. "We thought we'd given them the slip tonight."

Lemka burst into the room, her eyes large and round with excitement. "They're coming," she exclaimed. "Soldiers. A whole truck load!"

All of them stood motionless for a few seconds. Then Dawnay took the papers she had put in her waistband. "Hide these," she said, thrusting them into Lemka's hand. "Your husband can pick them up later and give them back."

Lemka took them and turned to Neilson. "My mother's room," she said firmly. "They won't go in there."

"I hope you're right," he smiled as he followed her.

There was a knock on the door, not violent or very loud. Lemka emerged from the rear room and opened the door. A corporal saluted and spoke in Arabic; two soldiers stood beside him. Their guns were still slung on their shoulders.

"He says they have come to fetch you and Dr. Fleming," Lemka interpreted, addressing Dawnay.

"Tell them we'll come right away," Dawnay said, with what

she hoped was a bright but casual smile. "We'll be all right, so don't worry. But you'll have to find a safer place for Dr. Neilson. We'll keep in touch somehow."

Lemka extended her hand and clasped Dawnay's affectionately. "My cousin will think of something. We had better not talk more, or the soldiers will suspect us."

One soldier insisted on coming in the car, and the corporal made signs to Fleming to drive close behind the army truck. The weather had cleared a little, the wind blowing strongly but steadily.

Back in the compound the computer block was a blaze of light. Two soldiers took over from the escort and led Fleming and Dawnay into the building. Kaufman was sitting at a desk in the office, his face a mask of suppressed anger. Abu was standing uneasily to one side.

"Now what's all this about?" the German barked at them as they entered. "Why were you outside without permission?"

"Permission from whom?" Dawnay demanded. "And why permission to visit friends; the family of a colleague?"

Kaufman tried to meet her look and failed. "You know you are not supposed to be without an escort," he blustered.

Fleming stepped forward, his fists clenched. "Now look here, you Teutonic gauleiter . . ." he began, but Abu Zeki stepped in front of him. "They sent for you because it was urgent. The girl collapsed while she was working in the sensory bay."

"Andre?" Fleming was already at the door. "I'll go to her," he called over his shoulder.

"How bad is she?" Dawnay asked Abu.

"She is very weak," he replied. "But there was a little more data from the printer before she collapsed." He picked up a sheaf of record sheets from the desk and gave them to Dawnay.

Kaufman cleared his throat. "You will be more carefully watched in future," he warned, but he seemed uncertain and worried. "How important is the girl to us?"

"About as important as your survival. You won't go on living for long if she doesn't finish this." Dawnay could hardly bear to speak to him, but when she saw the fear come into his eyes she realised for the first time that he was not invulnerable; that he might be able to be worked upon. "So for God's sake—and your own—try not to interfere more than you have to."

He looked at her doubtfully and went away without speaking.

Andre's corner of the sick bay was in darkness. The nurse, sitting beside a screened light, stood up when Fleming tip-toed in. She protested at the intrusion.

"It's all right," he told her. "I just want to see her. I shan't wake her."

The girl gave an annoyed sigh and walked across to the bed with him. As his eyes adjusted to the gloom he could make out the shape of Andre's emaciated body underneath the thin coverlet. Her head and hair were a vague shape in the centre of the white pillow. He bent down closer and saw that her eyes were open, watching him.

"I should have been here," he whispered, gently touching her hair. His fingers brushed her forehead. It was damp and cold.

Very faintly her voice came to him, slow and hesitant. "I have done what you wanted. Professor Dawnay has all she will need now."

His mind hardly registered what she had said. "I ought to have been with you," he said again.

He found her hand. It lay lifeless and unnaturally flexed on the coverlet. His thumb and forefinger felt for the pulse in her wrist. He could detect nothing.

"I am finished," she whispered, guessing what he was doing.

He withdrew his hand. "No, you're not," he said loudly. "We've a trick or two left. Neilson is here. The father of the man who built this computer. He made me realise what I ought to be doing. What we ought to be doing. We need some help from it for you as well as us."

He stood up. "Put yourself in my hands," he ordered. "You did before. Tonight you will sleep. Tomorrow I shall come for you. I will take you to the computer. Yes, I know," he exclaimed when he saw her attempt to protest. "You're weak. You collapsed this evening. But this time I'll be beside you, helping you."

He had very little belief that he could really do anything, but he hoped that some fresh strength had passed from him to her. She moved a little, as if relaxing and getting more comfortable. Her eyelids fluttered and closed. Her face took on the serenity of natural sleep.

Fleming went to the door, beckoning the nurse to follow. Outside he talked quietly to her, telling her that she was not to be frightened, and not to talk. "We're all in danger," he explained to her. "Your patient is trying to save us. It's up to us to save *her*. Trust me and we shall do it."

Half-heartedly the girl nodded that she understood. Fleming wished he could convince himself as easily.

He slept little that night, but lay trying to make a new plan of action for the little time they had left. With the light of morning he deliberately followed his usual routine of a shower, shave and breakfast to give Andre every precious minute to recuperate from her collapse the night before. Even then he was early. Sleepy guards, resigned to another couple of hours before the day reliefs took over, eyed him warily when, accompanied by the nurse, he pushed Andre in her wheelchair to the computer building.

After the boisterous, still stormy, weather outside the air inside the building seemed heavy and lifeless. Despite the air conditioning the familiar aroma of Kaufman's cigarellos hung around. Fleming half expected the man to come bustling up, demanding to know what was happening. But the offices were empty. Presumably the German had hung around for hours, thinking. Fleming hoped that whatever conscience he might still have had been at work.

Andre had said nothing when he had fetched her. Beyond a smile in answer to his greeting she might have been in a trance. After he had dismissed the nurse and had Andre sitting in front of the screen he resigned himself to the fact that he would just have to hope to instil his ideas in her mind, without getting a sign of reaction.

And so it was. He talked of what Dawnay believed was wrong with her, how guilty they both felt because of it. He painted a picture unreally optimistic, of what her life could be if she could help Dawnay to help her. In the end he simulated something very near anger, challenging her to prove her power.

She sat with her head drooped, her hands folded listlessly in her lap. Only the occasional fluttering of her eyelids showed that she was awake and listening. He stopped talking after a while, not knowing what else to say. He saw her try to brace herself. One hand was lifted with agonising slowness to the sensory control. The machine began to hum. A pin-point of light glowed in the centre of the screen; it dulled and expanded. Fleming stepped away, not taking his eyes off her, until he was against the wall. There he stood, tense, motionless, watching. The impossible was happening.

After a time he felt a pull on his sleeve. Abu was standing beside him looking puzzled and expectant. Fleming jerked his head towards the office and they walked quietly to it.

"What?" Abu began. "Is she . . . ?"

"I think so," Fleming replied, not really knowing what Abu was asking. He tugged his thoughts unwillingly away from Andre. "What's the news from you?"

"I went home after midnight," he said. "I had to pass through the guard room. But the officer seemed to think it was okay for me to go unescorted. My cousin Yusel got home just before me. We've fixed up Professor Neilson where he'll be safe enough. A cave high above the temple, where that rock fault is. He'll be comfortable enough there as he hasn't to move around much. It was hard going for him; the air is thinning here just as Yusel says it is even at sea level in England."

"He's got food and water?"

Abu nodded. "Lemka will visit him regularly, or her mother."

Fleming nodded, satisfied. "It's good of you all," he muttered.

"Young Doctor Neilson was kind to me," Abu said. "We liked him very much."

Both men stopped abruptly. The output printer had started to work. Fleming's thoughts raced back to Andre. "Get the nurse to take her back to bed," he ordered. He walked across to her and put his arm around her shoulders. "Good!" he said. "Now rest—and hang on."

He grabbed the paper coming from the printer, running down the short lines of figures. The details meant little to him, but the general purport was clear enough. It concerned the constituents in plasma. For ten minutes he stood watching the figures emerge. At last the motor died and the computer sank into silence.

Dawnay was working at her laboratory bench in her usual bewildering and seemingly haphazard array of apparatus. Fleming thrust the sheets of paper before her.

"What are those?" she asked, continuing to watch some fluid drip through a filter. "More bacterial formulae?"

"No," said Fleming. "Formulae for Andromeda."

She stopped her work and looked at him wonderingly. "Who programmed it?"

"She did. I more or less forced her. So far as I can judge it's a progression of figures that stands for the missing chemical constituents in her blood. Get it into chemical terms, and we can use it on her."

She took the paper and slumped in a chair. "It would take weeks of work," she muttered, running her eye over the data. "And I have this bigger job." She waved her hand almost helplessly at the jumble of retorts and test tubes on the bench.

"Which Andre got for us," he reminded her.

She was exasperated at the implied reproof. "Let's get this straight, John," she began in level tones. "First you were against me creating her. Then you wanted me to kill her when she was first made. Next you demanded that she was kept away from the computer. Now—"

"I want her to live."

"And the rest of us?" she asked him. "Do you want us to live? How much can I take on, do you imagine? My energy's limited. There's only one of me and I'm dead tired. Sometimes I think my brain is softening." She pulled herself together and smiled at him. "Do you think I wouldn't try to save her if I could? But there are millions of us, John, and our lives are in the balance. I don't even know if this is going to work. Still less that, even if it does, I'll have it made in quantity in time."

She leaned forward and held out the sheets of paper to him. He kept his hands deep in his trouser pockets, refusing to accept them. She let them fall to the floor.

He bent to pick them up and put them carefully on a clear corner of the bench. "You'll have to talk to Gamboul," he said quietly. "She won't see me and doesn't trust Abu Zeki any more. But she might listen to you. If you could persuade her to give us more freedom and more outside help. . . ."

Dawnay was lost in her own thoughts. "I don't know, I just don't know," she murmured.

Without warning there was a tremendous crack of thunder. It shook the building, making the apparatus on the bench shake and jangle. Immediately the noise died away there came the scream of wind.

"Even Gamboul must know that this weather thing isn't

something she can handle, that it wasn't part of her damned programme," Fleming said when the racket died down.

"All right," Dawnay agreed; "I'll try to explain to her."

An interview was not granted until the following morning. Gamboul sent an order for Dawnay to come to her private residence, the house which Salim had owned. From all accounts, Gamboul rarely visited the Presidential Palace any more, not even to go through the formalities of reporting the country's day-to-day activities. The President was kept a virtual prisoner. He did not seem greatly to mind; he was sick. The comparatively slight thinning of the atmosphere over Azaran was already affecting the older people. The President was suffering from bronchitis.

The Salim residence looked shabby and dilapidated. There had been some minor storm damage. No one had troubled to sweep up the rubble. The palm trees which had grown in the courtyard for more than fifty years had been broken by the wind.

An armed guard escorted Dawnay to Gamboul's office. She could see at once how the other woman had changed. The sensuality seemed to have drained out of Gamboul. Her face had become more beautiful in a haggard, almost aesthetic way, and there was something fanatical about her bright dark eyes. Something terrifyingly self-possessed and dedicated.

She was surprisingly friendly, asking what she could do. "You have everything you need for our work?" she enquired.

"For yours; not for mine," Dawnay corrected her. Then, without preamble she gave a factual and restrained report on the reasons for the state of the weather.

Gamboul listened quietly, without interrupting. She walked to the window and looked out across the city to the towering masses of cumulus beyond it over the desert.

She was quiet for a time after Dawnay had finished. "How shall we die?" she murmured, walking back to her desk and sitting down. Dawnay explained.

Gamboul waved an expressive hand. "That wasn't the meaning in the message," she protested. "It wasn't meant to happen. Everything was clear and logical. What I saw was—desolation, but not like this. And there was power too."

"What did you learn you had to do?" Dawnay prompted.

Gamboul's mind was far away, reviving that night in front of the computer screen. "Govern," she muttered. "Everyone knows that it has to be, but nobody will make the real effort. A few have tried. . . ."

"Hitler? Napoleon?" Dawnay suggested.

Gamboul was not insulted. "Yes," she agreed. "But they were not brilliant enough, or rather they did not have the help of the brain from out there. It will be necessary to sacrifice almost everything. But not like this! Not now! We're not ready!"

"How much power have you?" Dawnay asked.

"Enough here. But this was to be only a beginning."

"It still could be," said Dawnay. She could see now a way of appealing to the other woman's greed and fear.

Gamboul turned sharply to her. "What do you mean?" she demanded.

"It's possible," Dawnay explained, "that we may be able to find a way to save the atmosphere. Not probable, but just a chance. We're getting some help from the computer with a formula that looks like an anti-bacterium. We may be able to synthesise it. But I shall need help and equipment. If we succeed we shall have to mass produce it and then pump it in to the sea all over the world."

Gamboul gave her a look of suspicion. "How can you produce so much?"

Carefully Dawnay explained that with organisation the serum, once made, would increase naturally, possibly at a rate faster than the bacteria already in the sea. "Once we've bred bulk supplies we should have to send batches to all countries, where their own installations could all handle it simultaneously."

Gamboul began laughing. It was not a pleasant sound for there was no joy in it, only overweening exultation. "We will do it," she said, "but we shall not allow other governments to co-operate. Intel will build all the plant you need. Intel will offer the serum at its own price. This will give us the power I was told about. It is part of the message after all. I didn't understand. Now the world will be ours, held to ransom."

Dawnay rose, staring at her. "It's not for you!" She found herself shouting, too deeply shocked to care what risk she ran. "You're mad! It isn't part of the plan!"

But Gamboul seemed not to notice; only stared back at her with glazed eyes and spoke as if to a minion receiving orders.

"Indent for all the equipment you need, Professor. I assure you that there will be no restrictions about that."

A portable projector had been rigged up in the Cabinet Room at 10, Downing Street. The Prime Minister, a few of his senior colleagues including the Minister of Science, and Osborne were sitting at one end of the table watching the screen.

The Prime Minister raised his hand. "That's enough," he said wearily. "Put the lights on, will you?" The scene of a waste of water over what had once been Holland's most fertile farmland faded.

"The point is, sir, do we release it to the T.V. nets?" the Home Secretary enquired.

"Why not?" asked the Premier. "People who can do so, might as well see. Perhaps there'll be some sort of wry comfort in knowing that Europe's even worse off than we are. Anyway, not many will see them. I doubt whether a tenth of the country now has any electricity."

He fingered his pipe, then laid it down; smoking was almost impossible with breathing so difficult. "Any news from Neilson?" he enquired.

"Not yet, sir," Osborne replied. "Another report from Professor Dawnay brought on an Intel transport. It's a technical message the Director of Research is studying. But briefly, she claims that the bacterium is a bio-chemical thing put out by the Thorness computer."

"Is she doing anything?"

"She says she's working on it, sir. We're hoping she will give Neilson a lead and he can help her."

"Couldn't this Arab aviator or whatever he is smuggle Neilson back once there are some facts to work on?"

Osborne coughed deferentially. "I'm afraid the calculations would have to be done there, sir; they have the computer."

The Prime Minister gave Osborne a keen glance. "Thank you for reminding me of that," he snapped with uncharacteristic sharpness. "And what about the computer's minions, the fellow Fleming and the girl?"

"They're both there," the Minister of Science told him. "They're under guard."

The Prime Minister got up and walked to the head of the great table. "Perhaps it's time we moved in," he said quietly. "This isn't a Suez. We would have support from other quarters."

The Minister of Science shifted uneasily. "My experts have made an appreciation of that eventuality, sir. They advise against it. You will understand, sir, that the computer . . ."

". . . Has built them the sort of defence set-up it built us," the Prime Minister finished for him. "So we'll have to try appealing to their better nature, won't we?"

"Yes, sir," muttered the Minister of Science.

"Not a very profitable policy, I suspect," said the Premier. "But I doubt whether we or the Opposition can think up any other. I'll get the C.O.I. to draft something for the B.B.C. I suppose there's still some transmitter or other which can pump it out?"

"Daventry is still on the air, sir," the Minister of Science said. "The army's there with a group of mobile power units. We can reach Azaran on short-wave all right."

The special bulletin was broadcast in English and Arabic at hourly intervals throughout the night. Most of the first transmission got through to Azaran. After that, on Gamboul's personal orders, it was jammed.

She summoned Kaufman to her office to hear a tape transcription. The German sat impassively while the tape was played.

"This is London calling the government and people of Azaran," came the far-off, static-distorted voice. "We need your help. The continent of Europe has been devastated. The whole world is threatened by a series of climatic disturbances which have already begun to reach your own country. The air we breathe is being sucked into the sea. Within the next few weeks millions will die unless by some enormous effort it can be arrested. Tens of thousands are dying now. This country has been badly hit. Three quarters of Holland are inundated. Venice has been largely destroyed by a tidal wave. The cities of Rouen, Hamburg, and Dusseldorf no longer exist."

"Dusseldorf." Kaufman repeated the one word and the muscles of his face tightened.

Gamboul ignored him, listening to the tape. "At this moment

357

great storms are raging over the Atlantic, sweeping towards Europe. We need your help to check the course of events."

The voice was drowned in a welter of noise. Gamboul switched off the recorder. "That's where we began jamming," she explained.

"What I want to hear from you, Kaufman, is how they know that we are concerned with it."

Kaufman looked blankly at her. "Dusseldorf," he repeated. "It was my home. My old father . . ."

"We are supposed to have a good security service," snapped Gamboul. "And you are in charge of security, Herr Kaufman."

He roused himself as if from a dream. "We have done our best," he said stubbornly.

Gamboul shrugged. "It's no matter now. As soon as Dawnay has the new strain of bacteria we will make ourselves safe here. After that we will make it available to others—on our own terms."

"And meanwhile," said the German slowly, "the rest of the world must wait and die? You do not care? You think other people are not caring?"

She failed to notice the hatred in his eyes. "The world must wait," she agreed. "I know what has to be done. Others don't."

Kaufman was still looking fixedly at her. At long last she felt a little uneasy under his gaze.

"Remember, Herr Kaufman," she said. "You and I are not other people."

11

TORNADO

TRUE to her word, Janine Gamboul arranged priority for any order Dawnay gave. The resources of Intel were such that even in the chaotic conditions of Europe the materials were located, purchased and brought to Azaran by air. Even more remarkable was the speed with which young and brilliant chemists were found, specialists in bacteriology or the molecular construction of nucleic acids. Two were newly graduated students from Zurich, one a girl chemist from the research department of Germany's biggest drug firm. Questioning by Dawnay showed that they had come quite voluntarily, tempted not merely by the lavish salary but for the chance of doing what they had been told was an exciting new channel of research, in what they hoped was a less tempestuous part of the world. They had no idea of the true purposes of Intel, or of the potential nightmare that lay behind the weather disaster. The public everywhere still hoped that the worst would soon blow over.

Dawnay told her helpers the facts of the situation as it was; but she omitted the theories about the origin of the bacteria.

She worked them to the limit of endurance. They caught the sense of urgency and became her devoted servants. She was at work when they turned up in the morning, and was still there when they wearily went to their rest in the evening. Results began to show sooner than Dawnay had dared hope. Precisely ten days after they had begun in earnest the first droplet of synthetic bacterium was sprayed on a minute copper screen and placed in the electronic microscope. It was a dramatic moment as Dawnay adjusted the magnification, her assistants standing around her. Up to 500,000; then to a million. One and a quarter million. It was there: a many-sided formation, spiked, symmetrical. And it wasn't an inert crystal. It lived.

Silently she motioned to her staff to look. One after the other they shared in the triumph. Life, infinitely tiny, had been created.

Almost diffidently Dawnay had to bring herself and her assistants back to reality. This was really no more than a scientific curiosity. The real test lay ahead. The bacterium had to be bred in its billions—enough to fill a test tube. And then it had to be sent into battle against the organism which was its pre-destined enemy.

The precious and all too few droplets were sprayed into a dozen different culture soups. For six long hours there was nothing to do but wait. Tests showed dead bacteria in nine of the tubes; the other three had reached maximum saturation.

From these three, larger cultures were started. They all flourished. It was past midnight when Dawnay decided the real test could begin.

Dawnay drew a test tube of opaque bacteria-sodden sea water from the tank. It was sealed with a sterile rubber stopper. An assistant filled a hypodermic from the culture and handed it to Dawnay. The needle pierced the rubber stopper and the fluid produced a tiny swirl as it flowed into the opacity.

"Now another wait," said Dawnay. Only a slight tremor in her voice indicated the tension she felt. "So let's have some coffee."

She had not told anyone outside the laboratory how close she believed she was to success, dreading the risk of anti-climax. But Abu Zeki, drawn by the blaze of light from the laboratory windows, came over when the waiting period was almost over.

"Come in," Dawnay said, "you're in time to share in a success or help us find excuses for a failure."

"It's working?" he asked hopefully.

Dawnay laughed uncertainly. "In theory, yes. In practice—well, we'll know in a moment."

She crossed to the bench where the test tube had been clamped inside a sterile cabinet. Gingerly she withdrew it and held it to the light as the others grouped around her. Two-thirds of the water was clear and sparkling. She kept it aloft, staring, and even as they watched a few tiny heads of freed gas rose jauntily to the top of the tube.

Dawnay shook herself, bringing herself back to reality. "It's been in the tube for precisely 63 minutes," she murmured. "Now we will test it in the tank."

No need for sterility precautions or niceties of measurement now. Two tubes of culture were poured into the tank, and they all gathered round again to watch. Gradually little pools of clear water appeared, while fat, lazy bubbles appeared on the surface, burst, and were replaced by new bubbles.

"That's the nitrogen being released," Dawnay said. "The air pressure's altering."

It was true. The barograph needle was moving up slowly but steadily.

"You haf done it!" exclaimed the girl from Zurich.

"*We've* done it," Dawnay corrected. "The rest is simply mechanics. Producing on a large enough scale. We must get an hour or so's rest and then check growth rates, the effects of temperature and salinity." She turned to Abu. "They'd better start planning mass production. Go and see Gamboul or Kaufman. Tell them I must have an interview as soon as possible tomorrow—I mean—this morning."

She had no need to go into Baleb to see Gamboul. The Intel chief came to her, arriving at Dawnay's quarters while she was snatching a hurried breakfast. Gamboul asked merely for instructions, as if she were a secretary.

The result was that an hour later the Intel short-wave radio system was transmitting a long stream of orders to the cartel's headquarters in Vienna. Bulk chemical supplies of phosphates, proteins, and amino acids were to be sent by plane and ship irrespective of cost or country of origin. Engineers were to be recruited to work on the Azaran oil installations, clearing the tanks of petroleum and making them ready as breeding tanks. Old pipelines were to be adapted, and new ones laid, to pump the anti-bacteria straight into the Persian Gulf.

The message was merely acknowledged. There were no queries, no promises nor excuses. That night the first squadron of transports flew to Baleb with engineers and cargoes of chemicals. Two of them had crashed in a violent air storm over the eastern Mediterranean and a third blew up when a miniature whirlwind caught it just as it was touching down. The rest got through.

The air lift went on the next day without respite, and the first ocean freighter, hurriedly loaded at Capetown, radioed her estimated time of arrival.

A week after the original test the first bulk supplies of anti-bacteria were poured into the sea at ten points on the Azaran coast, carefully selected after a study of tidal currents. The effect was noticeable within twelve hours.

Fleming, who had been allowed to go with Dawnay to the coast, stood at the edge of the water, where the desert sloped down to make long golden beaches, and watched fascinated as the great nitrogen bubbles came bursting to the surface of the waves. Even the storminess of the sea could not hide them, and in his lungs he could feel a tingling freshness of regenerated air.

He and Dawnay drove back on the third day. "Now we must try to smuggle out some of the stuff with Neilson," she said. "This is all very fine, but it's merely local, and as you see, the weather remains quite unaffected by such a minor activity."

"No hope of Intel sending it?" Fleming peered through a windscreen opaque from a sudden downpour of hail and storm rain.

"Not a chance," Dawnay replied. "They won't release it to anyone except on their own terms. And what those terms are they haven't yet said. But I can imagine." Her words were drowned in a scream of wind which made the car shudder. "The weather's worse," she said, and there was a streak of alarm in her voice. "I wonder if we're doing right, after all. You see what's happening, John?"

He nodded, leaning forward to see the blurred image of the road. "We're treating the sea around here and nowhere else. Millions of cubic feet of nitrogen are being released. It's building up a cone of high pressure in a localised zone; everywhere else the pressure's dam' nigh a vacuum, and the original bacteria will be sucking in the nitrogen as fast as we can pump it out. We'll never win this way, all we'll do is breed hurricanes."

"God, how futile and helpless it all makes one feel," muttered Dawnay.

For an hour Fleming drove on in silence, concentrating on keeping the car going in a land which was just a kaleidoscope of rain, mud and wind.

Some ten miles from Baleb the wind dropped, though the rain continued. The air was abnormally clear, giving an illusion that objects were nearer than in fact they were.

"Look at that!" Fleming jerked his head towards the mountains along the horizon.

They stood out sharp and clear, lighter in colour than the purplish black clouds swirling above the crests. And right above them rose an immense spiral of greyish cloud, the top mushrooming and changing shape all the time.

"Tornado centre," said Dawnay. "We're in the calm area around it. Let's hope to God it doesn't move this way."

"That funnel is right over Abu's village, I think," muttered Fleming. "His family must be getting it badly, unless they saw the clouds building up and got to the caves where Neilson is."

But only Lemka had reached the cave when the tornado struck. She had clambered up the mountain with her daily basket of food for Neilson. He refused to let her go back when he noticed the abnormal calm and saw the clouds racing together towards the south.

At first Lemka protested. Her mother and the baby would be terrified by the storm. Besides, Yusel had promised to come with information about getting Neilson out with some contraband bacteria. But when the full fury of the tornado drove them into the recesses of the cave she subsided into frightened silence.

"He'll be all right, and your family," Neilson insisted with a cheerfulness he did not feel.

But things were not all right with any of them. Yusel had arrived at Abu's house shortly after Lemka had left with the food for Neilson. He had intended to set out earlier, hoping to accompany his sister because he had some good news for the American: he could smuggle a message to London the next day.

In his excitement he had not been very careful about his trip. He had not seen, through the rain and sandstorms, a car following a mile behind his.

Consequently he was absolutely unprepared when the door of Abu's house burst open and Kaufman pushed in with a couple of soldiers. Without orders, the soldiers pinioned Yusel and soon had him gagged and trussed in a chair, his arms and legs tied to it with rope.

While Lemka's mother cringed against the wall, holding the baby, Kaufman began methodically slapping Yusel's face with the back of his hand. The blows were not unduly severe, but they were relentlessly repeated, first on one side of the head, then on the other. Yusel grew dizzy, then half-conscious.

Kaufman stepped back, breathing heavily. The look in the

old woman's eyes above her veil made him uneasy. There had been people many years before who had looked like that—people who had perhaps cringed a little but whose spirit had still defied him. "Take the old woman and the child out of here," he growled.

As soon as a soldier had pushed the woman and baby into the kitchen Kaufman ungagged Yusel. "Now for some sense from you," he said, giving him another slap across the face to restore his senses. "I'm a reasonable man and I do not like to use force, but you must realise the unpleasant things which could happen. They won't if you answer a simple question. Who have you brought into the country?"

Yusel looked up at him with glazed eyes. He gulped and hesitated; Kaufman hit him again. Yusel's brain reeled. His head slumped forward and he began to lose consciousness. One of the guards revived him with a small, painful jab with a bayonet and Kaufman repeated his question.

"Professor Neilson," Yusel muttered.

Kaufman drew in his breath sharply. "Neilson!"

"The father," mumbled Yusel. "The father of the young scientist. . . ."

Kaufman closed his eyes in relief. For a split second he had had a vision of a ghost. "Why have you brought him?" he snarled. "Where is he?"

Yusel sat silent. He watched Kaufman's hands clench into fists and slowly rise to shoulder height. He bent his head in shame and fear. "He's in a cave above the temple," he whispered.

"More," ordered Kaufman.

Once he started talking, Yusel found it easy to go on. When he faltered Kaufman hit him again or a soldier prodded him with his bayonet, until they had the whole story.

Kaufman grunted with satisfaction and turned to the soldiers. "One of you take him down to the car. Keep him tied up. And you"—he turned to the second guard—"come with me. We'll get this American."

He walked outside, accompanied by the soldier. It was still calm, but there was a weird humming sound to the right, its note dropping steadily into a roar of wind. Eager to get to his quarry, Kaufman did no more than glance towards the spiralling mass of blackness sweeping along the distant mountain crests at the far end of the range.

The tornado hit them when they were within sight of the temple. Half drowned by an avalanche of water, unable to stand erect in the wind, they slithered forwards to the slight shelter the great fallen marble columns provided. And there they both lay shivering and in mortal fear, until the storm passed as abruptly as it had started.

"We'll get back," panted Kaufman, "before another storm. See if your comrade and the prisoner are still all right. I will go and see what's happened to the old woman and the child."

He had some vague idea of holding them as hostages, but when he got back to the village the house no longer existed. The flat stone roof had shifted in the wind and brought the walls down. Kaufman looked through the gaping hole where the window had been. He turned away abruptly: the crushed body of a woman was not a pleasant sight. . . .

He found the soldiers tinkering with the car. Water had got on the ignition leads and it was half an hour before they got the engine started. Yusel lay gagged and bound at the back. Kaufman spent the time standing around, looking up at the temple, then at the ruined house which was the tomb of the old woman and presumably the child. His mind was filled with fear and, though he would not let himself admit it, something like remorse.

The engine of the car coughed to life and began to run smoothly. Kaufman got in beside the driver. "As fast as you can go," he ordered, "before another storm catches us out in the desert. And drive straight to the residence of Mm'selle Gamboul. I'll take our prisoner. Mm'selle Gamboul will want to question him herself."

They made it just as the sky again darkened to the blackness of night. As he alighted he could hear the scream of a second tornado approaching from the far side of the city. He ran for the shelter of the house, leaving Yusel in the car.

Gamboul was seated at her desk as usual. Her face was a blur in the gloom. The electricity had failed, and the heavy curtains had been torn away from the windows where the little intricately shaped panes had been blown out.

She looked up as Kaufman came close to the desk. "Ah, there you are," she said impatiently. "I want you to get out to the compound as soon as the storm eases and phone Vienna. Tell them that we're in charge now and they must take orders from us."

He showed no surprise. "I shall not phone Vienna," he said slowly and deliberately. "There are some things you can't make a deal in, and this is one of them. I have been out in it. And I've important news."

She stood up and approached the window, moving to the side in case more glass was blown out. "You're afraid, you too, are you?" she sneered. "Everyone is afraid of responsibility, of taking risks. This afternoon I visited the girl. She is dying, that one. And raving as she dies. She told me that the computer was wrong, that the message did not tell me this. But I know, Herr Kaufman, I know! The power and the knowledge are all in my hands. No one else's."

Kaufman crossed the room and stood beside her. Somewhere in the town a fire had started. Despite the rain, the wind was whipping it into a small holocaust.

"Reports of everything you have done for the past month have been smuggled out of the country," he said. "There is a man who has been here for some time. He is waiting to take a specimen of the bacteria to London."

She wheeled on him. "You will stop him, of course," she warned.

He shook his head. "I shall not." His voice was almost gentle as he went on, "You are not sane. You would lead us all into destruction."

"You poor little man." She showed no anger, only contempt. "You are like all the rest. You have not the imagination to see. Come here!"

Abruptly she walked to the glass door leading to the balcony and turned the handle. She had to lean against it with all her weight to force it open against the wind.

"Come!" she repeated. "Come and see the elements at work. Working for me!" He stayed stubbornly where he was.

"You are frightened?" she laughed. "There is no need. It will not touch us. It cannot."

She walked majestically on to the balcony, her hair blowing back from her forehead, and paused at the balustrade, stretching her arms towards the sky. Kaufman caught the sound of her ecstatic laughter in the howling wind.

On an impulse he crossed to the door and pulled it shut. The bedlam outside lessened as if it had moved away. Suddenly there was a crescendo of noise and the great old house shook. A piece of coping crashed on the balcony, smashing into a score of pieces.

He saw Gamboul stare down at a lump of jagged marble just as a cascade of sand struck her. She bent quickly, rubbing her fists in her eyes. Blindly she stumbled to the door and began beating on it. The thick, decorative glass broke. Her fist ran with blood. He could see her mouth opening and shutting as she screamed at him.

He backed into the gloom of the room, watching impassively. The bursts of wind were coming faster now, until one merged into another. The house groaned and trembled. At last it came: a roaring, crumbling mass of stone which crashed on to the balcony and, tearing it out by its concrete roots, hurled it down into the courtyard below. The dust of debris mixed with the sand like eddying smoke. Kaufman walked forward, pressing his face myopically against the glass to see what had happened.

It was all very indistinct, but he thought he could see a twisted body among the rubble below. He kept on looking for a minute or so. He felt none of the disquiet that the sight of the old Arab woman had given him. Eventually he sought a chair well away from the crumbling walls. With a completely steady hand he lighted a cigarello.

"When the storm is past," he said aloud to the empty room, "I shall make myself a call to London. There is the matter of relations with the English."

He frowned, hoping that this would not be too great a problem. Professor Dawnay might be amenable; but Fleming was a formidable adversary. There had, after all, been so many unfortunate incidents between them in the past. The English mentality when it got obstinate ideas was something he had never understood.

The storm weakened, the clouds thinned and light returned though the wind blew nearly as hard as before. He went down to the courtyard. Yusel had been taken into the cellars, a guard reported. Kaufman heard himself giving orders for him to be kept under guard but decently treated, and then went and looked at Gamboul's body. It lay, twisted and broken, among the fallen stonework, and her dark eyes, rimmed with blood, stared lifelessly up at him.

One of her cars was undamaged, and Kaufman ordered the driver to take him to the computer compound. Damage on the route through the town's outskirts was appalling. A scattering of Arabs were looting destroyed shops; they fled at the sight of the car with the Intel insignia. There were no troops or police anywhere.

The squat, solid buildings inside the compound seemed reasonably intact; a few windows were blown in, and some of the garish, modernistic fripperies at the entrance to the executive building had toppled. Kaufman drove past them, straight to the laboratories.

Dawnay was alone, injecting bacteria into rows of test tubes. The disorderly array of apparatus occupying every bench and table she had been able to commandeer was strangely reassuring after the desolation outside.

"Ah, Professor Dawnay," Kaufman beamed, "you were not damaged by the storm, I trust?"

"No," she said shortly.

"I have to inform you," he went on, "that Fraulein Gamboul is dead." He enjoyed her look of amazement. "She was killed by the tornado. I am now the senior representative of Intel in this country. I ask you to help me. Our measures against the bacteria causing the storms: they are successful, yes?"

"It looks like it, for the moment, and in the sea here," she replied.

"Wonderbar!" he said. "Everywhere else things go from bad to worse—unless we give them your cure."

"And quickly."

Kaufman nodded. "That is what I have thought." He dropped his voice. "You know, Professor, Fraulein Gamboul was prepared to let it go on until the world accepted her terms, outrageous terms. She was insane, of course. Did you know that she killed Salim, shot him dead herself? She was a woman possessed. She would have left everything too late. We should all have perished."

Dawnay looked at him coldly. "We may still."

He licked his lips nervously and removed his glasses, polishing the lenses over and over again. "There has been an appeal from London over the radio. I shall answer it when communications are restored. And I shall prove we can help by sending your own personal report on the anti-bacterium. Professor Neilson shall take it on the first available plane."

He saw her startled look.

"Oh yes," he said triumphantly, replacing his glasses and staring at her. "I know all about Professor Neilson being here. He will not wish to trust me. He does not yet understand that I am just a business man, and a good business man sees through calamity to brighter things."

Dawnay could not disguise her relief. "So Neilson will explain how you can give bulk supplies to the world?"

He shook his head impatiently. "Not at once," he said. "People will be prepared to pay a great deal. I told you I am a business man." He turned to the door. His smile had gone. "You will have a typed report ready for despatch in an hour."

For a while Dawnay went on with her work like an automaton. She had not counted on Kaufman haggling over the price of life.

She crossed to the computer building in search of someone to talk to; there was superficial damage to the entrance bay and the cooling tower, but the computer appeared unharmed. No guards were left, but an electrician appeared from the staff rest room. He said he had no idea where Dr. Fleming was. Abu Zeki, he believed, had left immediately after the first of the afternoon's storms to visit his family.

Dawnay thanked him and made her way to the sick quarters.

The nurse had put up makeshift barricades of screens over the broken windows. The girl smiled with relief at seeing someone at last.

"Miss Andre has slept through it all," she whispered. "I think she is a little stronger."

Dawnay sat down by the bed. The nurse was right. Bad as the light was, Dawnay could see a better colour in Andre's cheeks.

"Is it—is it working?" Andre had not opened her eyes or moved when she whispered her question.

Dawnay clasped the fragile hand. "Yes, it's working," she murmured. "The barograph in the lab is still going up. How long it will last I don't know."

Andre struggled to sit up. "It was not in the message that we must . . ." She stopped and lay back, exhausted. "I tried to tell her. She would not listen. She came last night. I told her to listen to me, not to the computer. But——."

"Gamboul, you mean?" said Dawnay gently. "She's dead, Andre. Kaufman is now in charge."

Andre nodded slowly, as if she knew. Her fingers tried to find Dawnay's. "Do you believe me?" she asked. She saw Dawnay nod. The fingers relaxed and she lay back with her eyes closed once more. "Tell me all that has happened and I will tell you what to do."

As rapidly as she could, Dawnay gave a survey of the situation as far as she knew it. Before she had finished she thought Andre had fallen asleep or had lapsed into a coma, she was so utterly motionless. But after a full two minutes, the girl began speaking in a level monotone.

Dawnay listened intently. The responsibility Andre was thrusting on her shoulders was tremendous. It was intimidating; yet it was inspiring too. The rational, reasoned motives were all that her scientific mind needed. When Andre finished Dawnay made just one brief answer.

"I'll go right away," she said.

Half an hour later she was ordering a servant at the Presidential palace to take her immediately to his master. She had driven herself in a car she had found undamaged in the Intel parking lot. It was the first time she had been behind a car wheel since her young days as a student. Her erratic course did not matter. Flood water had destroyed the road in many places. Rubble from tottering houses had to be avoided or driven over. No guards stood outside the palace.

The President saw her immediately. He was seated in his high-backed chair, looking years older than when she had last taken her leave of him.

His ritualistic courtesy had not deserted him. He rose and bent over her hand, and indicated a chair. The faithful little negro boy was still there. The President told him to go and see if he could find someone to make coffee. Then he returned to his seat.

"The country is dying, Professor Dawnay," he said simply.

"The whole world may be," Dawnay replied. "That is why I have come. It is in your power to help. You have been informed that Miss Gamboul is dead? The President nodded. "So you are free."

370

"Free!" he said bitterly. "It is a little late."

"It may not be," she insisted. "It partly depends on you, your Excellency. If the anti-bacteria I have made is handled by Intel, and if it works, then it will be Intel's world. Kaufman will fix their price for them."

"I have been told very little, but I can gather the trend of events. And what can I do to stop this man Kaufman? He is like the others—Salim, Mm'selle Gamboul. . . ."

"We will deal with Kaufman," Dawnay promised. "While you send out the bacteria as a gift from Azaran. It will be the first action of a free nation."

He gazed at her with his sad, intelligent eyes. "Or the last," he suggested.

"Not if every laboratory in the world receives a supply. Then we've got a chance. If we can do it in the right way, through the right people." She thought back to their long battles with the authorities at Thorness. "Ever since the message was first picked up and a computer built to handle it, a few people have been struggling to keep this power out of the wrong hands and put it into the right ones."

"And what are mine?" he asked mildly.

"What we will make them for you!"

The boy entered with a tray. The President poured out some coffee and handed Dawnay a cup. He slowly sipped his own before he spoke again.

"So you are right?" he murmured, eyeing her keenly. "And to whom will you be responsible? Hundreds of thousands of people have died because—you will forgive me—of these experiments of yours."

Dawnay felt blood flooding into her neck and cheeks: a visible sign of her feeling of enormous guilt. "It was an accident," she said inadequately. "It could have happened with any experiment. I made a mistake."

Some of the fire of the revolutionary of years before flamed briefly in the President's face as he stood up and confronted her.

"Hundreds of thousands more may have to die correcting your mistake," he said. "The errors of politicians are sometimes expensive, and business men sometimes do their best to profit from them. But you scientists, you kill half the world. And the other half cannot live without you."

His anger faded. He sighed and permitted himself a slight

smile. "I am in your hands, Professor Dawnay. You will forgive me if I add that I wish I were not."

Dawnay drove back to the compound determined to mould events the way she knew they had to be; but the responsibility appalled her. She badly needed the catharsis of Fleming's critical mind.

She found him in the servicing bay behind the computer. He was working at the desk, which was a litter of papers.

"Hello," he said lazily. "I holed up here—safe from the desert breezes and from interruption." He glanced at his wrist watch. "God, is that the time? I've been trying to work out this thing for Andre. I've done most of the chemical conversions. They don't make a hell of a lot of sense."

He threw across some calculations. She read them cursorily. "It would be lethal if it's wrong," she said shortly.

"She's dying anyway, isn't she? I've been trying all ways . . ."

She interrupted him impatiently. "John, there isn't time for that."

He looked up at her. "Make 'em and break 'em, eh?"

Dawnay flushed. "There's something else that comes first. Or have you forgotten what's still raging over the greater part of the world?"

"No, I haven't forgotten," he said.

"We've made a lot of mistakes," she went on. "Both of us. I'm trying to get things right because it's the only hope we have. What happens to the world depends on us, on whether we take over or whether Kaufman does."

His grin was sardonic. "Have you been having the treatment, like Gamboul?"

"Gamboul is dead," she said evenly.

"Dead?" Fleming jumped to his feet. "Then the machine misfired! It's had a go at us and it's failed."

Dawnay shook her head.

"It hasn't done either. Gamboul was only supposed to protect us until we were in a position to use our own judgment."

He nodded towards the massive panels of the computer. "Or its . . ."

"Our own judgment, John," she repeated. "We make the decisions now. Don't you see that this can be the beginning of a new life?"

He gathered the papers on the desk into an untidy pile. "Except for Andre," he said harshly.

"She'll have to wait. There are other people dying besides her."

He had to accept the logic of the statement. It did not make him dislike it less. He admired and was fond of Madeleine Dawnay, and was all the more nauseated by the familiar, corrupting scent of power which he now sensed around her.

"To hell with everything," he said. "I can't think any more tonight. We may as well try to get a little sleep before the wind decides to blow the roof off."

They walked from the building together. The residential area was a shambles of mud and rubble. But their quarters provided makeshift shelter. Fleming wished Dawnay good-night and went to his own chalet. The windows had gone and he could look past the shattered palm trees to the building opposite where the sick quarters were. The nurse had found a hurricane lamp from somewhere. It was the only light in the pitch black darkness—a dull yellow blob which drew his eyes like a magnet, mesmerising his mind. He fell into a half sleep, thinking of the life that still flickered near that puny flame.

He was roused by Abu Zeki.

"Much has happened," Abu said, struggling to control his emotions. "The storm, yesterday, it was very bad in the mountains. My home has gone."

"Your family?" Fleming sat up.

"Lemka and Jan—they are alive. My mother-in-law. She is dead." Abu's voice faltered. "She had laid down with little Jan in her arms, beneath her. When I arrived—I, I thought they were both dead. Then Jan began crying. He was saturated in blood, his grandmother's blood."

"Where is Lemka?"

"She was in the cave with Professor Neilson. She'd gone up with food. Neilson made her stay when the storm came. They came down just after I'd rescued Jan. I'm afraid Lemka is very bitter—about all that Professor Dawnay and you—all that we have been doing here."

"Not bitter, Abu; just right." Fleming felt the familiar hopelessness closing down on him. "It's no use saying I'm sorry. What about Yusel and Neilson?"

"Yusel is safe, so far. He had gone to my house to talk to Neilson about taking out the bacteria on his next flight. But Kaufman followed him. Yusel was beaten up. Then they took him back to Baleb. I suppose he'd have been killed in the house if they hadn't. Then in the early hours, while we were getting my wife and the child settled in a neighbour's house, he arrived in an Intel car. Kaufman had sent him back, with a note for Neilson. Yusel gave us the news that Mm'selle Gamboul was dead."

"A note for Neilson!" Fleming exclaimed. "What did it say?"

"Kaufman wanted to see him. He promised there would be no danger. Yusel insisted it was a trap, but Mr. Neilson said he wanted to go. I brought him down with me. He's waiting in the reception building now for Kaufman to come from town."

Fleming sprang off the bed. "I'll get over there. You'd better come too, Abu. If it's one of Kaufman's usual pistol and dagger efforts I want to be around."

Both men hurried to the executive building. In the keen light of dawn the damaged facade looked cheap and tawdry. There had also been considerable damage in the vast entrance hall, some of it the obvious results of looting by the demoralised guards.

"Kaufman will be sitting in the seat of the mighty—in Gamboul's office. You'd better wait down here, Abu. Warn us if anyone arrives," Fleming ordered.

He ran lightly up the staircase. One of the double doors of the director's office was slightly ajar, and he sidled along the wall until he could listen.

Kaufman's guttural voice was unctuous and polite. "The plane is coming from Vienna, I hope, Herr Neilson," he was saying. "It should arrive very soon. It will be loaded immediately. You must expect an uncomfortable flight. Conditions are still bad everywhere."

"And some written proof of your proposals?" Neilson asked coldly.

"I have obtained a letter from the President," said Kaufman. "That makes this matter official, but of course, everything will be done by us."

It was the comment Fleming had expected; had been waiting for. He pushed open the door and walked in. Kaufman looked up, startled, and then went on talking as if he had seen no one.

"We, that is to say Intel, will make the anti-bacteria and market it, though we will not hold our fellow human beings to ransom. That was Fraulein Gamboul's idea. I stopped it."

Fleming strode forward. "You're not in a position to dispense charity, Kaufman."

"And you are not entitled to be in this office without permission," retorted Kaufman.

"There are no Azaran guards to protect you now," Fleming said; "not even a receptionist." He moved closer to Neilson so that they both faced the German.

Kaufman picked up his case and extracted a cigarello. He kept the match against the glowing end for longer than necessary. His hand was shaking a little.

"It is no use bearing old grudges," he said, removing the cigarello. "One does what one has to do for the superiors one works for. One does as they order. But at the same time one tries to do good." There was a whine in his voice as he uneasily watched his visitors.

Neilson stood up, clenching the edge of the desk. His knuckles were white with the pressure he put into the grip. "You killed my son," he said with deceptive quietness. "He was shot before the eyes of his mother and myself at your order. If I'd had the means and if you weren't still essential to fly me out I'd have killed you the moment I entered this office."

"Please!" said Kaufman.

"How did Gamboul die?" Fleming snapped.

"The balcony of her house. It fell. I was there. I saw it. She was mad, completely mad. I couldn't save her."

"Did you try?"

"No," the German yelled. "I could have dragged her inside when the building started to fall. But I didn't. I chose to save—"

"—Your own skin!"

"The world!" Kaufman stood up and faced them defiantly across the desk. He saw a faint derisive smile on Fleming's face and no smile at all on Neilson's, and before either man could move he had dodged round the chair and darted to a small door that led to a private staircase. He tore it open and then backed away. Yusel was standing there, expressionless, with a small curved Bedouin knife in his hand. Kaufman moved back to the desk. "You cannot get in my way like this!" His voice rose. "I am doing business fairly. I'm trying to help you all!"

Fleming moved nearer the window. "The weather is holding up," he said. "The plane should get through on time. Before it arrives, you'll provide the help you talk about. You'll confirm your orders for Professor Neilson's flight. You'll make quite certain that it flies to London. That's the last thing you'll organise here. Get on with it."

Kaufman hesitated, then nodded. He picked up a pen and reached to a side drawer in the desk as if to take a noteheading.

He moved amazingly quickly. In a split second he had leaped up, a gun in his hand, and moved backwards to the outer door.

"This is not your game, gentlemen," he taunted them. "You should not try it." Then he turned and ran for the stairs.

Fleming and Neilson were close on his heels, but he gained his lead as he leaped recklessly downstairs. Fleming saw Abu look up and start running towards the foot of the staircase. Fleming's shout of warning coincided with the bark of the pistol shot. Abu crumpled in a heap. Such was the onrush of Kaufman's flight that he was unable to stop in time, and he fell headlong over his victim's body.

Before he could rise Neilson was on him, quickly followed by Yusel. Fleming's thoughts were for Abu and he knelt down and lifted the Arab in his arms. The head fell backwards, blood vomiting from the mouth. Fleming could not be certain whether the staring eyes were sightless or trying to send him a message. Very gently he let the body rest prone on the floor.

Neilson was insanely pummelling into Kaufman. "Leave him," Fleming shouted. He went up to the weeping, yammering German. "We're not going to kill you," he said. "There's a murder charge for you to answer in Geneva and in other places, if the courts aren't all destroyed."

"I do not make these things happen," Kaufman whined. "I have to obey."

Fleming turned away, unable to stomach any more. "Keep hold of him, Yusel," he ordered. "Get him down to the airport. Take his gun. He'll give you no trouble."

"Wait!"

They spun around and saw Dawnay standing in the entrance.

"What are you all doing here?" she asked. Then she saw Abu's body. Fleming explained, and then allowed her to lead him back upstairs to the main offices.

"You come too," she commanded Neilson and Kaufman. Yusel had gone out and now returned with a white robe with which he covered the body of his dead cousin. They all went into Gamboul's room and Dawnay sat at Gamboul's desk with Kaufman facing her and guarded by Yusel. Fleming wandered uneasily over to the window, but she called him back.

"John," she said. "It's not as simple as you may think: we haven't finished with Herr Kaufman yet."

She looked up into Kaufman's bruised and dejected face. "To whom did you report in Vienna?"

Kaufman did not answer at once, but when Dawnay shifted her gaze from him to Yusel he changed his mind.

"The Board of Directors," he said sulkily.

"To whom you reported Gamboul's death?"

"Yes."

"And who is taking over here?"

Kaufman glanced away for a moment. "I am."

"But you are not a director."

He drew himself up with a return of assurance: "I am temporarily in charge."

"Until?" Dawnay asked. There was another pause.

"You'd better tell us the easy way," said Fleming.

"Or perhaps," Neilson added, "you'd rather I broke your neck."

"There are three directors coming on the plane to-day, from Vienna." Kaufman addressed himself entirely to Dawnay, as if to a judge whom he might expect to be lenient. Dawnay looked only mildly surprised.

"Three?"

"They should have come before!" He began to speak quickly, with mounting passion. "Fraulein Gamboul was not equal to it. It deranged her, but she would not have anyone else. We have been ridiculously understaffed for so great a project; but she had considerable influence with the Chairman." He gave a knowing, leering wink. "She was an attractive woman. But now it is different; I have put it all on proper business footings. We will have directors, and executives and assistants—they are bringing many to-day."

"Are they?" said Dawnay with interest.

"Oh yes. And any kind of reinforcements we need. So—" He turned triumphantly to Fleming and Neilson, but Dawnay cut him short.

"So we shall have to put you all under guard," she said calmly. "That can be arranged for. Meanwhile, as soon as the aircraft is in, you'll help us send a Telex in your own code to Vienna."

"To say what?"

"That they have arrived safely and that all is well and you need no further help. You will also give us the names and full particulars of your chairman and other directors in Europe, and all addresses and telephone numbers you can find here in the office." She turned to her American colleague. "I'll give you a report to take to London, Professor Neilson, and as much of the anti-bacterium as I can. They should be able to get you there by nightfall."

12

CLEAR SKY

THE Prime Minister received the emergency committee in his private study on the first floor of 10, Downing Street. Although he had insisted on the fact being kept secret, he had been in bed for two days. His doctors diagnosed the trouble as cardiac asthma, which was as good a description as any for the strain felt by everyone of more than middle age as breathing became more and more difficult. The news of Dawnay's miracle in Azaran had now reached Whitehall, but its effects were still unfelt.

However, he insisted on rising to greet the Minister of Science and Osborne when they arrived.

"Glad you made it," he wheezed. "Are things still bad?"

"A nightmare, sir," said the Minister. "All the low ground beyond Hammersmith is flooded; the roads are under water." He began coughing.

"It's no good for us, this business," said the Prime Minister. "We'll be the first to succumb. Which will solve many a political problem. We shall soon have the youngest cabinet in history, called The Survivors."

The Minister of Science managed a polite laugh. "One worrying matter, sir, is that London Airport is flooded out. Gatwick's been unserviceable for some time, of course. And Civil Aviation isn't too happy about Hurn. I'd like your authority to get the R.A.F. to clear Lyneham for a priority landing. With at least two helicopters standing by for a run direct to us here. Hyde Park is still fairly clear despite the feeding centres and casualty stations."

"This means you have more news, Bertie," said the Prime Minister. "I do wish you could restrain your sense of melodrama."

379

"We've picked up a signal from Azaran, sir," Osborne interposed. "Professor Neilson's on his way. He and Professor Dawnay have taken over from a Herr Kaufman, who we believe was involved in the security leak at Thorness."

"Quite so, Osborne," said the Prime Minister with an amused smile. That was an old wound now and, like Osborne's other wounds, it was healing over and being forgotten. Osborne had more than redeemed himself since then. "Thorness. But the anti-bacterium?"

"He's bringing all he can carry, sir. Not much because of the flight difficulties these days, but enough to distribute to about a thousand breeding centres."

"Through the international organisation?"

"Yes," said the Minister of Science. "I may say, Prime Minister, that the will to co-operate has been magnificent. Japan suggested moving every oil tanker still afloat into mid-ocean, straddling marine currents like the Gulf Stream. The Soviet Union has completely cleared five state chemical plants. Fifty per cent. of the United States oil refineries are now cleaned and waiting. Here the Royal Engineers expect to have every gasometer on the coast patched up and ready by Saturday; the dairy and petroleum firms have had all their road tankers commandeered and marshalled at the various centres we decided on."

"Good," wheezed the Prime Minister. "Let's hope, dear boy, that it's happening in time for some of us. You will want to confer with Neilson, of course, when he gets here. Afterwards, send him round here. I shall want to discuss his plans. Then a broadcast. The people deserve a few words of encouragement and hope."

But it was not until the following night that the Prime Minister felt justified in telling the world that hope was returning. Throughout the previous twenty-four hours there had been frantic activity. The thousand activated test tubes Neilson brought seemed pathetically few when allocation began. A hundred of them were first distributed to British breeding centres. To save time the chemists concerned were briefed verbally by Neilson. Multi-language instructions were then prepared while Army Signals contacted all nations concerned to report details of samples and estimated time of arrival.

The R.A.F. and the United States Air Force handled transportation. A little slice of history was made as a U.S. long-range reconnaissance jet dropped towards Moscow's military airfield with Russian fighters doing welcoming victory rolls around her.

In a gesture to the almost unknown man who had had the titular responsibility of saving the world thrust upon him the Prime Minister insisted that the broadcast should open with the statement by the President of Azaran.

The radio link was difficult and tenuous, but over most of the globe it held.

"For many centuries we of Azaran have been considered a backward people," came the soft sing-song tones of the President. "But now, if we can bring salvation to the rest of the world it will be our privilege and joy. Already over our own country the weather is improving, and the air once more satisfies our lungs. This, we pray and believe, will spread to all the stricken peoples of the earth."

A resourceful radio station operator had dug up a recording of the Azarani national anthem. Its plaintive discord surged out and faded.

Then the Prime Minister made his historic broadcast from London. "Strains of a newly synthesised bacterium, which we have received from Azaran, can be the means of banishing the evil which has inflicted itself on mankind. With the help of the scientists, in whose hands our fate now lies, the governments of all nations are doing all they can. Already strains of the bacterium are being bred in the United Kingdom and pumped into the sea. First batches have arrived in the laboratories of our sister nations in this crusade against annihilation. More are coming from Azaran and will be distributed as fast as is humanly possible. With a concerted effort in every quarter of the globe we may hope the content of the sea will change, and we will breathe our native air again."

The Prime Minister leaned back in his chair, exhausted. Speaking had been a great effort and he rested while translations of his speech were broadcast in the five working languages of the United Nations. Then he called for his car. He turned to the officials gathered around him and spoke in a voice which was hardly more than a whisper. "I would like to see, gentlemen, if those promises I've made are reasonable. They tell me there's a breeding plant down at the London docks."

A police car escorted the Prime Minister's limousine through the darkened city past Tower Bridge. It nosed a way through piles of debris, detouring round many a barricaded street, until it pulled up on an old shabby wharf.

A sullen drizzle was falling, a respite from the interminable storms and gales. Two raincoated men were standing at the water's edge, watching a man in a police launch. They started when they recognised the bent elderly man beside them as the Prime Minister.

"We're testing for nitrogen content, sir," one of the men explained. "Anti-bacteria were pumped into this water six hours ago."

"How's it doing?" asked the Prime Minister.

"Fine, sir. Come and look."

In the headlight of the police launch the filthy river water looked black and sullen. But while they watched a bubble formed and burst. Nearby two more bubbles formed.

"It's happening right across the river, sir. Been noticeable for the last two and a half hours. It's the nitrogen being released as the new bacterium kills off the old one."

Another car drew up on the wharf. Osborne, alerted by the Premier's P.A., had brought Neilson to the site. The Prime Minister greeted them quietly with a smile and a half-raised hand.

"The cure is not, I hope, as bad as the disease," he inquired of the American.

Neilson shook his head. "No sir. The anti-bacterium does not survive the conditions it creates; Professor Dawnay has tested this fact very thoroughly. It has only one enemy, one source of food, the bacteria emerging from Thorness. Once it has exhausted the supply of those it languishes and dies itself."

"Just as an antibiotic destroys germs and then is itself destroyed," put in Osborne.

"Except that in this case we think that the end will be more complete—"

The Prime Minister interrupted Neilson with another smile. "I see you have it under control."

He stood a little longer, watching the bubbles come and go. "Thank God! Thank God!" he whispered as he returned to his car.

Conditions in Azaran were completely transformed within

twenty-four hours of Neilson's arrival in Britain. Aircraft from a dozen nations flew in scientists and technicians to help Dawnay and to organise transportation and communications. A U.N. stand-by force was put on call but, by the President's wish, was only to enter Azaran in the event of a threat from Intel. Dawnay had engineered herself complete freedom.

But the whole entity of Intel was collapsing quietly and completely. The NKVD, Interpol and the FBI, working together on the report which Neilson had taken to London, raided and closed the main offices in Vienna and in Zurich and Hong Kong; and the names revealed in the documents they captured caused consternation in a dozen chancelleries. By general agreement among the great powers, no pressure was brought to force dismissal and arrest, but all the consortium's trading licences were withdrawn. There were a couple of suicides and a whole series of resignations on health grounds, hardly noticed in the world-wide drama of retreat from chaos, and what was left came rapidly to a standstill, leaving empty trading posts all over the world without credentials or trade, and useless unclaimed millions in safe deposits in Swiss banks. In Azaran, the main centre of anti-bacteria production and the computer which had evolved it were left respectively in the hands of Madeleine Dawnay and her associate, John Fleming, who had both become world-famous characters overnight.

The atmosphere of super-efficiency and the constant flattery bestowed on Dawnay and himself repelled Fleming. He wanted no part of it; nor, indeed, was there anything for him usefully to do. He avoided the eager, enthusiastic groups who gathered in the makeshift canteen. He evaded invitations to parties which were soon organised in Baleb.

Soon after he had seen Kaufman into Interpol's custody, Fleming had suffered an experience which he found he could not dismiss from his mind. He had collected the handful of personal things in Abu's desk and driven to Lemka's village, glad that an officer of the President's personal staff had gone earlier to break the news of Abu's death to her.

It was very quiet inside the ruined courtyard of the house. A line of washing fluttered in the wind. The baby's cot stood in the shade of a crumbling wall. A spiral of smoke eddied away from a cluster of faggots in a makeshift grate. He called and waited until Lemka appeared at the shattered doorway at the sound of footsteps.

"I came to say—" Fleming began.

"Do not tell me that you are sorry," she interrupted, moving to the clothes line and keeping her face averted. "And do not tell me it was not your fault."

"I didn't want to involve your husband," he muttered.

She turned round angrily. "You involved us all."

"I liked him, you know. Very much. I came to see what I could do," he pleaded.

She was fighting back her tears. "You've done enough. You've saved the world—from your own muddle. So now you think it is all right. How can you—all of you—be so arrogant? You don't believe in God. You don't accept life as His gift. You want to change it because you think you're greater than God."

"I tried to stop . . ." His voice trailed away.

"You tried, and we suffer. The girl—your girl—was right when she said you condemn us. Why don't you go back and listen to her?"

"She is dying."

"You kill her too?" She looked at him more with pity than with hatred. He could not answer. He laid the little parcel of Abu's possessions at the foot of the child's cot and walked away.

Back at the compound, he stole like an interloper by a round-about route to his own quarters. He took out the computer print-out and his own calculations from a drawer and began studying them.

He had put them away when Dawnay had refused to help him, because he felt that he could not possibly do them himself. He simply did not know enough bio-chemistry. For what seemed a lifetime he had avoided Andre's room, because he could no longer face the fact of her dying, and by now he had given up all hope of Dawnay having the time, energy or will to be able to help him.

Dawnay now was installed in the executive block, at the centre of a quickly-spun web of radio and cable communications, directing and advising struggling scientists all round the world. He did not know how she managed it, or whether she ever slept; he didn't even see her.

He sat in his little room and stared glumly at the mass of

figures. Then he opened a fresh bottle of whisky and started to try to make head or tail of them. It was close on midnight when he walked a little unsteadily across the deserted clearing to the laboratory.

With the experimental work over, the master breeding tanks had been transferred to the executive building where there was room for the regiments of assistants Dawnay could now direct. The laboratory where it had all begun was neat and lifeless. He groped for a switch. The light came on. Most of the circuits had been restored during the previous day.

Hardly knowing from what recesses of memory of his student days they came, or how much was inspired by the neat Scotch, he began to find the facts he needed arranging themselves in his mind. Slowly and laboriously, and a little drunkenly, he started to make a chemical synthesis out of the mess of calculation he had written down.

His own training kept him roughly on the right path, but he ruefully had to face the fact that the ordinary, plebeian routine of practical chemistry was really beyond him. He lacked patience and accuracy; but obstinacy, and the memory of Lemka's pitying eyes, drove him on. He did not notice that morning sunlight was outshining the bare electric bulbs, nor did he hear the door open.

"What a hell of a mess!" said Dawnay's voice. "Look at my laboratory. What do you think you're doing?"

He dropped off the high stool at the bench and stretched. "Hello, Madeleine," he said. "I've been trying to synthesise this thing for Andre. Most of the main chain seems to have jelled. But the side chains are all to hell."

Dawnay ran an expert eye over his work amid the litter spread across bench and desks. "I'm not surprised," she exclaimed. "You've achieved a glorious mess. Better leave it to me."

"I thought you hadn't time. I thought you were too busy setting the world to rights."

She ignored what he was saying and went on looking at the equations he had written down.

"Admittedly," she said slowly, "if there's a chemical deficiency in her blood or endocrine glands there must be a chemical answer, but we can't know whether this is it."

"It has to be, doesn't it?" he suggested. "Our electronic boss says so."

She considered for a time. "Why do you want to do this, John?" she enquired. "You've always been afraid of her. Always wanted her out of the way."

"Now I want her to live!"

She eyed him speculatively, a smile hovering around her mouth. "Because you're a scientist and you want to know what the message is really all about? You can't bear to think that Gamboul knew and you don't? That's really the reason, isn't it?"

"You've some funny old ideas," he smiled.

"Maybe," she answered, "maybe." She reached for an overall on the wall hook. "Go and get some breakfast, John. Then come back here. I'll have some work for you to do."

The two of them worked in perfect, almost instinctive cooperation, carefully avoiding any kind of moral or emotional argument. They were like enemies who were forced to live in the same cell. They talked of nothing but the enormous complication of the job, and for ten solid days, and most of the nights, they carried on. Messages about the world-wide improvements in barometric pressure, news bulletins reporting a noticeable lessening of wind violence, were just noted and then forgotten.

Because of her own forebodings of failure, Dawnay did not even tell Fleming that even before the checking was complete she had started injections on Andre. The ethics did not bother her. Andre's life was hovering near its end in any case.

Fleming still avoided the girl's sick room. He told himself that he would not see her until he could give her hope. He knew Dawnay was visiting her regularly, but he deliberately refrained from asking how she was.

And Dawnay, noting the slow improvement in her patient, hardly dared to believe that she had succeeded. Only when the doctor came and made prolonged and successful tests of muscular reflexes did she admit even to herself that the near-impossible had happened.

It was Andre herself who settled the matter. "I am getting well," she said one morning as she waited for another injection. "You have saved my life."

"You have saved yourself," Dawnay said gently. "You and John and the computer calculations."

"What will he do now—now that I'm to go on?" Andre asked.

"I don't know." Dawnay had wondered so much herself that she had been awaiting and dreading this question. "He's divided. One part wants to go on. The other is frightened. We're all like that. But fear doesn't entirely stop us going forward."

"And I stand for going forward?" Andre asked.

"For much more. Down here on our cosy little earth we used to think we were protected from the outside by sheer distance. Now we see that intelligence—pure, raw intelligence—can cross great gulfs of space and threaten us."

"You still think of me as a threat from outside?"

"No," Dawnay answered. "No, I don't."

Andre smiled. "Thank you for that. Can't I see him soon?"

"You're strong enough to get up," Dawnay agreed. "He should see you. Yes," she went on after a pause. "We'll go together when you can walk."

One evening the following week Fleming went back to the computer block. Partly to ease his conscience, and partly because he needed some fairly unskilled help, he had invited Yusel to work on the computer. The salary was good, which would help Lemka and the child.

When Dawnay found them there, the Arab excused himself and she was left alone with Fleming.

"John," she said, "Andre's here."

Fleming looked up in surprise.

"Where?"

"Outside." She smiled a little grimly at Fleming's amazement. "She's cured, John. We've done it. She'll be all right now."

At first she thought he was not going to say anything at all. Then he asked, in a hurt voice, "Why couldn't you have told me?"

"I wasn't sure which way it was going."

He stared at her with amazement. "So you've repaired her, and the first thing you do is to bring her here—back to the machine! It's all so easy, so planned, just as if we're being used." He turned away with a frown. "How can we go on competing with her, with this?"

"That depends on you," Dawnay replied. "I can't help you. My job here is finished. I'm flying home tomorrow."

"You can't!" he exclaimed.

"You wanted her well," she reminded him, but he looked at her and through her as though at a ghost.

"You can't leave me like this," he implored. "Not with her *here*."

She had never before seen him plead for help. "Look, John," she said kindly. "You're not a child that hides behind its mother's skirts. You're supposed to be a scientist. Andre didn't use you or me. It was we who turned the world upside down. It was Andre who saved it." She moved to the door, beckoning to the waiting girl. "I'll see you before I go."

Andre walked quickly towards Fleming, stopping before him and smiling like a happy schoolgirl. She was still thin and pale, and her eyes looked very big above her high, sharp cheek-bones; but she no longer looked ill. She was alive and vibrant, with a kind of fined-down beauty which touched him in spite of himself.

"I can hardly believe that you're like this," he said.

"You're not glad?"

"Of course I'm glad. . . ."

"Are you afraid of me?"

"So long as you're a puppet, a mechanical doll."

Colour suffused her cheeks and she tossed her hair away from her face. "And you're not? You still think of yourself as a divine, unique creation. Three thousand millions of you on this earth alone. They—we—are all puppets, dancing on strings."

"Let's dance then." He kept his hands in his pockets, his body motionless.

"I will do whatever you wish," she told him. "All I know is one certain thing. We cannot go separate ways."

He put out his hand and brushed it against hers. "Then let's leave here," he said. He turned and looked at the grey bulk of the computer. "After we've destroyed this. We'll make a real job of it this time. Then we'll find somewhere with peace, like that island we were on with old what-was-his-name—Preen."

"All right," she said. "We will do as you want. I have often told you that. But have you thought? Have you really thought? Do you think we'd be allowed to live in peace any more than Preen was? The only safe place for us is here. If we accept this and its protection we accept what is planned."

"Planned! That damned word. And what *is* planned?"

"What you want. It will be done here and in the rest of the world."

"I'm afraid I'm not cut out to be a dictator."

"The only possible sort of dictator is someone who is not cut out for it," she said. "Someone who knows."

"Knows what?" he asked.

She took hold of his arm and began to lead him across to the observation bay of the computer.

"I'll show you what I showed Mm'selle Gamboul," she said. "Stand close beside me."

Obediently he stood by the panel and brought in the phase switches as she called the numbers. She sat down, alert and expectant, with a hand on his.

The computer began to purr. Relays snicked into operation, the screen glowed. Like a film coming into focus the shadows grew smaller and sharper as they took form and perspective.

"It looks like the moon," Fleming murmured. "Dead mountains, dust-filled valleys."

"It isn't," Andre whispered, without looking away from the screen. "It isn't the moon. It's the planet from which the message came."

"You mean they're showing us themselves?" Fleming stared at the bizarre shadows and reflections. "The lighting's completely weird."

"Because of the source," she explained, "the light from their sun is blue."

She concentrated on the tube and the picture began to shift. The scenery moved horizontally at increasing speed until the screen became a blur of dazzling light. Again the scene slowed down and became stationary. There was a terrible stillness about it this time, the absolute rigidity of timeless age.

An enormous plain stretched into the background where it merged with the dark sky. In the foreground stood monstrous elongated shapes, placed haphazardly and apparently half buried in the level, soft-looking surface.

Fleming felt the skin on the back of his neck prickling. "My God," he whispered, "what are they?"

"They are the ones," said Andre. "The ones who sent it. The ones I'm supposed to be like."

"But they're lifeless." He corrected himself. "They're immobile."

She nodded, her eyes wide and fixed on the screen. "Of course," she said. "Really big brains cannot move around any more than this computer. There's no need."

"The surface of them seems solid. How do they see?"

"Eyes would be useless. The blue light would destroy all tissue and nerve fibre as you know them. They see by other means, just as their other senses are different from those people—" she hesitated "—people like us—have developed."

The picture began to crumble. Sections detached themselves and spun off the screen. Quickly everything faded.

"Is that all there is?" Fleming felt deprived of something.

Andre turned her face to him. It glistened with perspiration; her eyes were enormous, the pupils distended. "Yes," she smiled. "That's all. They are the ones. They wanted us to see their planet. They believed it would be enough. Perhaps as a warning. Perhaps to show what time brings and how to survive. How we could do the same."

Fleming glanced back at the dark screen. To him those shapes still stood clear and definite in their piteous immobility against the glass. "No," he said.

"Is it so much worse than the human race?" she asked him. "Which lives and reproduces and works and struggles by animal instinct. That's all human beings are—animals who spend their time competing for existence, keeping their bodies alive. And when the earth gets too crowded there is a holocaust and the survivors begin the cycle over again, and the brain never develops."

"Oh no?"

"Not really. Not fast enough. By the time the earth becomes no longer fit to live on, the human race will still be little struggling animals who die out."

"Unless we change?"

She nodded. "The brain from out there can guide us, and we can guide others. So long as we keep hold of the authority it gives us."

"And impose what it wants us to on the rest of the world?"

"We can only start to point a possible way," Andre answered. "It will be millions of years before the earth . . ."

"We haven't the right," he said.

"To use knowledge of what could be?" They argued for a long while, but in the end she said, "All right, then you're quite clear in your mind? You want to destroy all this?" She waved an expressive hand along the machine.

"Yes," he said firmly. "That's what I want."

She got up and crossed to the record cabinets. From the rear of a drawer she took a small roll of film and held it out to him.

"What's that?" he demanded, refusing to touch it.

"It's a roll of input negative. It writes zeros throughout the whole of the memory section. The computer has no will to stop it now. Feed this film in and in a few minutes it will be nothing but a mass of metal and glass."

He followed her to the programming console. He watched her slip the film on the spool holder and snap the flange shut. His eyes travelled upwards to the red button on the control panel. He was moving his hand to press it when Andre gently but firmly clasped his fingers.

"I'd rather that it wasn't you who did that," she said. "You see, I know it's a mistake. And I'd rather it wasn't yours."

He let his arm drop and stepped away from the panel. Andre bent over the operating desk and began writing on the memo pad clamped to one side.

"We'll leave a note," she explained. "But who for?"

He grinned happily. "For Yusel."

"Yes," she agreed. "Yusel. He'll start the input motor quite innocently when he sees this." In big capitals she wrote Yusel's name. "Now take me away please," she whispered, "if that's what you really want."

He did not move as she came close to him. Then very lightly he bent his head and kissed her, full on the mouth.

As he felt her lips warm and full against his, he sensed suddenly her full humanity. All the fear and strain of the past months fell away from him and he was simply alone at last with the woman he wanted.

He withdrew his mouth gently from hers and held her away from him at arms' length, and smiled at her. When she smiled back the grey panels of the computer cabinets became dim, unimportant shadows. He laughed out loud and took one of her hands in his.

"Now, let's go. I can get Kaufman's car. There's a place I'd like you to see."

She followed him unquestioningly. Outside it was dark and cool. The wind was just the night breeze of the desert. No clouds marred the serenity of the pale, peaceful light from an almost full moon.

In the car she snuggled against him. He drove steadily along the route which held such memories for him. When he neared the mountains he drove off the road, anxious to avoid arousing the sleeping people in Lemka's village. He stopped the car in the shadow of a great boulder.

Hand in hand they clambered up a goat track, making for the white mass of the temple ruins. The air became colder. Both of them panted with the effort, and the blood tingled in their faces and hands.

In silence Fleming stopped when his feet were on the great flight of steps which led up to the ruined portico. He kept his grip firmly on Andre's hand, making her stop too.

"Why have we come here?" she whispered.

"To breathe," he said, tilting his head back and inhaling deeply.

She looked upwards, too—into the vault of the sky, darkening at the edge of the mountain crest where the moonshine weakened. The Pole Star hung there like a brilliant lamp. Not far from it another star twinkled.

"Beta Cassiopeiae, it's called," said Fleming, knowing that their minds were so attuned that there was no need to doubt that she was looking just where he was. "A nicer name is the Lady in the Chair. Can you make out the shape?"

She laughed. "No, I can't." She continued looking upwards. "But now I know why you brought me here. That glimmer between the Pole Star and your Chair Lady."

"Yes," he said, putting his arm protectively around her.

"Andromeda," she whispered, "my namesake."

"The place where they are, the creatures without movement, without eyes; just with brains." He deliberately turned his head away from the stars. "It doesn't make sense. Think of the machine they made us build at Thorness. Remember what it did to you? Your hands?"

She nodded. "I remember. But if it had been very reasonable, very wise, would you have opposed it?" She saw him shake his head. "Then you'd have really fallen under its spell. You and everybody else. Just like Mademoiselle Gamboul."

"I suppose so."

"Therefore what are you afraid of? By making it brutal and

392

savage they forced you to take the control yourself. That's why we changed the decision circuits in this Azaran model. And that was intended too. It was all predictable."

"The nitrogen bug too?"

"Of course. That was to make absolutely sure that the control would be changed. That the decisions would not be the machine's."

Fleming was almost convinced. "But why run so close? It nearly did for us."

"That was a miscalculation."

"Don't kid yourself," he grinned. "That thing never made a mistake."

"They made just one; they hadn't reckoned on someone like you. They never thought that the first computer would be destroyed, only that it would be changed. If you hadn't done what you did that night in Scotland the marine bacteria could have been coped with much sooner."

"You've no proof," he protested lamely.

"I do know," she said softly. "I know you destroyed the only means of saving everything. At least that's what would have happened if your friend Bridger hadn't sold the design to Intel."

He was delighted with that. "Good old Denis," he exclaimed. "They ought to bury him in Westminster Abbey." He turned and put his hands on her shoulders. "And you, what was your purpose? To establish it here in a position of absolute power?"

"No. My job was to find someone who would understand how to use it." She fingered the button on his coat. "You wouldn't trust me. And yet—you expected a breakthrough into new knowledge."

Abruptly she stepped away.

"This is it, John. It's in your hands now."

"And you?" he asked, keeping his distance.

"I'm in your hands too."

"But what are you?"

She came back to him. "Flesh and blood," she said happily. "Dawnay's mixture."

He put his hands on either side of her face and tilted it so that the waning moon shone full on her. "It's the nearest thing to a miracle I've ever seen," he said.

They turned and walked down the mountain path, hand in

hand. "I remember the night the message first came through," Fleming said thoughtfully. "I started burbling about a New Renaissance. I was a bit tight. Old Bridger wasn't so cocky about it as I was. He said, 'When all the railings are down you have to have something to hang on to'."

His arm went round her waist, pulling her body close against his. "I'd better get used to hanging on to you, hadn't I?"

She smiled up at him, but she was not quite content.

"And the message?" she asked.

They had reached level ground, and he quickened his pace, once again taking her hand and pulling her along as he took long strides towards the car.

"Where are we going now?" she asked.

He looked back to her and laughed out loud again.

"To save it!" He shouted so that the hillside rang with his voice. "We've just about time to beat Yusel in to work. The new Renaissance begins in about an hour from now—if we get cracking."

He bundled Andre into the car. After he had walked round to the driving seat he paused for a second, looking up to the sky, already paling with the false dawn. The stars were going out. Very dimly, between the Lady in the Chair and the Pole Star he could make out the hazy light of the great Andromeda galaxy across the immensity of space.

Sir Fred Hoyle (1915–2001) was a famous English astronomer noted primarily for the theory of stellar nucleosynthesis and his often controversial stances on other scientific matters – in particular his rejection of the 'Big Bang' theory, a term coined by him on BBC radio. He has authored hundreds of technical articles, as well as textbooks, popular accounts of science and two autobiographies. In addition to his work as an astronomer, Hoyle was a writer of science fiction, including a number of books co-written with his son Geoffrey Hoyle. Hoyle spent most of his working life at the Institute of Astronomy at Cambridge and served as its director for a number of years. He was knighted in 1972 and died in Bournemouth, England, after a series of strokes.

John Herbert Elliot (1918–1997) was a British novelist, screenwriter and television producer. Between 1954 and 1960 Elliot scripted a succession of one-off television plays, and in 1961 he joined with astronomer Fred Hoyle – to ensure scientific authenticity – to write the science fiction serial *A for Andromeda*. The success of this serial prompted a sequel, *Andromeda Breakthrough*, a year later, followed by subsequent novelisations of both. His drama series *The Troubleshooters*, formerly *Mogul*, won the Shell International Award at the British Academy Television Awards in 1971. Elliot passed away in 1997.